THE

PHILIP K. DICK

The Golden Man

A Methuen Paperback

A Methuen Paperback

THE GOLDEN MAN
ISBN 0 417 06200 4

First published in Great Britain 1981
by Methuen Paperbacks (Magnum Books)
Reprinted 1983 and 1986

Printed in Great Britain for
Methuen London Ltd,
11 New Fetter Lane, London EC4P 4EE
by Cox & Wyman Ltd, Reading

ACKNOWLEDGMENTS

"The Golden Man," copyright © 1954 by Quinn Publishing Company, Inc., for *Worlds of IF Science Fiction*, April 1954.

"Return Match," copyright © 1966 by Galaxy Publishing Corporation for *Galaxy Science Fiction*, February 1967.

"The King of the Elves," copyright © 1953 by Galaxy Publishing Corporation for *Beyond Fantasy Fiction*, September 1953.

"The Mold of Yancy," copyright © 1955 by Quinn Publishing Company, Inc., for *Worlds of IF Science Fiction*, August 1955.

"Not By Its Cover," copyright © 1968 by Heath Knowledge, Inc., for *Famous Science Fiction*, Summer 1968.

"The Little Black Box," copyright © 1964 by Galaxy Publishing Corporation for *Worlds of Tomorrow*, August 1964.

"The Unreconstructed M," copyright © 1956 by Columbia Publications, Inc., for *The Original Science Fiction Stories*, January 1957.

"The War with the Fnools," copyright © 1968 by Galaxy Publishing Corporation for *Galaxy Magazine*, February 1969.

"The Last of the Masters," copyright © 1954 by Hanro Corporation for *Orbit Science Fiction*, November/December 1954.

"Meddler," copyright © 1954 by Columbia Publications, Inc., for *Future Science Fiction*, October 1954.

"A Game of Unchance," copyright © 1964 by Ziff-Davis Publishing Company for *Amazing Stories*, July 1964.

"Sales Pitch," copyright © 1954 by Columbia Publications, Inc., for *Future Science Fiction*, June 1954.

"Precious Artifact," copyright © 1964 by Galaxy Publishing Corporation for *Galaxy Magazine*, October 1964.

"Small Town," copyright © 1954 by Ziff-Davis Publishing Company for *Amazing Stories*, May 1954.

"The Pre-Persons," copyright © 1974 by Mercury Press, Inc., for *The Magazine of Fantasy and Science Fiction*, October 1974.

FOR MARK AND DIANE
WITH LOVE.

AND FOR RUSSELL GALEN
WHO GAVE ME FAITH
IN MYSELF.

CONTENTS

Foreword

By Mark Hurst

The stories in THE GOLDEN MAN appear here together for the first time anywhere. None of them have appeared in Phil Dick's previous single-author collections, although a couple have been included in subject anthologies.

In selecting the stories for THE GOLDEN MAN, I've tried to include a representative sampling of the themes that are repeated in Phil's novels. Each of these stories, however, stands on its own. The earliest, "The King of the Elves," appeared in *Beyond Fantasy Fiction* in September, 1953. The most recent, "The Pre-Persons," was published in *The Magazine of Fantasy and Science Fiction* in October, 1974.

I've known Phil Dick for several years. In 1969, a friend of mine turned me on to UBIK. Little did I know then that this would lead me to collect Phil's entire work, a process which took over ten years. Many of his novels are still out of print in this country and abroad, and digging up over one hundred stories ranging back to 1952 was an enormous undertaking. One of the stories in THE GOLDEN MAN, "Not By Its Cover," is so rare that I got my copy from Phil himself! He now tells me that other collectors would shoot on sight for it. It's in this book, so you won't have to resort to violence to read it.

The main reason why I put this book together is that I couldn't find many of these stories in my local bookstore when I wanted to read them. When I did find them from various sources, they were so good that I knew they must be restored to print.

I met Phil Dick through the mails after Fred Pohl gave me his address. I couldn't find a copy of MARTIAN

TIME-SLIP anywhere, so I wrote to Phil asking for one.
Damned if he didn't send one, too! Two years later, I
wrote to Judy-Lynn del Rey at Ballantine, asking her to
reissue it, and she did. Shortly thereafter, when I was at
Bantam, Doubleday offered Sydny Weinberg and me a
package deal for the reprint rights to UBIK, THE
THREE STIGMATA OF PALMER ELDRITCH and
A MAZE OF DEATH. We snapped them up, and
brought the trio back into print. Before leaving Bantam, I
bought Phil's latest novel, VALIS (which he worked on
for over three years and which is his best yet). Later,
Judy-Lynn del Rey asked for my freelance contributions
to a collection she and John Brunner were putting
together, THE BEST OF PHILIP K. DICK. I was struck
then by the quality of the stories we couldn't include (for
reasons of space), so I secretly planned this volume.

It wasn't until I started working at Berkley and met
David Hartwell that my plans became reality. It went like
this:

> DAVE: "Mark, do you think there are enough
>   unanthologized Phil Dick stories for a
>   new collection?"
> MARK: "Dave, there're *more* than enough."

That's how easy it was, and here it is.

I only have two Phil Dick episodes to relate here, but
both are meaningful and will tell you a lot about the kind
of person Phil is. When I went out to California a few
years ago to meet him and rough out ideas for his new
novel, I pulled in exhausted after two weeks of camping.
Phil immediately offered me a place to stay. "Sleep in my
bed, I insist," he said. He slept on the couch. There was no
talking him out of this, even though I tried. Also, Philip
K. Dick is the only SF writer I know who once used his
Hugo Award trophy (for THE MAN IN THE HIGH
CASTLE) to break up a fight on his front lawn! To this
day, the wooden stand is still missing, and the silver
rocket leans at a rakish angle on his mantel.

What I like most about Phil's work is that you can read
one of his books or stories, enjoy it, put it down, pick it up

a few years later, re-read it, and *still* find something new. This is a rare quality in fiction, and one which places Mr. Dick more in the "mainstream" of literature than even *he* would care to admit. His characters are people who might bump into you while you're waiting in line at four A.M. at the local "7-11." What often happens to them, however, you wouldn't wish on a cockroach! His settings, however futuristic they might seem, are often projections of the environment in which we live today. The most outstanding element in Phil's books, outside of his wild and crazy plots and fully-realized characters, is Phil's sense of humor, that unique quality reflected again and again in his work, and which I've included in THE GOLDEN MAN. The guy is funny, often hilarious.

I hope you enjoy reading this book as much as I've enjoyed putting it together. If you like it, read his other books. You'll love them. And remember, Philip K. Dick is The Original Space Captain.

Right now, I'd like to thank Tim Underwood, Lloyd Currey and Fred Patten for their help in finding many of the stories. I'd also like to thank David Hartwell and John Silbersack for their enthusiasm for the project. Most of all, I'd like to thank my wife, Diane, for making coffee and giving me loving support while I read and selected the stories in THE GOLDEN MAN.

And as for you, Phil: this book is a tribute to you from your greatest fan.

Introduction

By Philip K. Dick

When I see these stories of mine, written over three decades, I think of the Lucky Dog Pet Store. There's a good reason for that. It has to do with an aspect of not just my life but with the lives of most freelance writers. It's called poverty.

I laugh about it now, and even feel a little nostalgia, because in many ways those were the happiest goddam days of my life, especially back in the early Fifties when my writing career began. But we were poor; in fact we—my wife Kleo and I—were *poor* poor. We didn't enjoy it a bit. Poverty does not build character. That is a myth. But it does make you into a good bookkeeper; you count accurately and you count money, little money, again and again. Before you leave the house to grocery shop you know exactly what you can spend, and you know exactly what you are going to buy, because if you screw up you will not eat the next day and maybe not the day after that.

So anyhow there I am at the Lucky Dog Pet Store on San Pablo Avenue, in Berkeley, California in the Fifties, buying a pound of ground horsemeat. The reason why I'm a freelance writer and living in poverty is (and I'm admitting this for the first time) that I am terrified of Authority Figures like bosses and cops and teachers; I want to be a freelance writer so I can be my own boss. It makes sense. I had quit my job managing a record department at a music store; all night every night I was writing short stories, both SF and mainstream...and selling the SF. I don't really enjoy the taste or texture of horsemeat; it's too sweet...but I also do enjoy not having to be behind a counter at exactly nine A.M., wearing a suit

and tie and saying, "Yes ma'am, can I help you?" and so
forth . . . I enjoyed being thrown out of the University of
California at Berkeley because I wouldn't take ROTC—
boy, an Authority Figure in a uniform is *the* Authority
Figure!—and all of a sudden, as I hand over the 35¢ to the
Lucky Dog Pet Store man, I find myself once more facing
my personal nemesis. Out of the blue, I am once again
confronted by an Authority Figure. There is no escape
from your nemesis; I had forgotten that.

The man says, "You're buying this horsemeat and you
are eating it yourselves."

He now stands nine feet tall and weights three hundred
pounds. He is glaring down at me. I am, in my mind, five
years old again, and I have spilled glue on the floor in
kindergarten.

"Yes sir," I admit. I want to tell him, Look; I stay up all
night writing SF stories and I'm real poor but I know
things will get better, and I have a wife I love, and a cat
named Magnificat, and a little old house I'm buying at the
rate of $25-a-month payments which is all I can
afford—but this man is interested in only one aspect of
my desperate (but hopeful) life. I know what he is going to
tell me. I have always known. The horsemeat they sell at
the Lucky Dog Pet Store is only for animal consumption.
But Kleo and I are eating it ourselves, and now we are
before the judge; the Great Assize has come; I am caught
in another Wrong Act.

I half expect the man to say, "You have a bad attitude."

That was my problem then and it's my problem now: I
have a bad attitude. In a nutshell, I fear authority but at
the same time I resent it—the authority *and* my own
fear—so I rebel. And writing SF is a way to rebel. I
rebelled against ROTC at U.C. Berkeley and got expelled;
in fact told never to come back. I walked off my job at the
record store one day and never came back. Later on I was
to oppose the Vietnam War and get my files blown open
and my papers gone through and stolen, as was written
about in *Rolling Stone*. Everything I do is generated by
my bad attitude, from riding the bus to fighting for my
country. I even have a bad attitude toward publishers; I
am always behind in meeting deadlines (I'm behind in this
one, for instance).

Yet—SF is a rebellious art form and it needs writers and readers and bad attitudes—an attitude of, "Why?" Or, "How come?" Or, "Who says?" This gets sublimated into such themes as appear in my writing as, "Is the universe real?" Or, "Are we all really human, or are some of us just reflex machines?" I have a lot of anger in me. I always have had. Last week my doctor told me that my blood pressure is elevated again and there now seems to be a cardiac complication. I got mad. Death makes me mad. Human and animal suffering make me mad; whenever one of my cats dies I curse God and I mean it; I feel fury at him. I'd like to get him here where I could interrogate him, tell him that I think the world is screwed up, that man didn't sin and fall but was pushed—which is bad enough—but was then sold the lie that he is basically sinful, which I know he is not.

I have known all kinds of people (I turned fifty a while ago and I'm angry about that; I've lived a long time) and those were by and large good people. I model the characters in my novels and stories on them. Now and again one of these people dies, and that makes me mad—*really* mad, as mad as I can get. "You took my cat," I want to say to God, "and then you took my girlfriend. What are you doing? Listen to me; listen! It's wrong what you're doing."

Basically, I am not serene. I grew up in Berkeley and inherited from it the social consciousness which spread out over this country in the Sixties and got rid of Nixon and ended the Vietnam War, plus a lot of other good things, the whole civil rights movement. Everyone in Berkeley gets mad at the drop of a hat. I used to get mad at the FBI agents who dropped by to visit with me week after week (Mr. George Smith and Mr. George Scruggs of the Red Squad), and I got mad at friends of mine who were members of the Communist Party; I got thrown out of the only meeting of the CP-USA I ever attended because I leaped to my feet and vigorously (i.e. angrily) argued against what they were saying.

That was in the early Fifties and now here we are in the very late Seventies and I am still mad. Right now I am furious because of my best friend, a girl named Doris, 24 years old. She has cancer. I am in love with someone who could die any time, and it makes fury against God and the world race through me, elevating my blood pressure and stepping up my heart beat. And so I write. I want to write about people I love, and put them into a fictional world spun out of my own mind, not the world we actually have, because the world we actually have does not meet my standards. Okay, so I should revise my standards; I'm out of step. I should yield to reality. I have never yielded to reality. That's what SF is all about. If you wish to yield to reality, go read Philip Roth; read the New York literary establishment mainstream bestselling writers. But you are reading SF and I am writing it for you. I want to show you, in my writing, what I love (my friends) and what I savagely hate (what happens to them).

I have watched Doris suffer unspeakably, undergo torment in her fight against cancer to a degree that I cannot believe. One time I ran out of the apartment and up to a friend's place, literally ran. My doctor had told me that Doris wouldn't live much longer and I should say goodbye to her and tell her it was because she was dying. I tried to and couldn't and then I panicked and ran. At my friend's house we sat around and listened to weird records (I'm into weird music in general, both in classical and in rock; it's a comfort). He is a writer, too, a young SF writer named K.W. Jeter—a good one. We just sat there and then I said aloud, really just pondering aloud, "The worst part of it is I'm beginning to lose my sense of humor about cancer." Then I realized what I'd said, and he realized, and we both collapsed into laughter.

So I do get to laugh. Our situation, the human situation, is, in the final analysis, neither grim nor meaningful but funny. What else can you call it? The wisest people are the clowns, like Harpo Marx, who would not speak. If I could have anything I want I would like God to listen to what Harpo was not saying, and understand why Harpo would not talk. Remember, Harpo *could* talk. He just wouldn't. Maybe there was nothing to say; everything has been said. Or maybe, had he spoken, he would have pointed out something too terrible, something we should not be aware of. I don't know. Maybe you can tell me.

Writing is a lonely way of life. You shut yourself up in

your study and work and work. For instance, I have had the same agent for 27 years and I've never met him because he is in New York and I'm in California. (I saw him once on TV, on the Tom Snyder Tomorrow Show, and my agent is one mean dude. He really plays hardball, which is what an agent is supposed to do.) I've met many other SF writers and become close friends with a number of them. For instance, I've known Harlan Ellison since 1954. Harlan hates my guts. When we were at the Metz Second Annual SF Festival last year, in France, see, Harlan tore into me; we were in the bar at the hotel, and all kinds of people, mostly French, were standing around. Harlan shredded me. It was fine; I loved it. It was sort of like a bad acid trip; you just have to kick back and enjoy; there is no alternative.

But I love that little bastard. He is a person who really exists. Likewise Van Vogt and Ted Sturgeon and Roger Zelazny and, most of all, Norman Spinrad and Tom Disch, my two main men in all the world. The loneliness of the writing *per se* is offset by the fraternity of writers. Last year a dream of mine of almost forty years was realized: I met Robert Heinlein. It was his writing, and A.E. Van Vogt's, which got me interested in SF, and I consider Heinlein my spiritual father, even though our political ideologies are totally at variance. Several years ago, when I was ill, Heinlein offered his help, anything he could do, and we had never met; he would phone me to cheer me up and see how I was doing. He wanted to buy me an electric typewriter, God bless him—one of the few true gentlemen in this world. I don't agree with any ideas he puts forth in his writing, but that is neither here nor there. One time when I owed the IRS a lot of money and couldn't raise it, Heinlein loaned the money to me. I think a great deal of him and his wife; I dedicated a book to them in appreciation. Robert Heinlein is a fine-looking man, very impressive and very military in stance; you can tell he has a military background, even to the haircut. He knows I'm a flipped-out freak and still he helped me and my wife when we were in trouble. That is the best in humanity, there; that is who and what I love.

My friend Doris who has cancer used to be Norman Spinrad's girlfriend. Norman and I have been close for

years; we've done a lot of insane things together. Norman
and I both get hysterical and start raving. Norman has the
worst temper of any living mortal. He knows it.
Beethoven was the same way. I now have no temper at all,
which is probably why my blood pressure is so high; I
can't get any of my anger out of my system. I don't really
know—in the final analysis—who I'm mad at. I really
envy Norman his ability to get it out of his system. He is
an excellent writer and an excellent friend. This is what I
get from being a SF writer: not fame and fortune, but
good friends. That's what makes it worth it to me. Wives
come and go; girlfriends come and go; we SF writers stay
together until we literally die... which I may do at any
time (probably to my own secret relief). Meanwhile I am
writing this introduction to THE GOLDEN MAN,
rereading stories that span a thirty year period of writing,
thinking back, remembering the Lucky Dog Pet Store,
my days in Berkeley, my political involvement and how
The Man got on my ass because of it... I still have a
residual fear in me, but I do believe that the reign of police
intrigue and terror is over in this country (for a time,
anyhow). I now sleep okay. But there was a time when I
sat up all night in fear, waiting for the knock on the door. I
was finally asked to "come downtown," as they call it, and
for hours the police interrogated me. I was even called in
by OSI (Airforce Intelligence) and questioned by them; it
had to do with terrorist activities in Marin County—not
terrorist activities by the authorities this time, but by
black ex-cons from San Quentin. It turned out that the
house behind mine was owned by a group of them. The
police thought we were in league; they kept showing me
photos of black guys and asking did I know them? At that
point I wouldn't have been able to answer. That was a
really scary day for little Phil.

So if you thought writers live a bookish, cloistered life
you are wrong, at least in my case. I was even in the street
for a couple of years: the dope scene. Parts of that scene
were funny and wonderful and other parts were hideous. I
wrote about it in A SCANNER DARKLY, so I won't
write about it here. The one good thing about my being in
the street was that the people didn't know I was a

well-known SF writer, or if they did they didn't care. They just wanted to know what I had that they could rip off and sell. At the end of the two years everything I owned was gone—literally, including my house. I flew to Canada as Guest of Honor at the Vancouver SF Convention, lectured at the University of B.C., and decided to stay there. The hell with the dope scene. I had temporarily stopped writing; it was a bad time for me. I had fallen in love with several unscrupulous street girls... I drove an old Pontiac convertible modified with a four-barrel carb and wide tires, and no brakes, and we were always in trouble, always facing problems we couldn't handle. It wasn't until I left Canada and flew down here to Orange County that I got my head together and back to writing. I met a very straight girl and married her, and we had a little baby we call Christopher. He is now five. They left me a couple of years ago. Well, as Vonnegut says, so it goes. What else can you say? It's like the whole of reality: you either laugh or—I guess fold and die.

One thing I've found that I can do that I really enjoy is rereading my own writing, earlier stories and novels especially. It induces mental time travel, the same way certain songs you hear on the radio do (for instance, when I hear Don McLean sing "Vincent" I at once see a girl named Linda wearing a mini skirt and driving her yellow Camaro; we're on our way to an expensive restaurant and I am worrying if I'll be able to pay the bill and Linda is talking about how she is in love with an older SF writer and I imagine—oh vain folly!—that she means me, but it turns out she means Norman Spinrad who I introduced her to); the whole thing returns, an eerie feeling which I'm sure you've experienced. People have told me that everything about me, every facet of my life, psyche, experiences, dreams and fears, are laid out explicitly in my writing, that from the corpus of my work I can be absolutely and precisely inferred. This is true. So when I read my writing, like these stories in this collection, I take a trip through my own head and life, only it is my earlier head and my earlier life. I abreact, as the psychiatrists say. There's the dope theme. There's the philosophical theme, especially the vast epistemological doubts that began when I was briefly attending U.C. Berkeley. Friends who are dead are in my stories and novels. Names of streets! I even put my agent's address in one, as a character's address (Harlan once put his own phone number in a story, which he was to regret later). And of course, in my writing, there is the constant theme of music, love of, preoccupation with, music. Music is the single thread making my life into a coherency.

You see, had I not become a writer I'd be somewhere in the music industry now, almost certainly the record industry. I remember back in the mid-Sixties when I first heard Linda Ronstadt; she was a guest on Glen Campbell's TV show, and no one had ever heard of her. I went nuts listening to her and looking at her. I had been a buyer in retail records and it had been my job to spot new talent that was hot property, and, seeing and hearing Ronstadt, I knew I was hearing one of the great people in the business; I could see down the pipe of time into the future. Later, when she'd recorded a few records, none of them hits, all of which I faithfully bought, I calculated to the exact *month* when she'd make it big. I even wrote Capitol Records and told them; I said, the next record Ronstadt cuts will be the beginning of a career unparalleled in the record industry. Her next record was "Heart Like a Wheel." Capitol didn't answer my letter, but what the hell; I was right, and happy to be right. But, see, that's what I'd be into now, had I not gone into writing SF. My fantasy number which I run in my head is, I discover Linda Ronstadt, and am remembered as the scout for Capitol who signed her. I would have wanted that on my gravestone:

> HE DISCOVERED LINDA RONSTADT
> AND SIGNED HER UP!

My friends are caustically and disdainfully amused by my fantasy life about discovering Ronstadt and Grace Slick and Streisand and so forth. I have a good stereo system (at least my cartridge and speakers are good) and I own a huge record collection, and every night from eleven P.M. to five A.M. I write while wearing my Stax electrostatic top-of-line headphones. It's my job and my vice mixed together. You can't hope for better than that:

having your job and your sin comingled. There I am, writing away, and into my ears is pouring Bonnie Koloc and no one can hear it but me. The joker is, though, that there's no one but me here anyhow, all the wives and girlfriends having long since left. That's another of the ills of writing; because it is such a solitary occupation, and requires such long-term concentrated attention, it tends to drive your wife or girlfriend away, anyhow whoever you're living with. It's probably the most painful price the writer pays. All I have to keep me company are two cats. Like my doper friends (ex-doper friends, since most of them are dead now) my cats don't know I'm a well-known writer, and, as with my doper friends, I prefer it that way.

When I was in France, I had the interesting experience of being famous. I am the best-liked SF writer there, best of all in the entire whole complete world (I tell you that for what it's worth). I was Guest of Honor, at the Metz Festival which I mentioned, and I delivered a speech which, typically, made no sense whatever. Even the French couldn't understand it, despite a translation. Something goes haywire in my brain when I write speeches; I think I imagine I'm a reincarnation of Zoroaster bringing news of God. So I try to make as few speeches as possible. Call me up, offer me a lot of money to deliver a speech, and I'll give a tacky pretext to get out of doing it; I'll say anything, palpably a lie. But it was fantastic (in the sense of not real) to be in France and see all my books in expensive beautiful editions instead of little paperbacks with what Spinrad calls "peeled eyeball" covers. Owners of bookstores came to shake my hand. The Metz City Council had a dinner and a reception for us writers. Harlan was there, as I mentioned; so was Roger Zelazny and John Brunner and Harry Harrison and Robert Sheckley. I had never met Sheckley before; he is a gentle man. Brunner, like me, has gotten stout. We all had endless meals together; Brunner made sure everyone knew he spoke French. Harry Harrison sang the Fascist national anthem in Italian in a loud voice, which showed what he thought of prestige (Harry is the iconoclast of the known universe). Editors and publishers skulked everywhere, as well as the media. I got interviewed from eight in the morning until three-thirty the next morning, and, as always, I said things which will come back to haunt me. It was the best week of my life. I think that there at Metz I was really happy for the first time—not because I was famous but because there was so much excitement in those people. The French get wildly excited about ordering from a menu; it's like the old political discussions we used to have back in Berkeley, only it's simply food involved. Which street to walk up involves ten French people gesticulating and yelling, and then running off in different directions. The French, like me and Spinrad, see the most improbable possibility in every situation, which is certainly why I am popular there. Take a number of possibilities, and the French and I will select the wildest. So I had come home at last. I could get hysterical among people aculturated to hysteria, people never able to make decisions or execute actions because of the drama in the very process of choosing. That's me: paralyzed by imagination. For me a flat tire on my car is (a) The End of the World; and (b) An Indication of Monsters (although I forget why).

This is why I love SF. I love to read it; I love to write it. The SF writer sees not just possibilities but *wild* possibilities. It's not just "What if—" It's "*My God*; what if—" In frenzy and hysteria. The Martians are always coming. Mr. Spock is the only one calm. This is why Spock has become a cult god to us; he calms our normal hysteria. He balances the proclivity of SF people to imagine the impossible.

> KIRK (frantically): Spock, the *Enterprise* is about to blow up!
> SPOCK (calmly): Negative, Captain; it's merely a faulty fuse.

Spock is always right, even when he's wrong. It's the tone of voice, the supernatural reasonability; this is not a man like us; this is a god. God talks this way; everyone of us senses it instinctively. That's why they have Leonard Nimoy narrating pseudo-science TV programs. Nimoy can make anything sound plausible. They can be in search of a lost button or the elephants' graveyard, and Nimoy will calm our doubts and fears. I would like him as a psychotherapist; I would rush in frantically, filled with my usual hysterical fears, and he would banish them.

> PHIL (hysterically): Leonard, the sky is falling!
> NIMOY (calmly): Negative, Phil; it's merely a
> faulty fuse.

And I'd feel okay and my blood pressure would drop and I could resume work on the novel I'm three years behind on *vis-à-vis* my deadline.

In reading the stories included in this volume, you should bear in mind that most were written when SF was so looked down upon that it virtually was not there, in the eyes of all America. This was not funny, the derision felt toward SF writers. It made our lives wretched. Even in Berkeley—or especially in Berkeley—people would say, "But are you writing anything serious?" We made no money; few publishers published SF (Ace Books was the only regular book publisher of SF); and really cruel abuse was inflicted on us. To select SF writing as a career was an act of self-destruction; in fact, most *writers*, let alone other people, could not even conceive of someone considering it. The only non-SF writer who ever treated me with courtesy was Herbert Gold, who I met at a literary party in San Francisco. He autographed a file card to me this way: "To a colleague, Philip K. Dick." I kept the card until the ink faded and was gone, and I still feel grateful to him for this charity. (Yes, that was what it was, then, to treat an SF writer with courtesy.) To get hold of a copy of my first published novel, SOLAR LOTTERY, I had to special order it from the City Lights Bookshop in San Francisco, which specialized in the outré. So in my head I have to collate the experience in 1977 of the mayor of Metz shaking hands with me at an official city function, and the ordeal of the Fifties when Kleo and I lived on ninety-dollars-a-month, when we could not even pay the fine on an overdue library book, and when I wanted to read a magazine I had to go to the library because I could not afford to buy it, when we were literally living on dog food. But I think you should know this—specifically, in case you are, say, in your twenties and rather poor and perhaps becoming filled with despair, whether you are a SF writer or not, whatever you want to make of your life. There can be a lot of fear, and often it is a justified fear. People do starve in America. My financial ordeal did not end in the Fifties; as late as the mid-Seventies I still could not pay my rent, nor afford to take Christopher to the doctor, nor own a car, nor have a phone. In the month that Christopher and his mother left me I earned nine dollars, and that was just three years ago. Only the kindness of my agent, Scott Meredith, in loaning me money when I was broke got me through. In 1971 I actually had to beg friends for food. Now look; I don't want sympathy; what I am trying to do is tell you that your crisis, your ordeal, assuming you have one, is not something that is going to be endless, and I want you to know that you will probably survive it through your courage and wits and sheer drive to live. I have seen uneducated street girls survive horrors that beggar description. I have seen the faces of men whose brains had been burned-out by drugs, men who still could think enough to be able to realize what had happened to them; I watched their clumsy attempts to weather that which cannot be weathered. As in Heine's poem, "Atlas," this line: "I carry that which can't be carried." And the next line is, "And in my body my heart would like to break!" But this is not the sole constituent of life, and it is not the sole theme in fiction, mine or anyone else's, except perhaps for the nihilist French existentialists. Kabir, the sixteenth century Sufi poet, wrote, "If you have not lived through something, it is not true." So live through it; I mean, go all the way to the end. Only then can it be understood, not along the way.

If I had to come forth with an analysis of the anger that lies inside me, which expresses itself in so many sublimations, I would guess that probably what arouses my indignation is seeing the meaningless. That which is disorder, the force of entropy—there is no redemptive value of something that can't be understood, as far as I am concerned. My writing, in toto, is an attempt on my part to take my life and everything I've seen and done, and fashion it into a work which makes sense. I'm not sure I've been successful. First, I cannot falsify what I have seen. I see disorder and sorrow, and so I have to write about it; but I've seen bravery and humor, and so I put that in, too. But what does it all add up to? What is the vast overview which is going to impart sense into the entirety?

What helps for me—if help comes at all—is to find the mustard seed of the funny at the core of the horrible and futile. I've been researching ponderous and solemn theological matters for five years now, for my novel-in-progress, and much of the Wisdom of the World has passed from the printed page and into my brain, there to be processed and secreted in the form of more words: words in, words out, and a brain in the middle wearily trying to determine the meaning of it all. Anyhow, the other night I started on the article on Indian Philosophy in the *Encyclopedia of Philosophy*, an eight-volume learned reference set which I esteem. The time was four AM.; I was exhausted—I have been working endlessly like this on this novel, doing this kind of research. And there, at the heart of this solemn article, was this:

"The Buddhist idealists used various arguments to show that perception does not yield knowledge of external objects distinct from the percipient... The external world supposedly consists of a number of different objects, but they can be known as different only because there are different sorts of experiences 'of' them. Yet if the experiences are thus distinguishable, there is no need to hold the superfluous hypothesis of external objects..."

In other words, by applying Ockham's razor to the basic epistemological question of, "What is reality?" the Buddhist idealists reach the conclusion that belief in an external world is a "superfluous hypothesis"; i.e. it violates the Principle of Parsimony—which is the principle underlying all Western science. Thus the external world is abolished, and we can go about more important business—whatever that might be.

That night I went to bed laughing. I laughed for an hour. I am still laughing. Push philosophy and theology to their ultimate (and Buddhist idealism probably is the ultimate of both) and what do you wind up with? Nothing. Nothing exists (they also proved that the self doesn't exist, either). As I said earlier, there is only one way out: seeing it all as ultimately funny. Kabir, who I quoted, saw dancing and joy and love as ways out, too; and he wrote about the sound of "the anklets on the feet of an insect as it walks." I would like to hear that sound; perhaps if I could my anger and fear, and my high blood pressure, would go away.

THE GOLDEN MAN

The Golden Man

"Is it always hot like this?" the salesman demanded. He addressed everybody at the lunch counter and in the shabby booths against the wall. A middled-aged fat man with a good-natured smile, rumpled gray suit, sweat-stained white shirt, a drooping bowtie, and a panama hat.

"Only in the summer," the waitress answered.

None of the others stirred. The teen-age boy and girl in one of the booths, eyes fixed intently on each other. Two workmen, sleeves rolled up, arms dark and hairy, eating bean soup and rolls. A lean, weathered farmer. An elderly businessman in a blue-serge suit, vest and pocket watch. A dark rat-faced cab driver drinking coffee. A tired woman who had come in to get off her feet and put down her bundles.

The salesman got out a package of cigarettes. He glanced curiously around the dingy cafe, lit up, leaned his arms on the counter, and said to the man next to him: "What's the name of this town?"

The man grunted. "Walnut Creek."

The salesman sipped at his coke for awhile, cigarette held loosely between plump white fingers. Presently he reached in his coat and brought out a leather wallet. For a long time he leafed thoughtfully through cards and papers, bits of notes, ticket stubs, endless odds and ends, soiled fragments—and finally a photograph.

He grinned at the photograph, and then began to chuckle, a low moist rasp. "Look at this," he said to the man beside him.

The man went on reading his newspaper.

"Hey, look at this." The salesman nudged him with his

elbow and pushed the photograph at him. "How's that strike you?"

Annoyed, the man glanced briefly at the photograph. It showed a nude woman, from the waist up. Perhaps thirty-five years old. Face turned away. Body white and flabby. With eight breasts.

"Ever seen anything like that?" the salesman chuckled, his little red eyes dancing. His face broke into lewd smiles and again he nudged the man.

"I've seen that before." Disgusted, the man resumed reading his newspaper.

The salesman noticed the lean old farmer was looking at the picture. He passed it genially over to him. "How's that strike you, pop? Pretty good stuff, eh?"

The farmer examined the picture solemnly. He turned it over, studied the creased back, took a second look at the front, then tossed it to the salesman. It slid from the counter, turned over a couple of times, and fell to the floor face up.

The salesman picked it up and brushed it off. Carefully, almost tenderly, he restored it to his wallet. The waitress' eyes flickered as she caught a glimpse of it.

"Damn nice," the salesman observed, with a wink. "Wouldn't you say so?"

The waitress shrugged indifferently. "I don't know. I saw a lot of them around Denver. A whole colony."

"That's where this was taken. Denver DCA Camp."

"Any still alive?" the farmer asked.

The salesman laughed harshly. "You kidding?" He made a short, sharp swipe with his hand. "Not any more."

THEY WERE all listening. Even the high school kids in the booth had stopped holding hands and were sitting up straight, eyes wide with fascination.

"Saw a funny kind down near San Diego," the farmer said. "Last year, some time. Had wings like a bat. Skin, not feathers. Skin and bone wings."

The rat-eyed taxi driver chimed in. "That's nothing. There was a two-headed one in Detroit. I saw it on exhibit."

"Was it alive?" the waitress asked.

"No. They'd already euthed it."

"In sociology," the high school boy spoke up, "we saw tapes of a whole lot of them. The winged kind from down south, the big-headed one they found in Germany, an awful-looking one with sort of cones, like an insect. And—"

"The worst of all," the elderly businessman stated, "are those English ones. That hid out in the coal mines. The ones they didn't find until last year." He shook his head. "Forty years, down there in the mines, breeding and developing. Almost a hundred of them. Survivors from a group that went underground during the War."

"They just found a new kind in Sweden," the waitress said. "I was reading about it. Controls minds at a distance, they said. Only a couple of them. The DCA got there plenty fast."

"That's a variation of the New Zealand type," one of the workmen said. "It reads minds."

"Reading and controlling are two different things," the businessman said. "When I hear something like that I'm plenty glad there's the DCA."

"There was a type they found right after the War," the farmer said. "In Siberia. Had the ability to control objects. Psychokinetic ability. The Soviet DCA got it right away. Nobody remembers that any more."

"I remember that," the businessman said. "I was just a kid, then. I remember because that was the first deeve I ever heard of. My father called me into the living-room and told me and my brothers and sisters. We were still rebuilding the house. That was in the days when the DCA inspected everyone and stamped their arms." He held up his thin, gnarled wrist. "I was stamped there, sixty years ago."

"Now they just have the birth inspection," the waitress said. She shivered. "There was one in San Francisco this month. First in over a year. They thought it was over, around here."

"It's been dwindling," the taxi driver said. "Frisco wasn't too bad hit. Not like some. Not like Detroit."

"They still get ten or fifteen a year in Detroit," the high school boy said. "All around there. Lots of pools still left. People go into them, in spite of the robot signs."

"What kind was this one?" the salesman asked. "The

one they found in San Francisco."

The waitress gestured. "Common type. The kind with no toes. Bent-over. Big eyes."

"The nocturnal type," the salesman said.

"The mother had hid it. They say it was three years old. She got the doctor to forge the DCA chit. Old friend of the family."

The salesman had finished his coke. He sat playing idly with his cigarette, listening to the hum of talk he had set into motion. The high school boy was leaning excitedly toward the girl across from him, impressing her with his fund of knowledge. The lean farmer and the businessman were huddled together, remembering the old days, the last years of the War, before the first Ten-Year Reconstruction Plan. The taxi driver and the two workmen were swapping yarns about their own experiences.

The salesman caught the waitress' attention. "I guess," he said thoughtfully, "that one in Frisco caused quite a stir. Something like that happening so close."

"Yeah," the waitress murmured.

"This side of the Bay wasn't really hit," the salesman continued. "You never get any of them over here."

"No." The waitress moved abruptly. "None in this area. Ever." She scooped up dirty dishes from the counter and headed toward the back.

"Never?" the salesman asked, surprised. "You've never had any deeves on this side of the Bay?"

"No. None." She disappeared into the back, where the fry cook stood by his burners, white apron and tattooed wrists. Her voice was a little too loud, a little too harsh and strained. It made the farmer pause suddenly and glance up.

Silence dropped like a curtain. All sound cut off instantly. They were all gazing down at their food, suddenly tense and ominous.

"None around here," the taxi driver said, loudly and clearly, to no one in particular. "None ever."

"Sure," the salesman agreed genially. "I was only—"

"Make sure you get that straight," one of the workmen said.

The salesman blinked. "Sure, buddy. Sure." He fumbled nervously in his pocket. A quarter and a dime jangled to the floor and he hurriedly scooped them up. "No offense."

For a moment there was silence. Then the high school boy spoke up, aware for the first time that nobody was saying anything. "I heard something," he began eagerly, voice full of importance. "Somebody said they saw something up by the Johnson farm that looked like it was one of those—"

"Shut up," the businessman said, without turning his head.

SCARLET-FACED, the boy sagged in his seat. His voice wavered and broke off. He peered hastily down at his hands and swallowed unhappily.

The salesman paid the waitress for his coke. "What's the quickest road to Frisco?" he began. But the waitress had already turned her back.

The people at the counter were immersed in their food. None of them looked up. They ate in frozen silence. Hostile, unfriendly faces, intent on their food.

The salesman picked up his bulging briefcase, pushed open the screen door, and stepped out into the blazing sunlight. He moved toward his battered 1978 Buick, parked a few meters up. A blue-shirted traffic cop was standing in the shade of an awning, talking languidly to a young woman in a yellow silk dress that clung moistly to her slim body.

The salesman paused a moment before he got into his car. He waved his hand and hailed the policeman. "Say, you know this town pretty good?"

The policeman eyed the salesman's rumpled gray suit, bowtie, his sweat-stained shirt. The out-of-state license. "What do you want?"

"I'm looking for the Johnson farm," the salesman said. "Here to see him about some litigation." He moved toward the policeman, a small white card between his fingers. "I'm his attorney—from the New York Guild. Can you tell me how to get out there? I haven't been through here in a couple of years."

Nat Johnson gazed up at the noonday sun and saw that it was good. He sat sprawled out on the bottom step of the porch, a pipe between his yellowed teeth, a lithe, wiry man in red-checkered shirt and canvas jeans, powerful hands, iron-gray hair that was still thick despite sixty-five years of active life.

He was watching the children play. Jean rushed laughing in front of him, bosom heaving under her sweat shirt, black hair streaming behind her. She was sixteen, bright-eyed, legs strong and straight, slim young body bent slightly forward with the weight of the two horseshoes. After her scampered Dave, fourteen, white teeth and black hair, a handsome boy, a son to be proud of. Dave caught up with his sister, passed her, and reached the far peg. He stood waiting, legs apart, hands on his hips, his two horseshoes gripped easily. Gasping, Jean hurried toward him.

"Go ahead!" Dave shouted. "You shoot first. I'm waiting for you."

"So you can knock them away?"

"So I can knock them closer."

Jean tossed down one horseshoe and gripped the other with both hands, eyes on the distant peg. Her lithe body bent, one leg slid back, her spine arched. She took careful aim, closed one eye, and then expertly tossed the shoe. With a clang the shoe struck the distant peg, circled briefly around it, then bounced off again and rolled to one side. A cloud of dust rolled up.

"Not bad," Nat Johnson admitted, from his step. "Too hard, though. Take it easy." His chest swelled with pride as the girl's glistening, healthy body took aim and again threw. Two powerful, handsome children, almost ripe, on the verge of adulthood. Playing together in the hot sun.

And there was Cris.

Cris stood by the porch, arms folded. He wasn't playing. He was watching. He had stood there since Dave and Jean had begun playing, the same half-intent, half-remote expression on his finely-cut face. As if he were seeing past them, beyond the two of them. Beyond the field, the barn, the creek bed, the rows of cedars.

"Come on, Cris!" Jean called, as she and Dave moved across the field to collect their horseshoes. "Don't you want to play?"

No, Cris didn't want to play. He never played. He was off in a world of his own, a world into which none of them could come. He never joined in anything, games or chores or family activities. He was by himself always. Remote, detached, aloof. Seeing past everyone and everything—that is, until all at once something clicked and he momentarily rephased, reentered their world briefly.

NAT JOHNSON reached out and knocked his pipe against the step. He refilled it from his leather tobacco pouch, his eyes on his eldest son. Cris was now moving into life. Heading out onto the field. He walked slowly, arms folded calmly, as if he had, for the moment, descended from his own world into theirs. Jean didn't see him; she had turned her back and was getting ready to pitch.

"Hey," Dave said, startled. "Here's Cris."

Cris reached his sister, stopped, and held out his hand. A great dignified figure, calm and impassive. Uncertainly, Jean gave him one of the horseshoes. "You want this? You want to play?"

Cris said nothing. He bent slightly, a supple arc of his incredibly graceful body, then moved his arm in a blur of speed. The shoe sailed, struck the far peg, and dizzily spun around it. Ringer.

The corners of Dave's mouth turned down. "What a lousy darn thing."

"Cris," Jean reproved. "You don't play fair."

No, Cris didn't play fair. He had watched half an hour—then come out and thrown once. One perfect toss, one dead ringer.

"He never makes a mistake," Dave complained.

Cris stood, face blank. A golden statue in the mid-day sun. Golden hair, skin, a light down of gold fuzz on his bare arms and legs—

Abruptly he stiffened. Nat sat up, startled. "What is it?" he barked.

Cris turned in a quick circle, magnificent body alert. "Cris!" Jean demanded. "What—"

Cris shot forward. Like a released energy beam he bounded across the field, over the fence, into the barn and out the other side. His flying figure seemed to skim over the dry grass as he descended into the barren creek-bed, between the cedars. A momentary flash of gold—and he was gone. Vanished. There was no sound. No motion. He had utterly melted into the scenery.

"What was it this time?" Jean asked wearily. She came over to her father and threw herself down in the shade. Sweat glowed on her smooth neck and upper lip; her sweat shirt was streaked and damp. "What did he see?"

"He was after something," Dave stated, coming up.

Nat grunted. "Maybe. There's no telling."

"I guess I better tell Mom not to set a place for him," Jean said. "He probably won't be back."

Anger and futility descended over Nat Johnson. No, he wouldn't be back. Not for dinner and probably not the next day—or the one after that. He'd be gone God only knew how long. Or where. Or why. Off by himself, alone some place. "If I thought there was any use," Nat began, "I'd send you two after him. But there's no—"

He broke off. A car was coming up the dirt road toward the farmhouse. A dusty, battered old Buick. Behind the wheel sat a plump red-faced man in a gray suit, who waved cheerfully at them as the car sputtered to a stop and the motor died into silence.

"AFTERNOON," the man nodded, as he climbed out of the car. He tipped his hat pleasantly. He was middle-aged, genial-looking, perspiring freely as he crossed the dry ground toward the porch. "Maybe you folks can help me."

"What do you want?" Nat Johnson demanded hoarsely. He was frightened. He watched the creek bed out of the corner of his eye, praying silently. God, if only he *stayed* away. Jean was breathing quickly, sharp little gasps. She was terrified. Dave's face was expressionless, but all color had drained from it. "Who are you?" Nat demanded.

"Name's Baines. George Baines." The man held out his hand but Johnson ignored it. "Maybe you've heard of me. I own the Pacifica Development Corporation. We built all those little bomb-proof houses just outside town. Those little round ones you see as you come up the main highway from Lafayette."

"What do you want?" Johnson held his hands steady with an effort. He'd never heard of the man, although he'd noticed the housing tract. It couldn't be missed—a great ant-heap of ugly pill-boxes straddling the highway. Baines looked like the kind of man who'd own them. But what did he want here?

"I've bought some land up this way," Baines was explaining. He rattled a sheaf of crisp papers. "This is the deed, but I'll be damned if I can find it." He grinned good-naturedly. "I know it's around this way, someplace, this side of the State road. According to the clerk at the County Recorder's Office, a mile or so this side of that hill over there. But I'm no damn good at reading maps."

"It isn't around here," Dave broke in. "There's only farms around here. Nothing for sale."

"This is a farm, son," Baines said genially. "I bought it for myself and my missus. So we could settle down." He wrinkled his pug nose. "Don't get the wrong idea—I'm not putting up any tracts around here. This is strictly for myself. An old farm house, twenty acres, a pump and a few oak trees—"

"Let me see the deed." Johnson grabbed the sheaf of papers, and while Baines blinked in astonishment, he leafed rapidly through them. His face hardened and he handed them back. "What are you up to? This deed is for a parcel fifty miles from here."

"Fifty miles!" Baines was dumbfounded. "No kidding? But the clerk told me—"

Johnson was on his feet. He towered over the fat man. He was in top-notch physical shape—and he was plenty damn suspicious. "Clerk, hell. You get back into your car and drive out of here. I don't know what you're after, or what you're here for, but I want you off my land."

In Johnson's massive fist something sparkled. A metal tube that gleamed ominously in the mid-day sunlight. Baines saw it—and gulped. "No offense, mister." He backed nervously away. "You folks sure are touchy. Take it easy, will you?"

Johnson said nothing. He gripped the lash-tube tighter and waited for the fat man to leave.

But Baines lingered. "Look, buddy. I've been driving around this furnace five hours, looking for my damn place. Any objection to my using your—facilities?"

Johnson eyed him with suspicion. Gradually the suspicion turned to disgust. He shrugged. "Dave, show him where the bathroom is."

"Thanks." Baines grinned thankfully. "And if it wouldn't be too much trouble, maybe a glass of water. I'd be glad to pay you for it." He chuckled knowingly. "Never let the city people get away with anything, eh?"

"Christ." Johnson turned away in revulsion as the fat man lumbered after his son, into the house.

"Dad," Jean whispered. As soon as Baines was inside she hurried up onto the porch, eyes wide with fear. "Dad, do you think he—"

Johnson put his arm around her. "Just hold on tight. He'll be gone, soon."

The girl's dark eyes flashed with mute terror. "Every time the man from the water company, or the tax collector, some tramp, children, *anybody* come around, I get a terrible stab of pain—here." She clutched at her heart, hand against her breasts. "It's been that way thirteen years. How much longer can we keep it going? *How long?*"

THE MAN named Baines emerged gratefully from the bathroom. Dave Johnson stood silently by the door, body rigid, youthful face stony.

"Thanks, son," Baines sighed. "Now where can I get a glass of cold water?" He smacked his thick lips in anticipation. "After you've been driving around the sticks looking for a dump some red-hot real estate agent stuck you with—"

Dave headed into the kitchen. "Mom, this man wants a drink of water. Dad said he could have it."

Dave had turned his back. Baines caught a brief glimpse of the mother, gray-haired, small, moving toward the sink with a glass, face withered and drawn, without expression.

Then Baines hurried from the room down a hall. He passed through a bedroom, pulled a door open, found himself facing a closet. He turned and raced back, through the living room, into a dining room, then another bedroom. In a brief instant he had gone through the whole house.

He peered out a window. The back yard. Remains of a rusting truck. Entrance of an underground bomb shelter.

Tin cans. Chickens scratching around. A dog, asleep under a shed. A couple of old auto tires.

He found a door leading out. Soundlessly, he tore the door open and stepped outside. No one was in sight. There was a barn, a leaning, ancient wood structure. Cedar trees beyond, a creek of some kind. What had once been an outhouse.

BAINES moved cautiously around the side of the house. He had perhaps thirty seconds. He had left the door of the bathroom closed; the boy would think he had gone back in there. Baines looked into the house through a window. A large closet, filled with old clothing, boxes and bundles of magazines.

He turned and started back. He reached the corner of the house and started around it.

Nat Johnson's gaunt shape loomed up and blocked his way. "All right, Baines. You asked for it."

A pink flash blossomed. It shut out the sunlight in a single blinding burst. Baines leaped back and clawed at his coat pocket. The edge of the flash caught him and he half-fell, stunned by the force. His suit-shield sucked in the energy and discharged it, but the power rattled his teeth and for a moment he jerked like a puppet on a string. Darkness ebbed around him. He could feel the mesh of the shield glow white, as it absorbed the energy and fought to control it.

His own tube came out—and Johnson had no shield. "You're under arrest," Baines muttered grimly. "Put down your tube and your hands up. And call your family." He made a motion with the tube. "Come on, Johnson. Make it snappy."

The lash-tube wavered and then slipped from Johnson's fingers. "You're still alive." Dawning horror crept across his face. "Then you must be—"

Dave and Jean appeared. *"Dad!"*

"Come over here," Baines ordered. "Where's your mother?"

Dave jerked his head numbly. "Inside."

"Get her and bring her here."

"You're DCA," Nat Johnson whispered.

Baines didn't answer. He was doing something with his

neck, pulling at the flabby flesh. The wiring of a contact mike glittered as he slipped it from a fold between two chins and into his pocket. From the dirt road came the sound of motors, sleek purrs that rapidly grew louder. Two teardrops of black metal came gliding up and parked beside the house. Men swarmed out, in the dark gray-green of the Government Civil Police. In the sky swarms of black dots were descending, clouds of ugly flies that darkened the sun as they spilled out men and equipment. The men drifted slowly down.

"He's not here," Baines said, as the first man reached him. "He got away. Inform Wisdom back at the lab."

"We've got this section blocked off."

Baines turned to Nat Johnson, who stood in dazed silence, uncomprehending, his son and daughter beside him. "How did he know we were coming?" Baines demanded.

"I don't know," Johnson muttered. "He just—knew."

"A telepath?"

"I don't know."

Baines shrugged. "We'll know, soon. A clamp is out, all around here. He can't get past, no matter what the hell he can do. Unless he can dematerialize himself."

"What'll you do with him when you—if you catch him?" Jean asked huskily.

"Study him."

"And then kill him?"

"That depends on the lab evaluation. If you could give me more to work on, I could predict better."

"We can't tell you anything. We don't know anything more." The girl's voice rose with desperation. "He doesn't talk."

Baines jumped. *"What?"*

"He doesn't talk. He never talked to us. Ever."

"How old is he?"

"Eighteen."

"No communication." Baines was sweating. "In eighteen years there hasn't been any semantic bridge between you? Does he have *any* contact? Signs? Codes?"

"He—ignores us. He eats here, stays with us. Sometimes he plays when we play. Or sits with us. He's gone days on end. We've never been able to find out what he's doing—or where. He sleeps in the barn—by himself."

"Is he really gold-colored?"

"Yes."

"Skin, eyes, hair, nails. Everything."

"And he's large? Well-formed?"

It was a moment before the girl answered. A strange emotion stirred her drawn features, a momentary glow. "He's incredibly beautiful. A god come down to earth." Her lips twisted. "You won't find him. He can do things. Things you have no comprehension of. Powers so far beyond your limited—"

"You don't think we'll get him?" Baines frowned. "More teams are landing all the time. You've never seen an Agency clamp in operation. We've had sixty years to work out all the bugs. If he gets away it'll be the first time—"

Baines broke off abruptly. Three men were quickly approaching the porch. Two green-clad Civil Police. And a third man between them. A man who moved silently, lithely, a faintly luminous shape that towered above them.

"Cris!" Jean screamed.

"We got him," one of the police said.

Baines fingered his lash-tube uneasily. "Where? How?"

"He gave himself up," the policeman answered, voice full of awe. "He came to us voluntarily. Look at him. He's like a metal statue. Like some sort of—god."

The golden figure halted for a moment beside Jean. Then it turned slowly, calmly, to face Baines.

"Cris!" Jean shrieked. *"Why did you come back?"*

The same thought was eating at Baines, too. He shoved it aside—for the time being. "Is the jet out front?" he demanded quickly.

"Ready to go," one of the CP answered.

"Fine." Baines strode past them, down the steps and onto the dirt field. "Let's go. I want him taken directly to the lab." For a moment he studied the massive figure who stood calmly between the two Civil Policemen. Beside him, they seemed to have shrunk, become ungainly and repellent. Like dwarves... What had Jean said? *A god come to earth.* Baines broke angrily away. "Come on," he muttered brusquely. "This one may be tough; we've never run up against one like it before. We don't know what the hell it can do."

THE CHAMBER was empty, except for the seated figure. Four bare walls, floor and ceiling. A steady glare of white light relentlessly etched every corner of the chamber. Near the top of the far wall ran a narrow slot, the view windows through which the interior of the chamber was scanned.

The seated figure was quiet. He hadn't moved since the chamber locks had slid into place, since the heavy bolts had fallen from outside and the rows of bright-faced technicians had taken their places at the view windows. He gazed down at the floor, bent forward, hands clasped together, face calm, almost expressionless. In four hours he hadn't moved a muscle.

"Well?" Baines said. "What have you learned?"

Wisdom grunted sourly. "Not much. If we don't have him doped out in forty-eight hours we'll go ahead with the euth. We can't take any chances."

"You're thinking about the Tunis type," Baines said. He was, too. They had found ten of them, living in the ruins of the abandoned North African town. Their survival method was simple. They killed and absorbed other life forms, then imitated them and took their places. *Chameleons*, they were called. It had cost sixty lives, before the last one was destroyed. Sixty top-level experts, highly trained DCA men.

"Any clues?" Baines asked.

"He's different as hell. This is going to be tough." Wisdom thumbed a pile of tape-spools. "This is the complete report, all the material we got from Johnson and his family. We pumped them with the psych-wash, then let them go home. Eighteen years—and no semantic bridge. Yet, he looks fully developed. Mature at thirteen—a shorter, faster life-cycle than ours. But why the mane? All the gold fuzz? Like a Roman monument that's been gilded."

"Has the report come in from the analysis room? You had a wave-shot taken, of course."

"His brain pattern has been fully scanned. But it takes time for them to plot it out. We're all running around like lunatics while he just sits there!" Wisdom poked a stubby finger at the window. "We caught him easily enough. He can't have *much*, can he? But I'd like to know what it is. Before we euth him."

"Maybe we should keep him alive until we know."

"Euth in forty-eight hours," Wisdom repeated stubbornly. "Whether we know or not. I don't like him. He gives me the creeps."

Wisdom stood chewing nervously on his cigar, a red-haired, beefy-faced man, thick and heavy-set, with a barrel chest and cold, shrewd eyes deep-set in his hard face. Ed Wisdom was Director of DCA's North American Branch. But right now he was worried. His tiny eyes darted back and forth, alarmed flickers of gray in his brutal, massive face.

"You think," Baines said slowly, "this is *it?*"

"I always think so," Wisdom snapped. "I have to think so."

"I mean—"

"I know what you mean." Wisdom paced back and forth, among the study tables, technicians at their benches, equipment and humming computers. Buzzing tape-slots and research hookups. "This thing lived eighteen years with his family and *they* don't understand it. *They* don't know what it has. They know what it does, but not how."

"What does it do?"

"It knows things."

"What kind of things?"

Wisdom grabbed his lash-tube from his belt and tossed it on a table. "Here."

"What?"

"Here." Wisdom signalled, and a view window was slid back an inch. "Shoot him."

Baines blinked. "You said forty-eight hours."

With a curse, Wisdom snatched up the tube, aimed it through the window directly at the seated figure's back, and squeezed the trigger.

A blinding flash of pink. A cloud of energy blossomed in the center of the chamber. It sparkled, then died into dark ash.

"Good God!" Baines gasped. "You—"

He broke off. The figure was no longer sitting. As Wisdom fired, it had moved in a blur of speed, away from the blast, to the corner of the chamber. Now it was slowly coming back, face blank, still absorbed in thought.

"Fifth time," Wisdom said, as he put his tube away. "Last time Jamison and I fired together. Missed. He knew exactly when the bolts would hit. And where."

Baines and Wisdom looked at each other. Both of them were thinking the same thing. "But even reading minds wouldn't tell him where they were going to hit," Baines said. "When, maybe. But not where. Could you have called your own shots?"

"Not mine," Wisdom answered flatly. "I fired fast, damn near at random." He frowned. "Random. We'll have to make a test of this." He waved a group of technicians over. "Get a construction team up here. On the double." He grabbed paper and pen and began sketching.

WHILE construction was going on, Baines met his fiancee in the lobby outside the lab, the great central lounge of the DCA Building.

"How's it coming?" she asked. Anita Ferris was tall and blonde, blue eyes and a mature, carefully cultivated figure. An attractive, competent-looking woman in her late twenties. She wore a metal foil dress and cape—with a red and black stripe on the sleeve, the emblem of the A-Class. Anita was Director of the Semantics Agency, a top-level Government Coordinator. "Anything of interest, this time?"

"Plenty." Baines guided her from the lobby, into the dim recess of the bar. Music played softly in the background, a shifting variety of patterns formed mathematically. Dim shapes moved expertly through the gloom, from table to table. Silent, efficient robot waiters.

As Anita sipped her Tom Collins, Baines outlined what they had found.

"What are the chances," Anita asked slowly, "that he's built up some kind of deflection-cone? There was one kind that warped their environment by direct mental effort. No tools. Direct mind to matter."

"Psychokinetics?" Baines drummed restlessly on the

table top. "I doubt it. The thing has ability to predict, not to control. He can't stop the beams, but he can sure as hell get out of the way."

"Does he jump between the molecules?"

Baines wasn't amused. "This is serious. We've handled these things sixty years—longer than you and I have been around added together. Eighty-seven types of deviants have shown up, real mutants that could reproduce themselves, not mere freaks. This is the eighty-eighth. We've been able to handle each of them in turn. But this—"

"Why are you so worried about this one?"

"First, it's eighteen years old. That in itself is incredible. Its family managed to hide it that long."

"Those women around Denver were older than that. Those ones with—"

"They were in a Government camp. Somebody high up was toying with the idea of allowing them to breed. Some sort of industrial use. We withheld euth for years. But Cris Johnson stayed alive *outside our control*. Those things at Denver were under constant scrutiny."

"Maybe he's harmless. You always assume a deeve is a menace. He might even be beneficial. Somebody thought those women might work in. Maybe this thing has something that would advance the race."

"*Which* race? Not the human race. It's the old 'the operation was a success but the patient died' routine. If we introduce a mutant to keep us going it'll be mutants, not us, who'll inherit the earth. It'll be mutants surviving for their own sake. Don't think for a moment we can put padlocks on them and expect them to serve us. If they're really superior to homo sapiens, they'll win out in even competition. To survive, we've got to cold-deck them right from the start."

"In other words, we'll know homo superior when he comes—by definition. He'll be the one we won't be able to euth."

"That's about it," Baines answered. "Assuming there *is* a homo superior. Maybe there's just homo peculiar. Homo with an improved line."

"The Neanderthal probably thought the Cro-Magnon man had merely an improved line. A little more advanced ability to conjure up symbols and shape flint. From your description, this thing is more radical than a mere improvement."

"This thing," Baines said slowly, "has an ability to predict. So far, it's been able to stay alive. It's been able to cope with situations better than you or I could. How long do you think we'd stay alive in that chamber, with energy beams blazing down at us? In a sense it's got the ultimate survival ability. If it can always be accurate—"

A wall-speaker sounded. "Baines, you're wanted in the lab. Get the hell out of the bar and upramp."

Baines pushed back his chair and got to his feet. "Come along. You may be interested in seeing what Wisdom has got dreamed up."

A TIGHT GROUP of top-level DCA officials stood around in a circle, middle-aged, gray-haired, listening to a skinny youth in a white shirt and rolled-up sleeves explaining an elaborate cube of metal and plastic that filled the center of the view-platform. From it jutted an ugly array of tube snouts, gleaming muzzles that disappeared into an intricate maze of wiring.

"This," the youth was saying briskly, "is the first real test. It fires at random—as nearly random as we can make it, at least. Weighted balls are thrown up in an air stream, then dropped free to fall back and cut relays. They can fall in almost any pattern. The thing fires according to their pattern. Each drop produces a new configuration of timing and position. Ten tubes, in all. Each will be in constant motion."

"And *nobody* knows how they'll fire?" Anita asked.

"Nobody." Wisdom rubbed his thick hands together. "Mind-reading won't help him, not with this thing."

Anita moved over to the view windows, as the cube was rolled into place. She gasped. "Is that him?"

"What's wrong?" Baines asked.

Anita's cheeks were flushed. "Why, I expected a—a *thing*. My God, he's beautiful! Like a golden statue. Like a deity!"

Baines laughed. "He's eighteen years old, Anita. Too young for you."

The woman was still peering through the view window.

"Look at him. Eighteen? I don't believe it."

Cris Johnson sat in the center of the chamber, on the floor. A posture of contemplation, head bowed, arms folded, legs tucked under him. In the stark glare of the overhead lights his powerful body glowed and rippled, a shimmering figure of downy gold.

"Pretty, isn't he?" Wisdom muttered. "All right. Start it going."

"You're going to *kill* him?" Anita demanded.

"We're going to try."

"But he's—" She broke off uncertainly. "He's not a monster. He's not like those others, those hideous things with two heads, or those insects. Or those awful things from Tunis."

"What is he, then?" Baines asked.

"I don't know. But you can't just *kill* him. It's terrible!"

The cube clicked into life. The muzzles jerked, silently altered position. Three retracted, disappeared into the body of the cube. Others came out. Quickly, efficiently, they moved into position—and abruptly, without warning, opened fire.

A staggering burst of energy fanned out, a complex pattern that altered each moment, different angles, different velocities, a bewildering blur that cracked from the windows down into the chamber.

The golden figure moved. He dodged back and forth, expertly avoiding the bursts of energy that seared around him on all sides. Rolling clouds of ash obscured him; he was lost in a mist of crackling fire and ash.

"Stop it!" Anita shouted. "For God's sake, you'll destroy him!"

The chamber was an inferno of energy. The figure had completely disappeared. Wisdom waited a moment, then nodded to the technicians operating the cube. They touched guide buttons and the muzzles slowed and died. Some sank back into the cube. All became silent. The works of the cube ceased humming.

Cris Johnson was still alive. He emerged from the settling clouds of ash, blackened and singed. But unhurt. He had avoided each beam. He had weaved between them and among them as they came, a dancer leaping over glittering sword-points of pink fire. He had survived.

"No," Wisdom murmured, shaken and grim. "Not a telepath. Those were at random. No prearranged pattern."

THE THREE of them looked at each other, dazed and frightened. Anita was trembling. Her face was pale and her blue eyes were wide. "What, then?" She whispered. "What is it? What does he have?"

"He's a good guesser," Wisdom suggested.

"He's not guessing," Baines answered. "Don't kid yourself. That's the whole point."

"No, he's not guessing." Wisdom nodded slowly. "He *knew*. He predicted each strike. I wonder ... *Can* he err? *Can* he make a mistake?"

"We caught him," Baines pointed out.

"You said he came back voluntarily." There was a strange look on Wisdom's face. "Did he come back *after* the clamp was up?"

Baines jumped. "Yes, after."

"He couldn't have got through the clamp. So he came back." Wisdom grinned wryly. "The clamp must actually have been perfect. It was supposed to be."

"If there had been a single hole." Baines murmured, "he would have known it—gone through."

Wisdom ordered a group of armed guards over. "Get him out of there. To the euth stage."

Anita shrieked. "Wisdom, you can't—"

"He's too far ahead of us. We can't compete with him." Wisdom's eyes were bleak. "We can only guess what's going to happen. He *knows*. For him, it's a sure thing. I don't think it'll help him at euth, though. The whole stage is flooded simultaneously. Instantaneous gas, released throughout." He signalled impatiently to the guards. "Get going. Take him down right away. Don't waste any time."

"Can we?" Baines murmured thoughtfully.

The guards took up positions by one of the chamber locks. Cautiously, the tower control slid the lock back. The first two guards stepped cautiously in, lash-tubes ready.

Cris stood in the center of the chamber. His back was to them as they crept toward him. For a moment he was silent, utterly unmoving. The guards fanned out, as more of them entered the chamber. Then—

Anita screamed. Wisdom cursed. The golden figure spun and leaped forward, in a flashing blur of speed. Past the triple line of guards, through the lock and into the corridor.

"Get him!" Baines shouted.

Guards milled everywhere. Flashes of energy lit up the corridor, as the figure raced among them up the ramp.

"No use," Wisdom said calmly. "We can't hit him." He touched a button, then another. "But maybe this will help."

"What—" Baines began. But the leaping figure shot abruptly at him, straight at him, and he dropped to one side. The figure flashed past. It ran effortlessly, face without expression, dodging and jumping as the energy beams seared around it.

For an instant the golden face loomed up before Baines. It passed and disappeared down a side corridor. Guards rushed after it, kneeling and firing, shouting orders excitedly. In the bowels of the building, heavy guns were rumbling up. Locks slid into place as escape corridors were systematically sealed off.

"Good God," Baines gasped, as he got to his feet. "Can't he do anything but run?"

"I gave orders," Wisdom said, "to have the building isolated. There's no way out. Nobody comes and nobody goes. He's loose here in the building—but he won't get out."

"If there's one exit overlooked, he'll know it," Anita pointed out shakily.

"We won't overlook any exit. We got him once; we'll get him again."

A messenger robot had come in. Now it presented its message respectfully to Wisdom. "From analysis, sir."

Wisdom tore the tape open. "Now we'll know how it thinks." His hands were shaking. "Maybe we can figure out its blind spot. It may be able to out-think us, but that doesn't mean it's invulnerable. It only predicts the future—it can't change it. If there's only death ahead, its ability won't . . ."

Wisdom's voice faded into silence. After a moment he passed the tape to Baines.

"I'll be down in the bar," Wisdom said. "Getting a good stiff drink." His face had turned lead-gray. "All I can say is *I hope to hell this isn't the race to come.*"

"What's the analysis?" Anita demanded impatiently, peering over Baines' shoulder. "How does it think?"

"It doesn't," Baines said, as he handed the tape back to his boss. "It doesn't think at all. Virtually no frontal lobe. It's not a human being—it doesn't use symbols. It's nothing but an animal."

"An animal," Wisdom said. "With a single highly-developed faculty. Not a superior man. Not a man at all."

UP AND DOWN the corridors of the DCA Building, guards and equipment clanged. Loads of Civil Police were pouring into the building and taking up positions beside the guards. One by one, the corridors and rooms were being inspected and sealed off. Sooner or later the golden figure of Cris Johnson would be located and cornered.

"We were always afraid a mutant with superior intellectual powers would come along," Baines said reflectively. "A deeve who would be to us what we are to the great apes. Something with a bulging cranium, telepathic ability, a perfect semantic system, ultimate powers of symbolization and calculation. A development along our own path. A better human being."

"He acts by reflex," Anita said wonderingly. She had the analysis and was sitting at one of the desks studying it intently. "Reflex—like a lion. A golden lion." She pushed the tape aside, a strange expression on her face. "The lion god."

"Beast," Wisdom corrected tartly. "Blond beast, you mean."

"He runs fast," Baines said, "and that's all. No tools. He doesn't build anything or utilize anything outside himself. He just stands and waits for the right opportunity and then he runs like hell."

"This is worse than anything we've anticipated," Wisdom said. His beefy face was lead-gray. He sagged like an old man, his blunt hands trembling and uncertain. "To be replaced by an animal! Something that runs and hides. Something without a language!" He spat savagely. "That's why they weren't able to communicate with it. We wondered what kind of semantic system it had. It hasn't got any! No more ability to talk and think than a—dog."

"That means intelligence has failed," Baines went on huskily. "We're the last of our line—like the dinosaur. We've carried intelligence as far as it'll go. Too far, maybe. We've already got to the point where we know so much—think so much—we can't act."

"Men of thought," Anita said. "Not men of action. It's begun to have a paralyzing effect. But this thing—"

"This thing's faculty works better than ours ever did. We can recall past experiences, keep them in mind, learn from them. At best, we can make shrewd guesses about the future, from our memory of what's happened in the past. But we can't be certain. We have to speak of probabilities. Grays. Not blacks and whites. We're only guessing."

"Cris Johnson isn't guessing," Anita added.

"He can look ahead. See what's coming. He can—prethink. Let's call it that. He can see into the future. Probably he doesn't perceive it as the future."

"No," Anita said thoughtfully. "It would seem like the present. He has a broader present. But his present lies ahead, not back. Our present is related to the past. Only the past is certain, to us. To him, the future is certain. And he probably doesn't remember the past, any more than any animal remembers what's happened."

"As he develops," Baines said, "as his race evolves, it'll probably expand its ability to prethink. Instead of ten minutes, thirty minutes. Then an hour. A day. A year. Eventually they'll be able to keep ahead a whole lifetime. Each one of them will live in a solid, unchanging world. There'll be no variables, no uncertainty. No motion! They won't have anything to fear. Their world will be perfectly static, a solid block of matter."

"And when death comes," Anita said, "they'll accept it. There won't be any struggle; to them, it'll already have happened."

"Already have happened," Baines repeated. "To Cris, our shots had already been fired." He laughed harshly. "Superior survival doesn't mean superior man. If there were another world-wide flood, only fish would survive. If there were another ice age, maybe nothing but polar

bears would be left. When we opened the lock, he had already seen the men, seen exactly where they were standing and what they'd do. A neat faculty—but not a development of mind. A pure physical *sense*."

"But if every exit is covered," Wisdom repeated, "he'll see he can't get out. He gave himself up before—he'll give himself up again," He shook his head. "An animal. Without language. Without tools."

"With his new sense," Baines said, "he doesn't need anything else." He examined his watch. "It's after two. Is the building completely sealed off?"

"You can't leave," Wisdom stated. "You'll have to stay here all night—or until we catch the bastard."

"I meant her." Baines indicated Anita. "She's supposed to be back at Semantics by seven in the morning."

Wisdom shrugged. "I have no control over her. If she wants, she can check out."

"I'll stay," Anita decided. "I want to be here when he—when he's destroyed. I'll sleep here." She hesitated. "Wisdom, isn't there some other way? If he's just an animal couldn't we—"

"A zoo?" Wisdom's voice rose in a frenzy of hysteria. "Keep it penned up in the zoo? Christ no! It's got to be killed!"

FOR A LONG time the great gleaming shape crouched in the darkness. He was in a store room. Boxes and cartons stretched out on all sides, heaped up in orderly rows, all neatly counted and marked. Silent and deserted.

But in a few moments people burst in and searched the room. He could see this. He saw them in all parts of the room, clear and distinct, men with lash-tubes, grim-faced, stalking with murder in their eyes.

The sight was one of many. One of a multitude of clearly-etched scenes lying tangent to his own. And to each was attached a further multitude of interlocking scenes, that finally grew hazier and dwindled away. A progressive vagueness, each syndrome less distinct.

But the immediate one, the scene that lay closest to him, was clearly visible. He could easily make out the sight of the armed men. Therefore it was necessary to be out of the room before they appeared.

The golden figure got calmly to its feet and moved to the door. The corridor was empty; he could see himself already outside, in the vacant, drumming hall of metal and recessed lights. He pushed the door boldly open and stepped out.

A lift blinked across the hall. He walked to the lift and entered it. In five minutes a group of guards would come running along and leap into the lift. By that time he would have left it and sent it back down. Now he pressed a button and rose to the next floor.

He stepped out into a deserted passage. No one was in sight. That didn't surprise him. He couldn't be surprised. The element didn't exist for him. The positions of things, the space relationships of all matter in the immediate future, were as certain for him as his own body. The only thing that was unknown was that which had already passed out of being. In a vague, dim fashion, he had occasionally wondered where things went after he had passed them.

He came to a small supply closet. It had just been searched. It would be a half an hour before anyone opened it again. He had that long; he could see that far ahead. And then—

And then he would be able to see another area, a region farther beyond. He was always moving, advancing into new regions he had never seen before. A constantly unfolding panorama of sights and scenes, frozen land-scapes spread out ahead. All objects were fixed. Pieces on a vast chess board through which he moved, arms folded, face calm. A detached observer who saw objects that lay ahead of him as clearly as those under foot.

Right now, as he crouched in the small supply closet, he saw an unusually varied multitude of scenes for the next half hour. Much lay ahead. The half hour was divided into an incredibly complex pattern of separate configurations. He had reached a critical region; he was about to move through worlds of intricate complexity.

He concentrated on a scene ten minutes away. It showed, like a three dimensional still, a heavy gun at the end of the corridor, trained all the way to the far end. Men moved cautiously from door to door, checking each room again, as they had done repeatedly. At the end of the half hour they had reached the supply closet. A scene showed them looking inside. By that time he was gone, of course. He wasn't in that scene. He had passed on to another.

The next scene showed an exit. Guards stood in a solid line. No way out. He was in that scene. Off to one side, in a niche just inside the door. The street outside was visible, stars, lights, outlines of passing cars and people.

In the next tableau he had gone back, away from the exit. There was no way out. In another tableau he saw himself at other exits, a legion of golden figures, duplicated again and again, as he explored regions ahead, one after another. But each exit was covered.

In one dim scene he saw himself lying charred and dead; he had tried to run through the line, out the exit.

But that scene was vague. One wavering, indistinct still out of many. The inflexible path along which he moved would not deviate in that direction. It would not turn him that way. The golden figure in that scene, the miniature doll in that room, was only distantly related to him. It was himself, but a far-away self. A self he would never meet. He forgot it and went on to examine the other tableau.

The myriad of tableaux that surrounded him were an elaborate maze, a web which he now considered bit by bit. He was looking down into a doll's house of infinite rooms, rooms without number, each with its furniture, its dolls, all rigid and unmoving. The same dolls and furniture were repeated in many. He, himself, appeared often. The two men on the platform. The woman. Again and again the same combinations turned up; the play was redone frequently, the same actors and props moved around in all possible ways.

Before it was time to leave the supply closet, Cris Johnson had examined each of the rooms tangent to the one he now occupied. He had consulted each, considered its contents thoroughly.

He pushed the door open and stepped calmly out into the hall. He knew exactly where he was going. And what he had to do. Crouched in the stuffy closet, he had quietly and expertly examined each miniature of himself, observed which clearly-etched configuration lay along his inflexible path, the one room of the doll house, the one set out of legions, toward which he was moving.

ANITA slipped out of her metal-foil dress, hung it over a hanger, then unfastened her shoes and kicked them under the bed. She was just starting to unclip her bra when the door opened.

She gasped. Soundlessly, calmly, the great golden shape closed the door and bolted it after him.

Anita snatched up her lash-tube from the dressing table. Her hand shook; her whole body was trembling. "What do you want?" she demanded. Her fingers tightened convulsively around the tube. "I'll kill you."

The figure regarded her silently, arms folded. It was the first time she had seen Cris Johnson closely. The great dignified face, handsome and impassive. Broad shoulders. The golden mane of hair, golden skin, pelt of radiant fuzz—

"Why?" she demanded breathlessly. Her heart was pounding wildly. "What do you want?"

She could kill him easily. But the lash-tube wavered. Cris Johnson stood without fear; he wasn't at all afraid. Why not? Didn't he understand what it was? What the small metal tube could do to him?

"Of course," she said suddenly, in a choked whisper. "You can see ahead. You know I'm not going to kill you. Or you wouldn't have come here."

She flushed, terrified—and embarrassed. He knew exactly what she was going to do; he could see it as easily as she saw the walls of the room, the wall-bed with its covers folded neatly back, her clothes hanging in the closet, her purse and small things on the dressing table.

"All right." Anita backed away, then abruptly put the tube down on the dressing table. "I won't kill you. Why should I?" She fumbled in her purse and got out her cigarettes. Shakily, she lit up, her pulse racing. She was scared. And strangely fascinated. "Do you expect to stay here? It won't do any good. They've come through the dorm twice, already. They'll be back."

Could he understand her? She saw nothing on his face, only blank dignity. God, he was huge! It wasn't possible he was only eighteen, a boy, a child. He looked more like some great golden god, come down to earth.

She shook the thought off savagely. He wasn't a god.

He was a beast. *The blond beast*, come to take the place of man. To drive man from the earth.

Anita snatched up the lash-tube. "Get out of here! You're an animal! A big stupid animal! You can't even understand what I'm saying—you don't even have a language. You're not human."

Cris Johnson remained silent. As if he were waiting. Waiting for what? He showed no sign of fear or impatience, even though the corridor outside rang with the sound of men searching, metal against metal, guns and energy tubes being dragged around, shouts and dim rumbles as section after section of the building was searched and sealed off.

"They'll get you," Anita said. "You'll be trapped here. They'll be searching this wing any moment." She savagely stubbed out her cigarette. "For God's sake, what do you expect *me* to do?"

Cris moved toward her. Anita shrank back. His powerful hands caught hold of her and she gasped in sudden terror. For a moment she struggled blindly, desperately.

"Let go!" She broke away and leaped back from him. His face was expressionless. Calmly, he came toward her, an impassive god advancing to take her. "Get away!" She groped for the lash-tube, trying to get it up. But the tube slipped from her fingers and rolled onto the floor.

Cris bent down and picked it up. He held it out to her, in the open palm of his hand.

"Good God," Anita whispered. Shakily, she accepted the tube, gripped it hesitantly, then put it down again on the dressing table.

In the half-light of the room, the great golden figure seemed to glow and shimmer, outlined against the darkness. A god—no, not a god. An animal. A great golden beast, without a soul. She was confused. Which was he—or was he both? She shook her head, bewildered. It was late, almost four. She was exhausted and confused.

Cris took her in his arms. Gently, kindly, he lifted her face and kissed her. His powerful hands held her tight. She couldn't breathe. Darkness, mixed with the shimmering golden haze, swept around her. Around and around it spiraled, carrying her senses away. She sank down into it gratefully. The darkness covered her and dissolved her in a swelling torrent of sheer force that mounted in intensity each moment, until the roar of it beat against her and at last blotted out everything.

ANITA blinked, She sat up and automatically pushed her hair into place. Cris was standing before the closet. He was reaching up, getting something down.

He turned toward her and tossed something on the bed. Her heavy metal foil traveling cape.

Anita gazed down at the cape without comprehension. "What do you want?"

Cris stood by the bed, waiting.

She picked up the cape uncertainly. Cold creepers of fear plucked at her. "You want me to get you out of here," she said softly. "Past the guards and the CP."

Cris said nothing.

"They'll kill you instantly." She got unsteadily to her feet. "You can't run past them. Good God, don't you do anything but run? There must be a better way. Maybe I can appeal to Wisdom. I'm Class A—Director Class. I can go directly to the Full Directorate. I ought to be able to hold them off, keep back the euth indefinitely. The odds are a billion to one against us if we try to break past—"

She broke off.

"But you don't gamble," she continued slowly. "You don't go by odds. You *know* what's coming. You've seen the cards already." She studied his face intently. "No, you can't be cold-decked. It wouldn't be possible."

For a moment she stood deep in thought. Then with a quick, decisive motion, she snatched up the cloak and slipped it around her bare shoulders. She fastened the heavy belt, bent down and got her shoes from under the bed, snatched up her purse, and hurried to the door.

"Come on," she said. She was breathing quickly, cheeks flushed. "Let's go. While there are still a number of exits to choose from. My car is parked outside, in the lot at the side of the building. We can get to my place in an hour. I have a winter home in Argentina. If worst comes to worst we can fly there. It's in the back country, away from the cities. Jungle and swamps. Cut-off from almost everything." Eagerly she started to open the door.

Cris reached out and stopped her. Gently, patiently, he moved in front of her.

He waited a long time, body rigid. Then he turned the knob and stepped boldly out into the corridor.

The corridor was empty. No one was in sight. Anita caught a faint glimpse, the back of a guard hurrying off. If they had come out a second earlier—

Cris started down the corridor. She ran after him. He moved rapidly, effortlessly. The girl had trouble keeping up with him. He seemed to know exactly where to go. Off to the right, down a side hall, a supply passage. Onto an ascent freight-lift. They rose, then abruptly halted.

Cris waited again. Presently he slid the door back and moved out of the lift. Anita followed nervously. She could hear sounds: guns and men, very close.

They were near an exit. A double line of guards stood directly ahead. Twenty men, a solid wall—and a massive heavy-duty robot gun in the center. The men were alert, faces strained and tense. Watching wide-eyed, guns gripped tight. A Civil Police officer was in charge.

"We'll never get past," Anita gasped. "We wouldn't get ten feet." She pulled back. "They'll—"

Cris took her by the arm and continued calmly forward. Blind terror leaped inside her. She fought wildly to get away, but his fingers were like steel. She couldn't pry them loose. Quietly, irresistibly, the great golden creature drew her along beside him, toward the double line of guards.

"There he is!" Guns went up. Men leaped into action. The barrel of the robot cannon swung around. *"Get him!"*

Anita was paralyzed. She sagged against the powerful body beside her, tugged along helplessly by his inflexible grasp. The lines of guards came nearer, a sheer wall of guns. Anita fought to control her terror. She stumbled, half-fell. Cris supported her effortlessly. She scratched, fought at him, struggled to get loose—

"Don't shoot!" she screamed.

Guns wavered uncertainly. "Who is she?" The guards were moving around, trying to get a sight on Cris without including her. "Who's he got there?"

One of them saw the stripe on her sleeve. Red and

black. Director Class. Top-level.

"She's Class A." Shocked, the guards retreated. "Miss, get out of the way!"

Anita found her voice. "Don't shoot. He's—in my custody. You understand? I'm taking him out."

The wall of guards moved back nervously. "No one's supposed to pass. Director Wisdom gave orders—"

"I'm not subject to Wisdom's authority." She managed to edge her voice with a harsh crispness. "Get out of the way. I'm taking him to the Semantics Agency."

For a moment nothing happened. There was no reaction. Then slowly, uncertainly, one guard stepped aside.

Cris moved. A blur of speed, away from Anita, past the confused guards, through the breach in the line, out the exit, and onto the street. Bursts of energy flashed wildly after him. Shouting guards milled out. Anita was left behind, forgotten. The guards, the heavy-duty gun, were pouring out into the early morning darkness. Sirens wailed. Patrol cars roared into life.

Anita stood dazed, confused, leaning against the wall, trying to get her breath.

He was gone. He had left her. Good God—what had she done? She shook her head, bewildered, her face buried in her hands. She had been hypnotized. She had lost her will, her common sense. Her reason! The animal, the great golden beast, had tricked her. Taken advantage of her. And now he was gone, escaped into the night.

Miserable, agonized tears trickled through her clenched fingers. She rubbed at them futilely; but they keep on coming.

"HE'S GONE," Baines said. "We'll never get him, now. He's probably a million miles from here."

Anita sat huddled in the corner, her face to the wall. A little bent heap, broken and wretched.

Wisdom paced back and forth. "But where can he go? Where can he hide? Nobody'll hide him! Everybody knows the law about deeves!"

"He's lived out in the woods most of his life. He'll hunt—that's what he's always done. They wondered what he was up to, off by himself. He was catching game and sleeping under trees." Baines laughed harshly. "And the first woman he meets will be glad to hide him—as *she* was." He indicated Anita with a jerk of his thumb.

"So all that gold, that mane, that god-like stance, was *for* something. Not just ornament." Wisdom's thick lips twisted. "He doesn't have just one faculty—he has two. One is new, the newest thing in survival methods. The other is as old as life." He stopped pacing to glare at the huddled shape in the corner. "Plumage. Bright feathers, combs for the roosters, swans, birds, bright scales for the fish. Gleaming pelts and manes for the animals. An animal isn't necessarily *bestial*. Lions aren't bestial. Or tigers. Or any of the big cats. They're anything but bestial."

"He'll never have to worry," Baines said. "He'll get by—as long as human women exist to take care of him. And since he can see ahead, into the future, he already knows he's sexually irresistible to human females."

"We'll get him," Wisdom muttered. "I've had the Government declare an emergency. Military and Civil Police will be looking for him. Armies of men—a whole planet of experts, the most advanced machines and equipment. We'll flush him, sooner or later."

"By that time it won't make any difference," Baines said. He put his hand on Anita's shoulder and patted her ironically. "You'll have company, sweetheart. You won't be the only one. You're just the first of a long procession."

"Thanks," Anita grated.

"The oldest survival method and the newest. Combined to form one perfectly adapted animal. How the hell are we going to stop him? We can put *you* through a sterilization tank—but we can't pick them all up, all the women he meets along the way. And if we miss one we're finished."

"We'll have to keep trying," Wisdom said. "Round up as many as we can. Before they can spawn." Faint hope glinted in his tired, sagging face. "Maybe his characteristics are recessive. Maybe ours will cancel his out."

"I wouldn't lay any money on that," Baines said. "I think I know already which of the two strains is going to turn up dominant." He grinned wryly. "I mean, I'm making a good *guess*. It won't be us."

Return Match

IT WAS not an ordinary gambling casino. And this, for the police of S.L.A., posed a special problem. The outspacers who had set up the casino had placed their massive ship directly above the tables, so that in the event of a raid the jets would destroy the tables. Efficient, officer Joseph Tinbane thought to himself morosely. With one blast the outspacers left Terra and simultaneously destroyed all evidence of their illegal activity.

And, what was more, killed each and every human gameplayer who might otherwise have lived to give testimony.

He sat now in his parked aircar, taking pinch after pinch of fine imported Dean Swift inch-kenneth snuff, then switched to the yellow tin which contained wren's relish. The snuff cheered him, but not very much. To his left, in the evening darkness, he could make out the shape of the outspacers' upended ship, black and silent, with the enlarged walled space beneath it, equally dark and silent—but deceptively so.

"We can go in there," he said to his less experienced companion, "but it'll just mean getting killed." We'll have to trust the robots, he realized. Even if they are clumsy, prone to error. Anyhow they're not alive. And not being alive, in a project as this, constituted an advantage.

"The third has gone in," officer Falkes beside him said quietly.

The slim shape, in human clothing, stopped before the door of the casino, rapped, waited. Presently the door opened. The robot gave the proper code-word and was admitted.

"You think they'll survive the take-off blast?" Tinbane

asked. Falkes was an expert in robotics.

"Possibly one might. Not all, though. But one will be enough." Hot for the kill, officer Falkes leaned to peer past Tinbane; his youthful face was fixed in concentration. "Use the bull-horn now. Tell them they're under arrest. I see no point in waiting."

"The point I see," Tinbane said, "is that it's more comforting to see the ship inert and the action going on underneath. We'll wait."

"But no more robots are coming."

"Wait for them to send back their vid transmissions," Tinbane said. After all, that comprised evidence—of a sort. And at police HQ it was now being recorded in permanent form. Still, his companion officer assigned to this project did have a point. Since the last of the three humanoid plants had gone in, nothing more would take place, now. Until the outspacers realized they had been infiltrated and put their typical planned pattern of withdrawal into action. "All right," he said, and pushed down on the button which activated the bull-horn.

LEANING, Falkes spoke into the bull-horn. At once the bull-horn said, "AS ORDER-REPRESENTATIVES OF SUPERIOR LOS ANGELES I AND THE MEN WITH ME INSTRUCT EVERYONE INSIDE TO COME OUT ONTO THE STREET COLLECTIVELY; I FURTHER INSTRUCT—"

His voice, from the bull-horn, disappeared as the initial takeoff surge roared through the primary jets of the outspacers' ship. Falkes shrugged, grinned starkly at Tinbane. *It didn't take them long*, his mouth formed silently.

As expected no one came out. No one in the casino escaped. Even when the structure which composed the building melted. The ship detached itself, leaving a soggy, puddled mass of wax-like matter behind it. And still no one emerged.

All dead, Tinbane realized with mute shock.

"Time to go in," Falkes said stoically. He began to crawl into his neoasbestos suit, and, after a pause, so did Tinbane.

Together, the two officers entered the hot, dripping

puddle which had been the casino. In the center, forming a mound, lay two of the three humanoid robots; they had managed at the last moment to cover something with their bodies. Of the third Tinbane saw no sign; evidently it had been demolished along with everything else. Everything organic.

I wonder what they thought—in their own dim way—to be worth preserving, Tinbane thought as he surveyed the distorted remnants of the two robots. Something alive? One of the snail-like outspacers? Probably not. A gaming table, then.

"They acted fast," Falkes said, impressed. "For robots."

"But we got something," Tinbane pointed out. Gingerly, he poked at the hot fused metal which had been the two robots. A section, most likely a torso, slid aside, revealed what the robots had preserved.

A pinball machine.

Tinbane wondered why. What was this worth? Anything? Personally, he doubted it.

IN THE police lab on Sunset Avenue in downtown Old Los Angeles, a technician presented a long written analysis to Tinbane.

"Tell me orally," Tinbane said, annoyed; he had been too many years on the force to suffer through such stuff. He returned the clipboard and report to the tall, lean police technician.

"Actually it's not an ordinary construct," the technician said, glancing over his own report, as if he had already forgotten it; his tone, like the report itself, was dry, dull. This for him was obviously routine. He, too, agreed that the pinball machine salvaged by the humanoid robots was worthless—or so Tinbane guessed. "By that I mean it's not like any they've brought to Terra in the past. You can probably get more of an idea directly from the thing; I suggest you put a quarter in it and play through a game." He added, "The lab budget will provide you with a quarter which we'll retrieve from the machine later."

"I've got my own quarter," Tinbane said irritably. He followed the technician through the large, overworked

lab, past the elaborate—and in many cases obsolete—
assortment of analytical devices and partly broken-apart
constructs to the work area in the rear.

There, cleaned up, the damage done to it now repaired,
stood the pinball machine which the robots had
protected. Tinbane inserted a coin; five metal balls at once
spilled into the reservoir, and the board at the far end of
the machine lit up in a variety of shifting colors.

"Before you shoot the first ball," the technician said to
him, standing beside him so that he, too, could watch, "I
advise you to take a careful look at the terrain of the
machine, the components among which the ball will pass.
The horizontal area beneath the protective glass is
somewhat interesting. A miniature village, complete with
houses, lighted streets, major public buildings, overhead
sprintship runnels . . . not a Terran village, of course. An
Ionian village, of the sort they're used to. The detail work
is superb."

Bending, Tinbane peered. The technician was right; the
detail work on the scale-model structures astounded him.

"Tests that measure wear on the moving parts of this
machine," the technician informed him, "indicate that it
saw a great deal of use. There is considerable tolerance.
We estimate that before another thousand games could be
completed, the machine would have to go to the shop.
Their shop, back on Io. Which is where we understand
they build and maintain equipment of this variety." He
explained, "By that I mean gambling layouts in general."

"What's the object of the game?" Tinbane asked.

"We have here," the technician explained, "what we
call a full-shift set variable. In other words, the terrain
through which the steel ball moves is never the same. The
number of possible combinations is—" he leafed through
his report but was unable to find the exact figure—
"anyhow, quite great. In the millions. It's excessively
intricate, in our opinion. Anyhow, if you'll release the first
ball you'll see."

Depressing the plunger, Tinbane allowed the first ball
to roll from the reservoir and against the impulse-shaft.
He then drew back the springloaded shaft and snapped it
into release. The ball shot up the channel and bounced
free, against a pressure-cushion which imparted swift
additional velocity to it.

• • •

THE BALL now dribbled in descent, toward the upper perimeter of the village.

"The initial defense line," the technician said from behind him, "which protects the village proper, is a series of mounds colored, shaped and surfaced to resemble the Ionian landscape. The fidelity is quite obviously painstaking. Probably made from satellites in orbit around Io. You can easily imagine you're seeing an actual piece of that moon from a distance of ten or more miles up."

The steel ball encountered the perimeter of rough terrain. Its trajectory altered, and the ball wobbled uncertainly, no longer going in any particular direction.

"Deflected," Tinbane said, noting how satisfactorily the contours of the terrain acted to deprive the ball of is descending forward motion. "It's going to bypass the village entirely."

The ball, with severely decreased momentum, wandered into a side crease, followed the crease listlessly, and then, just as it appeared to be drifting into the lower take-up slot, abruptly hurtled from a pressure-cushion and back into play.

On the illuminated backboard a score registered. Victory, of a momentary sort, for the player. The ball once again menaced the village. Once again it dribbled through the rough terrain, following virtually the same path as before.

"Now you'll notice something moderately important," the technician said. "As it heads toward that same pressure-cushion which it just now hit. Don't watch the ball; watch the cushion."

Tinbane watched. And saw, from the cushion, a tiny wisp of gray smoke. He turned inquiringly toward the technician.

"Now watch the ball!" the technician said sharply.

Again the ball struck the pressure-cushion mounted slightly before the lower take-up slot. This time, however, the cushion failed to react to the ball's impact.

Tinbane blinked as the ball rolled harmlessly on, into the take-up slot and out of play.

"Nothing happened," he said presently.

"That smoke that you saw. Emerging from the wiring of the cushion. An electrical short. Because a rebound

from that spot placed the ball in a menacing position—
menacing to the village."

"In other words," Tinbane said, "something took note
of the effect the cushion was having on the ball. The
assembly operates so as to protect itself from the ball's
activity." He had seen this before, in other outspacer
gambling gear: sophisticated circuitry which kept the
gameboard constantly shifting in such a way as to seem
alive—in such a way as to reduce the chances of the player
winning. On this particular construct the player obtained
a winning score by inducing the five steel balls to pass into
the central layout: the replica of the Ionian hamlet. Hence
the hamlet had to be protected. Hence this particular
strategically located pressure-cushion required elimination. At least for the time being. Until the overall
configurations of topography altered decidedly.

"NOTHING NEW THERE," the technician said. "You've seen
it a dozen times before; I've seen it a hundred times before.
Let's say that this pinball machine has seen ten thousand
separate games, and each time there's been a careful
readjustment of the circuitry directed toward rendering
the steel balls neutralized. Let's say that the alterations are
cumulative. So by now any given player's score is
probably no more than a fraction of early scores, before
the circuits had a chance to react. The direction of
alteration—as in all outspacer gambling mechanisms—
has a zero win factor as the limit toward which it's
moving. Just *try* to hit the village, Tinbane. We set up a
constantly repeating mechanical ball-release and played
one hundred and forty games. At no time did a ball ever
get near enough to do the village any harm. We kept a
record of the scores obtained. A slight but significant
drop was registered each time." he grinned.

"So?" Tinbane said.

"So nothing. As I told you and as my report says." The
technician paused, then. "Except for one thing. Look at
this."

Bending, he traced his thin finger across the protective
glass of the layout, toward a construct near the center of
the replica village. A photographic record shows that with
each game that particular component becomes more

articulated. It's being erected by circuitry underneath—
obviously. As is every other change. But this configuration—doesn't it remind you of something?"

"Looks like a Roman catapult," Tinbane said. "But
with a vertical rather than a horizontal axis."

"That's our reaction, too. And look at the sling. In
terms of the scale of the village it's inordinately large.
Immense, in fact; specifically, *it's not to scale.*"

"It looks as if it would almost hold—"

"Not almost," the technician said. "We measured it.
The size of the sling is exact; one of those steel balls would
fit perfectly into it."

"And then?" Tinbane said, feeling chill.

"And then it would hurl the ball back at the player," the
lab technician said calmly. "It's aimed directly toward the
front of the machine, front and upward." He added, "And
it's been virtually completed."

THE BEST DEFENSE, Tinbane thought to himself as he
studied the outspacers' illegal pinball machine, is offense.
But whoever heard of it in this context?

Zero, he realized, isn't a low enough score to suit the
defensive circuitry of the thing. Zero won't do. It's got to
strive for less than zero. Why? Because, he decided, it's
not really moving toward zero as a limit; it's moving,
instead, toward the best defensive pattern. It's too well
designed.

Or is it?

"You think," he asked the lean, tall lab technician,
"That the outspacers intended this?"

"That doesn't matter. At least not from the immediate
standpoint. What matters is two factors: the machine was
exported—in violation of Terran law—to Terra, and it's
been played by Terrans. Intentionally or not, this could
be, in fact will soon be, a lethal weapon." He added, "We
calculate within the next twenty games. Every time a coin
is inserted, the building resumes. Whether a ball gets near
the village or not. All it requires is a flow of power from
the device's central helium battery. And that's automatic,
once play begins." He added, "It's at work building the
catapult right now, as we stand here. You better release
the remaining four balls, so it'll shut itself off. Or give us

permission to dismantle it—to at least take the power-supply out of the circuit."

"The outspacers don't have a very high regard for human life," Tinbane reflected. He was thinking of the carnage created by the ship taking off. And that, for them, was routine. But in view of that wholesale destruction of human life, this seemed unnecessary. What more did this accomplish?

Pondering, he said, "This is selective. This would eliminate only the game-player."

The technician said, "This would eliminate *every* gameplayer. One after another."

"But who would play the thing," Tinbane said, "after the first fatality?"

"People go there knowing that if there's a raid the outspacers will burn up everyone and everything," the technician pointed out. "The urge to gamble is an addictive compulsion; a certain type of person gambles no matter what the risk is. You ever hear of Russian Roulette?"

Tinbane released the second steel ball, watched it bounce and wander toward the replica village. This one managed to pass through the rough terrain; it approached the first house comprising the village proper. Maybe I'll get it, he thought savagely. Before it gets me. A strange, novel excitement filled him as he watched the ball thud against the tiny house, flatten the structure and roll on. The ball, although small to him, towered over every building, every structure, that made up the village.

—Every structure except the central catapult. He watched avidly as the ball moved dangerously close to the catapult, then, deflected by a major public building, rolled on and disappeared into the take-up slot. Immediately he sent the third ball hurtling up its channel.

"The stakes," the lab technician said softly, "are high, aren't they? Your life against its. Must be exceptionally appealing to someone with the right kind of temperament."

"I think," Tinbane said, "I can get the catapult before it's in action."

"Maybe. Maybe not."

"I'm getting the ball closer to it each time."

The technician said, "For the catapult to work, it requires one of the steel balls; that's its load. You're making it increasingly likely that it'll acquire use of one of the balls. You're actually helping it." He added somberly, "In fact it can't function without you; the gameplayer is not only the enemy, he's also essential. Better quit, Tinbane. The thing is using you."

"I'll quit," Tinbane said, "when I've gotten the catapult."

"You're damn right you will. You'll be dead." He eyed Tinbane narrowly. "Possibly this is why the outspacers built it. To get back at us for our raids. This very likely is what it's for."

"Got another quarter?" Tinbane said.

IN THE middle of his tenth game a surprising, unexpected alteration in the machine's strategy manifested itself. All at once it ceased routing the steel balls entirely to one side, away from the replica village.

Watching, Tinbane saw the steel ball roll directly—for the first time—through the center. Straight toward the proportionally massive catapult.

Obviously the catapult had been completed.

"I outrank you, Tinbane," the lab technician said tautly. "And I'm ordering you to quit playing."

"Any order from you to me," Tinbane said, "has to be in writing and has to be approved by someone in the department at inspector level." But, reluctantly, he halted play. "I can get it," he said reflectively, "but not standing here. I have to be away, far enough back so that it can't pick me off." So it can't distinguish me and aim, he realized.

Already he had noted it swivel slightly. Through some lens-system it had detected him. Or possibly it was thermotropic, had sensed him by his body heat.

If the latter, then defensive action for him would be relatively simple: a resistance coil suspended at another locus. On the other hand it might be utilizing a cephalic index of some sort, recording all nearby brain-emanations. But the police lab would know that already.

"What's its tropism?" he asked.

The technician said, "That assembly hadn't been built

up, at the time we inspected it. It's undoubtedly coming into existence now, in concert with the completion of the weapon."

Tinbane said thoughtfully, "I hope it doesn't possess equipment to *record* a cephalic index." Because, he thought, if it did, storing the pattern would be no trouble at all. It could retain a memory of its adversary for use in the event of future encounters.

Something about that notion frightened him—over and above the immediate menace of the situation.

"I'll make a deal," the technician said. "You continue to operate it until it fires its initial shot at you. Then step aside and let us tear it down. We need to know its tropism; this may turn up again in a more complex fashion. You agree? You'll be taking a calculated risk, but I believe its initial shot will be aimed with the idea of use as feedback; it'll correct for a second shot . . . which will never take place."

Should he tell the technician his fear?

"What bothers me," he said, "is the possibility that it'll retain a specific memory of me. For future purposes."

"What future purposes? It'll be completely torn down. As soon as it fires."

Reluctantly, Tinbane said, "I think I'd better make the deal." I may already have gone too far, he thought. You may have been right.

THE NEXT steel ball missed the catapult by only a matter of a fraction of an inch. But what unnerved him was not the closeness; it was the quick, subtle attempt on the part of the catapult to snare the ball as it passed. A motion so rapid that he might easily have overlooked it.

"It wants that ball," the technician observed. "It wants *you*." He, too, had seen.

With hesitation, Tinbane touched the plunger which would release the next—and for him possibly the last—steel ball.

"Back out," the technician advised nervously. "Forget the deal; stop playing. We'll tear it down as it is."

"We need the tropism," Tinbane said. And depressed the plunger.

The steel ball, suddenly seeming to him huge and hard

and heavy, rolled unhesitatingly into the waiting catapult; every contour of the machine's topography collaborated. The acquisition of the load took place before he even understood what had happened. He stood staring.

"Run!" the technician leaped back, bolted; crashing against Tinbane, he threw him bodily away from the machine.

With a clatter of broken glass the steel ball shot by Tinbane's right temple, bounced against the far wall of the lab, came to rest under a work table.

Silence.

After a time the technician said shakily, "It had plenty of velocity. Plenty of mass. Plenty of what it needed."

Haltingly, Tinbane stood up, took a step toward the machine.

"Don't release another ball," the technician said warningly.

Tinbane said, "I don't have to." He turned, then, sprinted away.

The machine had released the ball itself.

IN THE outer office, Tinbane sat smoking, seated across from Ted Donovan, the lab chief. The door to the lab had been shut, and every one of the several lab technicians had been bull-horned to safety. Beyond the closed door the lab was silent. Inert, Tinbane thought, and waiting.

He wondered if it was waiting for anyone, any human, any Terran, to come within reach. Or—just him.

The latter thought amused him even less than it had originally; even seated out here he felt himself cringe. A machine built on another world, sent to Terra empty of direction, merely capable of sorting among all its defensive possibilities until at last it stumbled onto the key. Randomness at work, through hundreds, even thousands of games...through person after person, player after player. Until at last it reached critical direction, and the last person to play it, also selected by the process of randomness, became welded to it in a contract of death. In this case, himself. Unfortunately.

Ted Donovan said, "We'll spear its power source from a distance; that shouldn't be hard. You go on home, forget about it. When we have its tropic circuit laid out we'll notify you. Unless of course it's late at night, in which case—"

"Notify me," Tinbane said, "whatever time it is. If you will." He did not have to explain; the lab chief understood.

"Obviously," Donovan said, "this construct is aimed at the police teams raiding the casinos. How they steered our robots onto it we don't of course know—yet. We may find *that* circuit, too." He picked up the already extant lab report, eyed it with hostility. "This was far too cursory, it would now appear. 'Just another outspacer gambling device.' The hell it is." He tossed the report away, disgusted.

"If that's what they had in mind," Tinbane said, "they got what they wanted; they got me completely." At least in terms of hooking him. Of snaring his attention. And his cooperation.

"You're a gambler; you've got the streak. But you didn't know it. Possibly it wouldn't have worked otherwise." Donovan added, "But it is interesting. A pinball machine that fights back. That gets fed up with steel balls rolling over it. I hope they don't build a skeet-shoot. This is bad enough."

"Dreamlike," Tinbane murmured.

"Pardon?"

"Not really real." But, he thought, it is real. He rose, then, to his feet. "I'll do what you say; I'll go on home to my conapt. You have the vidphone number." He felt tired and afraid.

"You look terrible," Donovan said, scrutinizing him. "It shouldn't get you to this extent; this is a relatively benign construct, isn't it? You have to attack it, to set it in motion. If left alone—"

"I'm leaving it alone," Tinbane said. "But I feel it's waiting. It wants me to come back." He felt it expecting him, anticipating his return. The machine was capable of learning and he had taught it—taught it about himself.

Taught it that he existed. That there was such a person on Terra as Joseph Tinbane.

And that was too much.

WHEN HE unlocked the door of his conapt the phone was already ringing. Leadenly, he picked up the receiver.

"Hello," he said.

"Tinbane?" It was Donovan's voice. "It's encephalo-tropic, all right. We found a pattern-print of your brain configuration, and of course we destroyed it. But—" Donovan hesitated. "We also found something else it had constructed since the initial analysis."

"A transmitter," Tinbane said hoarsely.

"Afraid so. Half-mile of broadcast, two miles if beamed. And it was cupped to beam, so we have to assume the two-mile transmission. We have absolutely no idea what the receiver consists of, naturally, whether it's even on the surface or not. Probably is. In an office somewhere. Or a hover-car such as they use. Anyhow, now you know. So it's decidedly a vengeance weapon; your emotional response was unfortunately correct. When our double-dome experts looked this over they drew the conclusion that you were waited-for, so to speak. It saw you coming. The instrument may never have functioned as an authentic gambling device in the first place; the tolerances which we noted may have been built in, rather than the result of wear. So that's about it."

Tinbane said, "What do you suggest I do?"

"'Do'?" A pause. "Not much. Stay in your conapt; don't report for work, not for a while."

So if they nail me, Tinbane thought, no one else in the department will get hit at the same time. More advantageous for the rest of you; hardly for me, though. "I think I'll get out of the area," he said aloud. "The structure may be limited in space, confined to S.L.A. or just one part of the city. If you don't veto it." He had a girl friend, Nancy Hackett, in La Jolla; he could go there.

"Suit yourself."

He said, "You can't do anything to help me, though."

"I tell you what," Donovan said. "We'll allocate some funds, a moderate sum, best we can, on which you can function. Until we track down the damn receiver and find out what it's tied to. For us, the main headache is that word of this matter has begun to filter through the department. It's going to be hard getting crack-down teams to tackle future outspacer gambling opera-tions ... which of course is specifically what they had in mind. One more thing we can do. We can have the lab build you a brain-shield so you no longer emanate a recognizable template. But you'd have to pay for it out of your own pocket. Possibly it could be debited against your salary, payments divided over several months. If you're interested. Frankly, if you want my personal opinion, I'd advise it."

"All right," Tinbane said. He felt dull, dead, tired and resigned; all of those at once. And he had the deep and acute intuition that his reaction was rational. "Anything else you suggest?" he asked.

"Stay armed. Even when you're asleep."

"What asleep?" he said. "You think I'm going to get any sleep? Maybe I will after that machine is totally destroyed." But that won't make any difference, he realized. Not now. Not after it's dispatched my brain-wave pattern to something else, something we know nothing about. God knows what equipment it might turn out to be; outspacers show up with all kinds of convoluted things.

HE HUNG up the phone, walked into his kitchen, and getting down a half-empty fifth of Antique bourbon, fixed himself a whiskey sour.

What a mess, he said to himself. Pursued by a pinball machine from another world. He almost—but not quite—had to laugh.

What do you use, he asked himself, to catch an angry pinball machine? One that has your number and is out to get you? Or more specifically, a pinball machine's nebulous friend . . .

Something went *tap tap* against the kitchen window.

Reaching into his pocket he brought out his regulation-issue laser pistol; walking along the kitchen wall he approached the window from an unseen side, peered out into the night. Darkness. He could make nothing out. Flashlight? He had one in the glove compartment of his aircar, parked on the roof of the conapt building. Time to get it.

A moment later, flashlight in hand, he raced downstairs, back to his kitchen.

The beam of the flashlight showed, pressed against the outer surface of the window, a buglike entity with projecting elongated pseudopodia. The two feelers had tapped against the glass of the window, evidently exploring in their blind, mechanical way.

The bug-thing had ascended the side of the building; he could perceive the suction-tread by which it clung.

His curiosity, at this point, became greater than his fear. With care he opened the window—no need of having to pay the building repair committee for it—and cautiously took aim with his laser pistol. The bug-thing did not stir; evidently it had stalled in midcycle. Probably its responses, he guessed, were relatively slow, much more so than a comparable organic equivalent. Unless, of course, it was set to detonate; in which case he had no time to ponder.

He fired a narrow-beam into the underside of the bug-thing.

Maimed, the bug-thing settled backward, its many little cups releasing their hold. As it fell away, Tinbane caught hold of it, lifted it swiftly into the room, dropped it onto the floor, meantime keeping his pistol pointed at it. But it was finished functionally; it did not stir.

Laying it on the small kitchen table he got a screwdriver from the tool-drawer beside the sink, seated himself, examined the object. He felt, now, that he could take his time; the pressure, momentarily at least, had abated.

It took him forty minutes to get the thing open; none of the holding screws fitted an ordinary screwdriver, and he found himself at last using a common kitchen knife. But finally he had it open before him on the table, its shell divided into two parts: one hollow and empty, the other crammed with components. A bomb? He tinkered with exceeding care, inspecting each assembly bit by bit.

No bomb—at least none which he could identify. Then a murder tool? No blade, no toxins or micro-organisms, no tube capable of expelling a lethal charge, explosive or otherwise. So then what in God's name did it do? He recognized the motor which had driven it up the side of the building, then the photo-electric steering turret by which it oriented itself. But that was all. Absolutely all.

From the standpoint of use, it was a fraud.

Or was it? He examined his watch. Now he had spent an entire hour on it; his attention had been diverted from everything else—and who knew what that else might be?

NERVOUSLY, he slid stiffly to his feet, collected his laser pistol, and prowled throughout the apartment, listening, wondering, trying to sense something, however small, that was out of its usual order.

It's giving them time, he realized. One entire hour! For whatever it is they're *really* up to.

Time, he thought, for me to leave the apartment. To get to La Jolla and the hell out of here, until this is all over with.

His vidphone rang.

When he answered it, Ted Donovan's face clicked grayly into view. "We've got a department aircar monitoring your conapt building," Donovan said. "And it picked up some activity; I thought you'd want to know."

"Okay," he said tensely.

"A vehicle, airborne, landed briefly on your roof parking lot. Not a standard aircar but something larger. Nothing we could recognize. It took right off again at great speed, but I think this is it."

"Did it deposit anything?" he asked.

"Yes. Afraid so."

Tight-lipped, he said, "Can you do anything for me at this late point? It would be appreciated very much."

"What do you suggest? We don't know what it is; you certainly don't know either. We're open to ideas, but I think we'll have to wait until you know the nature of the—hostile artifact."

Something bumped against his door, something in the hall.

"I'll leave the line open," Tinbane said. "Don't leave; I think it's happening now." He felt panic, at this stage; overt, childish panic. Carrying his laser pistol in a numb, loose grip he made his way step by step to the locked front door of his conapt, halted, then unlocked the door and opened it. Slightly. As little as he could manage.

An enormous, unchecked force pushed the door further; the knob left his hand. And, soundlessly, the vast steel ball resting against the half-open door rolled forward. He stepped aside—he had to—knowing that this was the adversary; the dummy wall-climbing gadget had deflected his attention from this.

He could not get out. He would not be going to La Jolla now. The great massed sphere totally blocked the way.

Returning to the vidphone he said to Donovan, "I'm encapsulated. Here in my own conapt." At the outer perimeter, he realized. Equal to the rough terrain of the pinball machine's shifting landscape. The first ball has been blocked there, has lodged in the doorway. But what about the second? The third?

Each would be closer.

"Can you build something for me?" he asked huskily. "Can the lab start working this late at night?"

"We can try," Donovan said. "It depends entirely on what you want. What you have in mind? What do you think would help?"

He hated to ask for it. But he had to. The next one might burst in through a window, or crash onto him from the roof. "I want," he said, "some form of catapult. Big enough, tough enough, to handle a spherical load with a diameter of between four and a half and five feet. You think you can manage it?" He prayed to God they could.

"Is that what you're facing?" Donovan said harshly.

"Unless it's an hallucination," Tinbane said. "A deliberate, artifically induced terror-projection, designed specifically to demoralize me."

"The department aircar saw something," Donovan said. "And it wasn't an hallucination; it had measurable mass. And—" He hesitated. "It did leave off something big. Its departing mass was considerably diminished. So it's real, Tinbane."

"That's what I thought," Tinbane said.

"WE'LL GET the catapult to you as soon as we possibly can," Donovan said. "Let's hope there's an adequate interval between each—attack. And you better figure on five at least."

Tinbane, nodding lit a cigarette, or at least tried to. But his hands were shaking too badly to get the lighter into place. He then got out a yellow-lacquered tin of dean's

own snuff, but found himself unable to force open the
tight tin; the tin hopped from his fingers and fell to the
floor. "Five," he said, *"per game."*

"Yes," Donovan said reluctantly, "there's that."

The wall of the living room shuddered.

The next one was coming at him from the adjoining
apartment.

The King of the Elves

It was raining and getting dark. Sheets of water blew along the row of pumps at the edge of the filling station; the tree across the highway bent against the wind.

Shadrach Jones stood just inside the doorway of the little building, leaning against an oil drum. The door was open and gusts of rain blew in onto the wood floor. It was late; the sun had set, and the air was turning cold. Shadrach reached into his coat and brought out a cigar. He bit the end off it and lit it carefully, turning away from the door. In the gloom, the cigar burst into life, warm and glowing. Shadrach took a deep draw. He buttoned his coat around him and stepped out onto the pavement.

"Darn," he said. "What a night!" Rain buffeted him, wind blew at him. He looked up and down the highway, squinting. There were no cars in sight. He shook his head, locked up the gasoline pumps.

He went back into the building and pulled the door shut behind him. He opened the cash register and counted the money he'd taken in during the day. It was not much.

Not much, but enough for one old man. Enough to buy him tobacco and firewood and magazines, so that he could be comfortable as he waited for the occasional cars to come by. Not very many cars came along the highway any more. The highway had begun to fall into disrepair; there were many cracks in its dry, rough surface, and most cars preferred to take the big state highway that ran beyond the hills. There was nothing in Derryville to attract them, to make them turn toward it. Derryville was a small town, too small to bring in any of the major industries, too small to be very important to anyone. Sometimes hours went by without—

Shadrach tensed. His fingers closed over the money.
From outside came a sound, the melodic ring of the signal
wire stretched along the pavement.

Dinggg!

SHADRACH dropped the money into the till and pushed
the drawer closed. He stood up slowly and walked toward
the door, listening. At the door, he snapped off the light
and waited in the darkness, staring out.

He could see no car there. The rain was pouring down,
swirling with the wind; clouds of mist moved along the
road. And something was standing beside the pumps.

He opened the door and stepped out. At first, his eyes
could make nothing out. Then the old man swallowed
uneasily.

Two tiny figures stood in the rain, holding a kind of
platform between them. Once, they might have been gaily
dressed in bright garments, but now their clothes hung
limp and sodden, dripping in the rain. They glanced
half-heartedly at Shadrach. Water streaked their tiny
faces, great drops of water. Their robes blew about them
with the wind, lashing and swirling.

On the platform, something stirred. A small head
turned wearily, peering at Shadrach. In the dim light, a
rain-streaked helmet glinted dully.

"Who are you?" Shadrach said.

The figure on the platform raised itself up. "I'm the
King of the Elves and I'm wet."

Shadrach stared in astonishment.

"That's right," one of the bearers said. "We're all wet."

A small group of elves came straggling up, gathering
around their king. They huddled together forlornly,
silently.

"The King of the Elves," Shadrach repeated. "Well, I'll
be darned."

Could it be true? They were very small, all right, and
their dripping clothes were strange and oddly colored.

But *Elves?*

"I'll be darned. Well, whatever you are, you shouldn't
be out on a night like this."

"Of course not," the king murmured. "No fault of our
own. No fault..." His voice trailed off into a choking

cough. The Elf soldiers peered anxiously at the platform.

"Maybe you better bring him inside," Shadrach said. "My place is up the road. He shouldn't be out in the rain."

"Do you think we like being out on a night like this?" one of the bearers muttered. "Which way is it? Direct us."

Shadrach pointed up the road. "Over there. Just follow me. I'll get a fire going."

He went down the road, feeling his way onto the first of the flat stone steps that he and Phineas Judd had laid during the summer. At the top of the steps, he looked back. The platform was coming slowly along, swaying a little from side to side. Behind it, the Elf soldiers picked their way, a tiny column of silent dripping creatures, unhappy and cold.

"I'll get the fire started," Shadrach said. He hurried them into the house.

WEARILY, the Elf King lay back against the pillow. After sipping hot chocolate, he had relaxed and his heavy breathing sounded suspiciously like a snore.

Shadrach shifted in discomfort.

"I'm sorry," the Elf King said suddenly, opening his eyes. He rubbed his forehead. "I must have drifted off. Where was I?"

"You should retire, Your Majesty," one of the soldiers said sleepily. "It is late and these are hard times."

"True," the Elf King said, nodding. "Very true." He looked up at the towering figure of Shadrach, standing before the fireplace, a glass of beer in his hand. "Mortal, we thank you for your hospitality. Normally, we do not impose on human beings."

"It's those Trolls," another of the soldiers said, curled up on a cushion of the couch.

"Right," another soldier agreed. He sat up, groping for his sword. "Those reeking Trolls, digging and croaking—"

"You see," the Elf King went on, "as our party was crossing from the Great Low Steps toward the Castle, where it lies in the hollow of the Towering Mountains—"

"You mean Sugar Ridge," Shadrach supplied helpfully.

"The Towering Mountains. Slowly we made our way.

A rain storm came up. We became confused. All at once a group of Trolls appeared, crashing through the underbrush. We left the woods and sought safety on the Endless Path—"

"The highway. Route Twenty."

"So that is why we're here." The Elf King paused a moment. "Harder and harder it rained. The wind blew around us, cold and bitter. For an endless time we toiled along. We had no idea where we were going or what would become of us."

The Elf King looked up at Shadrach. "We knew only this: Behind us, the Trolls were coming, creeping through the woods, marching through the rain, crushing everything before them."

He put his hand to his mouth and coughed, bending forward. All the Elves waited anxiously until he was done. He straightened up.

"It was kind of you to allow us to come inside. We will not trouble you for long. It is not the custom of the Elves—"

Again he coughed, covering his face with his hand. The Elves drew toward him apprehensively. At last the king stirred. He sighed.

"What's the matter?" Shadrach asked. He went over and took the cup of chocolate from the fragile hand. The Elf King lay back, his eyes shut.

"He has to rest," one of the soldiers said. "Where's your room? The sleeping room."

"Upstairs," Shadrach said. "I'll show you where."

LATE that night, Shadrach sat by himself in the dark, deserted living room, deep in meditation. The Elves were asleep above him, upstairs in the bedroom, the Elf King in the bed, the others curled up together on the rug.

The house was silent. Outside, the rain poured down endlessly, blowing against the house. Shadrach could hear the tree branches slapping in the wind. He clasped and unclasped his hands. What a strange business it was—all these Elves, with their old, sick king, their piping voices. How anxious and peevish they were!

But pathetic, too; so small and wet, with water

dripping down from them, and all their gay robes limp and soggy.

The Trolls—what were they like? Unpleasant and not very clean. Something about digging, breaking and pushing through the woods...

Suddenly, Shadrach laughed in embarrassment. What was the matter with him, believing all this? He put his cigar out angrily, his ears red. What was going on? What kind of joke was this?

Elves? Shadrach grunted in indignation. Elves in Derryville? In the middle of Colorado? Maybe there were Elves in Europe. Maybe in Ireland. He had heard of that. But here? Upstairs in his own house, sleeping in his own bed?

"I've heard just about enough of this," he said. "I'm not an idiot, you know."

He turned toward the stairs, feeling for the banister in the gloom. He began to climb.

Above him, a light went on abruptly. A door opened.

Two Elves came slowly out onto the landing. They looked down at him. Shadrach halted halfway up the stairs. Something on their faces made him stop.

"What's the matter?" he asked hesitantly.

They did not answer. The house was turning cold, cold and dark, with the chill of the rain outside and the chill of the unknown inside.

"What is it?" he said again. "What's the matter?"

"The king is dead," one of the Elves said. "He died a few moments ago."

Shadrach stared up, wide-eyed. "He did? But—"

"He was very cold and very tired." The Elves turned away, going back into the room, slowly and quietly shutting the door.

Shadrach stood, his fingers on the banister, hard, lean fingers, strong and thin.

He nodded his head blankly.

"I see," he said to the closed door. "He's dead."

THE ELF soldiers stood around him in a solemn circle. The living room was bright with sunlight, the cold white glare of early morning.

"But wait," Shadrach said. He plucked at his necktie. "I have to get to the filling station. Can't you talk to me when I come home?"

The faces of the Elf soldiers were serious and concerned.

"Listen," one of them said. "Please hear us out. It is very important to us."

Shadrach looked past them. Through the window he saw the highway, steaming in the heat of day, and down a little way was the gas station, glittering brightly. And even as he watched, a car came up to it and honked thinly, impatiently. When nobody came out of the station, the car drove off again down the road.

"We beg you," a soldier said.

Shadrach looked down at the ring around him, the anxious faces, scored with concern and trouble. Strangely, he had always thought of Elves as carefree beings, flitting without worry or sense—

"Go ahead," he said. "I'm listening." He went over to the big chair and sat down. The Elves came up around him. They conversed among themselves for a moment, whispering, murmuring distantly. Then they turned toward Shadrach.

The old man waited, his arms folded.

"We cannot be without a king," one of the soldiers said. "We could not survive. Not these days."

"The Trolls," another added. "They multiply very fast. They are terrible beasts. They're heavy and ponderous, crude, bad-smelling—"

"The odor of them is awful. They come up from the dark wet places, under the earth, where the blind, groping plants feed in silence, far below the surface, far from the sun."

"Well, you ought to elect a king, then," Shadrach suggested. "I don't see any problem there."

"We do not elect the King of the Elves," a soldier said. "The old king must name his successor."

"Oh," Shadrach replied. "Well, there's nothing wrong with that method."

"As our old king lay dying, a few distant words came forth from his lips," a soldier said. "We bent closer, frightened and unhappy, listening."

"Important, all right," agreed Shadrach. "Not something you'd want to miss."

"He spoke the name of him who will lead us."

"Good. You caught it, then. Well, where's the difficulty?"

"The name he spoke was—was your name."

Shadrach stared. *"Mine?"*

"The dying king said: 'Make him, the towering mortal, your king. Many things will come if he leads the Elves into battle against the Trolls. I see the rising once again of the Elf Empire, as it was in the old days, as it was before—'"

"Me!" Shadrach leaped up. "Me? King of the Elves?"

Shadrach walked about the room, his hands in his pockets. "Me, Shadrach Jones, King of the Elves." He grinned a little. "I sure never thought of it before."

He went to the mirror over the fireplace and studied himself. He saw his thin, graying hair, his bright eyes, dark skin, his big Adam's apple.

"King of the Elves," he said. "King of the Elves. Wait till Phineas Judd hears about this. Wait till I tell him!"

Phineas Judd would certainly be surprised!

ABOVE THE filling station, the sun shown, high in the clear blue sky.

Phineas Judd sat playing with the accelerator of his old Ford truck. The motor raced and slowed. Phineas reached over and turned the ignition key off, then rolled the window all the way down.

"What did you say?" he asked. He took off his glasses and began to polish them, steel rims between slender, deft fingers that were patient from years of practice. He restored his glasses to his nose and smoothed what remained of his hair into place.

"What was it, Shadrach?" he said. "Let's hear that again."

"I'm King of the Elves," Shadrach repeated. He changed position, bringing his other foot up on the runningboard. "Who would have thought it? Me, Shadrach Jones, King of the Elves."

Phineas gazed at him. "How long have you been— King of the Elves, Shadrach?"

"Since the night before last."

"I see. The night before last." Phineas nodded. "I see. And what, may I ask, occurred the night before last?"

"The Elves came to my house. When the old Elf king died, he told them that—"

A truck came rumbling up and the driver leaped out. "Water!" he said. "Where the hell is the hose?"

Shadrach turned reluctantly. "I'll get it." He turned back to Phineas. "Maybe I can talk to you tonight when you come back from town. I want to tell you the rest. It's very interesting."

"Sure," Phineas said, starting up his little truck. "Sure, Shadrach. I'm very interested to hear."

He drove off down the road.

Later in the day, Dan Green ran his flivver up to the filling station.

"Hey, Shadrach," he called. "Come over here! I want to ask you something."

Shadrach came out of the little house, holding a waste-rag in his hand.

"What is it?"

"Come here." Dan leaned out the window, a wide grin on his face, splitting his face from ear to ear. "Let me ask you something, will you?"

"Sure."

"Is it true? Are you really the King of the Elves?"

Shadrach flushed a little. "I guess I am," he admitted, looking away. "That's what I am, all right."

Dan's grin faded. "Hey, you trying to kid me? What's the gag?"

Shadrach became angry. "What do you mean? Sure, I'm the King of the Elves. And anyone who says I'm not—"

"All right, Shadrach," Dan said, starting up the flivver quickly. "Don't get mad. I was just wondering."

Shadrach looked very strange.

"All right," Dan said. "You don't hear me arguing, do you?"

BY THE end of the day, everyone around knew about Shadrach and how he had suddenly become King of the Elves. Pop Richey, who ran the Lucky Store in

Derryville, claimed Shadrach was doing it to drum up trade for the filling station.

"He's a smart old fellow," Pop said. "Not very many cars go along there any more. He knows what he's doing."

"I don't know," Dan Green disagreed. "You should hear him, I think he really believes it."

"King of the Elves?" They all began to laugh. "Wonder what he'll say next."

Phineas Judd pondered. "I've known Shadrach for years. I can't figure it out." He frowned, his face wrinkled and disapproving. "I don't like it."

Dan looked at him. "Then you think he believes it?"

"Sure," Phineas said. "Maybe I'm wrong, but I really think he does."

"But how could he believe it?" Pop asked. "Shadrach is no fool. He's been in business for a long time. He must be getting something out of it, the way I see it. But what, if it isn't to build up the filling station?"

"Why, don't you know what he's getting?" Dan said, grinning. He gold tooth shone.

"What?" Pop demanded.

"He's got a whole kingdom to himself, that's what—to do with like he wants. How would you like that, Pop? Wouldn't you like to be King of the Elves and not have to run this old store anymore?"

"There isn't anything wrong with my store," Pop said. "I ain't ashamed to run it. Better than being a clothing salesman."

Dan flushed. "Nothing wrong with that, either." He looked at Phineas. "Isn't that right? Nothing wrong with selling clothes, is there, Phineas?"

Phineas was staring down at the floor. He glanced up. "What? What was that?"

"What you thinking about?" Pop wanted to know. "You look worried."

"I'm worried about Shadrach," Phineas said. "He's getting old. Sitting out there by himself all the time, in the cold weather, with the rain water running over the floor—it blows something awful in the winter, along the highway—"

"Then you *do* think he believes it?" Dan persisted.

"You *don't* think he's getting something out of it?"

Phineas shook his head absently and did not answer.

The laughter died down. They all looked at one another.

THAT NIGHT, as Shadrach was locking up the filling station, a small figure came toward him from the darkness.

"Hey!" Shadrach called out. "Who are you?"

An Elf soldier came into the light, blinking. He was dressed in a little gray robe, buckled at the waist with a band of silver. On his feet were little leather boots. He carried a short sword at his side.

"I have a serious message for you," the Elf said. "Now, where did I put it?"

He searched his robe while Shadrach waited. The Elf brought out a tiny scroll and unfastened it, breaking the wax expertly. He handed it to Shadrach.

"What's it say?" Shadrach asked. He bent over, his eyes close to the vellum. "I don't have my glasses with me. Can't quite make out these little letters."

"The Trolls are moving. They've heard that the old king is dead, and they're rising, in all the hills and valleys around. They will try to break the Elf Kingdom into fragments, scatter the Elves—"

"I see," Shadrach said. "Before your new king can really get started."

"That's right." The Elf soldier nodded. "This is a crucial moment for the Elves. For centuries, our existence has been precarious. There are so many Trolls, and Elves are very frail and often take sick—"

"Well, what should I do? Are there any suggestions?"

"You're supposed to meet with us under the Great Oak tonight. We'll take you into the Elf Kingdom, and you and your staff will plan and map the defense of the Kingdom."

"What?" Shadrach looked uncomfortable. "But I haven't eaten dinner. And my gas station—tomorrow is Saturday, and a lot of cars—"

"But you are King of the Elves," the soldier said.

Shadrach put his hand to his chin and rubbed it slowly.

"That's right," he replied. "I am, ain't I?"

The Elf soldier bowed.

"I wish I'd known this sort of thing was going to happen," Shadrach said. "I didn't suppose being King of the Elves—"

He broke off, hoping for an interruption. The Elf soldier watched him calmly, without expression.

"Maybe you ought to have someone else as your king," Shadrach decided. "I don't know very much about war and things like that, fighting and all that sort of business." He paused, shrugged his shoulders. "It's nothing I've ever mixed in. They don't have wars here in Colorado. I mean they don't have wars between human beings."

STILL THE Elf soldier remained silent.

"Why was I picked?" Shadrach went on helplessly, twisting his hands. "I don't know anything about it. What made him go and pick me? Why didn't he pick somebody else?"

"He trusted you," the Elf said. "You brought him inside your house, out of the rain. He knew that you expected nothing for it, that there was nothing you wanted. He had known few who gave and asked nothing back."

"Oh." Shadrach thought it over. At last he looked up. "But what about my gas station? And my house? And what will they say, Dan Green and Pop down at the store—"

The Elf soldier moved away, out of the light. "I have to go. It's getting late, and at night the Trolls come out. I don't want to be too far away from the others."

"Sure," Shadrach said.

"The Trolls are afraid of nothing, now that the old king is dead. They forage everywhere. No one is safe."

"Where did you say the meeting is to be? And what time?"

"At the Great Oak. When the moon sets tonight, just as it leaves the sky."

"I'll be there, I guess," Shadrach said. "I suppose you're right. The King of the Elves can't afford to let his kingdom down when it needs him most."

He looked around, but the Elf soldier was already gone.

Shadrach walked up the highway, his mind full of doubts and wonderings. When he came to the first of the flat stone steps, he stopped.

"And the old oak tree is on Phineas's farm! What'll Phineas say?"

But he was the Elf King and the Trolls were moving in the hills. Shadrach stood listening to the rustle of the wind as it moved through the trees beyond the highway, and along the far slopes and hills.

Trolls? Were there really Trolls there, rising up, bold and confident in the darkness of the night, afraid of nothing, afraid of no one?

And this business of being Elf King...

Shadrach went on up the steps, his lips pressed tight. When he reached the top of the stone steps, the last rays of sunlight had already faded. It was night.

PHINEAS JUDD stared out the window. He swore and shook his head. Then he went quickly to the door and ran out onto the porch. In the cold moonlight a dim figure was walking slowly across the lower field, coming toward the house along the cow trail.

"Shadrach!" Phineas cried. "What's wrong? What are you doing out this time of night?"

Shadrach stopped and put his fists stubbornly on his hips.

"You go back home," Phineas said. "What's got into you?"

"I'm sorry, Phineas," Shadrach answered. "I'm sorry I have to go over your land. But I have to meet somebody at the old oak tree."

"At this time of night?"

Shadrach bowed his head.

"What's the matter with you, Shadrach? Who in the world you going to meet in the middle of the night on my farm?"

"I have to meet with the Elves. We're going to plan out the war with the Trolls."

"Well, I'll be damned," Phineas Judd said. He went back inside the house and slammed the door. For a long time he stood thinking. Then he went back out on the porch again. "What did you say you were doing? You don't have to tell me, of course, but I just—"

"I have to meet the Elves at the old oak tree. We must have a general council of war against the Trolls."

"Yes, indeed. The Trolls. Have to watch for the Trolls all the time."

"Trolls are everywhere," Shadrach stated, nodding his head. "I never realized it before. You can't forget them or ignore them. They never forget you. They're always planning, watching you—"

Phineas gaped at him, speechless.

"Oh, by the way," Shadrach said. "I may be gone for some time. It depends on how long this business is going to take. I haven't had much experience in fighting Trolls, so I'm not sure. But I wonder if you'd mind looking after the gas station for me, about twice a day, maybe once in the morning and once at night, to make sure no one's broken in or anything like that."

"You're going away?" Phineas came quickly down the stairs. "What's all this about Trolls? Why are you going?"

Shadrach patiently repeated what he had said.

"But what for?"

"Because I'm the Elf King. I have to lead them."

There was silence. "I see," Phineas said, at last. "That's right, you *did* mention it before, didn't you? But, Shadrach, why don't you come inside for a while and you can tell me about the Trolls and drink some coffee and—"

"Coffee?" Shadrach looked up at the pale moon above him, the moon and the bleak sky. The world was still and dead and the night was very cold and the moon would not be setting for some time.

Shadrach shivered.

"It's a cold night," Phineas urged. "Too cold to be out. Come on in—"

"I guess I have a little time," Shadrach admitted. "A cup of coffee wouldn't do any harm. But I can't stay very long . . ."

SHADRACH stretched his legs out and sighed. "This coffee sure tastes good, Phineas."

Phineas sipped a little and put his cup down. The living room was quiet and warm. It was a very neat little living room with solemn pictures on the walls, gray uninterest-

ing pictures that minded their own business. In the corner
was a small reed organ with sheet music carefully
arranged on top of it.

Shadrach noticed the organ and smiled. "You still
play, Phineas?"

"Not much any more. The bellows don't work right.
One of them won't come back up."

"I suppose I could fix it sometime. If I'm around, I
mean."

"That would be fine," Phineas said. "I was thinking of
asking you."

"Remember how you used to play 'Vilia' and Dan
Green came up with that lady who worked for Pop during
the summer? The one who wanted to open a pottery
shop?"

"I sure do," Phineas said.

Presently, Shadrach set down his coffee cup and
shifted in his chair.

"You want more coffee?" Phineas asked quickly. He
stood up. "A little more?"

"Maybe a little. But I have to be going pretty soon."

"It's a bad night to be outside."

Shadrach looked through the window. It was darker;
the moon had almost gone down. The fields were stark.
Shadrach shivered. "I wouldn't disagree with you," he
said.

Phineas turned eagerly. "Look, Shadrach. You go on
home where it's warm. You can come out and fight Trolls
some other night. There'll always be Trolls. You said so
yourself. Plenty of time to do that later, when the
weather's better. When it's not so cold."

Shadrach rubbed his forehead wearily. "You know, it
all seems like some sort of a crazy dream. When did I start
talking about Elves and Trolls? When did it all begin?"
His voice trailed off. "Thank you for the coffee." He got
slowly to his feet. "It warmed me up a lot. And I
appreciated the talk. Like old times, you and me sitting
here the way we used to."

"Are you going?" Phineas hesitated. *"Home?"*

"I think I better. It's late."

PHINEAS got quickly to his feet. He led Shadrach to the
door, one arm around his shoulder.

"All right, Shadrach, you go on home. Take a good hot bath before you go to bed. It'll fix you up. And maybe just a little snort of brandy to warm the blood."

Phineas opened the front door and they went slowly down the porch steps, onto the cold, dark ground.

"Yes, I guess I'll be going," Shadrach said. "Good night—"

"You go on home." Phineas patted him on the arm. "You run along home and take a good hot bath. And then go straight to bed."

"That's a good idea. Thank you, Phineas. I appreciate your kindness." Shadrach looked down at Phineas's hand on his arm. He had not been that close to Phineas for years.

Shadrach contemplated the hand. He wrinkled his brow, puzzled.

Phineas's hand was huge and rough and his arms were short. His fingers were blunt; his nails broken and cracked. Almost black, or so it seemed in the moonlight.

Shadrach looked up at Phineas. "Strange," he murmured.

"What's strange, Shadrach?"

In the moonlight, Phineas's face seemed oddly heavy and brutal. Shadrach had never noticed before how the jaw bulged, what a great protruding jaw it was. The skin was yellow and coarse, like parchment. Behind the glasses, the eyes were like two stones, cold and lifeless. The ears were immense, the hair stringy and matted.

Odd that he never noticed before. But he had never seen Phineas in the moonlight.

Shadrach stepped away, studying his old friend. From a few feet off, Phineas Judd seemed unusually short and squat. His legs were slightly bowed. His feet were enormous. And there was something else—

"What is it?" Phineas demanded, beginning to grow suspicious. "Is there something wrong?"

Something was completely wrong. And he had never noticed it, not in all the years they had been friends. All around Phineas Judd was an odor, a faint, pungent stench of rot, of decaying flesh, damp and moldy.

Shadrach glanced slowly about him. "Something wrong?" he echoed. "No, I wouldn't say that."

By the side of the house was an old rain barrel, half

fallen apart. Shadrach walked over to it.

"No, Phineas. I wouldn't exactly say there's something wrong."

"What are you doing?"

"Me?" Shadrach took hold of one of the barrel staves and pulled it loose. He walked back to Phineas, carrying the barrel stave carefully. "I'm King of the Elves. Who—or what—are you?"

Phineas roared and attacked with his great murderous shovel hands.

Shadrach smashed him over the head with the barrel stave. Phineas bellowed with rage and pain.

At the shattering sound, there was a clatter and from underneath the house came a furious horde of bounding, leaping creatures, dark bent-over things, their bodies heavy and squat, their feet and heads immense. Shadrach took one look at the flood of dark creatures pouring out from Phineas's basement. He knew what they were.

"Help!" Shadrach shouted. "Trolls! Help!"

THE TROLLS were all around him, grabbing hold of him, tugging at him, climbing up him, pummeling his face and body.

Shadrach fell to with the barrel stave, swung again and again, kicking Trolls with his feet, whacking them with the barrel stave. There seemed to be hundreds of them. More and more poured out from under Phineas's house, a surging black tide of pot-shaped creatures, their great eyes and teeth gleaming in the moonlight.

"Help!" Shadrach cried again, more feebly now. He was getting winded. His heart labored painfully. A Troll bit his wrist, clinging to his arm. Shadrach flung it away, pulling loose from the horde clutching his trouser legs, the barrel stave rising and falling.

One of the Trolls caught hold of the stave. A whole group of them helped, wrenching furiously, trying to pull it away. Shadrach hung on desperately. Trolls were all over him, on his shoulders, clinging to his coat, riding his arms, his legs, pulling his hair—

He heard a high-pitched clarion call from a long way off, the sound of some distant golden trumpet, echoing in the hills.

The Trolls suddenly stopped attacking. One of them dropped off Shadrach's neck. Another let go of his arm.

The call came again, this time more loudly.

"Elves!" a Troll rasped. He turned and moved toward the sound, grinding his teeth and spitting with fury.

"Elves!"

The Trolls swarmed forward, a growing wave of gnashing teeth and nails, pushing furiously toward the Elf columns. The Elves broke formation and joined battle, shouting with wild joy in their shrill, piping voices. The tide of Trolls rushed against them, Troll against Elf, shovel nails against golden sword, biting jaw against dagger.

"Kill the Elves!"

"Death to the Trolls!"

"Onward!"

"Forward!"

Shadrach fought desperately with the Trolls that were still clinging to him. He was exhausted, panting and gasping for breath. Blindly, he whacked on and on, kicking and jumping, throwing Trolls away from him, through the air and across the ground.

How LONG the battle raged, Shadrach never knew. He was lost in a sea of dark bodies, round and evil-smelling, clinging to him, tearing, biting, fastened to his nose and hair and fingers. He fought silently, grimly.

All around him, the Elf legions clashed with the Troll horde, little groups of struggling warriors on all sides.

Suddenly Shadrach stopped fighting. He raised his head, looking uncertainly around him. Nothing moved. Everything was silent. The fighting had ceased.

A few Trolls still clung to his arms and legs. Shadrach whacked one with the barrel stave. It howled and dropped to the ground. He staggered back, struggling with the last Troll, who hung tenaciously to his arm.

"Now you!" Shadrach gasped. He pried the Troll loose and flung it into the air. The Troll fell to the ground and scuttled off into the night.

There was nothing more. No Troll moved anywhere. All was silent across the bleak moon-swept fields.

Shadrach sank down on a stone. His chest rose and fell

painfully. Red specks swam before his eyes. Weakly, he got out his pocket handkerchief and wiped his neck and face. He closed his eyes, shaking his head from side to side.

When he opened his eyes again, the Elves were coming toward him, gathering their legion together again. The Elves were disheveled and bruised. Their golden armor was gashed and torn. Their helmets were bent or missing. Most of their scarlet plumes were gone. Those that still remained were drooping and broken.

But the battle was over. The war was won. The Troll hordes had been put to flight.

SHADRACH got slowly to his feet. The Elf warriors stood around him in a circle, gazing up at him with silent respect. One of them helped steady him as he put his handkerchief away in his pocket.

"Thank you," Shadrach murmured. "Thank you very much."

"The Trolls have been defeated," an Elf stated, still awed by what had happened.

Shadrach gazed around at the Elves. There were many of them, more than he had ever seen before. All the Elves had turned out for the battle. They were grim-faced, stern with the seriousness of the moment, weary from the terrible struggle.

"Yes, they're gone, all right," Shadrach said. He was beginning to get his breath. "That was a close call. I'm glad you fellows came when you did. I was just about finished, fighting them all by myself."

"All alone, the King of the Elves held off the entire Troll army," an Elf announced shrilly.

"Eh?" Shadrach said, taken aback. Then he smiled. "That's true, I *did* fight them alone for a while. I *did* hold off the Trolls all by myself. The whole darn Troll army."

"There is more," an Elf said.

Shadrach blinked. "More?"

"Look over here, O King, mightiest of all the Elves. This way. To the right."

The Elves led Shadrach over.

"What is it?" Shadrach murmured, seeing nothing at first. He gazed down, trying to pierce the darkness.

"Could we have a torch over here?"

Some Elves brought little pine torches.

There, on the frozen ground, lay Phineas Judd, on his back. His eyes were blank and staring, his mouth half open. He did not move. His body was cold and stiff.

"He is dead," an Elf said solemnly.

Shadrach gulped in sudden alarm. Cold sweat stood out abruptly on his forehead. "My gosh! My old friend! What have I done?"

"You have slain the Great Troll."

Shadrach paused.

"I *what?*"

You have slain the Great Troll, leader of all the Trolls."

"This has never happened before," another Elf exclaimed excitedly. "The Great Troll has lived for centuries. Nobody imagined he could die. This is our most historic moment."

All the Elves gazed down at the silent form with awe, awe mixed with more than a little fear.

"Oh, go on!" Shadrach said. "That's just Phineas Judd."

But as he spoke, a chill moved up his spine. He remembered what he had seen a little while before, as he stood close by Phineas, as the dying moonlight crossed his old friend's face.

"Look." One of the Elves bent over and unfastened Phineas's blue-serge vest. He pushed the coat and vest aside. "See?"

Shadrach bent down to look.

He gasped.

UNDERNEATH Phineas Judd's blue-serge vest was a suit of mail, an encrusted mesh of ancient, rusting iron, fastened tightly around the squat body. On the mail stood an engraved insignia, dark and time-worn, embedded with dirt and rust. A moldering half-obliterated emblem. The emblem of a crossed owl leg and toadstool.

The emblem of the Great Troll.

"Golly," Shadrach said. "And *I* killed him."

For a long time he gazed silently down. Then, slowly, realization began to grow in him. He straightened up, a smile forming on his face.

"What is it, O King?" an Elf piped.

"I just thought of something," Shadrach said. "I just realized that—that since the Great Troll is dead and the Troll army has been put to flight—"

He broke off. All the Elves were waiting.

"I thought maybe I—that is, maybe if you don't need me any more—"

The Elves listened respectfully. "What is it, Mighty King? Go on."

"I thought maybe now I could go back to the filling station and not be king any more." Shadrach glanced hopefully around at them. "Do you think so? With the war over and all. With him dead. What do you say?"

For a time, the Elves were silent. They gazed unhappily down at the ground. None of them said anything. At last they began moving away, collecting their banners and pennants.

"Yes, you may go back," an Elf said quietly. "The war is over. The Trolls have been defeated. You may return to your filling station, if that is what you want."

A flood of relief swept over Shadrach. He straightened up, grinning from ear to ear. "Thanks! That's fine. That's really fine. That's the best news I've heard in my life."

He moved away from the Elves, rubbing his hands together and blowing on them.

"Thanks an awful lot." He grinned around at the silent Elves. "Well, I guess I'll be running along, then. It's late. Late and cold. It's been a hard night. I'll—I'll see you around."

The Elves nodded silently.

"Fine. Well, good night." Shadrach turned and started along the path. He stopped for a moment, waving back at the Elves. "It was quite a battle, wasn't it? We really licked them." He hurried on along the path. Once again he stopped, looking back and waving. "Sure glad I could help out. Well, good night!"

One or two of the Elves waved, but none of them said anything.

SHADRACH JONES walked slowly toward his place. He could see it from the rise, the highway that few cars traveled, the filling station falling to ruin, the house that might not last as long as himself, and not enough money coming in to repair them or buy a better location.

He turned around and went back.

The Elves were still gathered there in the silence of the night. They had not moved away.

"I was hoping you hadn't gone," Shadrach said, relieved.

"And we were hoping you would not leave," said a soldier.

Shadrach kicked a stone. It bounced through the tight silence and stopped. The Elves were still watching him.

"Leave?" Shadrach asked. "And me King of the Elves?"

"Then you will remain our king?" an Elf cried.

"It's a hard thing for a man of my age to change. To stop selling gasoline and suddenly be a king. It scared me for a while. But it doesn't any more."

"You will? You *will*?"

"Sure," said Shadrach Jones.

The little circle of Elf torches closed in joyously. In their light, he saw a platform like the one that had carried the old King of the Elves. But this one was much larger, big enough to hold a man, and dozens of the soldiers waited with proud shoulders under the shafts.

A soldier gave him a happy bow. "For you, Sire."

Shadrach climbed aboard. It was less comfortable than walking, but he knew this was how they wanted to take him to the Kingdom of the Elves.

The Mold of Yancy

LEON SIPLING groaned and pushed away his work papers. In an organization of thousands he was the only employee not putting out. Probably he was the only yance-man on Callisto not doing his job. Fear, and the quick pluckings of desperation, made him reach up and wave on the audio circuit to Babson, the over-all office controller.

"Say," Sipling said hoarsely, "I think I'm stuck, Bab. How about running the gestalt through, up to my spot? Maybe I can pick up the rhythm . . ." He grinned weakly. "The hum of other creative minds."

After a speculative moment, Babson reached for the impulse synapsis, his massive face unsympathetic. "You holding up progress, Sip? This has to be integrated with the daily by six tonight. The schedule calls for the works to be on the vidlines during the dinner-hour stretch."

The visual side of the gestalt had already begun to form on the wall screen; Sipling turned his attention to it, grateful of a chance to escape Babson's cold glare.

The screen showed a 3-D of Yancy, the usual three quarter view, from the waist up. John Edward Yancy in his faded workshirt, sleeves rolled up, arms brown and furry. A middle-aged man in his late fifties, his face sunburned, neck slightly red, a good-natured smile on his face, squinting because he was looking into the sun. Behind Yancy was a still of his yard, his garage, his flower garden, lawn, the back of his neat little white plastic house. Yancy grinned at Sipling: a neighbor pausing in the middle of a summer day, perspiring from the heat and the exertion of mowing his lawn, about to launch into a few harmless remarks about the weather, the state of the planet, the condition of the neighborhood.

"Say," Yancy said, in the audio phones propped up on Sipling's desk. His voice was low, personal. "The darndest thing happened to my grandson Ralf, the other morning. You know how Ralf is; he's always getting to school half an hour early . . . says he likes to be in his seat before anybody else."

"That eager-beaver," Joe Pines, at the next desk, cat-called.

From the screen, Yancy's voice rolled on, confident, amiable, undisturbed. "Well, Ralf saw this squirrel; it was just sitting there on the sidewalk. He stopped for a minute and watched." The look on Yancy's face was so real that Sipling almost believed him. He could, almost, see the squirrel and the tow-headed youngest grandson of the Yancy family, the familiar child of the familiar son of the planet's most familiar—and beloved—person.

"This squirrel," Yancy explained, in his homey way, "was collecting nuts. And by golly, this was just the other day, only the middle of June. And here was this little squirrel—" with his hands he indicated the size, "collecting these nuts and carrying them off for winter."

And then, the amused, anecdote-look on Yancy's face faded. A serious, thoughtful look replaced it: the meaningful-look. His blue eyes darkened (good color work). His jaw became more square, more imposing (good dummy-switch by the android crew). Yancy seemed older, more solemn and mature, more impressive. Behind him, the garden-scene had been jerked and a slightly different backdrop filtered in; Yancy now stood firmly planted in a cosmic landscape, among mountains and winds and huge old forests.

"I got to thinking," Yancy said, and his voice was deeper, slower. "There was that little squirrel. How did he know winter was coming? There he was, working away, getting prepared for it." Yancy's voice rose. "Preparing for a winter he'd never seen."

Sipling stiffened and prepared *himself*; it was coming. At his desk, Joe Pines grinned and yelled: "Get set!"

"That squirrel," Yancy said solemnly, "had faith. No, he never saw any sign of winter. But he knew winter was coming." The firm jaw moved; one hand came slowly up . . .

And then the image stopped. It froze, immobile, silent. No words came from it; abruptly the sermon ended, in the middle of a paragraph.

"That's it," Babson said briskly, filtering the Yancy out. "Help you any?"

Sipling pawed jerkily at his work papers. "No," he admitted, "actually it doesn't. But—I'll get it worked out."

"I hope so." Babson's face darkened ominously and his small mean eyes seemed to grow smaller. "What's the matter with you? Home problems?"

"I'll be okay," Sipling muttered, sweating. "Thanks."

On the screen a faint impression of Yancy remained, still poised at the word *coming*. The rest of the gestalt was in Sipling's head: the continuing slice of words and gestures hadn't been worked out and fed to the composite. Sipling's contribution was missing, so the entire gestalt was stopped cold in its tracks.

"Say," Joe Pines said uneasily, "I'll be glad to take over, today. Cut your desk out of the circuit and I'll cut myself in."

"Thanks," Sipling muttered, "but I'm the only one who can get this damn part. It's the central gem."

"You ought to take a rest. You've been working too hard."

"Yes," Sipling agreed, on the verge of hysteria. "I'm a little under the weather."

That was obvious: everybody in the office could see that. But only Sipling knew why. And he was fighting with all his strength to keep from screaming out the reason at the top of his lungs.

BASIC ANALYSIS OF the political milieu at Callisto was laid out by Niplan computing apparatus at Washington D.C.; but the final evaluations were done by human technicians. The Washington computers could ascertain that the Callisto political structure was moving toward a totalitarian make-up, but they couldn't say what that indicated. Human beings were required to class the drift as malign.

"It isn't possible," Taverner protested. "There's constant industrial traffic in and out of Callisto; except for the Ganymede syndicate they've got out-plant commerce bottled up. We'd know as soon as anything phony got started."

"How would we know?" Police Director Kellman inquired.

Taverner indicated the data-sheets, graphs and charts of figures and percentages that covered the walls of the Niplan Police offices. "It would show up in hundreds of ways. Terrorist raids, political prisons, extermination camps. We'd hear about political recanting, treason, disloyalty...all the basic props of a dictatorship."

"Don't confuse a totalitarian society with a dictatorship," Kellman said drily. "A totalitarian state reaches into every sphere of its citizens' lives, forms their opinions on every subject. The government can be a dictatorship, *or* a parliament, *or* an elected president, *or* a council of priests. That doesn't matter."

"All right," Taverner said, mollified. "I'll go. I'll take a team there and see what they're doing."

"Can you make yourselves look like Callistotes?"

"What are they like?"

"I'm not sure," Kellman admitted thoughtfully, with a glance at the elaborate wall charts. "But whatever it is, they're all beginning to turn out alike."

AMONG ITS passengers the interplan commercial liner that settled down at Callisto carried Peter Taverner, his wife, and their two children. With a grimace of concern, Taverner made out the shapes of local officials waiting at the exit hatch. The passengers were going to be carefully screened; as the ramp descended, the clot of officials moved forward.

Taverner got to his feet and collected his family. "Ignore them," he told Ruth. "Our papers will get us by."

Expertly prepared documents identified him as a speculator in nonferric metals, looking for a wholesale outlet to handle his jobbing. Callisto was a clearing-point for land and mineral operations; a constant flood of wealth-hungry entrepreneurs streamed back and forth, carting raw materials from the underdeveloped moons, hauling mining equipment from the inner planets.

Cautiously, Taverner arranged his topcoat over his arm. A heavyset man, in his middle thirties, he could have passed for a successful business operator. His double-breasted business suit was expensive, but conservative. His big shoes were brightly shined. All things considered, he'd probably get by. As he and his family moved toward the exit ramp, they presented a perfect and exact imitation of the out-planet business-class.

"State your business," a green-uniformed official demanded, pencil poised. I-d tabs were being checked, photographed, recorded. Brain pattern comparisons were being made: the usual routine.

"Nonferric enterprises," Taverner began, but a second official cut him abruptly off.

"You're the third cop this morning. What's biting you people on Terra?" The official eyed Taverner intently. "We're getting more cops than ministers."

Trying to maintain his poise, Taverner answered evenly: "I'm here to take a rest. Acute alcoholism—nothing official."

"That's what your cohorts said." The official grinned humorlessly. "Well, what's one more Terran cop?" He slid the lock-bars aside and waved Taverner and his family through. "Welcome to Callisto. Have fun—enjoy yourselves. Fastest-growing moon in the system."

"Practically a planet," Taverner commented ironically.

"Any day, now." The official examined some reports. "According to our friends in your little organization, you've been pasting up wall graphs and charts about us. Are we that important?"

"Academic interest," Taverner said; if three spots had been made, then the whole team had been netted. The local authorities were obviously primed to detect infiltration . . . the realization chilled him.

But they were letting him through. Were they *that* confident?

Things didn't look good. Peering around for a cab, he grimly prepared to undertake the business of integrating the scattered team members into a functioning whole.

THAT EVENING, at the *Stay-Lit* bar on the main street of the commercial district of town, Taverner met with his two team members. Hunched over their whiskey sours, they compared notes.

"I've been here almost twelve hours," Eckmund stated, gazing impassively at the rows of bottles in the gloomy depths of the bar. Cigar smoke hovered in the air; the automatic music box in the corner banged away metallically. "I've been walking around town, looking at things, making observations."

"Me," Dorser said, "I've been at the tape-library. Getting official myth, comparing it to Callistote reality. And talking to the scholars—educated people hanging around the scanning rooms."

Taverner sipped his drink. "Anything of interest?"

"You know the primitive rule-of-thumb test," Eckmund said wryly. "I loafed around on a slum street corner until I got in a conversation with some people waiting for a bus. I started knocking the authorities: complaining about the bus service, the sewage disposal, taxes, everything. They chimed right in. Heartily. No hesitation. And no fear."

"The legal government," Dorser commented, "is set up in the usual archaic fashion. Two-party system, one a little more conservative than the other—no fundamental difference of course. But both elect candidates at open primaries, ballots circulated to all registered voters." A spasm of amusement touched him. "This is a model democracy. I read the text books. Nothing but idealistic slogans: freedom of speech, assembly, religion—the works. Same old grammar school stuff."

The three of them were temporarily silent.

"There are jails," Taverner said slowly. "Every society has law violations."

"I visited one," Eckmund said, belching. "Petty thieves, murderers, claim-jumpers, strong-arm hoods—the usual."

"No political prisoners?"

"No." Eckmund raised his voice. "We might as well discuss this at the top of our lungs. Nobody cares—the authorities don't care."

"Probably after we're gone they'll clap a few thousand people into prison," Dorser murmured thoughtfully.

"My God," Eckmund retorted, "people can leave Callisto any time they want. If you're operating a police state you have to keep your borders shut. And these borders are wide open. People pour in and out."

"Maybe it's a chemical in the drinking water," Dorser suggested.

"How the hell can they have a totalitarian society without terrorism?" Eckmund demanded rhetorically. "I'll swear to it—there are no thought-control cops here. There is absolutely no fear."

"Somehow, pressure is being exerted," Taverner persisted.

"Not by cops," Dorser said emphatically. "Not by force and brutality. Not by illegal arrest and imprisonment and forced labor."

"If this were a police state," Eckmund said thoughtfully, "there'd be some kind of resistance movement. Some sort of 'subversive' group trying to overthrow the authorities. But in this society you're free to complain; you can buy time on the t-v and radio stations, you can buy space in the newspapers—anything you want." He shrugged. "So how can there be a clandestine resistance movement? It's silly."

"Nevertheless," Taverner said, "these people are living in a one-party society, with a party line, with an official ideology. They show the effects of a carefully controlled totalitarian state. They're guinea pigs—whether they realize it or not."

"Wouldn't they realize it?"

Baffled, Taverner shook his head. "I would have thought so. There must be some mechanism we don't understand."

"It's all open. We can look everything over."

"We must be looking for the wrong thing." Idly, Taverner gazed at the television screen above the bar. The nude girlie song-and-dance routine had ended; now the features of a man faded into view. A genial, round-faced man in his fifties, with guileless blue eyes, an almost childish twitch to his lips, a fringe of brown hair playing around his slightly prominent ears.

"Friends," the t-v image rumbled, "it's good to be with you again, tonight. I thought I might have a little chat with you."

"A commercial," Dorser said, signalling the bartending machine for another drink.

"Who is that?" Taverner asked curiously.

"That kindly-looking geezer?" Eckmund examined his notes. "A sort of popular commentator. Name of Yancy."

"Is he part of the government?"

"Not that I know of. A kind of home-spun philosopher. I picked up a biography of him on a magazine stand." Eckmund passed the gaily-colored pamphlet to his boss. "Totally ordinary man, as far as I can see. Used to be a soldier; in the Mars-Jupiter War he distinguished himself—battlefield commission. Rose to the rank of major." He shrugged indifferently. "A sort of talking almanac. Pithy sayings on every topic. Wise old saws: how to cure a chest cold. What the trouble is back on Terra."

Taverner examined the booklet. "Yes, I saw his picture around."

"Very popular figure. Loved by the masses. Man of the people—speaks for them. When I was buying cigarettes I noticed he endorses one particular brand. Very popular brand, now; just about driven the others off the market. Same with beer. The Scotch in this glass is probably the brand Yancy endorses. The same with tennis balls. Only he doesn't play tennis—he plays croquet. All the time, every weekend." Accepting his fresh drink Eckmund finished, "So now everybody plays croquet."

"How can croquet be a planet-wide sport?" Taverner demanded.

"This isn't a planet," Dorser put in. "It's a pipsqueak moon."

"Not according to Yancy," Eckmund said. "We're supposed to think of Callisto as a planet."

"How?" Taverner asked.

"Spiritually, it's a planet. Yancy likes people to take a spiritual view of matters. He's strong on God and honesty in government and being hard-working and clean-cut. Warmed-over truisms."

The expression on Taverner's face hardened. "Interesting," he murmured. "I'll have to drop by and meet him."

"Why? He's the dullest, most mediocre man you could dream up."

"Maybe," Taverner answered, "that's why I'm interested."

• • •

BABSON, huge and menacing, met Taverner at the entrance of the Yancy Building. "Of course you can meet Mr. Yancy. But he's a busy man—it'll take awhile to squeeze in an appointment. Everybody wants to meet Mr. Yancy."

Taverner was unimpressed. "How long do I have to wait?"

As they crossed the main lobby to the elevators, Babson made a computation. "Oh, say four months."

"Four *months!*"

"John Yancy is just about the most popular man alive."

"Around here, maybe," Taverner commented angrily, as they entered the packed elevator. "I never heard of him before. If he's got so much on the ball, why isn't he piped all around Niplan?"

"Actually," Babson admitted, in a hoarse, confidential whisper, "I can't imagine what people see in Yancy. As far as I'm concerned he's just a big bag of wind. But people around here enjoy him. After all, Callisto is—provincial. Yancy appeals to a certain type of rural mind—to people who like their world simple. I'm afraid Terra would be too sophisticated for Yancy."

"Have you tried?"

"Not yet," Babson said. Reflectively, he added: "Maybe later."

While Taverner was pondering the meaning of the big man's words, the elevator ceased climbing. The two of them stepped off into a luxurious, carpeted hall, illuminated by recessed lights. Babson pushed open a door, and they entered a large, active office.

Inside, a screening of a recent Yancy gestalt was in progress. A group of yance-men watched it silently, faces alert and critical. The gestalt showed Yancy sitting at his old-fashioned oak desk, in his study. It was obvious that he had been working on some philosophical thoughts: spread out over the desk were books and papers. On Yancy's face was a thoughtful expression; he sat with his hand against his forehead, features screwed up into a solemn study of concentration.

"This is for next Sunday morning," Babson explained.

Yancy's lips moved, and he spoke. "Friends," he began,

in his deep, personal, friendly, man-to-man voice, "I've been sitting here at my desk—well, about the way you're sitting around your living rooms." A switch in camera work occurred; it showed the open door of Yancy's study. In the living room was the familiar figure of Yancy's sweet-faced middle-aged homey wife; she was sitting on the comfortable sofa primly sewing. On the floor their grandson Ralf played the familiar game of jacks. The family dog snoozed in the corner.

One of the watching yance-men made a note on his pad. Taverner glanced at him curiously, baffled.

"Of course, I was in there with them," Yancy continued, smiling briefly. "I was reading the funnies to Ralf. He was sitting on my knee." The background faded, and a momentary phantom scene of Yancy sitting with his grandson on his knee floated into being. Then the desk and the book-lined study returned. "I'm mighty grateful for my family," Yancy revealed. "In these times of stress, it's my family that I turn to, as my pillar of strength."

Another notation was made by a watching yance-man.

"Sitting here, in my study, this wonderful Sunday morning," Yancy rumbled on, "I realize how lucky we are to be alive, and to have this lovely planet, and the fine cities and houses, all the things God has given us to enjoy. But we've got to be careful. We've got to make sure we don't lose these things."

A change had come over Yancy. It seemed to Taverner that the image was subtly altering. It wasn't the same man; the good humor was gone. This was an older man, and larger. A firm-eyed father, speaking to his children.

"My friends," Yancy intoned, "there are forces that could weaken this planet. Everything we've built up for our loved ones, for our children, *could be taken away from us overnight*. We must learn to be vigilant. We must protect our liberties, our possessions, our way of life. If we become divided, and fall to bickering among each other, we will be easy prey for our enemies. We must work together, my friends.

"That's what I've been thinking about this Sunday morning. *Cooperation. Teamwork.* We've got to be secure, and to be secure, we must be one united people. That's the key, my friends, the key to a more abundant life." Pointing out the window at the lawn and garden, Yancy said: "You know, I was..."

The voice trailed off. The image froze. Full room lights came on, and the watching yance-men moved into muttering activity.

"Fine," one of them said. "So far, at least. But where's the rest?"

"Sipling, again," another answered. "His slice still hasn't come through. What's wrong with that guy?"

Scowling, Babson detached himself. "Pardon me," he said to Taverner. "I'll have to excuse myself—technical matters. You're free to look around, if you care to. Help yourself to any of the literature—anything you want."

"Thanks," Taverner said uncertainly. He was confused; everything *seemed* harmless, even trivial. But something basic was wrong.

Suspiciously, he began to prowl.

IT WAS obvious that John Yancy had pontificated on every known subject. A Yancy opinion on every conceivable topic was available...modern art, or garlic in cooking, or the use of intoxicating beverages, or eating meat, or socialism, or war, or education, or open-front dresses on women, or high taxes, or atheism, or divorce, or patriotism—every shade and nuance of opinion possible.

Was there any subject that Yancy *hadn't* expressed himself on?

Taverner examined the voluminous tapes that lined the walls of the offices. Yancy's utterances had run into billions of tape feet...could one man have an opinion on everything in the universe?

Choosing a tape at random, he found himself being addressed on the topic of table manners.

"You know," the miniature Yancy began, his voice tinny in Taverner's ears, "at dinner the other night I happened to notice how my grandson Ralf was cutting his steak." Yancy grinned at the viewer, as an image of the six-year-old boy sawing grimly away floated briefly into sight. "Well, I got to thinking, there was Ralf working away at that steak, not having any luck with it. And it seemed to me—"

Taverner snapped the tape off and returned it to the slot. Yancy had definite opinions on everything... or *were* they so definite?

A strange suspicion was growing in him. On some topics, yes. On minor issues, Yancy had exact rules, specific maxims drawn from mankind's rich storehouse of folklore. But major philosophical and political issues were something else again.

Getting out one of the many tapes listed under War, Taverner ran it through at random.

"...I'm against war," Yancy pronounced angrily. "And I ought to know; I've done my share of fighting."

There followed a montage of battle scenes: the Jupiter-Mars War in which Yancy had distinguished himself by his bravery, his concern for his comrades, his hatred of the enemy, his variety of proper emotions.

"But," Yancy continued staunchly, "I feel a planet must be strong. We must not surrender ourselves meekly... weakness invites attack and fosters aggression. By being weak we promote war. We must gird ourselves and protect those we love. With all my heart and soul I'm against useless wars; but I say again, as I've said many times before, a man must come forward and fight a *just* war. He must not shrink from his responsibility. War is a terrible thing. But sometimes we must..."

As he restored the tape, Taverner wondered just what the hell Yancy *had* said. What were his views on war? They took up a hundred separate reels of tape; Yancy was always ready to hold forth on such vital and grandiose subjects as War, the Planet, God, Taxation. But did he *say* anything?

A cold chill crawled up Taverner's spine. On specific—and trivial—items there were absolute opinions: dogs are better than cats, grapefruit is too sour without a dash of sugar, it's good to get up early in the morning, too much drinking is bad. But on big topics... an empty vacuum, filled with the vacant roll of high-sounding phrases. A public that agreed with Yancy on war and taxes and God and planet agreed with absolutely nothing. And with everything.

On topics of importance, they had no opinion at all. They only *thought* they had an opinion.

Rapidly, Taverner scanned tapes on various major subjects. It was the same all down the line. With one sentence Yancy gave; with the next he took away. The total effect was a neat cancellation, a skillful negation. But the viewer was left with the illusion of having consumed a rich and varied intellectual feast. It was amazing. And it was professional: the ends were tied up too slickly to be mere accident.

Nobody was as harmless and vapid as John Edward Yancy. He was just too damn good to be true.

Sweating, Taverner left the main reference room and poked his way toward the rear offices, where busy yance-men worked away at their desks and assembly tables. Activity whirred on all sides. The expression on the faces around him was benign, harmless, almost bored. The same friendly, trivial expression that Yancy himself displayed.

Harmless—and in its harmlessness, diabolical. And there wasn't a damn thing he could do. If people liked to listen to John Edward Yancy, if they wanted to model themselves after him—what could the Niplan Police do about it?

What crime was being committed?

No wonder Babson didn't care if the police prowled around. No wonder the authorities had freely admitted them. There weren't any political jails or labor gangs or concentration camps...there didn't have to be.

Torture chambers and extermination camps were needed only when persuasion failed. And persuasion was working perfectly. A police state, rule by terror, came about when the totalitarian apparatus began to break down. The earlier totalitarian societies had been incomplete; the authorities hadn't really gotten into every sphere of life. But techniques of communication had improved.

The first really successful totalitarian state was being realized before his eyes: harmless and trivial, it emerged. And the last stage—nightmarish, but perfectly logical— was when all the newborn boys were happily and voluntarily named John Edward.

Why not? They already lived, acted, and thought like John Edward. And there was Mrs. Margaret Ellen Yancy, for the women. She had her full range of opinions, too; she had her kitchen, her taste in clothes, her little recipes and advice, for all the women to imitate.

There were even Yancy children for the youth of the planet to imitate. The authorities hadn't overlooked anything.

Babson strolled over, a genial expression on his face. "How's it going, officer?" he chuckled wetly, putting his hand on Taverner's shoulder.

"Fine," Taverner managed to answer; he evaded the hand.

"You like our little establishment?" There was genuine pride in Babson's thick voice. "We do a good job. An artistic job—we have real standards of excellence."

Shaking with helpless anger, Taverner plunged out of the office and into the hall. The elevator took too long; furiously, he turned toward the stairs. He had to get out of the Yancy Building; he had to get away.

From the shadows of the hall a man appeared, face pale and taut. "Wait. Can—I talk to you?"

Taverner pushed past him. "What do you want?"

"You're from the Terran Niplan Police? I—" The man's Adam's apple bobbed. "I work here. My name's Sipling, Leon Sipling. I have to do something—I can't stand it any more."

"Nothing can be done," Taverner told him. "If they want to be like Yancy—"

"But there isn't any Yancy," Sipling broke in, his thin face twitching spasmodically. "We made him up . . . we invented him."

Taverner halted. "You *what?*"

"I've decided." Voice quavering excitedly, Sipling rushed on: "I'm going to do something—and I know exactly what." Catching hold of Taverner's sleeve he grated: "You've got to help me. I can stop all this, but I can't do it alone."

IN LEON SIPLING'S attractive, well-furnished living room, the two of them sat drinking coffee and watching their children scramble around on the floor, playing games. Sipling's wife and Ruth Taverner were in the kitchen, drying the dishes.

"Yancy is a synthesis," Sipling explained. "A sort of composite person. No such individual actually exists. We drew on basic prototypes from sociological records; we based the gestalt on various typical persons. So it's true to life. But we stripped off what we didn't want, and intensified what we did want." Broodingly, he added: "There could be a Yancy. There are a lot of Yancy-like people. In fact, that's the problem."

"You deliberately set out with the idea of remolding people along Yancy's line?" Taverner inquired.

"I can't precisely say what the idea is, at top level. I was an ad writer for a mouth wash company. The Callisto authorities hired me and outlined what they wanted me to do. I've had to guess as to the purpose of the project."

"By authorities, you mean the governing council?"

Sipling laughed sharply. "I mean the trading syndicates that own this moon: lock, stock, and barrel. But we're not supposed to call it a moon. It's a planet." His lips twitched bitterly. "Apparently, the authorities have a big program built up. It involves absorbing their trade rivals on Ganymede—when that's done, they'll have the out-planets sewed up tight."

"They can't get at Ganymede without open war," Taverner protested. "The Medean companies have their own population behind them." And then it dawned. "I see," he said softly. "They'd actually start a war. It would be worth a war, to them."

"You're damn right it would. And to start a war, they have to get the public lined up. Actually, the people here have nothing to gain. A war would wipe out all the small operators—it would concentrate power in fewer hands—and they're few enough already. To get the eighty million people here behind the war, they need an indifferent, sheep-like public. *And they're getting that.* When this Yancy campaign is finished, the people here on Callisto will accept anything. Yancy does all their thinking for them. He tells them how to wear their hair. What games to play. He tells the jokes the men repeat in their back rooms. His wife whips up the meal they all have for dinner. All over this little world—millions of duplicates of Yancy's day. Whatever he does, whatever he believes. We've been conditioning the public for eleven straight years. The important thing is the unvarying monotony of it. A whole generation is growing up looking to Yancy for an answer to everything."

"It's a big business, then," Taverner observed. "This project of creating and maintaining Yancy."

"Thousands of people are involved in just writing the material. You only saw the first stage—and it goes into every city. Tapes, films, books, magazines, posters, pamphlets, dramatic visual and audio shows, plants in the newspapers, sound trucks, kids' comic strips, word-of-mouth report, elaborate ads... the works. A steady stream of Yancy." Picking up a magazine from the coffee table he indicated the lead article. "'How is John Yancy's Heart?' Raises the question of what would we do without Yancy? Next week, an article on Yancy's stomach." Acidly, Sipling finished: "We know a million approaches. We turn it out of every pore. We're called yance-men; it's a new art-form."

"How do you—the corps, feel about Yancy?"

"He's a big sack of hot air."

"None of you is convinced?"

"Even Babson has to laugh. And Babson is at the top; after him come the boys who sign the checks. God, if we ever started believing in Yancy... if we got started thinking that trash *meant* something—" An expression of acute agony settled over Sipling's face. "That's it. That's why I can't stand it."

"Why?" Taverner asked, deeply curious. His throat-mike was taking it all in, relaying it back to the home office at Washington. "I'm interested in finding out why you broke away."

Sipling bent down and called his son. "Mike, stop playing and come on over here." To Taverner he explained: "Mike's nine years old. Yancy's been around as long as he's been alive."

Mike came dutifully over. "Yes, sir?"

"What kind of marks do you get in school?" his father asked.

The boy's chest stuck out proudly; he was a clear-eyed little miniature of Leon Sipling. "All A's and B's."

"He's a smart kid," Sipling said to Taverner. "Good in arithmetic, geography, history, all that stuff." Turning to the boy he said: "I'm going to ask you some questions; I want this gentleman to hear your answers. Okay?"

"Yes, sir," the boy said obediently.

His thin face grim, Sipling said to his son: "I want to know what you think about war. You've been told about war in school; you know about all the famous wars in history. Right?"

"Yes, sir. We learned about the American Revolution, and the First Global War, and then the Second Global War, and then the First Hydrogen War, and the War between the colonists on Mars and Jupiter."

"To the schools," Sipling explained tightly to Taverner, "we distribute Yancy material—educational subsidies in packet form. Yancy takes children through history, explains the meaning of it all. Yancy explains natural science. Yancy explains good posture and astronomy and every other thing in the universe. But I never thought my own son..." His voice trailed off unhappily, then picked up life. "So you know all about war. Okay, what do you think of war?"

Promptly, the boy answered: "War is bad. War is the most terrible thing there is. It almost destroyed mankind."

Eying his son intently, Sipling demanded: "Did anybody tell you to say that?"

The boy faltered uncertainly. "No, sir."

"You really believe those things?"

"Yes, sir. It's true, isn't it? Isn't war bad?"

Sipling nodded. "War is bad. But what about *just* wars?"

Without hesitation the boy answered: "We have to fight just wars, of course."

"Why?"

"Well, we have to protect our way of life."

"Why?"

Again, there was no hesitation in the boy's reedy answer. "We can't let them walk over us, sir. That would encourage aggressive war. We can't permit a world of brute power. We have to have a world of—" He searched for the exact word. "A world of *law*."

Wearily, half to himself, Sipling commented: "I wrote those meaningless, contradictory words myself, eight years ago." Pulling himself together with a violent effort he asked: "So war is bad. But we have to fight just wars. Well, maybe this—*planet*, Callisto, will get into a war with . . . let's pick Ganymede, at random." He was unable to keep the harsh irony from his voice. "Just at random. Now, we're at war with Ganymede. Is it a *just* war? Or only a war?"

This time, there was no answer. The boy's smooth face was screwed up in a bewildered, struggling frown.

"No answer?" Sipling inquired icily.

"Why, uh," the boy faltered. "I mean . . ." He glanced up hopefully. "When the time comes won't somebody say?"

"Sure," Sipling choked. "Somebody will say. Maybe even Mr. Yancy."

Relief flooded the boy's face. "Yes, sir. Mr. Yancy will say." He retreated back toward the other children. "Can I go now?"

As the boy scampered back to his game, Sipling turned miserably to Taverner. "You know what game they're playing? It's called Hippo-Hoppo. Guess whose grandson just loves it. Guess who invented the game."

There was silence.

"What do you suggest?" Taverner asked. "You said you thought something could be done."

A cold expression appeared on Sipling's face, a flash of deeply-felt cunning. "I know the project . . . I know how it can be pried apart. But somebody has to stand with a gun at the head of the authorities. In nine years I've come to see the essential key to the Yancy character . . . the key to the new type of person we're growing, here. It's simple. It's the element that makes that person malleable enough to be led around."

"I'll bite," Taverner said patiently, hoping the line to Washington was good and clear.

"All Yancy's beliefs are insipid. The key is *thinness*. Every part of his ideology is diluted: nothing excessive. We've come as close as possible to *no* beliefs . . . you've noticed that. Wherever possible we've cancelled attitudes out, left the person a-political. Without a viewpoint."

"Sure," Taverner agreed. "But with the illusion of a viewpoint."

"All aspects of personality have to be controlled; we want the total person. So a specific attitude has to exist for each concrete question. In every respect, our rule is: *Yancy believes the least troublesome possibility.* The most shallow. The simple, effortless view, the view that fails to go deep enough to stir any real thought."

Taverner got the drift. "Good solid lulling views." Excitedly he hurried on, "But if an extreme original view got in, one that took real effort to work out, something that was hard to live..."

"Yancy plays croquet. So everybody fools around with a mallet." Sipling's eyes gleamed. "But suppose Yancy had a preference for—Kriegspiel."

"For *what?*"

"Chess played on two boards. Each player has his own board, with a complete set of men. He never sees the other board. A moderator sees both; he tells each player when he's taken a piece, or lost a piece, or moved into an occupied square, or made an impossible move, or checked, or is in check himself."

"I see," Taverner said quickly. "Each player tries to infer his opponent's location on the board. He plays blind. Lord, it would take every mental faculty possible."

"The Prussians taught their officers military strategy that way. It's more than a game: it's a cosmic wrestling match. What if Yancy sat down in the evening with his wife and grandson, and played a nice lively six-hour game of Kriegspiel? Suppose his favorite books—instead of being western gun-toting anachronisms—were Greek tragedy? Suppose his favorite piece of music was Bach's *Art of the Fugue,* not *My Old Kentucky Home?*"

"I'm beginning to get the picture," Taverner said, as calmly as possible. "I think we can help."

BABSON squeaked once. "But this is—illegal!"

"Absolutely," Taverner acknowledged. "That's why we're here." He waved the squad of Niplan secret-servicemen into the offices of the Yancy Building, ignoring the stunned workers sitting bolt-upright at their desks. Into his throat-mike he said, "How's it coming with the big-shots?"

"Medium," Kellman's faint voice came, strengthened

by the relay system between Callisto and Earth. "Some slipped out of bounds to their various holdings, of course. But the majority never thought we'd take action."

"You can't!" Babson bleated, his great face hanging down in wattles of white dough. "What have we done? What law—"

"I think," Taverner interrupted, "we can get you on purely commercial grounds alone. You've used the name Yancy to endorse various manufactured products. There's no such person. That's a violation of statutes governing ethical presentation of advertising."

Babson's mouth closed with a snap, then slid feebly open. "No—such—person? But everybody knows John Yancy. Why, he's—" Stammering, gesturing, he finished, "He's everywhere."

Suddenly a wretched little pistol appeared in his pulpy hand; he was waving it wildly as Dorser stepped up and quietly knocked it skidding across the floor. Babson collapsed into fumbling hysterics.

Disgusted, Dorser clamped handgrapples around him. "Act like a man," he ordered. But there was no response; Babson was too far gone to hear him.

Satisfied, Taverner plunged off, past the knot of stunned officials and workers, into the inner offices of the project. Nodding curtly, Taverner made his way up to the desk where Leon Sipling sat surrounded by his work.

The first of the altered gestalts was already flickering through the scanner. Together, the two men stood watching it.

"Well?" Taverner said, when it was done. "You're the judge."

"I believe it'll do," Sipling answered nervously. "I hope we don't stir up too much . . . it's taken eleven years to build it up; we want to tear it down by degrees."

"Once the first crack is made, it should start swaying." Taverner moved toward the door. "Will you be all right on your own?"

Sipling glanced at Eckmund who lounged at the end of the office, eyes fixed on the uneasily working yance-men. "I suppose so. Where are you going?"

"I want to watch this as it's released. I want to be around when the public gets its first look at it." At the door, Taverner lingered. "It's going to be a big job for you, putting out the gestalt on your own. You may not get much help, for awhile."

Sipling indicated his co-workers; they were already beginning to pick up their tempo where they had left off. "They'll stay on the job," he disagreed. "As long as they get full salaries."

Taverner walked thoughtfully across the hall to the elevator. A moment later he was on his way downstairs.

At a nearby street corner, a group of people had collected around a public vid-screen. Anticipating the late-afternoon t-v cast of John Edward Yancy.

The gestalt began in the regular way. There was no doubt about it: when Sipling wanted to, he could put together a good slice. And in this case he had done practically the whole pie.

In rolled-up shirt sleeves and dirt-stained trousers, Yancy crouched in his garden, a trowel in one hand, straw hat pulled down over his eyes, grinning into the warm glare of the sun. It was so real that Taverner could hardly believe no such person existed. But he had watched Sipling's sub-crews laboriously and expertly constructing the thing from the ground up.

"Afternoon," Yancy rumbled genially. He wiped perspiration from his steaming, florid face and got stiffly to his feet. "Man," he admitted, "it's a hot day." He indicated a flat of primroses. "I was setting them out. Quite a job."

So far so good. The crowd watched impassively, taking their ideological nourishment without particular resistance. All over the moon, in every house, schoolroom, office, on each street corner, the same gestalt was showing. And it would be shown again.

"Yes," Yancy repeated, "it's really hot. Too hot for those primroses—they like the shade." A fast pan-up showed he had carefully planted his primroses in the shadows at the base of his garage. "On the other hand," Yancy continued, in his smooth, good-natured, over-the-back-fence conversational voice, "my dahlias need lots of sun."

The camera leaped to show the dahlias blooming frantically in the blazing sunlight.

Throwing himself down in a striped lawnchair, Yancy removed his straw hat and wiped his brow with a pocket handkerchief. "So," he continued genially, "if anybody asked me which is better, shade or sun, I'd have to reply it depends on whether you're a primrose or a dahlia." He grinned his famous guileless boyish grin into the cameras. "I guess I must be a primrose—I've had all the sun I can stand for today."

The audience was taking it in without complaint. An inauspicious beginning, but it was going to have long-term consequences. And Yancy was starting to develop them right now.

His genial grin faded. That familiar look, that awaited serious frown showing that deep thoughts were coming, faded into place. Yancy was going to hold forth: wisdom was on the way. But it was nothing ever uttered by him before.

"You know," Yancy said slowly, seriously, "that makes a person do some thinking." Automatically, he reached for his glass of gin and tonic—a glass which up until now would have contained beer. And the magazine beside it wasn't *Dog Stories Monthly*; it was *The Journal of Psychological Review*. The alteration of peripheral props would sink in subliminally; right now, all conscious attention was riveted on Yancy's words.

"It occurs to me," Yancy orated, as if the wisdom were fresh and brand-new, arriving just now, "that some people might maintain that, say, sunlight is *good* and shade is *bad*. But that's downright silly. Sunlight is good for roses and dahlias, but it would darn well finish off my fuchsias."

The camera showed his ubiquitous prize fuchsias.

"Maybe you know people like that. They just don't understand that—" And as was his custom, Yancy drew on folklore to make his point. "That one man's meat," he stated profoundly, "is another man's poison. Like, for instance, for breakfast I like a couple of eggs done sunny-side up, maybe a few stewed prunes, and a piece of of toast. But Margaret, she prefers a bowl of cereal. And Ralf, he won't take either. He likes flapjacks. And the fellow down the street, the one with the big front lawn, he likes a kidney pie and a bottle of stout."

Taverner winced. Well, they would have to feel their way along. But still the audience stood absorbing it, word after word. The first feeble stirrings of a radical idea: that each person had a different set of values, a unique style of life. That each person might believe, enjoy, and approve of different things.

It would take time, as Sipling said. The massive library of tapes would have to be replaced; injunctions built up in each area would have to be broken down. A new type of thinking was being introduced, starting with a trite observation about primroses. When a nine-year-old boy wanted to find out if a war was just or unjust, he would have to inquire into his own mind. There would be no ready answer from Yancy; a gestalt was already being prepared on that, showing that every war had been called just by some, unjust by others.

There was one gestalt Taverner wished he could see. But it wouldn't be around for a long time; it would have to wait. Yancy was going to change his taste in art, slowly but steadily. One of these days, the public would learn that Yancy no longer enjoyed pastoral calendar scenes.

That now he preferred the art of that fifteenth century Dutch master of macabre and diabolical horror, Hieronymus Bosch.

Not By Its Cover

THE ELDERLY, cross-tempered president of Obelisk Books said irritably, "I don't want to see him, Miss Handy. The item is already in print; if there's an error in the text we can't do anything about it now."

"But Mr. Masters," Miss Handy said, "it's such an important error, sir. *If* he's right. Mr. Brandice claims that the entire chapter—"

"I read his letter; I also talked to him on the vidphone. I know what he claims." Masters walked to the window of his office, gazed moodily out at the arid, crater-marred surface of Mars which he had witnessed so many decades. *Five thousand copies printed and bound,* he thought. *And of that, half in gold-stamped Martian wub-fur. The most elegant, expensive material we could locate. We were already losing money on the edition, and now this.*

On his desk lay a copy of the book. Lucretius' *De Rerum Natura*, in the lofty, noble John Dryden translation. Angrily, Barney Masters turned the crisp white pages. Who would expect anyone on Mars to know such an ancient text that well? he reflected. And the man waiting in the outer office consisted of only one out of eight who had written or called Obelisk Books about a disputed passage.

Disputed? There was no contest; the eight local Latin scholars were right. It was simply a question of getting them to depart quietly, to forget they had ever read through the Obelisk edition and found the fnugled up passage in question.

Touching the button of his desk intercom, Masters said to his receptionist, "Okay; send him." Otherwise the man would never leave; his type would stay parked outside.

95

Scholars were generally like that; they seemed to have infinite patience.

The door opened and a tall gray-haired man, wearing old-fashioned Terra-style glasses, loomed, briefcase in hand. "Thank you, Mr. Masters," he said, entering. "Let me explain, sir, why my organization considers an error such as this so important." He seated himself by the desk, unzipped his briefcase briskly. "We are after all a colony planet. All our values, mores, artifacts and customs come to us from Terra. WODAFAG considers your printing of this book..."

"'WODAFAG'?", Masters interrupted. He had never heard of it, but even so he groaned. Obviously one of the many vigilant crank outfits who scanned everything printed, either emanating locally here on Mars or arriving from Terra.

"Watchmen Over Distortion and Forged Artifacts Generally," Brandice explained. "I have with me an authentic, correct Terran edition of *De Rerum Natura*— the Dryden translation, as is your local edition." His emphasis on *local* made it sound slimy and second-rate; as if, Masters brooded, Obelisk Books was doing something unsavory in printing books at all. "Let us consider the inauthentic interpolations. You are urged to study first my copy—" He laid a battered, elderly, Terran-printed book open on Masters' desk. "—in which it appears correctly. And then, sir, a copy of your own edition; the same passage." Beside the little ancient blue book he laid one of the handsome large wub-fur bound copies which Obelisk Books had turned out.

"Let me get my copy editor in here," Masters said. Pressing the intercom buttom he said to Miss Handy, "Ask Jack Snead to step in here, please."

"Yes, Mr. Masters."

"To quote from the authentic edition," Brandice said, "we obtain a metric rendering of the Latin as follows. Ahem." He cleared his throat self-consciously, then began to read aloud.

"From sense of grief and pain we shall be free;
We shall not feel, because we shall not be.
Though earth in seas, and seas in heaven were lost,
We should not move, we only should be toss'd."

"I know the passage," Masters said sharply, feeling needled; the man was lecturing him as if he were a child.

"This quatrain," Brandice said, "is absent from your edition, and the following spurious quatrain—of God knows what origin—appears in its place. Allow me." Taking the sumptuous, wub-fur bound Obelisk copy, he thumbed through, found the place; then read.

"From sense of grief and pain we shall be free;

Which earth-bound man can neither qualify nor see.

Once dead, we fathom seas cast up from this:

Our stint on earth doth herald an unstopping bliss."

Glaring at Masters, Brandice closed the wub-fur bound copy noisily. "What is most annoying," Brandice said, "is that this quatrain preaches a message diametric to that of the entire book. Where did it come from? *Somebody* had to write it; Dryden didn't write it— Lucretius didn't." He eyed Masters as if he thought Masters personally had done it.

The office door opened and the firm's copy editor, Jack Snead, entered "He's right," he said resignedly to his employer. "And it's only one alteration in the text out of thirty or so; I've been ploughing through the whole thing, since the letters started arriving. And now I'm starting in on other recent catalog-items in our fall list." He added, grunting. "I've found alterations in several of them, too."

Masters said, "You were the last editor to proofread the copy before it went to the typesetters. Were these errors in it then?"

"Absolutely not," Snead said. "And I proofread the galleys personally; the changes weren't in the galleys, either. The changes don't appear until the final bound copies come into existence—if that makes any sense. Or more specifically, the ones bound in gold and wub-fur. The regular bound-in-boards copies—they're okay."

Masters blinked. "But they're all the same edition. They ran through the presses together. In fact we didn't originally plan an exclusive, higher-priced binding; it was only at the last minute that we talked it over and the business office suggested half the edition be offered in wub-fur."

"I think," Jack Snead said, "we're going to have to do

some close-scrutiny work on the subject of Martian wub-fur."

AN HOUR later aging, tottering Masters, accompanied by copy editor Jack Snead, sat facing Luther Saperstein, business agent for the pelt-procuring firm of Flawless, Incorporated; from them, Obelisk Books had obtained the wub-fur with which their books had been bound.

"First of all," Masters said in a brisk, professional tone, "what is wub-fur?"

"Basically," Saperstein said, "in the sense in which you're asking the question, it is fur from the Martian wub. I know this doesn't tell you much, gentlemen, but at least it's a reference point, a postulate on which we can all agree, where we can start and build something more imposing. To be more helpful, let me fill you in on the nature of the wub itself. The fur is prized because, among other reasons, it is rare. Wub-fur is rare because a wub very seldom dies. By that I mean, it is next to impossible to slay a wub—even a sick or old wub. And, even though a wub is killed, the hide lives on. That quality imparts its unique value to home-decoration, or, as in your case, in the binding of lifetime, treasured books meant to endure."

Masters sighed, dully gazed out the window as Saperstein droned on. Beside him, his copy editor made brief cryptic notes, a dark expression on his youthful, energetic face.

"What we supplied you," Saperstein said, "when you came to us—and remember: you came to us; we didn't seek you out—consisted of the most select, perfect hides in our giant inventory. These living hides shine with a unique luster all their own; nothing else either on Mars or back home on Terra resembles them. If torn or scratched, the hide repairs itself. It grows, over the months, a more and more lush pile, so that the covers of your volumes become progressively luxurious, and hence highly sought-after. Ten years from now the deep-pile quality of these wub-fur bound books—"

Interrupting, Snead said, "So the hide is still alive. Interesting. And the wub, as you say, is so deft as to be virtually impossible to kill." He shot a swift glance at Masters. "Every single one of the thirty-odd alterations

NOT BY ITS COVER

made in the texts in our books deals with immortality.
The Lucretius revision is typical; the original text teaches
that man is temporary, that even if he survives after death
it doesn't matter because he won't have any memory of his
existence here. In place of that, the spurious new passage
comes out and flatly talks about a future of life predicated
on this one; as you say, at complete variance with
Lucretius' entire philosophy. You realize what we're
seeing, don't you? The damn wub's philosophy superim-
posed on that of the various authors. That's it; beginning
and end." He broke off, resumed his note-scratching,
silently.

"How can a hide," Masters demanded, "even a
perpetually living one, exert influence on the contents of a
book? A text already printed—pages cut, folios glued and
sewed—it's against reason. Even *if* the binding, the damn
hide, is really alive, and I can hardly believe that." He
glared at Saperstein. "If it's alive, what does it live on?"

"Minute particles of food-stuffs in suspension in the
atmosphere," Saperstein said, blandly.

Rising to his feet, Masters said, "Let's go. This is
ridiculous."

"It inhales the particles," Saperstein said, "through its
pores." His tone was dignified, even reproving.

Studying his notes, not rising along with his employer,
Jack Snead said thoughtfully, "Some of the amended
texts are fascinating. They vary from a complete reversal
of the original passage—and the author's meaning—as in
the case of Lucretius, to very subtle, almost invisible
corrections—if that's the word—to texts more in accord
with the doctrine of eternal life. The real question is this.
Are we faced merely with the opinion of one particular life
form, *or does the wub know what it's talking about?*
Lucretius' poem, for instance; it's very great, very
beautiful, very interesting—as poetry. But as philosophy,
maybe it's wrong. I don't know. It's not my job; I simply
edit books; I don't write them. The last thing a good copy
editor does is editorialize, on his own, in the author's text.
But that is what the wub, or anyhow the post-wub pelt, is
doing." He was silent, then.

Saperstein said, "I'd be interested to know if it added
anything of value."

"Poetically? Or do you mean philosophically? From a poetic or literary, stylistic point of view its interpolations are no better and no worse than the originals; it manages to blend in with the author well enough so that if you didn't know the text already you'd never notice." He added broodingly, "You'd never know it was a pelt talking."

"I meant from a philosophical point of view."

"Well, it's always the same message, monotonously ground out. There is no death. We go to sleep; we wake up—to a better life. What it did to *De Rerum Natura*; that's typical. If you've read that you've read them all."

"It would be an interesting experiment," Masters said thoughtfully, "to bind a copy of the Bible in wub-fur."

"I had that done," Snead said.

"And?"

"Of course I couldn't take time to read it all. But I did glance over Paul's letters to the Corinthians. It made only one change. The passage that begins, 'Behold, I tell you a mystery—' it set all of that in caps. And it repeated the lines, 'Death, where is thy sting? Grave, where is thy victory?' ten times straight; ten whole times, all in caps. Obviously the wub agreed; that's its own philosophy, or rather theology." He said, then, weighing each word, "This basically is a theological dispute . . . between the reading public and the hide of a Martian animal that looks like a fusion between a hog and a cow. Strange." Again he returned to his notes.

After a solemn pause, Masters said, "You think the wub has inside information or don't you? As you said, this may not be just the opinion of one particular animal that's been successful in avoiding death; it may be the truth."

"What occurs to me," Snead said, "is this. The wub hasn't merely learned to avoid death; it's actually done what it preaches. By getting killed, skinned, and its hide—still alive—made into book covers—it has conquered death. It lives on. In what it appears to regard as a better life. We're not just dealing with an opinionated local life form; we're dealing with an organism that has already done what we're still in doubt about. Sure it knows. It's a living confirmation of its own doctrine. The facts speak for themselves. I tend to believe it."

"Maybe continual life for *it*," Masters disagreed, "but that doesn't mean necessarily for the rest of us. The wub, as Mr. Saperstein points out, is unique. The hide of no other life form either on Mars or on Luna or Terra lives on, imbibing life from microscopic particles in suspension in the atmosphere. Just because *it* can do it—"

"Too bad we can't communicate with a wub hide," Saperstein said. "We've tried, here at Flawless, ever since we first noticed the fact of its post-mortem survival. But we never found a way."

"But we at Obelisk," Snead pointed out, "have. As a matter of fact I've already tried an experiment. I had a one-sentence text printed up, a single line reading: 'The wub, unlike every other living creature, is immortal.'

"I then had it bound in wub-fur; then I read it again. It had been changed. Here." He passed a slim book, handsomely appointed, to Masters. "Read it as it is now."

Masters read aloud: "The wub, like every other living creature, is immortal."

Returning the copy to Snead he said, "Well, all it did was drop out the *un*; that's not much of a change, two letters."

"But from the standpoint of meaning," Snead said, "it constitutes a bombshell. We're getting feedback from beyond the grave—so to speak. I mean, let's fact it; wub-fur is technically dead because the wub that grew it is dead. This is awfully damn close to providing an indisputable verification of the survival of sentient life after death."

"Of course there is one thing," Saperstein said hesitantly. "I hate to bring it up; I don't know what bearing it has on all this. But the Martian wub, for all its uncanny—even miraculous—ability to preserve itself, is from a mentational standpoint a stupid creature. A Terran opossum, for example, has a brain one-third that of a cat. The wub has a brain one-fifth that of an opossum." He looked gloomy.

"Well," Snead said, "the Bible says, 'The last shall be the first.' Possibly the lowly wub is included under this rubric; let's hope so."

Glancing at him, Masters said, "You *want* eternal life?"

"Certainly," Snead said. "Everybody does."

"Not I," Masters said, with decisiveness. "I have enough troubles now. The last thing I want is to live on as the binding of a book—or in any fashion whatsoever." But inside, he had begun silently to muse. Differently. Very differently, in fact.

"It sounds like something a wub would like," Saperstein agreed. "Being the binding of a book; just lying there supine, on a shelf, year after year, inhaling minute particles from the air. And presumably meditating. Or whatever wubs do after they're dead."

"They think theology," Snead said. "They preach." To his boss he said, "I assume we won't be binding any more books in wub-fur."

"Not for trade purposes," Masters agreed. "Not to sell. But—" He could not rid himself of the conviction that some use lay, here. "I wonder," he said, "if it would impart the same high level of survival factor to anything it was made into. Such as window drapes. Or upholstery in a float-car; maybe it would eliminate death on the commute paths. Or helmet-liners for combat troops. And for baseball players." The possibilities, to him, seemed enormous . . . but vague. He would have to think this out, give it a good deal of time.

"Anyhow," Saperstein said, "my firm declines to give you a refund; the characteristics of wub-fur were known publically in a brochure which we published earlier this year. We categorically stated—"

"Okay, it's our loss," Masters said irritably, with a wave of his hand. "Let it go." To Snead he said, "And it definitely says, in the thirty-odd passages it's interpolated, that life after death is pleasant?"

"Absolutely. 'Our stint on earth doth herald an unstopping bliss.' That sums it up, that line it stuck into *De Rerum Natura*; it's all right there."

"'Bliss,'" Masters echoed, nodding. "Of course, we're actually not on Earth; we're on Mars. But I suppose it's the same thing; it just means life, wherever it's lived." Again, even more gravely, he pondered. "What occurs to me," he said thoughtfully, "is it's one thing to talk abstractly about 'life after death'. People have been doing that for fifty thousand years; Lucretius was, two thousand years ago. What interests me more is not the big overall—

philosophical picture but the concrete fact of the
wub-pelt; the immortality which it carried around with
it." To Snead he said, "What other books did you bind in
it?"

"Tom Paine's *Age of Reason*," Snead said, consulting
his list.

"What were the results?"

"Two-hundred-sixty-seven blank pages. Except right
in the middle the one word *bleh*."

"Continue."

"The *Britannica*. It didn't precisely change anything,
but it added whole articles. On the soul, on transmigra-
tion, on hell, damnation, sin, or immortality; the whole
twenty-four volume set became religiously oriented." He
glanced up. "Should I go on?"

"Sure," Masters said, listening and meditating simultaneously.

"The *Summa Theologica* of Thomas Aquinas. It left
the text intact, but it periodically inserted the biblical line,
'The letter killeth but the spirit giveth life.' Over and over
again.

"James Hilton's *Lost Horizon*. Shangri-La turns out to
be a vision of the after life which—"

"Okay," Masters said. "We get the idea. The question
is, what can we do with this? Obviously we can't bind
books with it—at least books which it disagrees with."
But he was beginning to see another use; a much more
personal one. And it far outweighed anything which the
wub-fur might do for or to books—in fact for any
inanimate object.

As soon as he got to a phone—

"Of special interest," Snead was saying, "is its reaction
to a volume of collected papers on psychoanalysis by
some of the greatest living Freudian analysts of our time.
It allowed each article to remain intact, but at the end of
each it added the same phrase." He chuckled. "Physician,
heal thyself.' Bit of a sense of humor, there."

"Yeah," Masters said. Thinking, unceasingly, of the
phone and the one vital call which he would make.

BACK IN his own office at Obelisk Books, Masters tried
out a preliminary experiment—to see if this idea would

work. Carefully, he wrapped a Royal Albert yellow bone-china cup and saucer in wub-fur, a favorite from his own personal collection. Then, after much soul-searching and trepidation, he placed the bundle on the floor of his office and, with all his declining might, stepped on it.

The cup did not break. At least it did not seem to.

He unwrapped the package, then, and inspected the cup. He had been right; wrapped in living wub-fur it could not be destroyed.

Satisfied, he seated himself at his desk, pondered one last time.

The wrapper of wub-fur had made a temporary, fragile object imperishable. So the wub's doctrine of external survival had worked itself out in practice—exactly as he had expected.

He picked up the phone, dialed his lawyer's number.

"This is about my will," he said to his lawyer, when he had him on the other end of the line. "You know, the latest one I made out a few months ago. I have an additional clause to insert."

"Yes, Mr. Masters," his lawyer said briskly. "Shoot."

"A small item," Masters purred. "Has to do with my coffin. I want it mandatory on my heirs—my coffin is to be lined throughout, top, bottom and sides, with wub-fur. From Flawless, Incorporated. I want to go to my Maker clothed, so to speak, in wub-fur. Makes a better impression that way." He laughed nonchalantly, but his tone was deadly serious—and his attorney caught it.

"If that's what you want," the attorney said.

"And I suggest you do the same," Masters said.

"Why?"

Masters said, "Consult the complete home medical reference library we're going to issue next month. And make certain you get a copy that's bound in wub-fur; it'll be different from the others." He thought, then, about his wub-fur-lined coffin once again. Far underground, with him inside it, with the living wub-fur growing, growing.

It would be interesting to see the version of himself which a choice wub-fur binding produced.

Especially after several centuries.

The Little Black Box

BOGART CROFTS of the State Department said, "Miss Hiashi, we want to send you to Cuba to give religious instruction to the Chinese population there. It's your oriental background. It will help."

With a faint moan, Joan Hiashi reflected that her Oriental background consisted of having been born in Los Angeles and having attended courses at UCSB, the University of Santa Barbara. But she was technically, from the standpoint of training, an Asian scholar, and she had properly listed this on her job-application form.

"Let's consider the word *caritas*," Crofts was saying. "In your estimation, what actually does it mean, as Jerome used it? Charity? Hardly. But then what? Friendliness? Love?"

Joan said, "My field is Zen Buddhism."

"But everybody," Crofts protested in dismay, "knows what caritas means in late Roman usage. The esteem of good people for one another; that's what it means." His gray, dignified eyebrows raised. "Do you want this job, Miss Hiashi? And if so, why?"

"I want to disseminate Zen Buddhist propaganda to the Communist Chinese in Cuba," Joan said, "because—" She hesitated. The truth was simply, that it meant a good salary for her, the first truly high-paying job she had ever held. From a career standpoint, it was a plum. "Aw, hell," she said. "What is the nature of the One Way? I don't have any answer."

"It's evident that your field has taught you a method of avoiding giving honest answers," Crofts said sourly. "And being evasive. However—" He shrugged. "Possibly that only goes to prove that you're well trained and the proper

105

person for the job. In Cuba you'll be running up against some rather worldly and sophisticated individuals, who in addition are quite well off even from the U.S. standpoint. I hope you can cope with them as well as you've coped with me."

Joan said, "Thank you, Mr. Crofts." She rose. "I'll expect to hear from you, then."

"I am impressed by you," Crofts said, half to himself. "After all, you're the young lady who first had the idea of feeding Zen Buddhist riddles to UCSB's big computers."

"I was the first to *do* it," Joan corrected. "But the idea came from a friend of mine, Ray Meritan. The gray-green jazz harpist."

"Jazz and Zen Buddhism," Crofts said. "State may be able to make use of you in Cuba."

To RAY MERITAN she said, "I have to get out of Los Angeles, Ray. I really can't stand the way we're living here." She walked to the window of his apartment and looked out at the monorail gleaming far off. The silver car made its way at enormous speed, and Joan hurriedly looked away.

If we only could suffer, she thought. That's what we lack, any real experience of suffering, because we can escape anything. Even this.

"But you are getting out." Ray said. "You're going to Cuba and convert wealthy merchants and bankers into becoming ascetics. And it's a genuine Zen paradox; you'll be paid for it." He chuckled. "Fed into a computer, a thought like that would do harm. Anyhow, you won't have to sit in the Crystal Hall every night listening to me play—if that's what you're anxious to get away from."

"No," Joan said, "I expect to keep on listening to you on TV. I may even be able to use your music in my teaching." From a rosewood chest in the far corner of the room she lifted out a .32 pistol. It had belonged to Ray Meritan's second wife, Edna, who had used it to kill herself, the previous February, late one rainy afternoon. "May I take this along?" she asked.

"For sentiment?" Ray said. "Because she did it on your account?"

"Edna did nothing on my account. Edna liked me. I'm

not taking any responsibility for your wife's suicide, even though she did find out about us—seeing each other, so to speak."

Ray said meditatively, "And you're the girl always telling people to accept blame and not to project it out on the world. What do you call your principle, dear? Ah." He grinned. "The Anti-paranoia Prinzip. Doctor Joan Hiashi's cure for mental illness; absorb all blame, take it all upon yourself." He glanced up at her and said acutely, "I'm surprised you're not a follower of Wilbur Mercer."

"That clown," Joan said.

"But that's part of his appeal. Here, I'll show you." Ray switched on the TV set across the room from them, the legless black oriental-style set with its ornamentation of Sung dynasty dragons.

"Odd you would know when Mercer is on," Joan said.

Ray, shrugging murmured, "I'm interested. A new religion, replacing Zen Buddhism, sweeping out of the Middle West to engulf California. You ought to pay attention, too, since you claim religion as your profession. You're getting a job because of it. Religion is paying your bills, my dear girl, so don't knock it."

THE TV had come on, and there was Wilbur Mercer.

"Why isn't he saying anything?" Joan said.

"Why, Mercer has taken a vow this week. Complete silence." Ray lit a cigarette. "State ought to be sending me, not you. You're a fake."

"At least I'm not a clown," Joan said, "or a follower of a clown."

Ray reminded her softly, "There's a Zen saying, 'The Buddha is a piece of toilet paper.' And another. 'The Buddha often—'"

"Be still," she said sharply. "I want to watch Mercer."

"You want to watch," Ray's voice was heavy with irony. "Is that what you want, for God's sake? No one *watches* Mercer; that's the whole point." Tossing his cigarette into the fireplace, he strode to the TV set; there, before it, Joan saw a metal box with two handles, attached by a lead of twin-cable wire to the TV set. Ray seized the two handles, and at once a grimace of pain shot across his face.

"What is it?" she asked, in anxiety.

"N-nothing." Ray continued to grip the handles. On the screen, Wilbur Mercer walked slowly over the barren, jagged surface of a desolate hillside, his face lifted, an expression of serenity—or vacuity—on his thin, middle-aged features. Gasping, Ray released the handles. "I could only hold them for forty-five seconds this time." To Joan, he explained, "This is the empathy box, my dear. I can't tell you how I got it—to be truthful I don't really know. *They* brought it by, the organization that distributes it— Wilcer, Incorporated. But I can tell you that when you take hold of these handles you're no longer watching Wilbur Mercer. You're actually participating in his apotheosis. Why, you're feeling what he feels."

Joan said, "It looks like it hurts."

Quietly, Ray Meritan said, "Yes. Because Wilbur Mercer is being killed. He's walking to the place where he's going to die."

In horror, Joan moved away from the box.

"You said that was what we needed," Ray said. "Remember, I'm a rather adequate telepath; I don't have to bestir myself very much to read your thoughts. 'If only we could suffer.' That's what you were thinking, just a little while ago. Well, here's your chance, Joan."

"It's—morbid!"

"Was your thought morbid?"

"Yes!" she said.

Ray Meritan said, "Twenty million people are followers of Wilbur Mercer now. All over the world. And they're suffering with him, as he walks along toward Pueblo, Colorado. At least that's where they're *told* he's going. Personally I have my doubts. Anyhow, Mercerism is now what Zen Buddhism was once; you're going to Cuba to teach the wealthy Chinese bankers a form of asceticism that's already obsolete, already seen its day."

Silently, Joan turned away from him and watched Mercer walking.

"You know I'm right," Ray said. "I can pick up your emotions. You may not even be aware of them, but they're there."

On the screen, a rock was thrown at Mercer. It struck him on the shoulder.

Everyone who's holding onto his empathy box, Joan realized, felt that along with Mercer.

Ray nodded. "You're right."

"And—what about when he's actually killed?" She shuddered.

"We'll see what happens then," Ray said quietly. "We don't know."

II

To BOGART CROFTS, Secretary of State Douglas Herrick said, "I think you're wrong, Boge. The girl may be Meritan's mistress but that doesn't mean she knows."

"We'll wait for Mr. Lee to tell us," Crofts said irritably. "When she gets to Havana he'll be waiting to meet her."

"Mr. Lee can't scan Meritan direct?"

"One telepath scan another?" Bogart Crofts smiled at the thought. It conjured up a nonsensical situation: Mr. Lee reading Meritan's mind, and Meritan, also being a telepath, would read Mr. Lee's mind and discover that Mr. Lee was reading his mind, and Lee, reading Meritan's mind, would discover that Meritan knew—and so forth. Endless regression, winding up with a fusion of minds, within which Meritan carefully guarded his thoughts so that he did not think about Wilbur Mercer.

"It's the similarity of names that convinces me," Herrick said. "Meritan, Mercer. The first three letters—"

Crofts said, "Ray Meritan is not Wilbur Mercer. I'll tell you how we know. Over at CIA, we made an Ampex video tape from Mercer's telecast, had it enlarged and analyzed. Mercer was shown against the usual dismal background of cactus plants and sand and rock . . . you know."

"Yes" Herrick said, nodding. "The Wilderness, as they call it."

"In the enlargement something showed up in the sky. It was studied. It's not Luna. It's a moon, but too small to be Luna. Mercer is not on Earth. I would guess that he is not a terrestrial at all."

Bending down, Crofts picked up a small metal box, carefully avoiding the two handles. "And these were not designed and built on Earth. The entire Mercer Movement is null-T all the way, and that's the fact we've got to contend with."

Herrick said, "If Mercer is not a Terran, then he may have suffered and even died before, on other planets."

"Oh, yes," Crofts said. "Mercer—or whatever his or its real name is—may be highly experienced in this. But we still don't know what we want to know." And that of course was, What happens to those people holding onto the handles of their empathy boxes?

Crofts seated himself at his desk and scrutinized the box resting directly before him, with its two inviting handles. He had never touched them, and he never intended to. But—

"How soon will Mercer die?" Herrick asked.

"They're expecting it some time late next week."

"And Mr. Lee will have gotten something from the girl's mind by then, you think? Some clue as to where Mercer really is?"

"I hope so," Crofts said, still seated at the empathy box but still not touching it. It must be a strange experience, he thought, to place your hands on two ordinary-looking metal handles and find, all at once, that you're no longer yourself; you're another man entirely, in another place, laboring up a long, dreary inclined plain toward certain extinction. At least, so they say. But hearing about it ... what does that actually convey? Suppose I tried it for myself.

The sense of absolute pain ... that was what appalled him, held him back.

It was unbelievable that people could deliberately seek it out, rather than avoiding it. Gripping the handles of the empathy box was certainly not the act of a person seeking escape. It was not the avoidance of something but the seeking of something. And not the pain as such; Crofts knew better than to suppose that the Mercerites were simple masochists who desired discomfort. It was, he knew, the meaning of the pain which attracted Mercer's followers.

THE FOLLOWERS were suffering for something.

Aloud, he said to his superior, "They want to suffer as a

means of denying their private, personal existences. It's a communion in which they all suffer and experience Mercer's ordeal together." Like the Last Supper, he thought. That's the real key: the communion, the participation that is behind all religion. Or ought to be. Religion binds men together in a sharing, corporate body, and leaves everyone else on the outside.

Herrick said, "But primarily it's a political movement, or must be treated as such."

"From our standpoint," Crofts agreed. "Not theirs."

The intercom on the desk buzzed and his secretary said, "Sir, Mr. John Lee is here."

"Tell him to come in."

The tall, slender young Chinese entered, smiling, his hand out. He wore an old-fashioned single-breasted suit and pointed black shoes. As they shook hands, Mr. Lee said, "She has not left for Havana, has she?"

"No," Crofts said.

"Is she pretty?" Mr. Lee said.

"Yes," Crofts said, with a smile at Herrick. "But—difficult. The snappish kind of woman. Emancipated, if you follow me."

"Oh, the suffragette type," Mr. Lee said, smiling. "I detest that type of female. It will be hard going. Mr. Crofts."

"Remember," Crofts said, "your job is simply to be converted. All you have to do is listen to her propaganda about Zen Buddhism, learn to ask a few questions such as, 'Is this stick the Buddha?' and expect a few inexplicable blows on the head—a Zen practice, I understand, supposed to instill sense."

With a broad grin, Mr. Lee said, "Or to instill nonsense. You see, I am prepared. Sense, nonsense; in Zen it's the same thing." He became sober, now. "Of course, I myself am a Communist," he said. "The only reason I'm doing this is because the Party at Havana has taken the official stand that Mercerism is dangerous and must be wiped out." He looked gloomy. "I must say, these Mercerites are fanatics."

"True," Crofts agreed. "And we must work for their extinction." He pointed to the empathy box. "Have you ever—?"

"Yes," Mr. Lee said. "It's a form of punishment. Self-imposed, no doubt for reasons of guilt. Leisure gleans such emotions from people if it is properly utilized; otherwise not."

Crofts thought, This man has no understanding of the issues at all. He's a simple materialist. Typical of a person born in a Communist family, raised in a Communist society. Everything is either black or white.

"You're mistaken," Mr. Lee said; he had picked up Crofts' thought.

Flushing, Crofts said, "Sorry, I forgot. No offense."

"I see in your mind," Mr. Lee said, "that you believe Wilbur Mercer, as he calls himself, may be non-T. Do you know the Party's position on this question? It was debated just a few days ago. The Party takes the stand that there are no non-T races in the solar system, that to believe remnants of once-superior races still exist is a form of morbid mysticism."

Crofts sighed. "Deciding an empirical issue by vote—deciding it on a strictly political basis. I can't understand that."

At that point, Secretary Herrick spoke up, soothing both men. "Please, let's not become sidetracked by theoretical issues on which we don't all agree. Let's stick to basics—the Mercerite Party and its rapid growth all over the planet."

Mr. Lee said, "You are right, of course."

III

AT THE Havana airfield Joan Hiashi looked around her as the other passengers walked rapidly from the ship to the entrance of the number twenty concourse.

Relatives and friends had surged cautiously out onto the field, as they always did, in defiance of field rulings. She saw among them a tall, lean young Chinese man with a smile of greeting on his face.

Walking toward him she called, "Mr. Lee?"

"Yes." He hurried toward her. "It's dinner time. Would you care to eat? I'll take you to the Hang Far Lo restaurant. They have pressed duck and bird's nest soup, all Canton-style . . . very sweet but good once in a long while."

Soon they were at the restaurant, in a red-leather and imitation teak booth. Cubans and Chinese chattered on all sides of them; the air smelled of frying pork and cigar smoke.

"You are President of the Havana Institute for Asian Studies?" she asked, just to be certain there had been no slip-ups.

"Correct. It is frowned on by the Cuban Communist Party because of the religious aspect. But many of the Chinese here on the island attend lectures or are on our mailing list. And as you know we've had many distinguished scholars from Europe and Southern Asia come and address us . . . By the way. There is a Zen parable which I do not understand. The monk who cut the kitten in half—I have studied it and thought about it, but I do not see how the Buddha could be present when cruelty was done to an animal." He hastened to add, "I'm not disputing with you. I am merely seeking information."

Joan said, "Of all the Zen parables that has caused the most difficulty. The question to ask is, Where is that kitten now?"

"That recalls the opening of the *Bhagavad-Gita*," Mr. Lee said, with a quick nod. "I recall Arjura saying,

The bow Gandiva slips from
my hand . . .
Omens of evil!

What can we hope from this killing of kinsmen?"

"Correct," Joan said, "And of course you remember Krishna's answer. It is the most profound statement in all pre-Buddhistic religion of the issue of death and of action."

The waiter came for their order. He was a Cuban, in khaki and a beret.

"Try the fried won ton," Mr. Lee advised. "And the chow yuk, and of course the egg roll. You have egg roll today?" he asked the waiter.

"Si, Senor Lee." The waiter picked at his teeth with a toothpick.

Mr. Lee ordered for both of them, and the waiter departed.

"You know," Joan said, "when you've been around a telepath as much as I have, you become conscious of intensive scanning going on ... I could always tell when Ray was trying to dig at something in me. You're a telepath. And you're very intensively scanning me right now."

Smiling, Mr. Lee said, "I wish I was, Miss Hiashi."

"I have nothing to hide," Joan said. "But I wonder why you are so interested in what I'm thinking. You know I'm an employee of the United States Department of State; there's nothing secret about that. Are you afraid I've come to Cuba as a spy? To study military installations? Is it something like that?" She felt depressed. "This is not a good beginning," she said. "You haven't been honest with me."

"You are a very attractive woman, Miss Hiashi," Mr. Lee said, losing none of his poise. "I was merely curious to see—shall I be blunt? Your attitude toward sex."

"You're lying," Joan said quietly.

Now the bland smile departed; he stared at her.

"Bird's nest soup, señor." The waiter had returned; he set the hot steaming bowl in the center of the table. "Tea." He laid out a teapot and two small white handleless cups. "Señorita, you want chopsticks?"

"No," she said absently.

From outside the booth came a cry of anguish. Both Joan and Mr. Lee leaped up. Mr. Lee pulled the curtain aside; the waiter was staring, too, and laughing.

At a table in the opposite corner of the restaurant sat an elderly Cuban gentleman with his hands gripping the handles of an empathy box.

"Here, too," Joan said.

"They are pests," Mr. Lee said. "Disturbing our meal."

The waiter said, "Loco." He shook his head, still chuckling.

"Yes," Joan said. "Mr. Lee, I will continue here, trying to do my job, despite what's occurred between us. I don't know why they deliberately sent a telepath to meet me—possibly it's Communist paranoid suspicions of outsiders—but in any case I have a job to do here and I mean to do it. So shall we discuss the dismembered kitten?"

"At meal time?" Mr. Lee said faintly.

"You brought it up," Joan said, and proceeded, despite the expression of acute misery on Mr. Lee's face as he sat spooning up his bird's nest soup.

AT THE Los Angeles studio of television station KKHF, Ray Meritan sat at his harp, waiting for his cue. *How High the Moon*, he had decided, would be his first number. He yawned, kept his eye on the control booth.

Beside him, at the blackboard, jazz commentator Glen Goldstream polished his rimless glasses with a fine linen handkerchief and said, "I think I'll tie in with Gustav Mahler tonight."

"Who the hell is he?"

"A great late nineteenth century composer. Very romantic. Wrote long peculiar symphonies and folk-type songs. I'm thinking, however, of the rhythmic patterns in *The Drunkard in Springtime* from *Song of the Earth*. You've never heard it?"

"Nope," Meritan said restlessly.

"Very gray-green."

Ray Meritan did not feel very gray-green tonight. His head still ached from the rock thrown at Wilbur Mercer. Meritan had tried to let go of the empathy box when he saw the rock coming, but he had not been quick enough. It had struck Mercer on the right temple, drawing blood.

"I've run into three Mercerites this evening," Glen said. "And all of them looked terrible. What happened to Mercer today?"

"How would I know?"

"You're carrying yourself the way they did today. It's your head, isn't it? I know you well enough, Ray. You'd be mixed up in anything new and odd—what do I care if you're a Mercerite? I just thought maybe you'd like a pain pill."

Brusquely, Ray Meritan said, "That would defeat the entire idea, wouldn't it? A pain pill. Here, Mr. Mercer, as you go up the hillside, how about a shot of morphine? You won't feel a thing." He rippled a few cadences on his harp, releasing his emotions.

"You're on," the producer said from the control room. Their theme, *That's a Plenty*, swelled from the tape deck in the control room, and the number two camera facing Goldstream lit up its red light. Arms folded, Goldstream said, "Good evening, ladies and gentlemen. What is jazz?"

That's what I say, Meritan thought. What is jazz? What is life? He rubbed his splintered, pain-racked forehead and wondered how he could endure the next week. Wilbur Mercer was getting close to it now. Each day it would become worse...

"And after a brief pause for an important message," Goldstream was saying, "we'll be back to tell you more about the world of gray-green men and women, those peculiar people, and the world of the artistry of the one and only Ray Meritan."

The tape of the commercial appeared on the TV monitor facing Meritan.

Meritan said to Goldstream, "I'll take the pain pill."

A yellow, flat, notched tablet was held out to him. "Paracodein," Goldstream said. "Highly illegal, but effective. An addictive drug... I'm surprised you, of all people, don't carry some."

"I used to," Ray said, as he got a dixie cup of water and swallowed the pill.

"And now you're on Mercerism."

"Now I'm—" He glanced at Goldstream; they had known each other, in their professional capacities, for years. "I'm not a Mercerite," he said, "so forget it, Glen. It's just coincidence I got a headache the night Mercer was hit on the temple by a sharp rock thrown by some moronic sadist who ought to be the one dragging his way up that hillside." He scowled at Goldstream.

"I UNDERSTAND," Goldstream said, "that the U. S. Department of Mental Health is on the verge of asking the Justice Department to pick up the Mercerites."

Suddenly he swung to face camera two. A faint smile touched his face and he said smoothly, "Gray-green began about four years ago, in Pinole, California, at the now justly-famous Double Shot Club where Ray Meritan played, back in 1993 and '4. Tonight, Ray will let us hear one of his best known and liked numbers, *Once in Love with Amy.*" He swung in Meritan's direction "Ray.... Meritan!"

Plunk-plunk, the harp went as Ray Meritan's fingers riffled the strings.

An object lesson, he thought as he played. That's what the FBI would make me into for the teenagers, to show them what not to grow up to be. First on Paracodein, now on Mercer. Beware, kids!

Off camera, Glen Goldstream held up a sign he had scribbled.

IS MERCER A NON-TERRESTRIAL?

Underneath this, Goldstream wrote with a marking pencil:

IT'S *THAT* THEY
WANT TO KNOW.

Invasion from outside there somewhere, Meritan thought to himself as he played. That's what they're afraid of. Fear of the unknown, like tiny children. That's our ruling circles: tiny, fear-ridden children playing ritualistic games with super-powerful toys.

A thought came to him from one of the network officials in the control room. *Mercer has been injured.*

At once, Ray Meritan turned his attention that way, scanned as hard as he could. His fingers strummed the harp reflexively.

Government outlawing so-called empathy boxes.

He thought immediately of his own empathy box, before his TV set in the living room of his apartment.

Organization which distributes and sells the empathy boxes declared illegal, and FBI making arrests in several major cities. Other countries expected to follow.

How badly injured? he wondered. Dying?

And—what about the Mercerites who had been holding onto the handles of their empathy boxes at that moment? How were they, now? Receiving medical attention?

Should we air the news now? the network official was thinking. *Or wait until the commercial?*

Ray Meritan ceased playing his harp and said clearly into the boom microphone, "Wilbur Mercer has been injured. This is what we've all expected but it's still a major tragedy. Mercer is a saint."

Wide-eyed, Glen Goldstream gawked at him.

"I believe in Mercer," Ray Meritan said, and all across the United States his television audience heard his confession of faith. "I believe his suffering and injury and death have meaning for each of us."

It was done; he had gone on record. And it hadn't even taken much courage.

"Pray for Wilbur Mercer," he said and resumed playing his gray-green style of harp.

You fool, Glen Goldstream was thinking. Giving yourself away! You'll be in jail within a week. Your career is ruined!

Plunk-plunk, Ray played on his harp, and smiled humorlessly at Glen.

IV

MR. LEE said, "Do you know the story of the Zen monk, who was playing hide and go seek with the children? Was it Basho who tells this? The monk hid in an outhouse and the children did not think of looking there, and so they forgot him. He was a very simple man. Next day—"

"I admit that Zen is a form of stupidity," Joan Hiashi said. "It extols the virtues of being simple and gullible. And remember, the original meaning of 'gullible' is one who is easily gulled, easily cheated." She sipped a little of her tea and found it now cold.

"Then you are a true practitioner of Zen," Mr. Lee said. "Because you have been gulled." He reached inside his coat and brought out a pistol, which he pointed at Joan. "You're under arrest."

"By the Cuban Government?" she managed to say.

"By the United States Government," Mr. Lee said. "I have read your mind and I learn that you know that Ray Meritan is a prominent Mercerite and you yourself are attracted to Mercerism."

"But I'm not!"

"Unconsciously you are attracted. You are about to switch over. I can pick up those thoughts, even if you deny them to yourself. We are going back to the Unites States, you and I, and there we will find Mr. Ray Meritan and he will lead us to Wilbur Mercer; it is as simple as that."

"And this is why I was sent to Cuba?"

"I am a member of the Central Committee of the Cuban Communist Party," Mr. Lee said. "And the sole telepath on that committee. We have voted to work in cooperation with the Unites States Department of State during this current Mercer crisis. Our plane, Miss Hiashi, leaves for Washington, D.C. in half an hour; let us get down to the airport at once."

Joan Hiashi looked helplessly about the restaurant. Other people eating, the waiters... nobody paid any attention. She rose to her feet as a waiter passed with a heavily-loaded tray. "This man," she said, pointing to Mr. Lee, "is kidnapping me. Help me, please."

The waiter glanced at Mr. Lee, saw who it was, smiled at Joan and shrugged. "Mr. Lee, he is an important man," the waiter said, and went on with his tray.

"What he says is true," Mr. Lee said to her.

Joan ran from the booth and across the restaurant. "Help me," she said to the elderly Cuban Mercerite who sat with his empathy box before him. "I'm a Mercerite. They're arresting me."

The lined old face lifted; the man scrutinized her.

"Help me," she said.

"Praise Mercer," the old man said.

You can't help me, she realized. She turned back to Mr. Lee, who had followed after her, still holding the pistol pointed at her. "This old man is not going to do a thing," Mr. Lee said. "Not even get to his feet."

She sagged. "All right. I know."

THE TELEVISION set in the corner suddenly ceased its yammering of day-time trash; the image of a woman's face and bottle of cleanser abruptly disappeared and there was only blackness. Then, in Spanish, a news announcer began to speak.

"Hurt," Mr. Lee said, listening. "But Mercer is not dead. How do you feel, Miss Hiashi, as a Mercerite? Does this affect you? Oh, but that's right. One must take hold of the handles first, for it to reach you. It must be a voluntary act."

Joan picked up the elderly Cuban's empathy box, held it for a moment, and then seized the handles. Mr. Lee stared at her in surprise; he moved toward her, reaching for the box...

It was not pain that she felt. Is this how it is? she wondered as she saw around her, the restaurant dim and fade. Maybe Wilbur Mercer is unconscious; that must be it. I'm escaping from you, she thought to Mr. Lee. You can't—or at least you won't—follow me where I've gone: into the tomb world of Wilbur Mercer, who is dying somewhere on a barren plain, surrounded by his enemies. Now I'm with him. And it is an escape from something worse. From you. And you're never going to be able to get me back.

She saw, around her, a desolate expanse. The air smelled of harsh blossoms; this was the desert, and there was no rain.

A man stood before her, a sorrowful light in his gray, pain-drenched eyes. "I am your friend," he said, "but you must go on as if I did not exist. Can you understand that?" He spread empty hands.

"No," she said, "I can't understand that."

"How can I save you," the man said, "if I can't save myself?" He smiled: "Don't you see? *There is no salvation.*"

"Then what's it all for?" she asked.

"To show you," Wilbur Mercer said, "that you aren't alone. I am here with you and always will be. Go back and face them. And tell them that."

She released the handles.

Mr. Lee, holding his gun to her, said, "Well?"

"Let's go," she said. "Back to the United States. Turn me over to the FBI. It doesn't matter."

"What did you see?" Mr. Lee said, with curiosity.

"I won't tell you."

"But I can learn it anyhow. From your mind." He was probing, now, listening with his head cocked on one side. The corners of his mouth turned down as if he was pouting.

"I don't call that much," he said. "Mercer looks you in the face and says he can't do anything for you—is this the man you'd lay down your life for, you and the others? You're ill."

"In the society of the insane," Joan said, "the sick are well."

"What nonsense!" Mr. Lee said.

To BOGART CROFTS Mr. Lee said, "It was interesting. She became a Mercerite directly in front of me. The latency transforming itself into actuality... it proved I was correct in what I previously read in her mind."

"We'll have Meritan picked up any time now," Crofts said to his superior, Secretary Herrick. "He left the television studio in Los Angeles, where he got news of Mercer's severe injury. After that, no one seems to know what he did. He did *not* return to his apartment. The local police picked up his empathy box, and he was beyond a doubt not on the premises."

"Where is Joan Hiashi?" Crofts asked.

"Being held now in New York," Mr. Lee said.

"On what charge?" Crofts asked Secretary Herrick.

"Political agitation inimical to the safety of the United States."

Smiling, Mr. Lee said, "And arrested by a Communist official in Cuba. It is a Zen paradox which no doubt fails to delight Miss Hiashi."

Meanwhile, Bogart Crofts reflected, empathy boxes were being collected in huge quantities. Soon their destruction would begin. Within forty-eight hours most of the empathy boxes in the United States would no longer exist, including the one here in his office.

It still rested on his desk, untouched. It was he who originally had asked that it be brought in, and in all this time he had kept his hands off it, had never yielded. Now he walked over to it.

"What would happen," he asked Mr. Lee, "if I took hold of these two handles? There's no television set here. I have no idea what Wilbur Mercer is doing right now; in fact for all that I know, now he's finally dead."

Mr. Lee said, "If you grip the handles, sir, you will enter a—I hesitate to use the word but it seems to apply. A mystical communion. With Mr. Mercer, wherever he is;

you will share his suffering, as you know, but that is not all. You will also participate in his—" Mr. Lee reflected. "'World-view' is not the correct term. Ideology? No."

Secretary Herrick suggested, "What about *trance-state*?"

"Perhaps that is it," Mr. Lee said, frowning. "No, that is not it either. No word will do, and that is the entire point. It cannot be described—it must be experienced."

"I'll try," Crofts decided.

"No," Mr. Lee said. "Not if you are following my advice. I would warn you away from it. I saw Miss Hiashi do it, and I saw the change in her. Would you have tried Paracodein when it was popular with rootless cosmopolite masses?" He sounded angry.

"I have tried Paracodein," Crofts said. "It did absolutely nothing for me."

"What do you want done, Boge?" Secretary Herrick asked him.

Shrugging, Bogart Crofts said, "I mean I could see no reason for anyone liking it, wanting to become addicted to it." And at last he took hold of the two handles of the empathy box.

V

WALKING SLOWLY in the rain, Ray Meritan said to himself, They got my empathy box and if I go back to the apartment they'll get me.

His telepathic talent had saved him. As he entered the building he had picked up the thoughts of the gang of city police.

It was now past midnight. The trouble is I'm too well-known, he realized, from my damned TV show. No matter where I go I'll be recognized.

At least anywhere on Earth.

Where is Wilbur Mercer? he asked himself. In this solar system or somewhere beyond it, under a different sun entirely? Maybe we'll never know. Or at least *I'll* never know.

But did it matter? Wilbur Mercer was somewhere; that was all that was important. And there was always a way to reach him. The empathy box was always there—or at least had been, until the police raids. And Meritan had a feeling that the distribution company which had supplied the empathy boxes, and which led a shadowy existence anyhow, would find a way around the police. If he was right about them—

Ahead in the rainy darkness he saw the red lights of a bar. He turned and entered it.

To the bartender he said, "Look, do you have an empathy box? I'll pay you one hundred dollars for the use of it."

The bartender, a big burly man with hairy arms, said, "Naw, I don't have nuthin like that. Go on."

The people at the bar watched, and one of them said, "Those are illegal now."

"Hey, it's Ray Meritan," another said. "The jazz man."

Another man said lazily, "Play some gray-green jazz for us, jazz man." He sipped at his mug of beer.

Meritan started out of the bar.

"Wait," the bartender said. "Hold on, buddy. Go to this address." He wrote on a match folder, then held it out to Meritan.

"How much do I owe you?" Meritan said.

"Oh, five dollars ought to do it."

Meritan paid and left the bar, the match folder in his pocket. It's probably the address of the local police station, he said to himself. But I'll give it a try anyhow. If I could get to an empathy box one more time—

The address which the bartender had given him was an old, decaying wooden building in downtown Los Angeles. He rapped on the door and stood waiting.

The door opened. A middle-aged heavy woman in bathrobe and furry slippers peeped out at him. "I'm not the police," he said. "I'm a Mercerite. Can I use your empathy box?"

The door gradually opened; the woman scrutinized him and evidently believed him, although she said nothing.

"Sorry to bother you so late," he apologized.

"What happened to you, mister?" the woman said. "You look bad."

"It's Wilbur Mercer," Ray said. "He's hurt."

"Turn it on," the woman said, leading him with

shuffling into a dark, cold parlor where a parrot slept in a huge, bent, brass-wire cage. There, on an old-fashioned radio cabinet, he saw the empathy box. He felt relief creep over him at the sight of it.

"Don't be shy," the woman said.

"Thanks." he said, and took hold of the handles.

A voice said in his ear, "We'll use the girl. She'll lead us to Meritan. I was right to hire her in the first place."

Ray Meritan did not recognize the voice. It was not that of Wilbur Mercer. But even so, bewildered, he held tightly onto the handles, listening; he remained frozen there, hands extended, clutching.

"The non-T force has appealed to the most credulous segment of our community, but this segment—I firmly believe—is being manipulated by a cynical minority of opportunists at the top, such as Meritan. They're cashing in on this Wilbur Mercer craze for their own pocketbooks." The voice, self-assured, droned on.

Ray Meritan felt fear as he heard it. For this was someone on the other side, he realized. Somehow he had gotten into empathic contact with him, and not with Wilbur Mercer.

Or had Mercer done this deliberately, arranged this? He listened on, and now he heard:

". . . have to get the Hiashi girl out of New York and back here, where we can quiz her further." The voice added, "As I told Herrick . . ."

Herrick, the Secretary of State. This was someone in the State Department thinking, Meritan realized, thinking about Joan. Perhaps this was the official at State who had hired her.

Then she wasn't in Cuba. She was in New York. What had gone wrong? The whole implication was that State had merely made use of Joan to get at him.

He released the handles and the voice faded from his presence.

"Did you find him?" the middle-aged woman asked.

"Y-yes," Meritan said, disconcerted, trying to orient himself in the unfamiliar room.

"How is he? Is he well?"

"I—don't know right now." Meritan answered, truthfully. He thought, I must go to New York. And try to help Joan. She's in this because of me; I have no choice. Even if they catch me because of it . . . how can I desert her?

BOGART CROFTS said, "I didn't get Mercer."

He walked away from the empathy box, then turned to glare at it, balefully. "I got Meritan. But I don't know where he is. At the moment I took hold of the handles of this box, Meritan took hold somewhere else. We were connected and now he knows everything I know. And we know everything he knows, which isn't much." Dazed he turned to Secretary Herrick. "He doesn't know any more about Wilbur Mercer than we do; he was trying to reach him. He definitely is *not* Mercer." Crofts was silent then.

"There's more," Herrick said, turning to Mr. Lee. "What else did he get from Meritan, Mr. Lee?"

"Meritan is coming to New York to try to find Joan Hiashi," Mr. Lee said, obligingly reading Crofts' mind. "He got that from Mr. Meritan during the moment their minds were fused."

"We'll prepare to receive Mr. Meritan," Secretary Herrick said, with a grimace.

"Did I experience what you telepaths engage in all the time?" Crofts asked Mr. Lee.

"Only when one of us comes close to another telepath," Mr. Lee said. "It can be unpleasant. We avoid it, because if the two minds are thoroughly dissimilar and hence clash, it is psychologically harmful. I would assume you and Mr. Meritan clashed."

Crofts said, "Listen, how can we continue with this? I know now that Meritan is innocent. He doesn't know a damn thing about Mercer or the organization that distributes these boxes except its name."

There was momentary silence.

"But he is one of the few celebrities who has joined the Mercerites," Secretary Herrick pointed out. He handed a teletype dispatch to Crofts. "And he has done it openly. If you'll take the trouble to read this—"

"I know he affirmed his loyalty to Mercer on this evening's TV program," Crofts said, trembling.

"When you're dealing with a non-T force originating from another solar system entirely," Secretary Herrick said, "you must move with care. We will still try to take Meritan, and definitely through Miss Hiashi. We'll release her from jail and have her followed. When Meritan makes contact with her—"

To Crofts, Mr. Lee said, "Don't say what you intend, Mr. Crofts. It will permanently damage your career."

Crofts said, "Herrick, this is wrong. Meritan is innocent and so is Joan Hiashi. If you try to trap Meritan I'll resign from State."

"Write out your resignation and hand it to me," Secretary Herrick said. His face was dark.

"This is unfortunate," Mr. Lee said. "I would guess that your contact with Mr. Meritan warped your judgment, Mr. Crofts. He has influenced you malignly; shake it off, for the sake of your long career and country, not to mention your family."

"What we're doing is wrong," Crofts repeated.

SECRETLY HERRICK stared at him angrily. "No wonder those empathy boxes have done harm! Now I've seen it with my own eyes. I wouldn't turn back on any condition now."

He picked up the empathy box which Crofts had used. Lifting it high he dropped it to the floor. The box cracked open and then settled in a heap of irregular surfaces. "Don't consider that a childish act," he said. "I want any contact between us and Meritan broken. It can only be harmful."

"If we capture him," Crofts said, "he may continue to exert influence over us." He amended his statement: "Or rather, over me."

"Be that as it may, I intend to continue," Secretary Herrick said. "And please present your resignation. Mr. Crofts, I intend to act on that matter as well." He looked grim and determined.

Mr. Lee said, "Secretary, I can read Mr. Crofts' mind and I see that he is stunned at this moment. He is the innocent victim of a situation, arranged perhaps by Wilbur Mercer to spread confusion among us. And if you accept Mr. Crofts' resignation, Mercer will have succeeded."

"It doesn't matter whether he accepts it or not," Crofts

said. "Because in any case I'm resigning."

Sighing, Mr. Lee said, "The empathy box made you suddenly into an involuntary telepath and it was just too much." He patted Mr. Crofts on the shoulder. "Telepathic power and empathy are two versions of the same thing. Should be called 'telepathic box.' Amazing, those non-T invididuals; they can build what we can only evolve."

"Since you can read my mind," Crofts said to him, "you know what I'm planning to do. I have no doubt you'll tell Secretary Herrick."

Grinning blandly, Mr. Lee said, "The Secretary and I are cooperating in the interest of world peace. We both have our instructions." To Herrick he said, "This man is so upset that he now actually considers switching over. Joining the Mercerites before all the boxes are destroyed. He *liked* being an involuntary telepath."

"If you switch," Herrick said, "you'll be arrested. I promise it."

Crofts said nothing.

"He has not changed his mind," Mr. Lee said urbanely, nodding to both men, apparently amused by the situation.

But underneath, Mr. Lee was thinking, A brilliant bold type of stroke by the thing that calls itself Wilbur Mercer, this hooking up of Crofts with Meritan direct. It undoubtedly foresaw that Crofts would receive the strong emanations from the movement's core. The next step is that Crofts will again consult an empathy box—if he can find one—and this time Mercer itself will address him personally. Address its new disciple.

They have gained a man, Mr. Lee realized. They are ahead.

But ultimately we will win. Because ultimately we will manage to destroy all the empathy boxes, and without them Wilbur Mercer can do nothing. This is the only way he has—or *it* has—of reaching and controlling people, as it has done here with unfortunate Mr. Crofts. *Without the empathy boxes the movement is helpless.*

VI

AT THE UWA desk, at Rocky Field in New York City, Joan Hiashi said to the uniformed clerk, "I want to buy a one-way ticket to Los Angeles on the next flight. Jet or rocket; it doesn't matter. I just want to get there."

"First class or tourist?" the clerk asked.

"Aw, hell," Joan said wearily, "just sell me a ticket. Any kind of a ticket." She opened her purse.

As she started to pay for the ticket a hand stopped hers. She turned—and there stood Ray Meritan, his face twisting with relief.

"What a place to try to pick up your thoughts," he said. "Come on, let's go where it's quiet. You have ten minutes before your flight."

They hurried together through the building until they came to a deserted ramp. There they stopped, and Joan said, "Listen, Ray I know it's a trap for you. That's why they let me out. But where else can I go except to you?"

Ray said, "Don't worry about it. They were bound to pick me up sooner or later. I'm sure they know I left California and came here." He glanced around. "No FBI agents near us yet. At least I don't pick up anything suggesting it." He lit a cigarette.

"I don't have any reason to go back to L. A.," Joan said, "now that you're here. I might as well cancel my flight."

"You know they're picking up and destroying all the empathy boxes they can," Ray said.

"No," she said. "I didn't know, I was just released half an hour ago. That's dreadful. They really mean business."

Ray laughed. "Let's say they're really frightened." He put his arm around her and kissed her. "I tell you what we'll do. We'll try to sneak out of this place, go to the lower East Side and rent a little cold-water walk-up. We'll hide out and find an empathy box they missed." But, he thought, it's unlikely; they probably have them all by now. There weren't that many to start with.

"Anything you say," Joan said drably.

"Do you love me?" he asked her. "I can read your mind; you do." And then he said quietly, "I can also read the mind of a Mr. Lewis Scanlan, an FBI man who's now at the UWA desk. What name did you give?"

"Mrs. George McIsaacs," Joan said. "I think." She examined her ticket and envelope. "Yes, that's right."

"But Scanlan is asking if a Japanese woman has been at the desk in the last fifteen minutes," Ray said. "And the clerk remembers you. So—" He took hold of Joan's arm. "We better get started."

They hurried down the deserted ramp, passed through an electric-eye operated door and came out in a baggage lobby. Everyone there was far too busy to pay any attention as Ray Meritan and Joan threaded their way to the street door and, a moment later, stepped out onto the chill gray sidewalk where cabs had parked in a long double row. Joan started to hail a cab...

"Wait," Ray said, pulling her back. "I'm getting a jumble of thoughts. One of the cab drivers is an FBI man but I can't tell which." He stood uncertainly, not knowing what to do.

"We can't get away, can we?" Joan said.

"It's going to be hard." To himself he thought, More like impossible; you're right. He experienced the girl's confused, frightened thoughts, her anxiety about him, that she had made it possible for them to locate and capture him, her fierce desire not to return to jail, her pervasive bitterness at having been betrayed by Mr. Lee, the Chinese Communist bigshot who had met her in Cuba.

"What a life," Joan said, standing close to him.

And still he did not know which cab to take. One precious second after another escaped as he stood there. "Listen," he said to Joan, "maybe we should separate."

"No," she said clinging to him. "I can't stand to do it alone any more. Please."

A BEWHISKERED peddler walked up to them with a tray suspended by a cord which ran about his neck. "Hi, folks," he mumbled.

"Not now," Joan said to him.

"Free sample of breakfast cereal," the peddler said. "No cost. Just take a box, miss. You mister. Take one." He extended the tray of small, gaily colored cartons toward Ray.

Strange, Ray thought. I'm not picking up anything

from this man's mind. He stared at the peddler, saw—or
thought he saw—a peculiar insubstantiality to the man. A
diffused quality.

Ray took one of the samples of breakfast cereal.

"Merry Meal, it's called," the peddler said. "A new
product they're introducing to the public. There's a free
coupon inside. Entitles you to—"

"Okay," Ray said, sticking the box in his pocket. He
took hold of Joan and led her along the line of cabs. He
chose one at random and opened the rear door. "Get in,"
he said urgently to her.

"I took a sample of Merry Meal, too," she said with a
wan smile as he seated himself beside her. The cab started
up, left the line and pulled past the entrance of the airfield
terminal. "Ray, there was something strange about that
salesman. It was as if he wasn't actually there, as if he was
nothing more than—a picture."

As the cab drove down the auto ramp, away from the
terminal, another cab left the line and followed after
them. Twisting, Ray saw riding in the back of it two
well-fed men in dark business suits. FBI men, he said to
himself.

Joan said, "Didn't that cereal salesman remind you of
anyone?"

"Who?"

"A little of Wilbur Mercer. But I haven't seen him
enough to—"

Ray grabbed the cereal box from her hand, tore the
cardboard top from it. Poking up from the dry cereal he
saw the corner of the coupon the peddler had spoken
about; he lifted out the coupon, held it up and studied it.
The coupon said in large clear printing:

HOW TO ASSEMBLE AN
EMPATHY BOX FROM
ORDINARY HOUSEHOLD
OBJECTS

"It was them," he said to Joan.

He put the coupon carefully away in his pocket, then he
changed his mind. Folding it up, he tucked it in the cuff of
his trousers. Where the FBI possibly wouldn't find it.

Behind them, the other cab came closer, and now he picked up the thoughts of the two men. They were FBI agents; he had been right. He settled back against the seat.

There was nothing to do but wait.

Joan said, "Could I have the other coupon?"

"Sorry." He got out the other cereal package. She opened it, found the coupon inside and, after a pause, folded it and hid it in the hem of her skirt.

"I wonder how many there are of those so-called peddlers," Ray said musingly. "I'd be interested to know how many free samples of Merry Meal they're going to manage to give away before they're caught."

The first ordinary household object needed was a common radio set; he had noticed that. The second, the filament from a five-year light-bulb. And next—he'd have to look again, but now was not the time. The other cab had drawn abreast with theirs.

Later. And if the authorities found the coupon in the cuff of his trousers, *they*, he knew, would somehow manage to bring him another.

He put his arm around Joan. "I think we'll be all right."

The other cab, now, was nosing theirs to the curb and the two FBI men were waving in a menacing, official manner to the driver to stop.

"Shall I stop?" the driver said tensely to Ray.

"Sure," he said. And, taking a deep breath, prepared himself.

The Unreconstructed M

I

THE MACHINE was a foot wide and two feet long; it looked like an oversized box of crackers. Silently, with great caution, it climbed the side of a concrete building; it had lowered two rubberized rollers and was now beginning the first phase of its job.

From its rear, a flake of blue enamel was exuded. The machine pressed the flake firmly against the rough concrete and then continued on. Its upward path carried it from vertical concrete to vertical steel: it had reached a window. The machine paused and produced a micro-scopic fragment of cloth fabric. The cloth, with great care, was embedded in the fitting of the steel window frame.

In the chill darkness, the machine was virtually invisible. The glow of a distant tangle of traffic briefly touched it, illuminated its polished hull, and departed. The machine resumed its work.

It projected a plastic pseudopodium and incinerated the pane of window glass. There was no response from within the gloomy apartment: nobody was home. The machine, now dulled with particles of glass-dust, crept over the steel frame and raised an inquisitive receptor.

While it received, it exerted precisely two hundred pounds pressure on the steel window frame, the frame obediently bent. Satisfied, the machine descended the inside of the wall to the moderately thick carpet. There it began the second phase of its job.

ONE SINGLE human hair—follicle and speck of scalp included—was deposited on the hardwood floor by the lamp. Not far from the piano, two dried grains of tobacco were ceremoniously laid out. The machine waited an

interval of ten seconds and then, as an internal section of
magnetic tape clicked into place, it suddenly said. "Ugh!
Damn it ..."

Curiously, its voice was husky and masculine.

The machine made its way to the closet door, which
was locked. Climbing the wood surface, the machine
reached the lock mechanism, and, inserting a thin section
of itself, caressed the tumblers back. Behind the row of
coats was a small mound of batteries and wires: a
self-powered video recorder. The machine destroyed the
reservoir of film—which was vital—and then, as it left the
closet, expelled a drop of blood on the jagged tangle that
had been the lens-scanner. The drop of blood was even
more vital.

While the machine was pressing the artificial outline of
a heel mark into the greasy film that covered the flooring
of the closet, a sharp sound came from the hallway. The
machine ceased its work and became rigid. A moment
later a small, middle-aged man entered the apartment,
coat over one arm, briefcase in the other.

"Good God," he said, stopping instantly as he saw the
machine. "What are you?"

THE MACHINE lifted the nozzle of its front section and shot
an explosive pellet at the man's half-bald head. The pellet
traveled into the skull and detonated. Still clutching his
coat and briefcase, bewildered expression on his face, the
man collapsed to the rug. His glasses, broken, lay twisted
beside his ear. His body stirred a little, twitched, and then
was satisfactorily quiet.

Only two steps remained to the job, now that the main
part was done. The machine deposited a bit of burnt
match in one of the spotless ashtrays resting on the
mantel, and entered the kitchen to search for a water
glass. It was starting up the side of the sink when the noise
of human voices startled it.

"This is the apartment," a voice said, clear and close.

"Get ready—he ought to still be here." Another voice, a
man's voice, like the first. The hall door was pushed open
and two individuals in heavy overcoats sprinted purpose-
fully into the apartment. At their approach, the machine
dropped to the kitchen floor, the water glass forgotten.

Something had gone wrong. Its rectangular outline flowed and wavered; pulling itself into an upright package it fused its shape into that of a conventional t-v unit.

It was holding that emergency form when one of the men—tall, red-haired—peered briefly into the kitchen.

"Nobody in here," the man declared, and hurried on.

"The window," his companion said, panting. Two more figures entered the apartment, an entire crew. "The glass is gone—missing. He got in that way."

"But he's gone." The red-haired man reappeared at the kitchen door; he snapped on the light and entered, a gun visible in his hand. "Strange . . . we got here right away, as soon as we picked up the rattle." Suspiciously, he examined his wristwatch. "Rosenburg's been dead only a few seconds . . . how could he have got out again so fast?"

STANDING in the street entrance, Edward Ackers listened to the voice. During the last half hour the voice had taken on a carping, nagging whine; sinking almost to inaudibility, it plodded along, mechanically turning out its message of complaint.

"You're tired," Ackers said. "Go home. Take a hot bath."

"No," the voice said, interrupting its tirade. The locus of the voice was a large illuminated blob on the dark sidewalk, a few yards to Ackers' right. The revolving neon sign read:

BANISH IT!

Thirty times—he had counted—within the last few minutes the sign had captured a passerby and the man in the booth had begun his harangue. Beyond the booth were several theaters and restaurants: the booth was well-situated.

But it wasn't for the crowd that the booth had been erected. It was for Ackers and the offices behind him; the tirade was aimed directly at the Interior Department. The nagging racket had gone on so many months that Ackers was scarcely aware of it. Rain on the roof. Traffic noises. He yawned, folded his arms, and waited.

"Banish it," the voice complained peevishly. "Come

on, Ackers. Say something; do something."

"I'm waiting," Ackers said complacently.

A GROUP of middle-class citizens passed the booth and were handed leaflets. The citizens scattered the leaflets after them, and Ackers laughed.

"Don't laugh," the voice muttered. "It's not funny; it costs us money to print those."

"Your personal money?" Ackers inquired.

"Partly." Garth was lonely, tonight. "What are you waiting for? What's happened? I saw a police team leave your roof a few minutes ago..."

"We may take in somebody," Ackers said, "there's been a killing."

Down the dark sidewalk the man stirred in his dreary propaganda booth. "Oh?" Harvey Garth's voice came. He leaned forward and the two looked directly at each other: Ackers, carefully-groomed, well-fed, wearing a respectable overcoat... Garth, a thin man, much younger, with a lean, hungry face composed mostly of nose and forehead.

"So you see," Ackers told him, "we do need the system. Don't be utopian."

"A man is murdered; and you rectify the moral imbalance by killing the killer." Garth's protesting voice rose in a bleak spasm. "Banish it! Banish the system that condemns men to certain extinction!"

"Get your leaflets here," Ackers parodied drily. "And your slogans. Either or both. What would you suggest in place of the system?"

GARTH'S VOICE was proud with conviction. "Education."

Amused, Ackers asked: "Is that all? You think that would stop anti-social activity? Criminals just don't—*know* better?"

"And psychotherapy, of course." His projected face bony and intense, Garth peered out of his booth like an aroused turtle. "They're sick... that's why they commit crimes, healthy men don't commit crimes. And you compound it; you create a sick society of punitive cruelty." He waggled an accusing finger. "You're the real culprit, you and the whole Interior Department. You and the whole Banishment System."

Again and again the neon sign blinked BANISH IT!
Meaning, of course, the system of compulsory ostracism
for felons, the machinery that projected a condemned
human being into some random backwater region of the
sidereal universe, into some remote and out-of-the-way
corner where he would be of no harm.

"No harm to us, anyhow," Ackers mused aloud.

Garth spoke the familiar argument. "Yes, but what
about the local inhabitants?"

Too BAD about the local inhabitants. Anyhow, the
banished victim spent his energy and time trying to find a
way back to the Sol System. If he got back before old age
caught up with him he was readmitted by society. Quite a
challenge ... especially to some cosmopolite who had
never set foot outside Greater New York. There
were—probably—many involuntary expatriates cutting
grain in odd fields with primitive sickles. The remote
sections of the universe seemed composed mostly of dank
rural cultures, isolated agrarian enclaves typified by
small-time bartering of fruit and vegetables and hand-
made artifacts.

"Did you know," Ackers said, "that in the Age of
Monarchs, a pickpocket was usually hanged?"

"Banish it," Garth continued monotonously, sinking
back into his booth. The sign revolved; leaflets were
passed out. And Ackers impatiently watched the
late-evening street for sign of the hospital truck.

He knew Heimie Rosenburg. A sweeter little guy there
never was ... although Heimie had been mixed up in one
of the sprawling slave combines that illegally transported
settlers to out-system fertile planets. Between them, the
two largest slavers had settled virtually the entire Sirius
System. Four out of six emigrants were hustled out in
carriers registered as "freighters". It was hard to picture
gentle little Heimie Rosenburg as a business agent for
Tirol Enterprises, but there it was.

As HE WAITED, Ackers conjectured on Heimie's murder.
Probably one element of the incessant subterranean war
going on between Paul Tirol and his major rival. David
Lantano was a brilliant and energetic newcomer ... but

murder was anybody's game. It all depended on how it
was done; it could be commerical hack or the purest art.

"Here comes something," Garth's voice sounded,
carried, to his inner ear by the delicate output transformers of the booth's equipment. "Looks like a freezer."

It was; the hospital truck had arrived. Ackers stepped
forward as the truck halted and the back was let down.

"How soon did you get there?" he asked the cop who
jumped heavily to the pavement.

"Right away," the cop answered, "but no sign of the
killer. I don't think we're going to get Heimie back . . . they
got him dead-center, right in the cerebellum. Expert
work, no amateur stuff."

Disappointed, Ackers clambered into the hospital
truck to inspect for himself.

VERY TINY and still, Heimie Rosenburg lay on his back,
arms at his sides, gazing sightlessly up at the roof of the
truck. On his face remained the expression of bewildered
wonder. Somebody—one of the cops—had placed his
bent glasses in his clenched hand. In falling he had cut his
cheek. The destroyed portion of his skull was covered by a
moist plastic web.

"Who's back at the apartment?" Ackers asked
presently.

"The rest of my crew," the cop answered. "And an
independent researcher. Leroy Beam."

"Him," Ackers said, with aversion. "How is it he
showed up?"

"Caught the rattle, too, happened to be passing with
his rig. Poor Heimie had an awful big booster on that
rattle . . . I'm surprised it wasn't picked up here at the main
offices."

"They say Heimie had a high anxiety level," Ackers
said. "Bugs all over his apartment. You're starting to
collect evidence?"

"The teams are moving in," the cop said. "We should
begin getting specifications in half an hour. The killer
knocked out the vid bug set up in the closet. But—" He
grinned. "He cut himself breaking the circuit. A drop of
blood, right on the wiring; it looks promising."

•   •   •

AT THE apartment, Leroy Beam watched the Interior police begin their analysis. They worked smoothly and thoroughly, but Beam was dissatisfied.

His original impression remained: he was suspicious. Nobody could have gotten away so quickly. Heimie had died, and his death—the cessation of his neural pattern—had triggered off an automatic squawk. A rattle didn't particularly protect its owner, but its existence ensured (or usually ensured) detection of the murderer. Why had it failed Heimie?

Prowling moodily, Leroy Beam entered the kitchen for the second time. There, on the floor by the sink, was a small portable t-v unit, the kind popular with the sporting set: a gaudy little packet of plastic and knobs and multi-tinted lenses.

"Why this?" Beam asked, as one of the cops plodded past him. "This t-v unit sitting here on the kitchen floor. It's out of place."

The cop ignored him. In the living room, elaborate police detection equipment was scraping the various surfaces inch by inch. In the half hour since Heimie's death, a number of specifications had been logged. First, the drop of blood on the damaged vid wiring. Second, a hazy heel mark where the murderer had stepped. Third, a bit of burnt match in the ashtray. More were expected; the analysis had only begun.

It usually took nine specifications to delineate the single individual.

LEROY BEAM glanced cautiously around him. None of the cops was watching, so he bent down and picked up the t-v unit; it felt ordinary. He clicked the *on* switch and waited. Nothing happened; no image formed. Strange.

He was holding it upside down, trying to see the inner chassis, when Edward Ackers from Interior entered the apartment. Quickly, Beam stuffed the t-v unit into the pocket of his heavy overcoat.

"What are you doing here?" Ackers asked.

"Seeking," Beam answered, wondering if Ackers noticed his tubby bulge. "I'm in business, too."

"Did you know Heimie?"

"By reputation," Beam answered vaguely. "Tied in

with Tirol's combine, I hear; some sort of front man. Had an office on Fifth Avenue."

"Swank place, like the rest of those Fifth Avenue feather merchants." Ackers went on into the livingroom to watch the detectors gather up evidence.

There was a vast nearsightedness to the wedge grinding ponderously across the carpet. It was scrutinizing at a microscopic level, and its field was sharply curtailed. As fast as material was obtained, it was relayed to the Interior offices, to the aggregate file banks where the civil population was represented by a series of punch cards, cross-indexed infinitely.

Lifting the telephone, Ackers called his wife. "I won't be home," he told her. "Business."

A lag, and then Ellen responded. "Oh?" she said distantly. "Well, thanks for letting me know."

OVER IN the corner, two members of the police crew were delightedly examining a new discovery, valid enough to be a specification. "I'll call you again," he said hurriedly to Ellen, "before I leave. Goodbye."

"Goodbye," Ellen said curtly, and managed to hang up before he did.

The new discovery was the undamaged aud bug, which was mounted under the floor lamp. A continuous magnetic tape—still in motion—gleamed amiably; the murder episode had been recorded sound-wise in its entirety.

"Everything," a cop said gleefully to Ackers. "It was going before Heimie got home."

"You played it back?"

"A portion. There's a couple words spoken by the murderer, should be enough."

Ackers got in touch with Interior. "Have the specifications on the Rosenburg case been fed, yet?"

"Just the first," the attendant answered. "The file discriminates the usual massive category—about six billion names."

Ten minutes later the second specification was fed to the files. Persons with type O blood, with size 11½ shoes, numbered slightly over a billion. The third specification brought in the element of smoker-nonsmoker. That dropped the number to less than a billion, but not much less. Most adults smoked.

"The aud tape will drop it fast," Leroy Beam· commented, standing beside Ackers, his arms folded to conceal his bulging coat. "Ought to be able to get age, at least."

THE AUD TAPE, analyzed, gave thirty to forty years as the conjectured age. And—timbre analysis—a man of perhaps two hundred pounds. A little later the bent steel window frame was examined, and the warp noted. It jibed with the specification of the aud tape. There were now six specifications, including that of sex (male). The number of persons in the in-group was falling rapidly.

"It won't be long," Ackers said genially. "And if he tacked one of those little buckets to the building side, we'll have a paint scrape."

Beam said: "I'm leaving. Good luck."

"Stick around."

"Sorry." Beam moved toward the hall door. "This is yours, not mine. I've got my own business to attend to . . . I'm doing research for a hot-shot nonferrous mining concern."

Ackers eyed his coat. "Are you pregnant?"

"Not that I know of," Beam said, coloring. "I've led a good clean life." Awkwardly, he patted his coat. "You mean this?"

By the window, one of the police gave a triumphant yap. The two bits of pipe tobacco had been discovered: a refinement for the third specification. "Excellent," Ackers said, turning away from Beam and momentarily forgetting him.

Beam left.

Very shortly he was driving across town toward his own labs, the small and independent research outfit that he headed, unsupported by a government grant. Resting on the seat beside him was the portable t-v unit, it was still silent.

"FIRST of all," Beam's gowned technician declared, "it has a power supply approximately seventy times that of a

portable t-v pack. We picked up the Gamma radiation."
He displayed the usual detector. "So you're right, it's not a
t-v set."

Gingerly, Beam lifted the small unit from the lab
bench. Five hours had passed, and still he knew nothing
about it. Taking firm hold of the back he pulled with all
his strength. The back refused to come off. It wasn't stuck:
there were no seams. The back was not a back; it only
looked like a back.

"Then what is it?" he asked.

"Could be lots of things," the technician said
non-committally; he had been roused from the privacy of
his home, and it was now two-thirty in the morning.
"Could be some sort of scanning equipment. A bomb. A
weapon. Any kind of gadget."

Laboriously, Beam felt the unit all over, searching for a
flaw in the surface. "It's uniform," he murmured. "A single surface."

"You bet. The breaks are false—it's a poured
substance. And," the technician added, "it's hard. I tried
to chip off a representative sample but—" He gestured.
"No results."

"Guaranteed not to shatter when dropped," Beam said
absently. "New extra-tough plastic." He shook the unit
energetically; the muted noise of metal parts in motion
reached his ear. "It's full of guts."

"We'll get it open," the technician promised, "but not
tonight."

BEAM REPLACED the unit on the bench. He could, with bad
luck work days on this one item—to discover, after all,
that it had nothing to do with the murder of Heimie
Rosenburg. On the other hand . . .

"Drill me a hole in it," he instructed. "So we can see in."

His technician protested: "I drilled, the drill broke. I've
sent out for an improved density. This substance is
imported; somebody hooked it from a white dwarf
system. It was conceived under stupendous pressure."

"You're stalling," Beam said, irritated. "That's how
they talk in the advertising media."

The technician shrugged. "Anyhow, it's extra hard. A

naturally-evolved element, or an artificially-processed product from somebody's labs. Who has funds to develop a metal like this?"

"One of the big slavers," Beam said. "That's where the wealth winds up. And they hop around to various systems... they'd have access to raw materials. Special ores."

"Can't I go home?" the technician asked. "What's so important about this?"

"This device either killed or helped kill Heimie Rosenburg. We'll sit here, you and I, until we get it open." Beam seated himself and began examining the check sheet showing which tests had been applied. "Sooner or later it'll fly open like a clam—if you can remember that far back."

BEHIND THEM, a warning bell sounded.

"Somebody in the anteroom," Beam said, surprised and wary. "At two-thirty?" He got up and made his way down the dark hall to the front of the building. Probably it was Ackers. His conscience stirred guiltily: somebody had logged the absence of the t-v unit.

But it was not Ackers.

Waiting humbly in the cold, deserted anteroom was Paul Tirol, with him was an attractive young woman unknown to Beam. Tirol's wrinkled face broke into smiles, and he extended a hearty hand. "Beam," he said. They shook. "Your front door said you were down here. Still working?"

Guardedly, wondering who the woman was and what Tirol wanted, Beam said: "Catching up on some slipshod errors. Whole firm's going broke."

Tirol laughed indulgently. "Always the japer." His deep-set eyes darted; Tirol was a powerfully-built person, older than most, with a somber, intensely-creased face. "Have room for a few contracts? I thought I might slip a few jobs your way... if you're open."

"I'm always open," Beam countered, blocking Tirol's view of the lab proper. The door, anyhow, had slid itself shut. Tirol had been Heimie's boss... he no doubt felt entitled to all extant information on the murder. Who did it? When? How? Why? But that didn't explain why he was *here*.

"TERRIBLE THING," Tirol said crudely. He made no move to introduce the woman; she had retired to the couch to light a cigaret. She was slender, with mahogany-colored hair, she wore a blue coat, and a kerchief tied around her head.

"Yes," Beam agreed. "Terrible."

"You were there, I understand."

That explained some of it. "Well," Beam conceded, "I showed up."

"But you didn't actually see it?"

"No," Beam admitted, "nobody saw it. Interior is collecting specification material. They should have it down to one card before morning."

Visibly, Tirol relaxed. "I'm glad of that. I'd hate to see the vicious criminal escape. Banishment's too good for him; he ought to be gassed."

"Barbarism," Beam murmured drily. "The days of the gas chamber. Medieval."

Tirol peered past him. "You're working on—" Now he was overtly beginning to pry. "Come now, Leroy. Heimie Rosenburg—God bless his soul—was killed tonight and tonight I find you burning the midnight oil. You can talk openly with me; you've got something relevant to his death, haven't you?"

"That's Ackers you're thinking of."

TIROL CHUCKLED. "Can I take a look?"

"Not until you start paying me, I'm not on your books yet."

In a strained, unnatural voice, Tirol bleated: "I want it."

Puzzled, Beam said: "You want what?"

With a grotesque shudder, Tirol blundered forward, shoved Beam aside, and groped for the door. The door flew open and Tirol started noisily down the dark corridor, feeling his way by instinct toward the research labs.

"Hey!" Beam shouted, outraged. He sprinted after the old man, reached the inner door, and prepared to fight it out. He was shaking, partly with amazement, partly with anger. "What the hell?" he demanded breathlessly. "You don't own me!"

Behind him the door mysteriously gave way. Foolishly, he sprawled backward, half-falling into the lab. There, stricken with helpless paralysis, was his technician. And, coming across the floor of the lab was something small and metallic. It looked like an oversized box of crackers, and it was going lickety-split toward Tirol. The object—metal and gleaming—hopped up into Tirol's arms, and the old man turned and lumbered back up the hall to the anteroom.

"What was it?" the technician said, coming to life.

Ignoring him, Beam hurried after Tirol. "He's got it!" he yelled futilely.

"It—" the technician mumbled. "It was the t-v set. And it *ran*."

II

THE FILE BANKS at Interior were in agitated flux.

The process of creating a more and more restricted category was tedious, and it took time. Most of the Interior staff had gone home to bed; it was almost three in the morning, and the corridors and offices were deserted. A few mechanical cleaning devices crept here and there in the darkness. The sole source of life was the study chamber of the file banks. Edward Ackers sat patiently waiting for the results, waiting for specifications to come in, and for the file machinery to process them.

To his right a few Interior police played a benign lottery and waited stoically to be sent out for the pick-up. The lines of communication to Heimie Rosenburg's apartment buzzed ceaselessly. Down the street, along the bleak sidewalk, Harvey Garth was still at his propaganda booth, still flashing his BANISH IT! sign and muttering in people's ears. There were virtually no passersby, now, but Garth went on. He was tireless; he never gave up.

"Psychopath," Ackers said resentfully. Even where he sat, six floors up, the tinny, carping voice reached his middle ear.

"Take him in," one of the game-playing cops suggested. The game, intricate and devious, was a version of a Centauran III practice. "We can revoke his vendor's license."

• • •

ACKERS HAD, when there was nothing else to do, concocted and refined an indictment of Garth, a sort of lay analysis of the man's mental aberrations. He enjoyed playing the psychoanalytic game; it gave him a sense of power.

Garth, Harvey
Prominent compulsive syndrome. Has assumed role of ideological anarchist, opposing legal and social system. No rational expression, only repetition of key words and phrases. Idee fixe is *Banish the banishment system*. Cause dominates life. Rigid fanatic, probably of manic type, since...

Ackers let the sentence go, since he didn't really know what the structure of the manic type was. Anyhow, the analysis was excellent, and someday it would be resting in an official slot instead of merely drifting through his mind. And, when that happened, the annoying voice would conclude.

"Big turmoil," Garth droned. "Banishment system in vast upheaval... crisis moment has arrived."

"Why crisis?" Ackers asked aloud.

DOWN BELOW on the pavement Garth responded. "All your machines are humming. Grand excitement reigns. Somebody's head will be in the basket before sun-up." His voice trailed off in a weary blur. "Intrigue and murder. Corpses... the police scurry and a beautiful woman lurks."

To his analysis Ackers added an amplifying clause.

... "Garth's talents are warped by his compulsive sense of *mission*. Having designed an ingenious communication device he sees only its propaganda possibility. Whereas Garth's voice-ear mechanism could be put to work for All Humanity.

That pleased him. Ackers got up and wandered over to the attendant operating the file. "How's it coming?" he asked.

"Here's the situation," the attendant said. There was a

line of gray stubble smeared over his chin, and he was
bleary-eyed. "We're gradually paring it down."

ACKERS, as he resumed his seat, wished he were back in
the days of the almighty fingerprint. But a print hadn't
shown up in months, a thousand techniques existed for
print-removal and print alteration. There was now no
single specification capable, in itself, of delineating the
individual. A composite was needed, a gestalt of the
assembled data.

1) blood sample (type 0) 6, 139, 481, 601
2) shoe size (11½) 1,268,303,431
3) smoker 791,992,386
3a) smoker (pipe) 52,774,853
4) sex (male) 26,449,094
5) age (30-40 years) 9,221,397
6) weight (200 lbs) 488,290
7) fabric of clothing 17,459
8) hair variety 866
9) ownership of utilized weapon 40

A vivid picture was emerging from the data. Ackers
could see him clearly. The man was practically standing
there, in front of his desk. A fairly young man, somewhat
heavy, a man who smoked a pipe and wore an extremely
expensive tweed suit. An individual created by nine
specifications; no tenth had been listed because no more
data of specification level had been found.

Now, according to the report, the apartment had been
thoroughly searched. The detection equipment was going
outdoors.

"One more should do it," Ackers said, returning the
report to the attendant. He wondered if it would come in
and how long it would take.

To waste time he telephoned his wife, but instead of
getting Ellen he got the automatic response circuit. "Yes,
sir," it told him. "Mrs. Ackers has retired for the night.
You may state a thirty-second message which will be
transcribed for her attention tomorrow morning. Thank
you."

•   •   •

ACKERS RAGED at the mechanism futilely and then hung
up. He wondered if Ellen were really in bed; maybe she
had, as often before, slipped out. But, after all, it was
almost three o'clock in the morning. Any sane person
would be asleep: only he and Garth were still at their little
stations, performing their vital duties.

What had Garth meant by a *"beautiful woman"*?

"Mr. Ackers," the attendant said, "there's a tenth
specification coming in over the wires."

Hopefully, Ackers gazed up at the file bank. He could
see nothing, of course; the actual mechanism occupied the
underground levels of the building, and all that existed
here was the input receptors and throw-out slots. But just
looking at the machinery was in itself comforting. At this
moment the bank was accepting the tenth piece of
material. In a moment he would know how many citizens
fell into the ten categories . . . he would know if already he
had a group small enough to be sorted one by one.

"Here it is," the attendant said, pushing the report to
him.

type of utilized vehicle (color) 7

"My God," Ackers said mildly. "That's low enough.
Seven persons—we can go to work."

"You want the seven cards popped?"

"Pop them," Ackers said.

A MOMENT later, the throw-out slot deposited seven neat
white cards in the tray. The attendant passed them to
Ackers and he quickly riffled them. The next step was
personal motive and proximity: items that had to be
gotten from the suspects themselves.

Of the seven names six meant nothing to him. Two
lived on Venus, one in the Centaurus System, one was
somewhere in Sirius, one was in a hospital, and one lived
in the Soviet Union. The seventh, however, lived within a
few miles, on the outskirts of New York.

LANTANO, DAVID

That cinched, it. The gestalt, in Ackers' mind, locked
clearly in place, the image hardened to reality. He had half

expected, even prayed to see Lantano's card brought up.

"Here's your pick-up," he said shakily to the game-playing cops. "Better get as large a team together as possible, this one won't be easy." Momentously, he added: "Maybe I'd better come along."

BEAM REACHED the anteroom of his lab as the ancient figure of Paul Tirol disappeared out the street door and onto the dark sidewalk. The young woman, trotting ahead of him, had climbed into a parked car and started it forward; as Tirol emerged, she swept him up and at once departed.

Panting, Beam stood impotently collecting himself on the deserted pavement. The ersatz t-v unit was gone; now he had nothing. Aimlessly, he began to run down the street. His heels echoed loudly in the cold silence. No sign of them; no sign of anything.

"I'll be damned," he said, with almost religious awe. The unit—a robot device of obvious complexity—clearly belonged to Paul Tirol; as soon as it had identified his presence it had sprinted gladly to him. For . . . protection?

It had killed Heimie; and it belonged to Tirol. So, by a novel and indirect method, Tirol had murdered his employee, his Fifth Avenue front man. At a rough guess, such a highly-organized robot would cost in the neighborhood of a hundred thousand dollars.

A lot of money, considering that murder was the easiest of criminal acts. Why not hire an itinerant goon with a crowbar?

Beam started slowly back toward his lab. Then, abruptly, he changed his mind and turned in the direction of the business area. When a free-wheeling cab came by, he hailed it and clambered in.

"Where to, sport?" the starter at cab relay asked. City cabs were guided by remote control from one central source.

He gave the name of a specific bar. Settling back against the seat he pondered. Anybody could commit a murder; an expensive, complicated machine wasn't necessary.

The machine had been built to do something else. The murder of Heimie Rosenburg was incidental.

•   •   •

AGAINST the nocturnal skyline, a huge stone residence loomed. Ackers inspected it from a distance. There were no lights burning; everything was locked up tight. Spread out before the house was an acre of grass. David Lantano was probably the last person on Earth to own an acre of grass outright; it was less expensive to buy an entire planet in some other system.

"Let's go," Ackers commanded; disgusted by such opulence, he deliberately trampled through a bed of roses on his way up the wide porch steps. Behind him flowed the team of shock-police.

"Gosh," Lantano rumbled, when he had been roused from his bed. He was a kindly-looking, rather youthful fat man, wearing now an abundant silk dressing robe. He would have seemed more in place as director of a boy's summer camp; there was an expression of perpetual good-humor on his soft, sagging face. "What's wrong, officer?"

Ackers loathed being called officer. "You're under arrest," he stated.

"Me?" Lantano echoed feebly. "Hey, officer, I've got lawyers to take care of these things." He yawned voluminously. "Care for some coffee?" Stupidly, he began puttering around his front room, fixing a pot.

IT HAD BEEN years since Ackers had splurged and bought himself a cup of coffee. With Terran land covered by dense industrial and residential installations there was no room for crops, and coffee had refused to "take" in any other system. Lantano probably grew his somewhere on an illicit plantation in South America—the pickers probably believed they had been transported to some remote colony.

"No thanks," Ackers said. "Let's get going."

Still dazed, Lantano plopped himself down in an easy chair and regarded Ackers with alarm. "You're serious." Gradually his expression faded; he seemed to be drifting back to sleep. "Who?" he murmured distantly.

"Heimie Rosenburg."

"No kidding." Lantano shook his head listlessly. "I always wanted him in my company. Heimie's got real charm. Had, I mean."

It made Ackers nervous to remain here in the vast lush

mansion. The coffee was heating, and the smell of it tickled his nose. And, heaven forbid—there on the table was a basket of *apricots*.

"Peaches," Lantano corrected, noticing his fixed stare. "Help yourself."

"Where—did you get them?"

LANTANO shrugged. "Synthetic dome. Hydroponics. I forget where . . . I don't have a technical mind."

"You know what the fine is for possessing natural fruit?"

"Look," Lantano said earnestly, clasping his mushy hands together. "Give me the details on this affair, and I'll prove to you I had nothing to do with it. Come on, officer."

"Ackers," Ackers said.

"Okay, Ackers. I thought I recognized you, but I wasn't sure; didn't want to make a fool of myself. When was Heimie killed?"

Grudgingly, Ackers gave him the pertinent information.

For a time Lantano was silent. Then, slowly, gravely, he said: "You better look at those seven cards again. One of those fellows isn't in the Sirius System . . . he's back here."

Ackers calculated the chances of successfully banishing a man of David Lantano's importance. His organization—Interplan Export—had fingers all over the galaxy; there'd be search crews going out like bees. But nobody went out banishment distance. The condemned, temporarily ionized, rendered in terms of charged particles of energy, radiated outward at the velocity of light. This was an experimental technique that had failed; it worked only one way.

"Consider," Lantano said thoughtfully. "If I *was* going to hill Heimie—*would I do it myself?* You're not being logical, Ackers. I'd send somebody." He pointed a fleshy finger at Ackers. "You imagine I'd risk my own life? I know you pick up everybody . . . you usually turn up enough specifications."

"We have ten on you," Ackers said briskly.

"So you're going to banish me?"

"If you're guilty, you'll have to face banishment like

anyone else. Your particular prestige has no bearing."

• • •

NETTLED, Ackers said: "Obviously, you'll be released. You'll have plenty of opportunity to prove your innocence; you can question each of the ten specifications in turn."

He started to go on and describe the general process of court procedure employed in the twenty-first century, but something made him pause. David Lantano and his chair seemed to be gradually sinking into the floor. Was it an illusion? Blinking Ackers rubbed his eyes and peered. At the same time, one of the policemen yelped a warning of dismay; Lantano was quietly leaving them.

"Come back!" Ackers demanded; he leaped forward and grabbed hold of the chair. Hurriedly, one of his men shorted out the power supply of the building; the chair ceased descending and groaned to a halt. Only Lantano's head was visible above the floor level. He was almost entirely submerged in a concealed escape shaft.

"What seedy, useless—" Ackers began.

"I know," Lantano admitted, making no move to drag himself up. He seemed resigned; his mind was again off in clouds of contemplation. "I hope we can clear all this up. Evidently I'm being framed. Tirol got somebody who looks like me, somebody to go in and murder Heimie."

Ackers and the police crew helped him up from his depressed chair. He gave no resistance; he was too deep in his brooding.

THE CAB let Leroy Beam off in front of the bar. To his right, in the next block, was the Interior Building ... and, on the sidewalk, the opaque blob that was Harvey Garth's propaganda booth.

Entering the bar, Beam found a table in the back and seated himself. Already he could pick up the faint, distorted murmur of Garth's reflections. Garth, speaking to himself in a directionless blur, was not yet aware of him.

"Banish it," Garth was saying. "Banish all of them. Bunch of crooks and thieves." Garth, in the miasma of his booth, was rambling vitriologically.

"What's going on?" Beam asked. "What's the latest?"

Garth's monologue broke off as he focussed his attention on Beam. "You in there? In the bar?"

"I want to find out about Heimie's death."

"Yes," Garth said. "He's dead; the files are moving, kicking out cards."

"When I left Heimie's apartment," Beam said, "they had turned up six specifications." He punched a button on the drink selector and dropped in a token.

"That must have been earlier," Garth said; "they've got more."

"How many?"

"Ten in all."

TEN. That was usually enough. And all ten of them laid out by a robot device ... a little procession of hints strewn along its path: between the concrete side of the building and the dead body of Heimie Rosenburg.

"That's lucky," he said speculatively. "Helps out Ackers."

"Since you're paying me," Garth said, "I'll tell you the rest. They've already gone out on their pick-up; Ackers went along."

Then the device had been successful. Up to a point, at least. He was sure of one thing: the device should have been out of the apartment. Tirol hadn't known about Heimie's death rattle; Heimie had been wise enough to do the installation privately.

Had the rattle not brought persons into the apartment, the device would have scuttled out and returned to Tirol. Then, no doubt, Tirol would have detonated it. Nothing would remain to indicate that a machine could lay down a trail of synthetic clues: blood type, fabric, pipe tobacco, hair ... all the rest, and all spurious.

"Who's the pick-up on?" Beam asked.

"David Lantano."

Beam winced. "Naturally. That's what the whole thing's about; he's being framed!"

GARTH WAS indifferent; he was a hired employee, stationed by the pool of independent researchers to syphon information from the Interior Department. He had no actual interest in politics; his *Banish It!* was sheer window-dressing.

THE UNRECONSTRUCTED M   153

"I know it's a frame," Beam said, "and so does Lantano. But neither of us can prove it . . . unless Lantano has an absolutely airtight alibi."

"Banish it," Garth murmured, reverting to his routine. A small group of late-retiring citizens had strolled past his booth, and he was masking his conversation with Beam. The conversation, directed to the one listener, was inaudible to everyone else; but it was better not to take risks. Sometimes, very close to the booth, there was an audible feedback of the signal.

Hunched over his drink, Leroy Beam contemplated the various items he could try. He could inform Lantano's organization, which existed relatively intact . . . but the result would be epic civil war. And, in addition, he didn't really care if Lantano was framed; it was all the same to him. Sooner or later one of the big slavers had to absorb the other: cartel is the natural conclusion of big business. With Lantano gone, Tirol would painlessly swallow his organization; everybody would be working at his desk as always.

ON THE other hand, there might someday be a device—now half-completed in Tirol's basement—that left a trail of *Leroy Beam* clues. Once the idea caught on, there was no particular end.

"And I had the damn thing," he said fruitlessly. "I hammered on it for five hours. It was a t-v unit, then, but it was still the device that killed Heimie."

"You're positive it's gone?"

"It's not only gone—it's out of existence. Unless she wrecked the car driving Tirol home."

"She?" Garth asked.

"The woman." Beam pondered; "she saw it. Or she knew about it; she was with him." But, unfortunately, he had no idea who the woman might be.

"What'd she look like?" Garth asked.

"Tall, mahogany hair. Very nervous mouth."

"I didn't realize she was working with him openly. They must have really needed the device." Garth added: "You didn't identify her? I guess there's no reason why you should; she's kept out of sight."

"Who is she?"

"That's Ellen Ackers."

• • •

BEAM LAUGHED sharply. "And she's driving Paul Tirol around?"

"She's—well, she's driving Tirol around, yes. You can put it that way."

"How long?"

"I thought you were in on it. She and Ackers split up; that was last year. But he wouldn't let her leave; he wouldn't give her a divorce. Afraid of the publicity. Very important to keep up respectability . . . keep the shirt fully stuffed."

"He knows about Paul Tirol and her?"

"Of course not. He knows she's—spiritually hooked up. But he doesn't care . . . as long as she keeps it quiet. It's his position he's thinking about."

"If Ackers found out," Beam murmured. "If he saw the link between his wife and Tirol . . . he'd ignore his ten interoffice memos. He'd *want* to haul in Tirol. The hell with the evidence; he could always collect that later." Beam pushed away his drink; the glass was empty, anyhow. "Where is Ackers?"

"I told you. Out at Lantano's place, picking him up."

"He'd come back here? He wouldn't go home?"

"Naturally he'd come back here." Garth was silent a moment. "I see a couple of Interior vans turning into the garage ramp. That's probably the pick-up crew returning."

Beam waited tensely. "Is Ackers along?"

"Yes, he's there. *Banish It!*" Garth's voice rose in stentorian frenzy. *"Banish the system of Banishment! Root out the crooks and pirates!"*

Sliding to his feet, Beam left the bar.

A DULL LIGHT showed in the rear of Edward Ackers' apartment: probably the kitchen light. The front door was locked. Standing in the carpeted hallway, Beam skillfully tilted with the door mechanism. It was geared to respond to specific neural patterns: those of it's owners and a limited circle of friends. For him there was no activity.

Kneeling down, Beam switched on a pocket oscillator and started sine wave emission. Gradually, he increased the frequency. At perhaps 150,000 cps the lock guiltily clicked; that was all he needed. Switching the oscillator off, he rummaged through his supply of skeleton patterns until he located the closet cylinder. Slipped into the turret of the oscillator, the cylinder emitted a synthetic neural pattern close enough to the real thing to affect the lock.

The door swung open. Beam entered.

In half-darkness the living room seemed modest and tasteful. Ellen Ackers was an adequate housekeeper. Beam listened. Was she home at all? And if so, where? Awake? Asleep?

He peeped into the bedroom. There was the bed, but nobody was in it.

If she wasn't here she was at Tirol's. But he didn't intend to follow her; this was as far as he cared to risk.

HE INSPECTED the dining room. Empty. The kitchen was empty, too. Next came an upholstered general-purpose rumpus room; on one side was a gaudy bar and on the other a wall-to-wall couch. Tossed on the couch was a woman's coat, purse, gloves. Familiar clothes: Ellen Ackers had worn them. So she had come here after leaving his research lab.

The only room left was the bathroom. He fumbled with the knob; it was locked from the inside. There was no sound, but somebody was on the other side of the door. He could sense her in there.

"Ellen," he said, against the panelling. "Mrs. Ellen Ackers; is that you?"

No answer. He could sense her not making any sound at all: a stifled, frantic silence.

While he was kneeling down, fooling with his pocketful of magnetic lock-pullers, an explosive pellet burst through the door at head level and splattered into the plaster of the wall beyond.

Instantly the door flew open; there stood Ellen Ackers, her face distorted with fright. One of her husband's government pistols clenched in her small, bony hand. She was less than a foot from him. Without getting up, Beam grabbed her wrist; she fired over his head, and then the two of them deteriorated into harsh, labored breathing.

"COME ON," Beam managed finally. The nozzle of the gun was literally brushing the top of his head. To kill him, she would have to pull the pistol back against her. But he didn't let her; he kept hold of her wrist until finally, reluctantly, she dropped the gun. It clattered to the floor and he got stiffly up.

"You were sitting down," she whispered, in a stricken, accusing voice.

"Kneeling down: picking the lock. I'm glad you aimed for my brain." He picked up the gun and succeeded in getting it into his overcoat pocket; his hands were shaking.

Ellen Ackers gazed at him starkly; her eyes were huge and dark, and her face was an ugly white. Her skin had a dead cast, as if it were artificial, totally dry, thoroughly sifted with talc. She seemed on the verge of hysteria; a harsh, muffled shudder struggled up inside her, lodging finally in her throat. She tried to speak but only a rasping noise came out.

"Gee, lady," Beam said, embarrassed. "Come in the kitchen and sit down."

She stared at him as if he had said something incredible or obscene or miraculous; he wasn't sure which.

"Come on." He tried to take hold of her arm but she jerked frantically away. She had on a simple green suit, and in it she looked very nice; a little too thin and terribly tense, but still attractive. She had on expensive earrings, an imported stone that seemed always in motion... but otherwise her outfit was austere.

"You—were the man at the lab," she managed, in a brittle, choked voice.

"I'M LEROY BEAM. An independent." Awkwardly guiding her, he led her into the kitchen and seated her at the table. She folded her hands in front of her and studied them fixedly; the bleak boniness of her face seemed to be increasing rather than receding. He felt uneasy.

"Are you all right?" he asked.

She nodded.

"Cup of coffee?" He began searching the cupboards for a bottle of Venusian-grown coffee substitute. While he was looking, Ellen Ackers said tautly: "You better go in there. In the bathroom. I don't think he's dead, but he might be."

Beam raced into the bathroom. Behind the plastic

shower curtain was an opaque shape. It was Paul Tirol, lying wadded up in the tub, fully clothed. He was not dead but he had been struck behind the left ear and his scalp was leaking a slow, steady trickle of blood. Beam took his pulse, listened to his breathing, and then straightened up.

At the doorway Ellen Ackers materialized, still pale with fright. "Is he? Did I kill him?"

"He's fine."

VISIBLY, she relaxed. "Thank God. It happened so fast—he stepped ahead of me to take the *M* inside his place, and then I did it. I hit him as lightly as I could. He was so interested in it...he forgot about me." Words spilled from her, quick, jerky sentences, punctuated by rigid tremors of her hands. "I lugged him back in the car and drove here; it was all I could think of."

"What are you in this for?"

Her hysteria rose in a spasm of convulsive muscle-twitching. "It was all planned—I had *everything* worked out. As soon as I got hold of it I was going to—" She broke off.

"Blackmail Tirol?" he asked, fascinated.

She smiled weakly. "No, not Paul. It was Paul who gave me the idea...it was his first idea, when his researchers showed him the thing. The—*unreconstructed M*, he calls it. *M* stands for machine. He means it can't be educated, morally corrected."

Incredulous, Beam said: "You were going to blackmail your husband."

Ellen Ackers nodded. "So he'd let me leave."

Suddenly Beam felt sincere respect for her. "My God—the rattle. Heimie didn't arrange that; *you* did. So the device would be trapped in the apartment."

"Yes," she agreed. "I was going to pick it up. But Paul showed up with other ideas; he wanted it, too."

"What went haywire? You have it, don't you?"

Silently she indicated the linen closet. "I stuffed it away when I heard you."

Beam opened the linen closet. Resting primly on the neatly-folded towels was a small, familiar, portable t-v unit.

"It reverted," Ellen said, from behind him, in an utterly

defeated monotone. "As soon as I hit Paul it changed. For half an hour I've been trying to get it to shift. It won't. It'll stay that way forever."

III

BEAM WENT to the telephone and called a doctor. In the bathroom, Tirol groaned and feebly thrashed his arms. He was beginning to return to consciousness.

"Was that necessary?" Ellen Ackers demanded. "The doctor—did you have to call?"

Beam ignored her. Bending, he lifted the portable t-v unit and held it in his hands; he felt its weight move up his arms like a slow, leaden fatigue. The ultimate adversary, he thought; too stupid to be defeated. It was worse than an animal. It was a rock, solid and dense, lacking all qualities. Except, he thought, the quality of determination. It was determined to persist, to survive; a rock with will. He felt as if he were holding up the universe, and he put the unreconstructed M down.

FROM BEHIND him Ellen said: "It drives you crazy." Her voice had regained tone. She lit a cigaret with a silver cigaret lighter and then shoved her hands in the pockets of her suit.

"Yes," he said.

"There's nothing you can do, is there? You tried to get it open before. They'll patch Paul up, and he'll go back to his place, and Lantano will be banished—" She took a deep shuddering breath. "And the Interior Department will go on as always."

"Yes," he said. Still kneeling, he surveyed the M. Now, with what he knew, he did not waste time struggling with it. He considered it impassively; he did not even bother to touch it.

In the bathroom, Paul Tirol was trying to crawl from the tub. He slipped back, cursed and moaned, and started his laborious ascent once again.

"Ellen?" his voice quavered, a dim and distorted sound, like dry wires rubbing.

"Take it easy," she said between her teeth; not moving

she stood smoking rapidly on her cigaret.

"Help me, Ellen," Tirol muttered. "Something happened to me...I don't remember what. Something hit me."

"He'll remember," Ellen said.

BEAM SAID: "I can take this thing to Ackers as it is. You can tell him what it's for—what it did. That ought to be enough; he won't go through with Lantano."

But he didn't believe it, either. Ackers would have to admit a mistake, a basic mistake, and if he had been wrong to pick up Lantano, he was ruined. And so, in a sense, was the whole system of delineation. It could be fooled; it had been fooled. Ackers was rigid, and he would go right on in a straight line: the hell with Lantano. The hell with abstract justice. Better to preserve cultural continuity and keep society running on an even keel.

"Tirol's equipment," Beam said. "Do you know where it is?"

She shrugged wildly. "What equipment?"

"This thing—" he jabbed at the M— "was made somewhere."

"Not here, Tirol didn't make it."

"All right," he said reasonably. They had perhaps six minutes more before the doctor and the emergency medical carrier arrived on rooftop. "Who did make it?"

"The alloy was developed on Bellatrix." She spoke jerkily, word by word. "The rind...forms a skin on the outside, a bubble that gets sucked in and out of a reservoir. That's its rind, the t-v shape. It sucks it back and becomes the M; it's ready to act."

"Who made it?" he repeated.

"A Bellatrix machine tool syndicate...a subsidary of Tirol's organization. They're made to be watchdogs. The big plantations on outplanets use them; they patrol. They get poachers."

BEAM SAID: "Then originally they're not set for one person."

"No."

"Then *who* set this for Heimie? Not a machine tool syndicate."

"That was done here."

He straightened up and lifted the portable t-v unit. "Let's go. Take me there, where Tirol had it altered."

For a moment the woman did not respond. Grabbing her arm he hustled her to the door. She gasped and stared at him mutely.

"Come on," he said, pushing her out into the hall. The portable t-v unit bumped against the door as he shut it; he held the unit tight and followed after Ellen Ackers.

THE TOWN was slatternly and run-down, a few retail stores, fuel station, bars and dance halls. It was two hours' flight from Greater New York and it was called Olum.

"Turn right," Ellen said listlessly. She gazed out at the neon signs and rested her arm on the window sill of the ship.

They flew above warehouses and deserted streets. Lights were few. At an intersection Ellen nodded and he set the ship down on a roof.

Below them was a sagging, fly-specked wooden frame store. A peeling sign was propped up in the window: FULTON BROTHERS LOCKSMITHS. With the sign were doorknobs, locks, keys, saws, and spring-wound alarm clocks. Somewhere in the interior of the store a yellow night light burned fitfully.

"This way," Ellen said. She stepped from the ship and made her way down a flight of rickety wooden stairs. Beam laid the portable t-v unit on the floor of the ship, locked the doors, and then followed after the woman. Holding onto the railing, he descended to a back porch on which were trash cans and a pile of sodden newspapers tied with string. Ellen was unlocking a door and feeling her way inside.

First he found himself in a musty, cramped storeroom. Pipe and rolls of wire and sheets of metal were heaped everywhere; it was like a junkyard. Next came a narrow corridor and then he was standing in the entrance of a workshop. Ellen reached overhead and groped to find the hanging string of a light. The light clicked on. To the right was a long and littered workbench with a hand grinder at one end, a vise, a keyhole saw; two wooden stools were before the bench and half-assembled machinery was stacked on the floor in no apparent order. The workshop was chaotic, dusty, and archaic. On the wall was a threadbare blue coat hung from a nail: the workcoat of a machinist.

"Here," Ellen said, with bitterness. "This is where Paul had it brought. This outfit is owned by the Tirol organization; this whole slum is part of their holdings."

BEAM WALKED to the bench. "To have altered it," he said, "Tirol must have had a plate of Heimie's neural pattern." He overturned a heap of glass jars; screws and washers poured onto the pitted surface of the bench.

"He got it from Heimie's door," Ellen said, "He had Heimie's lock analyzed and Heimie's pattern inferred from the setting of the tumblers."

"And he had the M opened?"

"There's an old mechanic," Ellen said. "A little dried-up old man; he runs this shop. Patrick Fulton. He installed the bias on the M."

"A bias," Beam said, nodding.

"A bias against killing people. Heimie was the exception, for everybody else it took its protective form. Out in the wilds they would have set it for something else, not a t-v unit." She laughed, a sudden ripple close to hysteria. "Yes, that would have looked odd, it sitting out in a forest somewhere, a t-v unit. They would have made it into a rock or a stick."

"A rock," Beam said. He could imagine it. The M waiting, covered with moss, waiting for months, years, and then weathered and corroded, finally picking up the presence of a human being. Then the M ceasing to be a rock, becoming, in a quick blur of motion, a box one foot wide and two feet long. An oversized cracker box that started forward—

BUT THERE was something missing. "The fakery," he said. "Emitting flakes of paint and hair and tobacco. How did that come in?"

In a brittle voice Ellen said: "The landowner murdered the poacher, and he was culpable in the eyes of the law. So the M left clues. Claw marks. Animal blood. Animal hair."

"God," he said, revolted. "Killed by an animal."

"A bear, a wildcat—whatever was indigenous, it varied. The predator of the region, a natural death." With her toe she touched a cardboard carton under the workbench. "It's in there, it used to be, anyhow. The neural plate, the transmitter, the discarded parts of the M, the schematics."

The carton had been a shipping container for power packs. Now the packs were gone, and in their place was a carefully-wrapped inner box, sealed against moisture and insect infestation. Beam tore away the metal foil and saw that he had found what he wanted. He gingerly carried the contents out and spread them on the workbench among the soldering irons and drills.

"It's all there," Ellen said, without emotion.

"MAYBE," he said, "I can leave you out of this. I can take this and the t-v unit to Ackers and try it without your testimony."

"Sure," she said wearily.

"What are you going to do?"

"Well," she said, "I can't go back to Paul, so I guess there's not much I can do."

"The blackmail bit was a mistake," he said.

Her eyes glowed. "Okay."

"If he releases Lantano," Beam said, "he'll be asked to resign. Then he'll probably give you your divorce, it won't be important to him one way or another."

"I—" she began. And then she stopped. Her face seemed to fade, as if the color and texture of her flesh was vanishing from within. She lifted one hand and half-turned, her mouth open and the sentence still unfinished.

Beam, reaching, slapped the overhead light out; the workroom winked into darkness. He had heard it too, heard it at the same time as Ellen Ackers. The rickety outside porch had creaked and now the slow, ponderous motion was past the storeroom and into the hall.

A HEAVY MAN, he thought. A slow-moving man, sleepy, making his way step by step, his eyes almost shut, his great body sagging beneath his suit. Beneath, he thought, his expensive tweed suit. In the darkness the man's shape was looming; Beam could not see it but he could sense it there, filling up the doorway as it halted. Boards creaked under its weight. In a daze he wondered if Ackers already knew, if his order had already been rescinded. Or had the man got out on his own, worked through his own organization?

The man, starting forward again, spoke in a deep, husky voice. "Ugh," Lantano said. "Damn it."

Ellen began to shriek. Beam still did not realize what it was; he was still fumbling for the light and wondering stupidly why it did not come on. He had smashed the bulb, he realized. He lit a match. The match went out and he grabbed for Ellen Ackers' cigaret lighter. It was in her purse, and it took him an agonized second to get it out.

The unreconstructed M was approaching them slowly, one receptor stalk extended. Again it halted, swiveled to the left until it was facing the workbench. It was not now in the shape of a portable t-v unit; it had retaken its crackerbox shape.

"The plate," Ellen Ackers whispered. "It responded to the plate."

THE M had been aroused by Heimie Rosenburg's looking for it. But Beam still felt the presence of David Lantano. The big man was still here in the room; the sense of heaviness, the proximity of weight and ponderousness had arrived with the machine, as it moved, sketched Lantano's existence. As he fixedly watched, the machine produced a fragment of cloth fabric and pressed it into a nearby heap of grid-mesh. Other elements, blood and tobacco and hair, were being produced, but they were too small for him to see. The machine pressed a heelmark into the dust of the floor and then projected a nozzle from its anterior section.

Her arm over her eyes, Ellen Ackers ran away. But the machine was not interested in her; revolving in the direction of the workbench it raised itself and fired. An explosive pellet, released by the nozzle, traveled across the workroom and entered the debris heaped across the bench. The pellet detonated; bits of wire and nails showered in particles.

Heimie's dead, Beam thought, and went on watching. The machine was searching for the plate, trying to locate and destroy the synthetic neural emission. It swiveled, lowered its nozzle hesitantly, and then fired again. Behind the workbench, the wall burst and settled into itself.

Beam, holding the cigaret lighter, walked toward the M. A receptor stalk waved toward him and the machine retreated. Its lines wavered, flowed, and then painfully reformed. For an interval, the device struggled with itself; then, reluctantly, the portable t-v unit again became visible. From the machine a high-pitched whine emerged, an anguished squeal. Conflicting stimuli were present; the machine was unable to make a decision.

THE MACHINE was developing a situation neurosis and the ambivalence of its response was destroying it. In a way its anguish had a human quality, but he could not feel sorry for it. It was a mechanical contraption trying to assume a posture of disguise and attack at the same time; the breakdown was one of relays and tubes, not of a living brain. And it had been a living brain into which it had fired its original pellet. Heimie Rosenburg was dead, and there were no more like him and no possibility that more could be assembled. He went over to the machine and nudged it onto its back with his foot.

The machine whirred snake-like and spun away. "Ugh, damn it!" it said. It showered bits of tobacco as it rolled off; drops of blood and flakes of blue enamel fell from it as it disappeared into the corridor. Beam could hear it moving about, bumping into the walls like a blind, damaged organism. After a moment he followed after it.

In the corridor, the machine was traveling in a slow circle. It was erecting around itself a wall of particles: cloth and hairs and burnt matches and bits of tobacco, the mass cemented together with blood.

"Ugh, damn it," the machine said in its heavy masculine voice. It went on working, and Beam returned to the other room.

"Where's a phone?" he said to Ellen Ackers.

She stared at him vacantly.

"It won't hurt you," he said. He felt dull and worn-out. "It's in a closed cycle. It'll go on until it runs down."

"It went crazy," she said, she shuddered.

"No," he said. "Regression. It's trying to hide."

From the corridor the machine said, "Ugh. Damn it."
Beam found the phone and called Edward Ackers.

BANISHMENT for Paul Tirol meant first a procession of
bands of darkness and then a protracted, infuriating
interval in which empty matter drifted randomly around
him, arranging itself into first one pattern and then
another.

The period between the time Ellen Ackers attacked
him and the time banishment sentence had been
pronounced was vague and dim in his mind. Like the
present shadows, it was hard to pin down.

He had—he thought—awakened in Ackers' apartment. Yes, that was it; and Leroy Beam was there, too. A
sort of transcendental Leroy Beam who hovered robustly
around, arranging everybody in configurations of his
choice. A doctor had come. And finally Edward Ackers
had shown up to face his wife and the situation.

Bandaged, and on his way into Interior, he had caught
a glimpse of a man going out. The ponderous, bulbous
shape of David Lantano, on his way home to his
luxurious stone mansion and acre of grass.

At sight of him Tirol had felt a goad of fear. Lantano
hadn't even noticed him; an acutely thoughtful expression
on his face, Lantano padded into a waiting car and
departed.

"YOU HAVE one thousand dollars," Edward Ackers was
saying wearily, during the final phase. Distorted, Ackers'
face bloomed again in the drifting shadows around Tirol,
an image of the man's last appearance. Ackers, too, was
ruined, but in a different way. "The law supplies you with
one thousand dollars to meet your immediate needs, also
you'll find a pocket dictionary of representative out-
system dialects."

Ionization itself was painless. He had no memory of it;
only a blank space darker than the blurred images on
either side.

"You hate me," he had declared accusingly, his last
words to Ackers. "I destroyed you. But . . . it wasn't you."

He had been confused. "Lantano. Maneuvered but not. How? You did . . ."

But Lantano had had nothing to do with it. Lantano had shambled off home, a withdrawn spectator throughout. The hell with Lantano. The hell with Ackers and Leroy Beam and—reluctantly—the hell with Mrs. Ellen Ackers.

"Wow," Tirol babbled, as his drifting body finally collected physical shape. "We had a lot of good times . . . didn't we, Ellen?"

And then a roaring hot field of sunlight was radiating down on him. Stupefied, he sat slumped over, limp and passive. Yellow, scalding sunlight . . . everywhere. Nothing but the dancing heat of it, blinding him, cowing him into submission.

He was sprawled in the middle of a yellow clay road. To his right was a baking, drying field of corn wilted in the midday heat. A pair of large, disreputable-looking birds wheeled silently overhead. A long way off was a line of blunted hills: ragged troughs and peaks that seemed nothing more than heaps of dust. At their base was a meager lump of man-made buildings.

At least he *hoped* they were man-made.

As he climbed shakily to his feet, a feeble noise drifted to his ears. Coming down the hot, dirty road was a car of some sort. Apprehensive and cautious, Tirol walked to meet it.

The driver was human, a thin, almost emaciated youth with pebbled black skin and a heavy mass of weed-colored hair. He wore a stained canvas shirt and overalls. A bent, unlit cigaret hung from his lower lip. The car was a combustion-driven model and had rolled out of the twentieth century; battered and twisted, it rattled to a halt as the driver critically inspected Tirol. From the car's radio yammered a torrent of tinny dance music.

"You a tax collector?" the driver asked.

"Certainly not," Tirol said, knowing the bucolic hostility toward tax collectors. But—he floundered. He couldn't confess that he was a banished criminal from Earth; that was an invitation to be massacred, usually in some picturesque way. "I'm an inspector," he announced, "Department of Health."

Satisfied, the driver nodded. "Lots of scuttly cutbeetle, these days. You fellows got a spray, yet? Losing one crop after another."

TIROL GRATEFULLY climbed into the car. "I didn't realize the sun was so hot," he murmured.

"You've got an accent," the youth observed, starting up the engine. "Where you from?"

"Speech impediment," Tirol said cagily. "How long before we reach town?"

"Oh, maybe an hour," the youth answered, as the car wandered lazily forward.

Tirol was afraid to ask the name of the planet. It would give him away. But he was consumed with the need to know. He might be two star-systems away or two million; he might be a month out of Earth or seventy years. Naturally, he had to get back; he had no intention of becoming a sharecropper on some backwater colony planet.

"Pretty swip," the youth said, indicating the torrent of noxious jazz pouring from the car radio. "That's Calamine Freddy and his Woolybear Creole Original Band. Know that tune?"

"No," Tirol muttered. The sun and dryness and heat made his head ache, and he wished to God he knew where he was.

THE TOWN was miserably tiny. The houses were dilapidated; the streets were dirt. A kind of domestic chicken roamed here and there, pecking in the rubbish. Under a porch a bluish quasi-dog lay sleeping. Perspiring and unhappy, Paul Tirol entered the bus station and located a schedule. A series of meaningless entries flashed by: names of towns. The name of the planet, of course, was not listed.

"What's the fare to the nearest port?" he asked the indolent official behind the ticket window.

The official considered. "Depends on what sort of port you want. Where you planning to go?"

"Toward Center," Tirol said. "Center" was the term used in out-systems for the Sol Group.

Dispassionately, the official shook his head. "No inter-system port around here."

Tirol was baffled. Evidently, he wasn't on the hub planet of this particular system. "Well," he said, "then the nearest interplan port."

The official consulted a vast reference book. "You want to go to which system-member?"

"Whichever one has the intersystem port," Tirol said patiently. He would leave from there.

"That would be Venus."

ASTONISHED, Tirol said: "Then this system—" He broke off, chagrined, as he remembered. It was the parochial custom in many out-systems, especially those a long way out, to name their member planets after the original nine. This one was probably called "Mars" or "Jupiter" or "Earth," depending on its position in the group. "Fine," Tirol finished. "One-way ticket to—Venus."

Venus, or what passed for Venus, was a dismal orb no larger than an asteroid. A bleak cloud of metallic haze hung over it, obscuring the sun. Except for mining and smelting operations the planet was deserted. A few dreary shacks dotted the barren countryside. A perpetual wind blew, scattering debris and trash.

But the intersystem port was here, the field which linked the planet to its nearest star-neighbor and, ultimately, with the balance of the universe. At the moment a giant freighter was taking ore.

Tirol entered the ticket office. Spreading out most of his remaining money he said: "I want a one-way ticket taking me toward center. As far as I can go."

The clerk calculated. "You care what class?"

"No," he said, mopping his forehead.

"How fast?"

"No."

The clerk said: "That'll carry you as far as the Betelgeuse System."

"Good enough," Tirol said, wondering what he did then. But at least he could contact his organization from there; he was already back in the charted universe. But now he was almost broke. He felt a prickle of icy fear, despite the heat.

THE HUB PLANET of the Betelgeuse System was called Plantagenet III. It was a thriving junction for passenger

carriers transporting settlers to undeveloped colony
planets. As soon as Tirol's ship landed he hurried across
the field to the taxi stand.

"Take me to Tirol Enterprises," he instructed, praying
there was an outlet here. There had to be, but it might be
operating under a front name. Years ago he lost track of
the particulars of his sprawling empire.

"Tirol Enterprises," the cab driver repeated thoughtfully. "Nope, no such outfit, mister."

Stunned, Tirol said: "Who does the slaving around
here?"

The driver eyed him. He was a wizened, dried-up little
man with glasses; he peered turtle-wise, without compassion. "Well," he said, "I've been told you can get carried
out-system without papers. There's a shipping contrac-
tor ... called—" He reflected. Tirol, trembling, handed
him a last bill.

"The Reliable Export-Import," the driver said.

That was one of Lantano's fronts. In horror Tirol said:
"And that's it?"

The driver nodded.

DAZED, Tirol moved away from the cab. The buildings of
the field danced around him; he settled down on a bench
to catch his breath. Under his coat his heart pounded
unevenly. He tried to breathe, but his breath caught
painfully in his throat. The bruise on his head where Ellen
Ackers had hit him began to throb. It was true, and he was
gradually beginning to understand and believe it. He was
not going to get to Earth; he was going to spend the rest of
his life here on this rural world, cut off from his
organization and everything he had built up over the
years.

And, he realized, as he sat struggling to breathe, the
rest of his life was not going to be very long.

He thought about Heimie Rosenburg.

"Betrayed," he said, and coughed wrackingly. "You
betrayed me. You hear that? Because of you I'm here. It's
your fault; I never should have hired you."

He thought about Ellen Ackers. "You too," he gasped,
coughing. Sitting on the bench he alternately coughed
and gasped and thought about the people who had
betrayed him. There were hundreds of them.

THE LIVINGROOM of David Lantano's house was furnished in exquisite taste. Priceless late nineteenth century Blue Willow dishes lined the walls in a rack of wrought iron. At his antique yellow plastic and chrome table, David Lantano was eating dinner, and the spread of food amazed Beam even more than the house.

Lantano was in good humor and he ate with enthusiasm. His linen napkin was tucked under his chin and once, as he sipped coffee, he dribbled and belched. His brief period of confinement was over; he ate to make up for the ordeal.

He had been informed first by his own apparatus and now by Beam, that banishment had successfully carried Tirol past the point of return. Tirol would not be coming back and for that Lantano was thankful. He felt expansive toward Beam; he wished Beam would have something to eat.

Moodily, Beam said: "It's nice here."

"You could have something like this," Lantano said.

On the wall hung a framed folio of ancient paper protected by helium-filled glass. It was the first printing of a poem of Ogden Nash, a collector's item that should have been in a museum. It aroused in Beam a mixed feeling of longing and aversion.

"Yes," Beam said. "I could have this." This, he thought, or Ellen Ackers or the job at Interior or perhaps all three at once. Edward Ackers had been retired on pension and he had given his wife a divorce. Lantano was out of jeopardy. Tirol had been banished. He wondered what he did want.

"You could go a long way," Lantano said sleepily.

"As far as Paul Tirol?"

Lantano chuckled and yawned.

"I wonder if he left any family," Beam said. "Any children." He was thinking about Heimie.

LANTANO reached across the table toward the bowl of fruit. He selected a peach and carefully brushed it against the sleeve of his robe. "Try a peach," he said.

"No thanks," Beam said irritably.

Lantano examined the peach but he did not eat it. The

peach was made of wax; the fruit in the bowl was imitation. He was not really as rich as he pretended, and many of the artifacts about the living room were fakes. Each time he offered fruit to a visitor he took a calculated risk. Returning the peach to the bowl he leaned back in his chair and sipped his coffee.

If Beam did not have plans at least *he* had, and with Tirol gone the plans had a better than even chance of working out. He felt peaceful. Someday, he thought, and not too far off, the fruit in the bowl would be real.

The War with the Fnools

CAPTAIN EDGAR LIGHTFOOT of CIA said, "Darn it, the Fnools are back again, Major. They've taken over Provo, Utah."

With a groan, Major Hauk signaled his secretary to bring him the Fnool dossier from the locked archives. "What form are they assuming this time?" he asked briskly.

"Tiny real-estate salesmen," Lightfoot said.

Last time, Major Hauk reflected, it had been filling station attendants. That was the thing about the Fnools. When one took a particular shape they all took that shape. Of course, it made detection for CIA fieldmen much easier. But it did make the Fnools look absurd, and Hauk did not enjoy fighting an absurd enemy; it was a quality which tended to diffuse over both sides and even up to his own office.

"Do you think they'd come to terms?" Hauk said, half-rhetorically. "We could afford to sacrifice Provo, Utah, if they'd be willing to circumscribe themselves there. We could even add those portions of Salt Lake City which are paved with hideous old red brick."

Lightfoot said, "Fnools never compromise, Major. Their goal is Sol System domination. For all time."

Leaning over Major Hauk's shoulder, Miss Smith said, "Here is the Fnool dossier, sir." With her free hand she pressed the top of her blouse against her in a gesture indicating either advanced tuberculosis or advanced modesty. There were certain indications that it was the latter.

"Miss Smith," Major Hauk complained, "here are the Fnools trying to take over the Sol System and I'm handed

172

their dossier by a woman with a forty-two inch bosom. Isn't that a trifle schizophrenic—for me, at least?" He carefully averted his eyes from her, remembering his wife and the two children. "Wear something else from here on out," he told her. "Or swaddle yourself. I mean, my God, let's be reasonable: let's be realistic."

"Yes, Major," Miss Smith said. "But remember, I was selected at random from the CIA employees pool. I didn't *ask* to be your secretary."

With Captain Lightfoot beside him, Major Hauk laid out the documents that made up the Fnool dossier.

In the Smithsonian there was a huge Fnool, standing three feet high, stuffed and preserved in a natural habitat-type cubicle. School children for years had marveled at this Fnool, which was shown with pistol aimed at Terran innocents. By pressing a button, the school children caused the Terrans (not stuffed but imitation) to flee, whereupon the Fnool extinguished them with its advanced solar-powered weapon...and the exhibit reverted to its original stately scene, ready to begin all over again.

Major Hauk had seen the exhibit, and it made him uneasy. The Fnools, he had declared time and time again, were no joke. But there was something about a Fnool that—well, a Fnool was an idiotic life form. That was the basis of it. No matter what it imitated it retained its midget aspect; a Fnool looked like something given away free at supermarket openings, along with balloons and moist purple orchids. No doubt, Major Hauk had ruminated, it was a survival factor. It disarmed the Fnool's opponents. Even the name. It was just not possible to take them seriously, even at this very moment when they were infesting Provo, Utah, in the form of miniature real-estate salesmen.

Hauk instructed, "Capture a Fnool in this current guise, Lightfoot, bring it to me and I'll parley. I feel like capitulating, this time. I've been fighting them for twenty years now. I'm worn out."

"If you get one face to face with you," Lightfoot cautioned, "it may successfully imitate you and that would be the end. We would have to incinerate both of you, just to be on the safe side."

Gloomily, Hauk said, "I'll set up a key password situation with you right now, Captain. The word is *masticate*. I'll use it in a sentence . . . for instance, 'I've got to thoroughly masticate these data.' The Fnool won't know that—correct?"

"Yes, Major," Captain Lightfoot sighed and left the CIA office at once, hurrying to the 'copter field across the street to begin his trip to Provo, Utah.

But he had a feeling of foreboding.

WHEN his 'copter landed at the end of Provo Canyon on the outskirts of the town, he was at once approached by a two-foot-high man in a gray business suit carrying a briefcase.

"Good morning, sir," the Fnool piped. "Care to look at some choice lots, all with unobstructed views? Can be subdivided into—"

"Get in the 'copter," Lightfoot said, aiming his Army-issue .45 at the Fnool.

"Listen, my friend," the Fnool said, in a jolly tone of voice. "I can see you've never really given any hard-headed thought to the meaning of our race having landed on your planet. Why don't we step into the office a moment and sit down?" The Fnool indicated a nearby small building in which Lightfoot saw a desk and chairs. Over the office there was a sign:

EARLY BIRD
LAND DEVELOPMENT
INCORPORATED

"'The early bird catches the worm,'" the Fnool declared. "And the spoils go to the winner, Captain Lightfoot. By nature's laws, if we manage to infest your planet and pre-empt you, we've got all the forces of evolution and biology on our side." The Fnool beamed cheerily.

Lightfoot said, "There's a CIA major back in Washington, D.C. who's on to you."

"Major Hauk has defeated us twice," the Fnool admitted. "We respect him. But he's a voice crying in the wilderness, in this country, at least. You know perfectly

well, Captain, that the average American viewing that
exhibit at the Smithsonian merely smiles in a tolerant
fashion. There's just no awareness of the *menace*."

By now two other Fnools, also in the form of tiny
real-estate salesmen in gray business suits carrying
briefcases, had approached. "Look," one said to the
other. "Charley's captured a Terran."

"No," its companion disagreed, "the Terran captured
him."

"All three of you get in the CIA 'copter," Lightfoot
ordered, waving his .45 at them.

"You're making a mistake," the first Fnool said,
shaking its head. "But you're a young man; you'll mature
in time." It walked to the 'copter. Then, all at once, it spun
and cried, *"Death to the Terrans!"*

Its briefcase whipped up, a bolt of pure solar energy
whined past Lightfoot's right ear. Lightfoot dropped to
one knee and squeezed the trigger of the .45; the Fnool, in
the doorway of the 'copter, pitched head-forward and lay
with its briefcase beside it. The other two Fnools watched
as Lightfoot cautiously kicked the briefcase away.

"Young," one of the remaining Fnools said, "but with
quick reflexes. Did you see the way he dropped on one
knee?"

"Terrans are no joke," the other agreed. "We've got an
uphill battle ahead of us."

"As long as you're here," the first of the remaining
Fnools said to Lightfoot, "why don't you put a small
deposit down on some valuable unimproved land we've
got a listing for? I'll be glad to run you out to have a look
at it. Water and electricity available at a slight additional
cost."

"Get in the 'copter," Lightfoot repeated, aiming his gun
steadily at them.

IN BERLIN, an *Oberstleutnant* of the SHD, the
Sicherheitsdienst—the West German Security Service—
approaching his commanding officer, saluted in what is
termed Roman style and said, *"General, die Fnoolen sind
wieder zuruck. Was sollen wir jetz tun?"*

"The Fnools are *back*?" Hochflieger said, horrified.
"Already? But it was only three years ago that we

uncovered their network and eradicated them." Jumping
to his feet General Hochflieger paced about his cramped
temporary office in the basement of the *Bundesrat
Gebaude*, his large hands clasped behind his back. "And
what guise this time? Assistant Ministers of Domestic
Finance, as before?"

"No sir," the *Oberstleutnant* said. "They have come as
gear inspectors of the VW works. Brown suit, clipboard,
thick glasses, middle-aged. Fussy. And, as before, *nur*
six-tenth of a meter high."

"What I detest about the Fnools," Hochflieger said, "is
their ruthless use of science in the service of destruction,
especially their medical techniques. They almost defeated
us with that virus infection suspended in the gum on the
backs of multi-color commemorative stamps."

"A desperate weapon," his subordinate agreed, "but
rather too fantastic to be successful, ultimately. This time
they'll probably rely on crushing force combined with an
absolutely snychronized timetable."

"Selbsverstandlich," Hochflieger agreed. "But we've
nonetheless got to react and defeat them. Inform Terpol."
That was the Terra-wide organization of counter-
intelligence with headquarters on Luna. "Where, specifically, have they been detected?"

"In Schweinfurt only, so far."

"Perhaps we should obliterate the Schweinfurt area."

"They'll only turn up elsewhere."

"True." Hochflieger brooded. "What we must do is
pursue Operation *Hundefutter* to successful culmina-
tion." *Hundefutter* had developed for the West German
Government a sub-species of Terrans six-tenths of a
meter high and capable of assuming a variety of forms.
They would be used to penetrate the network of Fnool
activity and destroy it from within. *Hundefutter*, financed
by the Krupp family, had been held in readiness for just
this moment.

"I'll activate *Kommando Einsatzgruppe II*," his
subordinate said. "As counter-Fnools they can begin to
drop behind Fnool lines near the Schweinfurt area
immediately. By nightfall the situation should be in our
hands."

"Gruss Gott," Hochfleiger prayed, nodding. "Well, get

the *kommando* started, and we'll keep our ears open to see how it proceeds."

If it failed, he realized, more desperate measures would have to be initiated.

The survival of our race is at stake, Hochflieger said to himself. The next four thousand years of history will be determined by the brave act of a member of the SHD at this hour. Perhaps myself.

He paced about, meditating on that.

IN WARSAW the local chief of the People's Protective Agency for Preserving the Democratic Process—the NNBNDL—read the coded teletype dispatch several times as he sat at his desk drinking tea and eating a late breakfast of sweet rolls and Polish ham. This time disguised as chess players, Serge Nicov said to himself. And each Fnool making use of the queen's pawn opening, Qp to Q3 . . . a weak opening, he reflected, especially against Kp to K4, even if they draw white. But—

Still a potentially dangerous situation.

On a piece of official stationery he wrote *select out class of chess players employing queen's pawn opening.* For Invigorating Forest-renewal Team, he decided. Fnools are small, but they can plant saplings . . . we must get some use out of them. Seeds; they can plant sunflower seeds for our tundra-removal vegetable-oil venture.

A year of hard physical work, he decided, and they'll think twice before they invade Terra again.

On the other hand, we could make a deal with them, offer them an alternative to invigorating forest-renewal activity. They could enter the Army as a special brigade and be used in Chile, in the rugged mountains. Being only sixty-one centimeters high, many of them could be packed into a single nuclear sub for transport . . . but can Fnools be trusted?

The thing he hated most about Fnools—and he had learned to know them in their previous invasions of Terra—was their deceitfulness. Last time they had taken the physical form of a troupe of ethnic dancers . . . and what dancers they had turned out to be. They had massacred an audience in Leningrad before anyone could intervene, men, women and children all dead on the spot by weapons of ingenious design and sturdy although monotonous construction which had masqueraded as folk-instruments of a five-stringed variety.

It could never happen again; all Democratic lands were alert, now; special youth groups had been set up to keep vigil. But something new—such as this chess-player deception—could succeed as well, especially in small towns in the East republics, where chess players were enthusiatically welcomed.

From a hidden compartment in his desk Serge Nicov brought out the special non-dial phone, picked up the receiver and said into the mouthpiece, "Fnools back, in North Caucasus area. Better get as many tanks as possible lined up to accept their advance as they attempt to spread out. Contain them and then cut directly through their center, bisecting them repeatedly until they're splintered and can be dealt with in small bands."

"Yes, Political Officer Nicov."

Serge Nicov hung up and resumed eating his—now cold—late breakfast.

As CAPTAIN LIGHTFOOT piloted the 'copter back to Washington, D.C. one of the two captured Fnools said, "How is it that no matter what guise we come in, you Terrans can always detect us? We've appeared on your planet as filling station attendants, Volkswagen gear inspectors, chess champions, folk singers complete with native instruments, minor government officials, and now real-estate salesmen—"

Lightfoot said, "It's your size."

"That concept conveys nothing to us."

"You're only two feet tall!"

The two Fnools conferred, and then the other Fnool patiently explained, "But size is relative. We have all the absolute qualities of Terrans embodied in our temporary forms, and according to obvious logic—"

"Look," Lightfoot said, "stand here next to me." The Fnool, in its gray business suit, carrying its briefcase, came cautiously up to stand beside him. "You just come up to my knee cap," Lightfoot pointed out. "I'm six feet high. You're only one-third as tall as I. In a group of Terrans you Fnools stand out like an egg in a barrel of kosher pickles."

"Is that a folk saying?" the Fnool asked. "I'd better write that down." From its coat pocket it produced a tiny ball point pen no longer than a match. "Egg in barrel of pickles. Quaint. I hope, when we've wiped out your civilization, that some of your ethnic customs will be preserved by our museums."

"I hope so, too," Lightfoot said, lighting a cigarette.

The other Fnool, pondering, said, "I wonder if there's any way we can grow taller. Is it a racial secret preserved by your people?" Noticing the burning cigarette dangling between Lightfoot's lips, the Fnool said, "Is that how you achieve unnatural height. By burning that stick of compressed dried vegetable fibers and inhaling the smoke?"

"Yes," Lightfoot said, handing the cigarette to the two-foot-high Fnool. "That's our secret. Cigarette-smoking makes you grow. We have all our offspring, especially teen-agers, smoke. Everyone that's young."

"I'm going to try it," the Fnool said to its companion. Placing the cigarette between its lips, it inhaled deeply.

Lightfoot blinked. Because the Fnool was now four feet high, and its companion instantly imitated it; both Fnools were twice as high as before. Smoking the cigarette had augmented the Fnools' height incredibly by two whole feet.

"Thank you," the now four foot-high real-estate salesman said to Lightfoot, in a much deeper voice than before. "We are certainly making bold strides, are we not?"

Nervously, Lightfoot said, "Gimme back the cigarette."

IN HIS office at the CIA building, Major Julius Hauk pressed a button on his desk, and Miss Smith alertly opened the door and entered the room, dictation pad in hand.

"Miss Smith," Major Hauk said, "Captain Lightfoot's away. Now I can tell you. The Fnools are going to win this time. As senior officer in charge of defeating them, I'm about to give up and go down to the bomb-proof shelter constructed for hopeless situations such as this."

"I'm sorry to hear that, sir," Miss Smith said, her long eyelashes fluttering. "I've enjoyed working for you."

"But you, too," Hauk explained. "*All* Terrans are wiped out; our defeat is planet-wide." Opening a drawer of his desk he brought out an unopened fifth of Bullock & Lade Scotch which he had been given as a birthday present. "I'm going to finish this B&L Scotch off first," he informed Miss Smith. "Will you join me?"

"No thank you, sir," Miss Smith said. "I'm afraid I don't drink, at least during the daylight hours."

Major Hauk drank for a moment from a dixie cup, then tried a little more from the bottle just to be sure it was Scotch all the way to the bottom. At last he put it down and said, "It's hard to believe that our backs could be put to the wall by creatures no larger than domestic orange-striped tomcats, but such is the case." He nodded courteously to Miss Smith. "I'm off for the concrete sub-surface bomb-proof shelter, where I hope to hold out after the general collapse of life as we know it."

"Good for you, Major Hauk," Miss Smith said, a little uneasily. "But are you—just going to *leave* me here to become a captive of the Fnools? I mean—" Her sharply pointed breasts quivered in becoming unison beneath her blouse. "It seems sort of mean."

"You have nothing to fear from the Fnools, Miss Smith," Major Hauk said. "After all, two feet tall—" He gestured. "Even a neurotic young woman could scarcely—" He laughed. "Really."

"But it's a terrible feeling," Miss Smith said, "to be abandoned in the face of what we know to be an unnatural enemy from another planet entirely."

"I tell you what," Major Hauk said thoughtfully. "Perhaps I'll break a series of strict CIA rulings and allow you to go below to the shelter with me."

Putting down her pad and pencil and hurrying over to him, Miss Smith breathed, "Oh, Major, how can I thank you!"

"Just come along," Major Hauk said, leaving the bottle of B&L Scotch behind in his haste, the situation being what it was.

Miss Smith clung to him as he made his way a trifle unsteadily down the corridor to the elevator.

"Drat that Scotch," he murmured. "Miss Smith, Vivian, you were wise not to touch it. Given the cortico-thalamic reaction we are all experiencing in the face of the Fnoolian peril, Scotch isn't the beneficial balm it generally is."

"Here," his secretary said, sliding under his arm to help prop him up as they waited for the elevator. "Try to stand firm, Major. It won't be long now."

"You have a point there," Major Hauk agreed. "Vivian, my dear."

THE ELEVATOR came at last. It was the self-service type.

"You're being really very kind to me," Miss Smith said, as the major pressed the proper button and the elevator began to descend.

"Well, it may prolong your life," Major Hauk agreed. "Of course, that far underground . . . the average temperature is much greater than at the Earth's surface. Like a deep mine shaft, it runs in the near-hundreds."

"But at least we'll be alive," Miss Smith pointed out.

Major Hauk removed his coat and tie. "Be prepared for the humid warmth," he told her. "Here, perhaps you would like to remove your coat."

"Yes," Miss Smith said, allowing him in his gentlemanly way to remove her coat.

The elevator arrived at the shelter. No one was there ahead of them, fortunately; they had the shelter all to themselves.

"It *is* stuffy down here," Miss Smith said as Major Hauk switched on one dim yellow light. "Oh dear." She stumbled over something in the gloom. "It's so hard to see." Again she stumbled over some object; this time she half-fell. "Shouldn't we have more light, Major?"

"What, and attract the Fnools?" In the dark, Major Hauk felt about until he located her; Miss Smith had toppled onto one of the shelter's many bunks and was groping about for her shoe.

"I think I broke the heel off," Miss Smith said.

"Well, at least you got away with your life," Major Hauk said. "If nothing else." In the gloom he began to assist her in removing her other shoe, it being worthless, now.

"How long will we be down here?" Miss Smith asked.

"As long as the Fnools are in control," Major Hauk

informed her. "You'd better change into radiation-proof garb in case the rotten little non-terrestrials try H-bombing the White House. Here, I'll take your blouse and skirt—there should be overalls somewhere around."

"You're being really kind to me," Miss Smith breathed, as she handed him her blouse and skirt. "I can't get over it."

"I think," Major Hauk said, "I'll change my mind and go back up for that Scotch; we'll be down here longer than I anticipated and we'll need something like that as the solitude frays our nerves. You stay here." He felt his way back to the elevator.

"Don't be gone long," Miss Smith called anxiously after him. "I feel terribly exposed and unprotected down here alone, and what is more I can't seem to find that radiation-proof garb you spoke of."

"Be right back," Major Hauk promised.

AT THE field opposite the CIA Building, Captain Lightfoot landed the 'copter with the two captive Fnools aboard. "Get moving," he instructed them, digging the muzzle of his Service .45 into their small ribs.

"It's because he's bigger than us, Len," one of the Fnools said to the other. "If we were the same size he wouldn't dare treat us this way. But now we understand—finally—the nature of the Terrans' superiority."

"Yes." the other Fnool said. "The mystery of twenty years has been cleared up."

"Four feet tall is still suspicious-looking," Captain Lightfoot said, but he was thinking, If they grow from two feet to four feet in one instant, just by smoking a cigarette, what's to stop them from growing two feet more? Then they'll be six feet and look exactly like us.

And it's all my fault, he said to himself miserably.

Major Hauk will destroy me, career-wise if not body-wise.

However, he continued on as best he could; the famous tradition of the CIA demanded it. "I'm taking you directly to Major Hauk," he told the two Fnools. "He'll know what to do with you."

When they reached Major Hauk's office, no one was there.

"This is strange," Captain Lightfoot said.

"Maybe Major Hauk has beaten a hasty retreat," one of the Fnools said. "Does this tall amber bottle indicate anything?"

"That's a tall amber bottle of Scotch," Lightfoot said, scrutinizing it. "And it indicates nothing. However—" he removed the cap—"I'll try it. Just to be on the safe side."

After he had tried it, he found the two Fnools staring at him intently.

"This is what Terrans deem drink," Lightfoot explained. "It would be bad for you."

"Possibly," one of the two Fnools said, "but while you were drinking from that bottle I obtained your .45 Service revolver. Hands up."

Lightfoot, reluctantly, raised his hands.

"Give us that bottle," the Fnool said. "And let us try it for ourselves; we will be denied nothing. For in point of fact, Terran culture lies open before us."

"Drink will put an end to you," Lightfoot said desperately.

"As that burning tube of aged vegetable matter did?" the nearer of the two Fnools said with contempt.

It and its companion drained the bottle as Lightfoot watched.

Sure enough, they now stood six feet high. And, he knew, everywhere in the world, all Fnools had assumed equal stature. Because of him, the invasion of the Fnools would this time be successful. He had destroyed Terra.

"Cheers," the first Fnool said.

"Down the hatch," the other said. "Ring-a-ding." They studied Lightfoot. "You've shrunk to our size."

"No, Len," the other said. "We have expanded to his."

"Then at last we're all equal," Len said. "We're finally a success. The magic defense of the Terrans—their unnatural size—has been eradicated."

AT THAT point a voice said, "Drop that .45 Service revolver." And Major Hauk stepped into the room behind the two thoroughly drunken Fnools.

"Well I'll be goddamned," the first Fnool mumbled. "Look, Len, it's the man most responsible for previously defeating us."

"And he's little," Len said. "Little, like us. We're all little, now. I mean, we're all huge; goddamn it, it's the same thing. Anyhow we're equal." It lurched toward Major Hauk—

Major Hauk fired. And the Fnool named Len dropped. It was absolutely undeniably dead. Only one of the captured Fnools remained.

"Edgar, they've increased in size," Major Hauk said, pale. "Why?"

"It's due to me," Lightfoot admitted. "First because of the cigarette, then second because of the Scotch—your Scotch, Major, that your wife gave you on your last birthday. I admit their now being the same size as us makes them undistinguishable from us... but consider this, sir. *What if they grew once more?*"

"I see your idea clearly," Major Hauk said, after a pause. "If eight feet tall, the Fnools would be as conspicuous as they were when—"

The captured Fnool made a dash for freedom.

Major Hauk fired, low, but it was too late; the Fnool was out into the corridor and racing toward the elevator.

"Get it!" Major Hauk shouted.

The Fnool reached the elevator and without hesitation pressed the button; some extra-terrestrial Fnoolian knowledge guided its hand.

"It's getting away," Lightfoot grated.

Now the elevator had come. "It's going down to the bomb-proof shelter," Major Hauk yelled in dismay.

"Good," Lightfoot said grimly. "We'll be able to capture it with no trouble."

"Yes, but—" Major Hauk began, and then broke off. "You're right, Lightfoot; we must capture it. Once out on the street—It would be like any other man in a gray business suit carrying a briefcase."

"How can it be made to grow again?" Lightfoot said, as he and Major Hauk descended by means of the stairs. "A cigarette started it, then the Scotch—both new to Fnools. What would complete their growth, make them a bizarre eight feet tall?" He racked his brain as they dashed down and down, until at last the concrete and steel entrance of the shelter lay before them.

The Fnool was already inside.

"That's, um, Miss Smith you hear," Major Hauk admitted. "She was, or rather actually, we were—well, we were taking refuge from the invasion down here."

Putting his weight against the door, Lightfoot swung it aside.

Miss Smith at once hopped up, ran toward them and a moment later clung to the two men, safe now from the Fnool. "Thank God," she gasped. "I didn't realize what it was until—" She shuddered.

"Major," Captain Lightfoot said, "I think we've stumbled on it."

Rapidly, Major Hauk said, "Captain, you get Miss Smith's clothes, I'll take care of the Fnool. There's no problem now."

The Fnool, eight feet high, came slowly toward them, its hands raised.

The Last of the Masters

CONSCIOUSNESS COLLECTED around him. He returned with reluctance; the weight of centuries, an unbearable fatigue, lay over him. The ascent was painful. He would have shrieked if there were anything to shriek with. And anyhow, he was beginning to feel glad.

Eight thousand times he had crept back thus, with ever-increasing difficulty. Someday he wouldn't make it. Someday the black pool would remain. But not this day. He was still alive; above the aching pain and reluctance came joyful triumph.

"Good morning," a bright voice said. "Isn't it a nice day? I'll pull the curtains and you can look out."

He could see and hear. But he couldn't move. He lay quietly and allowed the various sensations of the room to pour in on him. Carpets, wallpaper, tables, lamps, pictures. Desk and vidscreen. Gleaming yellow sunlight streamed through the window. Blue sky. Distant hills. Fields, buildings, roads, factories. Workers and machines.

Peter Green was busily straightening things, his young face wreathed with smiles. "Lots to do today. Lots of people to see you. Bills to sign. Decisions to make. This is Saturday. There will be people coming in from the remote sectors. I hope the maintenance crew has done a good job." He added quickly, "They have, of course. I talked to Fowler on my way over here. Everything's fixed up fine."

The youth's pleasant tenor mixed with the bright sunlight. Sounds and sights, but nothing else. He could feel nothing. He tried to move his arm but nothing happened.

"Don't worry," Green said, catching his terror. "They'll

186

soon be along with the rest. You'll be all right. You *have* to be. How could we survive without you?"

He relaxed. God knew, it had happened often enough before. Anger surged dully. Why couldn't they coordinate? Get it up all at once, not piecemeal. He'd have to change their schedule. Make them organize better.

Past the bright window a squat metal car chugged to a halt. Uniformed men piled out, gathered up heavy armloads of equipment, and hurried toward the main entrance of the building.

"Here they come," Green exclaimed with relief. "A little late, eh?"

"Another traffic tie-up," Fowler snorted, as he entered. "Something wrong with the signal system again. Outside flow got mixed up with the urban stuff; tied up on all sides. I wish you'd change the law."

Now there was motion all around him. The shapes of Fowler and McLean loomed, two giant moons abruptly ascendant. Professional faces that peered down at him anxiously. He was turned over on his side. Muffled conferences. Urgent whispers. The clank of tools.

"Here," Fowler muttered. "Now here. No, that's later. Be careful. Now run it up through here."

The work continued in taut silence. He was aware of their closeness. Dim outlines occasionally cut off his light. He was turned this way and that, thrown around like a sack of meal.

"Okay," Fowler said. "Tape it."

A long silence. He gazed dully at the wall, at the slightly-faded blue and pink wallpaper. An old design that showed a woman in hoopskirts, with a little parasol over her dainty shoulder. A frilly white blouse, tiny tips of shoes. An astoundingly clean puppy at her side.

Then he was turned back, to face upward. Five shapes groaned and strained over him. Their fingers flew, their muscles rippled under their shirts. At last they straightened up and retreated. Fowler wiped sweat from his face; they were all tense and bleary-eyed.

"Go ahead," Fowler rasped. "Throw it."

Shock hit him. He gasped. His body arched, then settled slowly down.

His body. He could feel. He moved his arms

experimentally. He touched his face, his shoulder, the wall. The wall was real and hard. All at once the world had become three-dimensional again.

Relief showed on Fowler's face. "Thank—God." He sagged wearily. "How do you feel?"

After a moment he answered, "All right."

Fowler sent the rest of the crew out. Green began dusting again, off in the corner. Fowler sat down on the edge of the bed and lit his pipe. "Now listen to me," he said. "I've got bad news. I'll give it to you the way you always want it, straight from the shoulder."

"What is it?" he demanded. He examined his fingers. He already knew.

There were dark circles under Fowler's eyes. He hadn't shaved. His square-jawed face was drawn and unhealthy. "We were up all night. Working on your motor system. We've got it jury-rigged, but it won't hold. Not more than another few months. The thing's climbing. The basic units can't be replaced. When they wear they're gone. We can weld in relays and wiring, but we can't fix the five synapsis-coils. There were only a few men who could make those, and they've been dead two centuries. If the coils burn out—"

"Is there any deterioration in the synapsis-coils?" he interrupted.

"Not yet. Just motor areas. Arms, in particular. What's happening to your legs will happen to your arms and finally all your motor system. You'll be paralyzed by the end of the year. You'll be able to see, hear, and think. And broadcast. But that's all." He added, "Sorry, Bors. We're doing all we can."

"All right," Bors said. "You're excused. Thanks for telling me straight. I—guessed."

"Ready to go down? A lot of people with problems, today. They're stuck until you get there."

"Let's go." He focused his mind with an effort and turned his attention to the details of the day. "I want the heavy metals research program speeded. It's lagging, as usual. I may have to pull a number of men from related work and shift them to the generators. The water level will be dropping soon. I want to start feeding power along the lines while there's still power to feed. As soon as I turn my back everything starts falling apart."

Fowler signalled Green and he came quickly over. The two of them bent over Bors and, grunting, hoisted him up and carried him to the door. Down the corridor and outside.

They deposited him in the squat metal car, the new little service truck. Its polished surface was a startling contrast to his pitted, corroded hull, bent and splotched and eaten away. A dull, patina-covered machine of archaic steel and plastic that hummed faintly, rustily, as the men leaped in the front seat and raced the car out onto the main highway.

EDWARD TOLBY perspired, pushed his pack up higher, hunched over, tightened his gun belt, and cursed.

"Daddy," Silvia reproved. "Cut that."

Tolby spat furiously in the grass at the side of the road. He put his arm around his slim daughter. "Sorry, Silv. Nothing personal. The damn heat."

Mid-morning sun shimmered down on the dusty road. Clouds of dust rose and billowed around the three as they pushed slowly along. They were dead tired. Tolby's heavy face was flushed and sullen. An unlit cigarette dangled between his lips. His big, powerfully built body was hunched resentfully forward. His daughter's canvas shirt clung moistly to her arms and breasts. Moons of sweat darkened her back. Under her jeans her thigh muscles rippled wearily.

Robert Penn walked a little behind the two Tolbys, hands deep in his pockets, eyes on the road ahead. His mind was blank; he was half asleep from the double shot of hexobarb he had swallowed at the last League camp. And the heat lulled him. On each side of the road fields stretched out, pastures of grass and weeds, a few trees here and there. A tumbled-down farmhouse. The ancient rusting remains of a bomb shelter, two centuries old. Once, some dirty sheep.

"Sheep," Penn said. "They eat the grass too far down. It won't grow back."

"Now he's a farmer," Tolby said to his daughter.

"Daddy," Silvia snapped. "Stop being nasty."

"It's this heat. This damn heat." Tolby cursed again,

loudly and futilely. "It's not worth it. For ten pinks I'd go back and tell them it was a lot of pig swill."

"Maybe it is, at that," Penn said mildly.

"All right, you go back," Tolby grunted. "You go back and tell them it's a lot of pig swill. They'll pin a medal on you. Maybe raise you up a grade."

Penn laughed. "Both of you shut up. There's some kind of town ahead."

Tolby's massive body straightened eagerly. "Where?" He shielded his eyes. "By God, he's right. A village. And it isn't a mirage. You see it, don't you?" His good humor returned and he rubbed his big hands together. "What say, Penn. A couple of beers, a few games of throw with some of the local peasants—maybe we can stay overnight." He licked his thick lips with anticipation. "Some of those village wenches, the kind that hang around the grog shops—"

"I know the kind you mean," Penn broke in. "The kind that are tired of doing nothing. Want to see the big commercial centers. Want to meet some guy that'll buy them mecho-stuff and take them places."

At the side of the road a farmer was watching them curiously. He had halted his horse and stood leaning on his crude plow, hat pushed back on his head.

"What's the name of this town?" Tolby yelled.

The farmer was silent a moment. He was an old man, thin and weathered. "This town?" he repeated.

"Yeah, the one ahead."

"That's a nice town." The farmer eyed the three of them. "You been through here before?"

"No, sir," Tolby said. "Never."

"Team break down?"

"No, we're on foot."

"How far you come?"

"About a hundred and fifty miles."

The farmer considered the heavy packs strapped on their backs. Their cleated hiking shoes. Dusty clothing and weary, sweat-streaked faces. Jeans and canvas shirts. Ironite walking staffs. "That's a long way," he said. "How far you going?"

"As far as we feel like it," Tolby answered. "Is there a place ahead we can stay? Hotel? Inn?"

"That town," the farmer said, "is Fairfax. It has a lumber mill, one of the best in the world. A couple of pottery works. A place where you can get clothes put together by machines. Regular mecho-clothing. A gun shop where they pour the best shot this side of the Rockies. And a bakery. Also there's an old doctor living there, and a lawyer. And some people with books to teach the kids. They came here with t.b. They made a school house out of an old barn."

"How large a town?" Penn asked.

"Lot of people. More born all the time. Old folks die. Kids die. We had a fever last year. About a hundred kids died. Doctor said it came from the water hole. We shut the water hole down. Kids died anyhow. Doctor said it was the milk. Drove off half the cows. Not mine. I stood out there with my gun and I shot the first of them came to drive off my cow. Kids stopped dying as soon as fall came. I think it was the heat."

"Sure is hot," Tolby agreed.

"Yes, it gets hot around here. Water's pretty scarce." A crafty look slid across his old face. "You folks want a drink? The young lady looks pretty tired. Got some bottles of water down under the house. In the mud. Nice and cold." He hesitated. "Pink a glass."

Tolby laughed. "No, thanks."

"Two glasses a pink," the farmer said.

"Not interested," Penn said. He thumped his canteen and the three of them started on. "So long."

The farmer's face hardened. "Damn foreigners," he muttered. He turned angrily back to his plowing.

The town baked in silence. Flies buzzed and settled on the backs of stupefied horses, tied up at posts. A few cars were parked here and there. People moved listlessly along the sidewalks. Elderly lean-bodied men dozed on porches. Dogs and chickens slept in the shade under houses. The houses were small, wooden, chipped and peeling boards, leaning and angular—and old. Warped and split by age and heat. Dust lay over everything. A thick blanket of dry dust over the cracking houses and the dull-faced men and animals.

Two lank men approached them from an open doorway. "Who are you? What do you want?"

They stopped and got out their identification. The men examined the sealed-plastic cards. Photographs, fingerprints, data. Finally they handed them back.

"AL," one said. "You really from the Anarchist League?"

"That's right," Tolby said.

"Even the girl?" The men eyed Silvia with languid greed. "Tell you what. Let us have the girl a while and we'll skip the head tax."

"Don't kid me," Tolby grunted. "Since when does the League pay head tax or any other tax?" He pushed past them impatiently. "Where's the grog shop? I'm dying!"

A two-story white building was on their left. Men lounged on the porch, watching them vacantly. Penn headed toward it and the Tolbys followed. A faded, peeling sign lettered across the front read: *Beer, Wine on Tap*.

"This is it," Penn said. He guided Silvia up the sagging steps, past the men, and inside. Tolby followed; he unstrapped his pack gratefully as he came.

The place was cool and dark. A few men and women were at the bar; the rest sat around tables. Some youths were playing throw in the back. A mechanical tune-maker wheezed and composed in the corner, a shabby, half-ruined machine only partially functioning. Behind the bar a primitive scene-shifter created and destroyed vague phantasmagoria: seascapes, mountain peaks, snowy valleys, great rolling hills, a nude woman that lingered and then dissolved into one vast breast. Dim, uncertain processions that no one noticed or looked at. The bar itself was an incredibly ancient sheet of transparent plastic, stained and chipped and yellow with age. Its n-grav coat had faded from one end; bricks now propped it up. The drink mixer had long since fallen apart. Only wine and beer were served. No living man knew how to mix the simplest drink.

Tolby moved up to the bar. "Beer," he said. "Three beers." Penn and Silvia sank down at a table and removed their packs, as the bartender served Tolby three mugs of thick, dark beer. He showed his card and carried the mugs over to the table.

The youths in the back had stopped playing. They were watching the three as they sipped their beer and unlaced their hiking boots. After a while one of them came slowly over.

"Say," he said. "You're from the League."

"That's right," Tolby murmured sleepily.

Everyone in the place was watching and listening. The youth sat down across from the three; his companions flocked excitedly around and took seats on all sides. The juveniles of the town. Bored, restless, dissatisfied. Their eyes took in the ironite staffs, the guns, the heavy metal-cleated boots. A murmured whisper rustled through them. They were about eighteen. Tanned, rangy.

"How do you get in?" one demanded bluntly.

"The League?" Tolby leaned back in his chair, found a match, and lit his cigarette. He unfastened his belt, belched loudly, and settled back contentedly. "You get in by examination."

"What do you have to know?"

Tolby shrugged. "About everything." He belched again and scratched thoughtfully at his chest, between two buttons. He was conscious of the ring of people around on all sides. A little old man with a beard and horn-rimmed glasses. At another table, a great tub of a man in a red shirt and blue-striped trousers, with a bulging stomach.

Youths. Farmers. A Negro in a dirty white shirt and trousers, a book under his arm. A hard-jawed blonde, hair in a net, red nails and high heels, tight yellow dress. Sitting with a gray-haired businessman in a dark brown suit. A tall young man holding hands with a young black-haired girl, huge eyes, in a soft white blouse and skirt, little slippers kicked under the table. Under the table her bare, tanned feet twisted; her slim body was bent forward with interest.

"You have to know," Tolby said, "how the League was formed. You have to know how we pulled down the governments that day. Pulled them down and destroyed them. Burned all the buildings. And all the records. Billions of microfilms and papers. Great bonfires that burned for weeks. And the swarms of little white things that poured out when we knocked the buildings over."

"You killed them?" the great tub of a man asked, lips twitching avidly.

"We let them go. They were harmless. They ran and

hid. Under rocks." Tolby laughed. "Funny little scurrying things. Insects. Then we went in and gathered up all the records and equipment for making records. By God, we burned everything."

"And the robots," a youth said.

"Yeah, we smashed all the government robots. There weren't many of them. They were used only at high levels. When a lot of facts had to be integrated."

The youth's eyes bulged. "You saw them? You were there when they smashed the robots?"

Penn laughed. "Tolby means the League. That was two hundred years ago."

The youth grinned nervously. "Yeah. Tell us about the marches."

Tolby drained his mug and pushed it away. "I'm out of beer."

The mug was quickly refilled. He grunted his thanks and continued, voice deep and furry, dulled with fatigue. "The marches. That was really something, they say. All over the world, people getting up, throwing down what they were doing—"

"It started in East Germany," the hard-jawed blonde said. "The riots."

"Then it spread to Poland," the Negro put in shyly. "My grandfather used to tell me how everybody sat and listened to the television. His grandfather used to tell him. It spread to Czechoslovakia and then Austria and Roumania and Bulgaria. Then France. And Italy."

"France was first!" the little old man with beard and glasses cried violently. "They were without a government a whole month. The people saw they could live without a government!"

"The marches started it," the black-haired girl corrected. "That was the first time they started pulling down the government buildings. In East Germany and Poland. Big mobs of unorganized workers."

"Russia and America were the last," Tolby said. "When the march on Washington came there was close to twenty million of us. We were big in those days! They couldn't stop us when we finally moved."

"They shot a lot," the hard-faced blonde said.

"Sure. But the people kept coming. And yelling to the

soldiers. 'Hey, Bill! Don't shoot!' 'Hey, Jack! It's me, Joe.'
'Don't shoot—we're your friends!' 'Don't kill us, join us!'
And by God, after a while they did. They couldn't keep
shooting their own people. They finally threw down their
guns and got out of the way."

"And then you found the place," the little black-haired
girl said breathlessly.

"Yeah. We found the place. *Six* places. Three in
America. One in Britain. Two in Russia. It took us ten
years to find the last place—and make sure it was the last
place."

"What then?" the youth asked, bug-eyed.

"Then we busted every one of them." Tolby raised
himself up, a massive man, beer mug clutched, heavy face
flushed dark red. "Every damn A-bomb in the whole
world."

THERE WAS an uneasy silence.

"Yeah," the youth murmured. "You sure took care of
those war people."

"Won't be any more of them," the great tub of a man
said. "They're gone for good."

Tolby fingered his ironite staff. "Maybe so. And maybe
not. There just might be a few of them left."

"What do you mean?" the tub of a man demanded.

Tolby raised his hard gray eyes. "It's time you people
stopped kidding us. You know damn well what I mean.
We've heard rumors. Someplace around this area there's
a bunch of them. Hiding out."

Shocked disbelief, then anger hummed to a roar.
"That's a lie!" the tub of a man shouted.

"Is it?"

The little man with beard and glasses leaped up.
"There's nobody here has anything to do with governments! We're all good people!"

"You better watch your step," one of the youths said
softly to Tolby. "People around here don't like to be
accused."

Tolby got unsteadily to his feet, his ironite staff
gripped. Penn got up beside him and they stood together.
"If any of you knows something," Tolby said, "you better
tell it. Right now."

"Nobody knows anything," the hard-faced blonde said. "You're talking to honest folks."

"That's so," the Negro said, nodding his head. "Nobody here's doing anything wrong."

"You saved our lives," the black-haired girl said. "If you hadn't pulled down the governments we'd all be dead in the war. Why should we hold back something?"

"That's true," the great tub of a man grumbled. "We wouldn't be alive if it wasn't for the League. You think we'd do anything against the League?"

"Come on," Silvia said to her father. "Let's go." She got to her feet and tossed Penn his pack.

Tolby grunted belligerently. Finally he took his own pack and hoisted it to his shoulder. The room was deathly silent. Everyone stood frozen, as the three gathered their things and moved toward the door.

The little dark-haired girl stopped them. "The next town is thirty miles from here," she said.

"The road's blocked," her tall companion explained. "Slides closed it years ago."

"Why don't you stay with us tonight? There's plenty of room at our place. You can rest up and get an early start tomorrow."

"We don't want to impose," Silvia murmured.

Tolby and Penn glanced at each other, then at the girl. "If you're sure you have plenty of room—"

The great tub of a man approached them. "Listen. I have ten yellow slips. I want to give them to the League. I sold my farm last year. I don't need any more slips; I'm living with my brother and his family." He pushed the slips at Tolby. "Here."

Tolby pushed them back. "Keep them."

"This way," the tall young man said, as they clattered down the sagging steps, into a sudden blinding curtain of heat and dust. "We have a car. Over this way. An old gasoline car. My dad fixed it so it burns oil."

"You should have taken the slips," Penn said to Tolby, as they got into the ancient, battered car. Flies buzzed around them. They could hardly breathe; the car was a furnace. Silvia fanned herself with a rolled-up paper. The black-haired girl unbuttoned her blouse.

"What do we need money for?" Tolby laughed

good-naturedly. "I haven't paid for anything in my life. Neither have you."

The car sputtered and moved slowly forward, onto the road. It began to gain speed. Its motor banged and roared. Soon it was moving surprisingly fast.

"You saw them," Silvia said, over the racket. "They'd give us anything they had. We saved their lives." She waved at the fields, the farmers and their crude teams, the withered crops, the sagging old farmhouses. "They'd all be dead, if it hadn't been for the League." She smashed a fly peevishly. "They depend on us."

The black-haired girl turned toward them, as the car rushed along the decaying road. Sweat streaked her tanned skin. Her half-covered breasts trembled with the motion of the car. "I'm Laura Davis. Pete and I have an old farmhouse his dad gave us when we got married."

"You can have the whole downstairs," Pete said.

"There's no electricity, but we've got a big fireplace. It gets cold at night. It's hot in the day, but when the sun sets it gets terribly cold."

"We'll be all right," Penn murmured. The vibration of the car made him a little sick.

"Yes," the girl said, her black eyes flashing. Her crimson lips twisted. She leaned toward Penn intently, her small face strangely alight. "Yes, we'll take good care of you."

At that moment the car left the road.

Silvia shrieked. Tolby threw himself down, head between his knees, doubled up in a ball. A sudden curtain of green burst around Penn. Then a sickening emptiness, as the car plunged down. It struck with a roaring crash that blotted out everything. A single titanic cataclysm of fury that picked Penn up and flung his remains in every direction.

"PUT ME DOWN," Bors ordered. "On this railing for a moment before I go inside."

The crew lowered him onto the concrete surface and fastened magnetic grapples into place. Men and women hurried up the wide steps, in and out of the massive building that was Bors' main offices.

The sight from these steps pleased him. He liked to stop

here and look around at his world. At the civilization he
had carefully constructed. Each piece added painstak-
ingly, scrupulously. with infinite care, throughout the
years.

It wasn't big. The mountains ringed it on all sides. The
valley was a level bowl, surrounded by dark violet hills.
Outside, beyond the hills, the regular world began.
Parched fields. Blasted, poverty-stricken towns. Decayed
roads. The remains of houses, tumbled-down farm
buildings. Ruined cars and machinery. Dust-covered
people creeping listlessly around in hand-made clothing,
dull rags and tatters.

He had seen the outside. He knew what it was like. At
the mountains the blank faces, the disease, the withered
crops, the crude plows and ancient tools all ended here.
Here, within the ring of hills, Bors had constructed an
accurate and detailed reproduction of a society two
centuries gone. The world as it had been in the old days.
The time of governments. The time that had been pulled
down by the Anarchist League.

Within his five synapsis-coils the plans, knowledge,
information, blueprints of a whole world existed. In the
two centuries he had carefully recreated that world, had
made this miniature society that glittered and hummed on
all sides of him. The roads, buildings, houses, industries
of a dead world, all a fragment of the past, built with his
own hands, his own metal fingers and brain.

"Fowler," Bors said.

Fowler came over. He looked haggard. His eyes were
red-rimmed and swollen. "What is it? You want to go
inside?"

Overhead, the morning patrol thundered past. A string
of black dots against the sunny, cloudless sky. Bors
watched with satisfaction. "Quite a sight."

"Right on the nose," Fowler agreed, examining his
wristwatch. To their right, a column of heavy tanks
snaked along a highway between green fields. Their
gun-snouts glittered. Behind them a column of foot
soldiers marched, faces hidden behind bacteria masks.

"I'm thinking," Bors said, "that it may be unwise to
trust Green any longer."

"Why the hell do you say that?"

"Every ten days I'm inactivated. So your crew can see what repairs are needed." Bors twisted restlessly. "For twelve hours I'm completely helpless. Green takes care of me. Sees nothing happens. But—"

"But what?"

"It occurs to me perhaps there'd be more safety in a squad of troops. It's too much of a temptation for one man, alone."

Fowler scowled. "I don't see that. How about me? I have charge of inspecting you. I could switch a few leads around. Send a load through your synapsis-coils. Blow them out."

Bors whirled wildly, then subsided. "True. You could do that." After a moment he demanded, "But what would you gain? You know I'm the only one who can keep all this together. I'm the only one who knows how to maintain a planned society, not a disorderly chaos! If it weren't for me, all this would collapse, and you'd have dust and ruins and weeds. The whole outside would come rushing in to take over!"

"Of course. So why worry about Green?"

Trucks of workers rumbled past. Loads of men in blue-green, sleeves rolled up, armloads of tools. A mining team, heading for the mountains.

"Take me inside," Bors said abruptly.

Fowler called McLean. They hoisted Bors and carried him past the throngs of people, into the building, down the corridor and to his office. Officials and technicians moved respectfully out of the way as the great pitted, corroded tank was carried past.

"All right," Bors said impatiently. "That's all. You can go."

Fowler and McLean left the luxurious office, with its lush carpets, furniture, drapes and rows of books. Bors was already bent over his desk, sorting through heaps of reports and papers.

Fowler shook his head, as they walked down the hall. "He won't last much longer."

"The motor system? Can't we reinforce the—"

"I don't mean that. He's breaking up mentally. He can't take the strain any longer."

"None of us can," McLean muttered.

"Running this thing is too much for him. Knowing it's all dependent on him. Knowing as soon as he turns his back or lets down it'll begin to come apart at the seams. A hell of a job, trying to shut out the real world. Keeping his model universe running."

"He's gone on a long time," McLean said.

Fowler brooded. "Sooner or later we're going to have to face the situation." Gloomily, he ran his fingers along the blade of a large screwdriver. "He's wearing out. Sooner or later somebody's going to have to step in. As he continues to decay . . ." He stuck the screwdriver back in his belt, with his pliers and hammer and soldering iron. "One crossed wire."

"What's that?"

Fowler laughed. "Now he's got me doing it. One crossed wire and—*poof*. But what then? That's the big question."

"Maybe," McLean said softly, "you and I can then get off this rat race. You and I and all the rest of us. And live like human beings."

"*Rat race,*" Fowler murmured. "Rats in a maze. Doing tricks. Performing chores thought up by somebody else."

McLean caught Fowler's eye. "By somebody of another species."

TOLBY STRUGGLED VAGUELY. Silence. A faint dripping close by. A beam pinned his body down. He was caught on all sides by the twisted wreck of the car. He was head down. The car was turned on its side. Off the road in a gully, wedged between two huge trees. Bent struts and smashed metal all around him. And bodies.

He pushed up with all his strength. The beam gave, and he managed to get to a sitting position. A tree branch had burst in the windshield. The black-haired girl, still turned toward the back seat, was impaled on it. The branch had driven through her spine, out her chest, and into the seat; she clutched at it with both hands, head limp, mouth half-open. The man beside her was also dead. His hands were gone; the windshield had burst around him. He lay in a heap among the remains of the dashboard and the bloody shine of his own internal organs.

Penn was dead. Neck snapped like a rotten broom

handle. Tolby pushed his corpse aside and examined his daughter. Silvia didn't stir. He put his ear to her shirt and listened. She was alive. Her heart beat faintly. Her bosom rose and fell against his ear.

He wound a handkerchief around her arm, where the flesh was ripped open and oozing blood. She was badly cut and scratched; one leg was doubled under her, obviously broken. Her clothes were ripped, her hair matted with blood. But she was alive. He pushed the twisted door open and stumbled out. A fiery tongue of afternoon sunlight struck him and he winced. He began to ease her limp body out of the car, past the twisted door-frame.

A sound.

Tolby glanced up, rigid. Something was coming. A whirring insect that rapidly descended. He let go of Silvia, crouched, glanced around, then lumbered awkwardly down the gully. He slid and fell and rolled among the green vines and jagged gray boulders. His gun gripped, he lay gasping in the moist shadows, peering upward.

The insect landed. A small air-ship, jet-driven. The sight stunned him. He had heard about jets, seen photographs of them. Been briefed and lectured in the history-indoctrination courses at the League Camps. But to *see* a jet!

Men swarmed out. Uniformed men who started from the road, down the side of the gully, bodies crouched warily as they approached the wrecked car. They lugged heavy rifles. They looked grim and experienced, as they tore the car doors open and scrambled in.

"One's gone," a voice drifted to him.

"Must be around somewhere."

"Look, this one's alive! This woman. Started to crawl out. The rest all dead."

Furious cursing. "Damn Laura! She should have leaped! The fanatic little fool!"

"Maybe she didn't have time. God's sake, the thing's all the way through her." Horror and shocked dismay. "We won't hardly be able to get her loose."

"Leave her." The officer directing things waved the men back out of the car. "Leave them all."

"How about this wounded one?"

The leader hesitated. "Kill her," he said finally. He snatched a rifle and raised the butt. "The rest of you fan out and try to get the other one. He's probably—"

Tolby fired, and the leader's body broke in half. The lower part sank down slowly; the upper dissolved in ashy fragments. Tolby turned and began to move in a slow circle, firing as he crawled. He got two more of them before the rest retreated in panic to their jet-powered insect and slammed the lock.

He had the element of surprise. Now that was gone. They had strength and numbers. He was doomed. Already, the insect was rising. They'd be able to spot him easily from above. But he had saved Silvia. That was something.

He stumbled down a dried-up creek bed. He ran aimlessly; he had no place to go. He didn't know the countryside, and he was on foot. He slipped on a stone and fell headlong. Pain and billowing darkness beat at him as he got unsteadily to his knees. His gun was gone, lost in the shrubbery. He spat broken teeth and blood. He peered wildly up at the blazing afternoon sky.

The insect was leaving. It hummed off toward the distant hills. It dwindled, became a black ball, a fly-speck, then disappeared.

Tolby waited a moment. Then he struggled up the side of the ravine to the wrecked car. They had gone to get help. They'd be back. Now was his only chance. If he could get Silvia out and down the road, into hiding. Maybe to a farmhouse. Back to town.

He reached the car and stood, dazed and stupefied. Three bodies remained, the two in the front seat, Penn in the back. But Silvia was gone.

They had taken her with them. Back where they came from. She had been dragged to the jet-driven insect; a trail of blood led from the car up the side of the gully to the highway.

With a violent shudder Tolby pulled himself together. He climbed into the car and pried loose Penn's gun from his belt. Silvia's ironite staff rested on the seat; he took that, too. Then he started off down the road, walking without haste, carefully, slowly.

An ironic thought plucked at his mind. He had found

what they were after. The men in uniform. They were organized, responsible to a central authority. In a newly-assembled jet.

Beyond the hills was a government.

"SIR," GREEN SAID. He smoothed his short blond hair anxiously, his young face twisting.

Technicians and experts and ordinary people in droves were everywhere. The officers buzzed and echoed with the business of the day. Green pushed through the crowd and to the desk where Bors sat, propped up by two magnetic frames.

"Sir," Green said. "Something's happened."

Bors looked up. He pushed a metal-foil slate away and laid down his stylus. His eye cells clicked and flickered; deep inside his battered trunk motor gears whined. "What is it?"

Green came close. There was something in his face, an expression Bors had never seen before. A look of fear and glassy determination. A glazed, fanatic cast, as if his flesh had hardened to rock. "Sir, scouts contacted a League team moving North. They met the team outside Fairfax. The incident took place directly beyond the first road block."

Bors said nothing. On all sides, officials, experts, farmers, workmen, industrial managers, soldiers, people of all kinds buzzed and murmured and pushed forward impatiently. Trying to get to Bors' desk. Loaded down with problems to be solved, situations to be explained. The pressing business of the day. Roads, factories, disease control. Repairs. Construction. Manufacture. Design. Planning. Urgent problems for Bors to consider and deal with. Problems that couldn't wait.

"Was the League team destroyed?" Bors asked.

"One was killed. One was wounded and brought here." Green hesitated. "One escaped."

For a long time Bors was silent. Around him the people murmured and shuffled; he ignored them. All at once he pulled the vidscanner to him and snapped the circuit open. "One escaped? I don't like the sound of that."

"He shot three members of our scout unit. Including the leader. The others got frightened. They grabbed the injured girl and returned here."

Bors' massive head lifted. "They made a mistake. They should have located the one who escaped."

"This was the first time the situation—"

"I know," Bors said. "But it was an error. Better not to have touched them at all, than to have taken two and allowed the third to get away." He turned to the vidscanner. "Sound an emergency alert. Close down the factories. Arm the work crews and any male farmers capable of using weapons. Close every road. Remove the women and children to the undersurface shelters. Bring up the heavy guns and supplies. Suspend all non-military production and—" He considered. "Arrest everyone we're not sure of. On the C sheet. Have them shot." He snapped the scanner off.

"What'll happen?" Green demanded, shaken.

"The thing we've prepared for. Total war."

"We have weapons!" Green shouted excitedly. "In an hour there'll be ten thousand men ready to fight. We have jet-driven ships. Heavy artillery. Bombs. Bacteria pellets. What's the League? A lot of people with packs on their backs!"

"Yes," Bors said. "A lot of people with packs on their backs."

"How can they do anything? How can a bunch of anarchists organize? They have no structure, no control, no central power."

"They have the whole world. A billion people."

"*Individuals!* A club, not subject to law. Voluntary membership. We have a disciplined organization. Every aspect of our economic life operates at maximum efficiency. We—you—have your thumb on everything. All you have to do is give the order. Set the machine in motion."

Bors nodded slowly. "It's true the anarchist can't coordinate. The League can't organize in an efficient structure. It's a paradox. Government by anarchists... Anti-government, actually. Instead of governing the world they tramp around to make sure no one else does."

"Dog in the manger."

"As you say, they're actually a voluntary club of totally

unorganized individuals. Without law or central authority. They maintain no society—they can't govern. All they can do is interfere with anyone else who tries. Trouble-makers. But—"

"But what?"

"It was this way before. Two centuries ago. They were unorganized. Unarmed. Vast mobs, without discipline or authority. Yet they pulled down all the governments. All over the world."

"We've got a whole army. All the roads are mined. Heavy guns. Bombs. Pellets. Every one of us is a soldier. We're an armed camp!"

Bors was deep in thought. "You say one of them is here? One of the League agents?"

"A young woman."

Bors signalled the nearby maintenance crew. "Take me to her. I want to talk to her in the time remaining."

SILVIA WATCHED SILENTLY, as the uniformed men pushed and grunted their way into the room. They staggered over to the bed, pulled two chairs together, and carefully laid down their massive armload.

Quickly they snapped protective struts into place, locked the chairs together, threw magnetic grapples into operation, and then warily retreated.

"All right," the robot said. "You can go." The men left. Bors turned to face the woman on the bed.

"A machine," Silvia whispered, white-faced. "You're a machine."

Bors nodded slightly without speaking.

Silvia shifted uneasily on the bed. She was weak. One leg was in a transparent plastic cast. Her face was bandaged and her right arm ached and throbbed. Outside the window, the late afternoon sun sprinkled through the drapes. Flowers bloomed. Grass. Hedges. And beyond the hedges, buildings and factories.

For the last hour the sky had been filled with jet-driven ships. Great flocks that raced excitedly across the sky toward distant hills. Along the highway cars hurtled, dragging guns and heavy military equipment. Men were marching in close rank, rows of gray-clad soldiers, guns and helmets and bacteria masks. Endless lines of figures, identical in their uniforms, stamped from the same matrix.

"There are a lot of them," Bors said, indicating the marching men.

"Yes." Silvia watched a couple of soldiers hurry by the window. Youths with worried expressions on their smooth faces. Helmets bobbing at their waists. Long rifles. Canteens. Counters. Radiation shields. Bacteria masks wound awkwardly around their necks, ready to go into place. They were scared. Hardly more than kids. Others followed. A truck roared into life. The soldiers were swept off to join the others.

"They're going to fight," Bors said, "to defend their homes and factories."

"All this equipment. You manufacture it, don't you?"

"That's right. Our industrial organization is perfect. We're totally productive. Our society here is operated rationally. Scientifically. We're fully prepared to meet this emergency."

Suddenly Silvia realized what the emergency was. "The League! One of us must have got away." She pulled herself up. "Which of them? Penn or my father?"

"I don't know," the robot murmured indifferently.

Horror and disgust choked Silvia. "My God," she said softly. "You have no understanding of us. You run all this, and you're incapable of empathy. You're nothing but a mechanical computer. One of the old government integration robots."

"That's right. Two centuries old."

She was appalled. "And you've been alive all this time. We thought we destroyed all of you!"

"I was missed. I had been damaged. I wasn't in my place. I was in a truck, on my way out of Washington. I saw the mobs and escaped."

"Two hundred years ago. Legendary times. You actually saw the events they tell us about. The old days. The great marches. The day the governments fell."

"Yes. I saw it all. A group of us formed in Virginia. Experts, officials, skilled workmen. Later we came here. It was remote enough, off the beaten path."

"We heard rumors. A fragment...Still maintaining itself. But we didn't know where or how."

"I was fortunate," Bors said. "I escaped by a fluke. All the others were destroyed. It's taken a long time to organize what you see here. Fifteen miles from here is a ring of hills. This valley is a bowl—mountains on all sides. We've set up road blocks in the form of natural slides. Nobody comes here. Even in Fairfax, thirty miles off, they know nothing."

"That girl. Laura."

"Scouts. We keep scout teams in all inhabited regions within a hundred mile radius. As soon as you entered Fairfax, word was relayed to us. An air unit was dispatched. To avoid questions, we arranged to have you killed in an auto wreck. But one of you escaped."

Silvia shook her head, bewildered. "How?" she demanded. "How do you keep going? Don't the people revolt?" She struggled to a sitting position. "They must know what's happened everywhere else. How do you control them? They're going out now, in their uniforms. But—*will they fight? Can you count on them*?"

Bors answered slowly. "They trust me," he said. "I brought with me a vast amount of knowledge. Information and techniques lost to the rest of the world. Are jet-ships and vidscanners and power cables made anywhere else in the world? I retain all that knowledge. I have memory units, synapsis-coils. Because of me they have these things. Things you know only as dim memories, vague legends."

"What happens when you die?"

"I won't die! I'm eternal!"

"You're wearing out. You have to be carried around. And your right arm. You can hardly move it!" Silvia's voice was harsh, ruthless. "Your whole tank is pitted and rusty."

The robot whirred; for a moment he seemed unable to speak. "My knowledge remains," he grated finally. "I'll always be able to communicate. Fowler has arranged a broadcast system. Even when I talk—" He broke off. "Even then. Everything is under control. I've organized every aspect of the situation. I've maintained this system for two centuries. It's got to be kept going!"

Silvia lashed out. It happened in a split second. The boot of her cast caught the chairs on which the robot rested. She thrust violently with her foot and hands; the chairs teetered, hesitated—

"Fowler!" the robot screamed.

Silvia pushed with all her strength. Blinding agony seared through her leg; she bit her lip and threw her shoulder against the robot's pitted hulk. He waved his arms, whirred wildly, and then the two chairs slowly collapsed. The robot slid quietly from them, over on his back, his arms still waving helplessly.

Silvia dragged herself from the bed. She managed to pull herself to the window; her broken leg hung uselessly, a dead weight in its transparent plastic cast. The robot lay like some futile bug, arms waving, eye-lens clicking, its rusty works whirring in fear and rage.

"Fowler!" it screamed again. "Help me!"

Silvia reached the window. She tugged at the locks; they were sealed. She grabbed up a lamp from the table and threw it against the glass. The glass burst around her, a shower of lethal fragments. She stumbled forward—and then the repair crew was pouring into the room.

Fowler gasped at the sight of the robot on its back. A strange expression crossed his face. "Look at him!"

"Help me!" the robot shrilled. "Help me!"

One of the men grabbed Silvia around the waist and lugged her back to the bed. She kicked and bit, sunk her nails into the man's cheek. He threw her on the bed, face down, and drew his pistol. "Stay there," he gasped.

The others were bent over the robot, getting him to an upright position.

"What happened?" Fowler said. He came over to the bed, his face twisting. "Did he fall?"

Silvia's eyes glowed with hatred and despair. "I pushed him over. I almost got there." Her chest heaved. "The window. But my leg—"

"Get me back to my quarters!" Bors cried.

The crew gathered him up and carried him down the hall, to his private office. A few moments later he was sitting shakily at his desk, his mechanism pounding wildly, surrounded by his papers and memoranda.

He forced down his panic and tried to resume his work. He had to keep going. His vidscreen was alive with activity. The whole system was in motion. He blankly watched a subcommander sending up a cloud of black dots, jet bombers that shot up like flies and headed quickly off.

The system had to be preserved. He repeated it again and again. He had to save it. Had to organize the people and make *them* save it. If the people didn't fight, wasn't everything doomed?

Fury and desperation overwhelmed him. The system couldn't preserve itself; it wasn't a thing apart, something that could be separated from the people who lived it. Actually it *was* the people. They were identical; when the people fought to preserve the system they were fighting to preserve nothing less than themselves.

They existed only as long as the system existed.

He caught sight of a marching column of white-faced troops, moving toward the hills. His ancient synapsis-coils radiated and shuddered uncertainly, then fell back into pattern. He was two centuries old. He had come into existence a long time ago, in a different world. That world had created him; through him that world still lived. As long as he existed, that world existed. In miniature, it still functioned. His model universe, his recreation. His rational, controlled world, in which each aspect was fully organized, fully analyzed and integrated.

He kept a rational, progressive world alive. A humming oasis of productivity on a dusty, parched planet of decay and silence.

Bors spread out his papers and went to work on the most pressing problem. The transformation from a peace-time economy to full military mobilization. Total military organization of every man, woman, child, piece of equipment and dyne of energy under his direction.

EDWARD TOLBY emerged cautiously. His clothes were torn and ragged. He had lost his pack, crawling through the brambles and vines. His face and hands were bleeding. He was utterly exhausted.

Below him lay a valley. A vast bowl. Fields, houses, highways. Factories. Equipment. Men.

He had been watching the men three hours. Endless streams of them, pouring from the valley into the hills, along the roads and paths. On foot, in trucks, in cars, armored tanks, weapons carriers. Overhead, in fast little jet-fighters and great lumbering bombers. Gleaming ships that took up positions above the troops and prepared for battle.

Battle in the grand style. The two-centuries-old full-scale war that was supposed to have disappeared. But here it was, a vision from the past. He had seen this in the old tapes and records, used in the camp orientation courses. A ghost army resurrected to fight again. A vast host of men and guns, prepared to fight and die.

Tolby climbed down cautiously. At the foot of a slope of boulders a soldier had halted his motorcycle and was setting up a communications antenna and transmitter. Tolby circled, crouched, expertly approached him. A blond-haired youth, fumbling nervously with the wires and relays, licking his lips uneasily, glancing up and grabbing for his rifle at every sound.

Tolby took a deep breath. The youth had turned his back; he was tracing a power circuit. It was now or never. With one stride Tolby stepped out, raised his pistol and fired. The clump of equipment and the soldier's rifle vanished.

"Don't make a sound," Tolby said. He peered around. No one had seen; the main line was half a mile to his right. The sun was setting. Great shadows were falling over the hills. The fields were rapidly fading from brown-green to a deep violet. "Put your hands up over your head, clasp them, and get down on your knees."

The youth tumbled down in a frightened heap. "What are you going to do?" He saw the ironite staff, and the color left his face. "You're a League agent!"

"Shut up," Tolby ordered. "First, outline your system of responsibility. *Who's your superior?*"

The youth stuttered forth what he knew. Tolby listened intently. He was satisfied. The usual monolithic structure. Exactly what he wanted.

"At the top," he broke in. "At the top of the pillar. Who has ultimate responsibility?"

"Bors."

"Bors!" Tolby scowled. "That doesn't sound like a name. Sounds like—" He broke off, staggered. "We should have guessed! An old government robot. Still functioning."

The youth saw his chance. He leaped up and darted frantically away.

Tolby shot him above the left ear. The youth pitched over on his face and lay still. Tolby hurried to him and quickly pulled off his dark gray uniform. It was too small for him of course. But the motorcycle was just right. He'd seen tapes of them; he'd wanted one since he was a child. A fast little motorcycle to propel his weight around. Now he had it.

Half an hour later he was roaring down a smooth, broad highway toward the center of the valley and the buildings that rose against the dark sky. His headlights cut into the blackness; he still wobbled from side to side, but for all practical purposes he had the hang of it. He increased speed; the road shot by, trees and fields, haystacks, stalled farm equipment. All traffic was going against him, troops hurrying to the front.

The front. Lemmings going out into the ocean to drown. A thousand, ten thousand, metal-clad fingers, armed and alert. Weighted down with guns and bombs and flame throwers and bacteria pellets.

There was only one hitch. No army opposed them. A mistake had been made. It took two sides to make a war, and only one had been resurrected.

A mile outside the concentration of buildings he pulled his motorcycle off the road and carefully hid it in a haystack. For a moment he considered leaving his ironite staff. Then he shrugged and grabbed it up, along with his pistol. He always carried his staff, it was the League symbol. It represented the walking Anarchists who patrolled the world on foot, the world's protection agency.

He loped through the darkness toward the outline ahead. There were fewer men here. He saw no women or children. Ahead, charged wire was set up. Troops crouched behind it, armed to the teeth. A searchlight moved back and forth across the road. Behind it, radar vanes loomed and behind them an ugly square of concrete. The great offices from which the government was run.

For a time he watched the searchlight. Finally he had its motion plotted. In its glare, the faces of the troops stood out, pale and drawn. Youths. They had never fought. This was their first encounter. They were terrified.

When the light was off him, he stood up and advanced toward the wire. Automatically, a breach was slid back for him. Two guards raised up and awkwardly crossed bayonets ahead of him.

"Show your papers!" one demanded. Young lieutenants. Boys, white-lipped, nervous. Playing soldier.

Pity and contempt made Tolby laugh harshly and push forward. "Get out of my way."

One anxiously flashed a pocket light. "Halt! What's the code-key for this watch?" He blocked Tolby's way with his bayonet, hands twisting convulsively.

Tolby reached in his pocket, pulled out his pistol, and as the searchlight started to swerve back, blasted the two guards. The bayonets clattered down and he dived forward. Yells and shapes rose on all sides. Anguished, terrified shouts. Random firing. The night was lit up, as he dashed and crouched, turned a corner past a supply warehouse, raced up a flight of stairs and into the massive building ahead.

He had to work fast. Gripping his ironite staff, he plunged down a gloomy corridor. His boots echoed. Men poured into the building behind him. Bolts of energy thundered past him; a whole section of the ceiling burst into ash and collapsed behind him.

He reached stairs and climbed rapidly. He came to the next floor and groped for the door handle. Something flickered behind him. He half-turned, his gun quickly up—

A stunning blow sent him sprawling. He crashed against the wall; his gun flew from his fingers. A shape bent over him, rifle gripped. "Who are you? What are you doing here?"

Not a soldier. A stubble-chinned man in stained shirt and rumpled trousers. Eyes puffy and red. A belt of tools, hammer, pliers, screwdriver, a soldering iron, around his waist.

Tolby raised himself up painfully. "If you didn't have that rifle—"

Fowler backed warily away. "Who are you? This floor is forbidden to troops of the line. You know this—" Then he saw the ironite staff. "By God," he said softly. "You're the one they didn't get." He laughed shakily. "You're the one who got away."

Tolby's fingers tightened around the staff, but Fowler reacted instantly. The snout of the rifle jerked up, on a line with Tolby's face.

"Be careful," Fowler warned. He turned slightly; soldiers were hurrying up the stairs, boots drumming, echoing shouts ringing. For a moment he hesitated, then waved his rifle toward the stairs ahead. "Up. Get going."

Tolby blinked. "What—"

"Up!" The rifle snout jabbed into Tolby. "Hurry!"

Bewildered, Tolby hurried up the stairs, Fowler close behind him. At the third floor Fowler pushed him roughly through the doorway, the snout of his rifle digging urgently into his back. He found himself in a corridor of doors. Endless offices.

"Keep going," Fowler snarled. "Down the hall. Hurry!"

Tolby hurried, his mind spinning. "What the hell are you—"

"I could never do it," Fowler gasped, close to his ear. "Not in a million years. But it's got to be done."

Tolby halted. "What is this?"

They faced each other defiantly, faces contorted, eyes blazing. "He's in there," Fowler snapped, indicating a door with his rifle. "You have one chance. Take it."

For a fraction of a second Tolby hesitated. Then he broke away. "Okay. I'll take it."

Fowler followed after him. "Be careful. Watch your step. There's a series of check points. Keep going straight, in all the way. As far as you can go. And for God's sake, hurry!"

His voice faded, as Tolby gained speed. He reached the door and tore it open.

Soldiers and officials ballooned. He threw himself against them; they sprawled and scattered. He scrambled on, as they struggled up and stupidly fumbled for their guns. Through another door, into an inner office, past a desk where a frightened girl sat, eyes wide, mouth open. Then a third door, into an alcove.

A wild-faced youth leaped up and snatched frantically for his pistol. Tolby was unarmed, trapped in the alcove.

Figures already pushed against the door behind him. He gripped his ironite staff and backed away as the blond-haired fanatic fired blindly. The bolt burst a foot away; it flicked him with a tongue of heat.

"You dirty anarchist!" Green screamed. His face distorted, he fired again and again. "You murdering anarchist spy!"

Tolby hurled his ironite staff. He put all his strength in it; the staff leaped through the air in a whistling arc, straight at the youth's head. Green saw it coming and ducked. Agile and quick, he jumped away, grinning humorlessly. The staff crashed against the wall and rolled clanging to the floor.

"Your walking staff!" Green gasped and fired.

The bolt missed him on purpose. Green was playing games with him. Tolby bent down and groped frantically for the staff. He picked it up. Green watched, face rigid, eyes glittering. "Throw it again!" he snarled.

Tolby leaped. He took the youth by surprise. Green grunted, stumbled back from the impact, then suddenly fought with maniacal fury.

Tolby was heavier. But he was exhausted. He had crawled hours, beat his way through the mountains, walked endlessly. He was at the end of his strength. The car wreck, the days of walking. Green was in perfect shape. His wiry, agile body twisted away. His hands came up. Fingers dug into Tolby's windpipe; he kicked the youth in the groin. Green staggered back, convulsed and bent over with pain.

"All right," Green gasped, face ugly and dark. His hand fumbled with his pistol. The barrel came up.

Half of Green's head dissolved. His hands opened and his gun fell to the floor. His body stood for a moment, then settled down in a heap, like an empty suit of clothes.

Tolby caught a glimpse of a rifle snout pushed past him—and the man with the tool belt. The man waved him on frantically. "Hurry!"

Tolby raced down a carpeted hall, between two great flickering yellow lamps. A crowd of officials and soldiers stumbled uncertainly after him, shouting and firing at random. He tore open a thick oak door and halted.

He was in a luxurious chamber. Drapes, rich

wallpaper. Lamps. Bookcases. A glimpse of the finery of the past. The wealth of the old days. Thick carpets. Warm radiant heat. A vidscreen. At the far end, a huge mahogany desk.

At the desk a figure sat. Working on heaps of papers and reports, piled masses of material. The figure contrasted starkly with the lushness of the furnishings. It was a great pitted, corroded tank of metal. Bent and greenish, patched and repaired. An ancient machine.

"It that you, Fowler?" the robot demanded.

Tolby advanced, his ironite staff gripped.

The robot turned angrily. "Who is it? Get Green and carry me down into the shelter. One of the roadblocks has reported a League agent already—" The robot broke off. Its cold, mechanical eye-lens bored up at the man. It clicked and whirred in uneasy astonishment. "I don't know you."

It saw the ironite staff.

"League agent," the robot said. "You're the one who got through." Comprehension came. *The third one. You came here. You didn't go back.*" Its metal fingers fumbled clumsily at the objects on the desk, then in the drawer. It found a gun and raised it awkwardly.

Tolby knocked the gun away; it clattered to the floor. "Run!" he shouted at the robot. "Start running!"

It remained. Tolby's staff came down. The fragile, complex brain-unit of the robot burst apart. Coils, wiring, relay fluid, spattered over his arms and hands. The robot shuddered. Its machinery thrashed. It half-rose from its chair, then swayed and toppled. It crashed full length on the floor, parts and gears rolling in all directions.

"Good God," Tolby said, suddenly seeing it for the first time. Shakily, he bent over its remains. "It was crippled."

Men were all around him. "He's killed Bors!" Shocked, dazed faces. "Bors is dead!"

Fowler came up slowly. "You got him, all right. There's nothing left now."

Tolby stood holding his ironite staff in his hands. "The poor blasted thing," he said softly. "Completely helpless. Sitting there and I came and killed him. He didn't have a chance."

THE BUILDING was bedlam. Soldiers and officials scurried crazily about, grief-stricken, hysterical. They bumped into each other, gathered in knots, shouted and gave meaningless orders.

Tolby pushed past them; nobody paid any attention to him. Fowler was gathering up the remains of the robot. Collecting the smashed pieces and bits. Tolby stopped beside him. Like Humpty-Dumpty, pulled down off his wall he'd never be back together, not now.

"Where's the woman?" he asked Fowler. "The League agent they brought in."

Fowler straightened up slowly. "I'll take you." He led Tolby down the packed, surging hall, to the hospital wing of the building.

Silvia sat up apprehensively as the two men entered the room. "What's going on?" She recognized her father. "Dad! Thank God! It was you who got out."

Tolby slammed the door against the chaos of sound hammering up and down the corridor. "How are you? How's your leg?"

"Mending. What happened?"

"I got him. The robot. He's dead."

For a moment the three of them were silent. Outside, in the halls, men ran frantically back and forth. Word had already leaked out. Troops gathered in huddled knots outside the building. Lost men, wandering away from their posts. Uncertain. Aimless.

"It's over," Fowler said.

Tolby nodded. "I know."

"They'll get tired of crouching in their foxholes," Fowler said. "They'll come filtering back. As soon as the news reaches them, they'll desert and throw away their equipment."

"Good," Tolby grunted. "The sooner the better." He touched Fowler's rifle. "You, too, I hope."

Silvia hesitated. "Do you think—"

"Think what?"

"Did we make a mistake?"

Tolby grinned wearily. "Hell of a time to think about that."

"He was doing what he thought was right. They built up their homes and factories. This whole area . . . They turn out a lot of goods. I've been watching through the window. It's made me think. They've done so much. Made so much."

"Made a lot of guns," Tolby said.

"We have guns, too. We kill and destroy. We have all the disadvantages and none of the advantages."

"We don't have war," Tolby answered quietly. "To defend this neat little organization there are ten thousand men up there in those hills. All waiting to fight. Waiting to drop their bombs and bacteria pellets, to keep this place running. But they won't. Pretty soon they'll give up and start to trickle back."

"This whole system will decay rapidly," Fowler said. "He was already losing his control. He couldn't keep the clock back much longer."

"Anyhow, it's done," Silvia murmured. "We did our job." She smiled a little. "Bors did his job and we did ours. But the times were against him and with us."

"That's right," Tolby agreed. "We did our job. And we'll never be sorry."

Fowler said nothing. He stood with his hands in his pockets, gazing silently out the window. His fingers were touching something. Three undamaged synapsis-coils. Intact memory elements from the dead robot, snatched from the scattered remains.

Just in case, he said to himself. *Just in case the times change.*

Meddler

THEY ENTERED the great chamber. At the far end, technicians hovered around an immense illuminated board, following a complex pattern of lights that shifted rapidly, flashing through seemingly endless combinations. At long tables machines whirred—computers, human-operated and robot. Wall-charts covered every inch of vertical space. Hasten gazed around him in amazement.

Wood laughed. "Come over here and I'll really show you something. You recognize *this,* don't you?" He pointed to a hulking machine surrounded by silent men and women in white lab robes.

"I recognize it," Hasten said slowly. "It's something like our own Dip, but perhaps twenty times larger. What do you haul up? And *when* do you haul?" He fingered the surface-plate of the Dip, then squatted down, peering into the maw. The maw was locked shut; the Dip was in operation. "You know, if we had any idea this existed, Histo-Research would have—"

"You know now." Wood bent down beside him. "Listen. Hasten, you're the first man from outside the Department ever to get into this room. You saw the guards. No one gets in here unauthorized; the guards have orders to kill anyone trying to enter illegally."

"To hide this? A machine? You'd shoot to—"

They stood, Wood facing him, his jaw hard. "*Your* Dip digs back into antiquity. Rome. Greece. Dust and old volumes." Wood touched the big Dip beside them. "This Dip is different. We guard it with our lives, and anyone else's lives; do you know why?"

Hasten stared at it.

"This Dip is set, not for antiquity, but—for the future."

Wood looked directly into Hasten's face. "Do you understand? The future."

"You're dredging the future? But you can't! It's forbidden by law; you know that!" Hasten drew back. "If the Executive Council knew this they'd break this building apart. You know the dangers. Berkowsky himself demonstrated them in his original thesis."

Hasten paced angrily. "I can't understand you, using a future oriented Dip. When you pull material from the future you automatically introduce new factors into the present; the future is altered—you start a never-ending shift. The more you dip the more new factors are brought in. You create unstable conditions for centuries to come. That's why the law was passed."

Wood nodded. "I know."

"And you still keep dipping?" Hasten gestured at the machine and the technicians. "Stop, for God's sake! Stop before you introduce some lethal element that can't be erased. Why do you keep—"

Wood sagged suddenly. "All right, Hasten, don't lecture us. It's too late; it's already happened. A lethal factor was introduced in our first experiments. We thought we knew what we were doing..." He looked up. "And that's why you were brought here. Sit down— you're going to hear all about it."

THEY FACED each other across the desk. Wood folded his hands. "I'm going to put it straight on the line. You are considered an expert, *the* expert at Histo-Research. You know more about using a Time Dip than anyone alive; that's why you've been shown our work, our illegal work."

"And you've already got into trouble?"

"Plenty of trouble, and every attempt to meddle further makes it that much worse. Unless we do something, we'll be the most culpable organization in history."

"Please start at the beginning," Hasten said.

"The Dip was authorized by the Political Science Council; they wanted to know the results of some of their decisions. At first we objected, giving Berkowsky's theory; but the idea is hypnotic, you know. We gave in, and the Dip was built—secretly, of course.

"We made our first dredge about one year hence. To

protect ourselves against Berkowsky's factor we tried a subterfuge; we actually brought nothing back. This Dip is geared to pick up nothing. No object is scooped; it merely photographs from a high altitude. The film comes back to us and we make enlargements and try to gestalt the conditions.

"Results were all right, at first. No more wars, cities growing, much better looking. Blow-ups of street scenes show many people, well-content, apparently. Pace a little slower.

"Then we went ahead fifty years. Even better: cities on the decrease. People not so dependent on machines. More grass, parks. Same general conditions, peace, happiness, much leisure. Less frenetic waste, hurry.

"We went on, skipping ahead. Of course, with such an indirect viewing method we couldn't be certain of anything, but it all looked fine. We relayed out information to the Council and they went ahead with their planning. And then it happened."

"What, exactly?" Hasten said, leaning forward.

"We decided to revisit a period we had already photographed, about a hundred years hence. We sent out the Dip, got it back with a full reel. The men developed it and we watched the run." Wood paused.

"And?"

"And it wasn't the same. It was different. Everything was changed. War—war and destruction everywhere." Wood shuddered. "We were appalled; we sent the Dip back at once to make absolutely certain."

"And what did you find this time?"

WOOD'S FISTS clenched. "Changed again, and for worse! Ruins, vast ruins. People poking around. Ruin and death everywhere. Slag. The *end* of war, the last phase."

"I see," Hasten said, nodding.

"That's not the worst! We conveyed the news to the Council. It ceased all activity and went into a two-week conference; it canceled all ordinances and withdrew every plan formed on the basis of our reports. It was a month before the Council got in touch with us again. The members wanted us to try once more, take one more Dip to the same period. We said no, but they insisted. It could be no worse, they argued.

"So we sent the Dip out again. It came back and we ran the film. Hasten, there are things worse than war. You wouldn't believe what we saw. There was no human life; none at all, not a single human being."

"Everything was destroyed?"

"No! No destruction, cities big and stately, roads, buildings, lakes, fields. But no human life; the cities empty, functioning mechanically, every machine and wire untouched. But no living people."

"What was it?"

"We sent the Dip on ahead, at fifty year leaps. Nothing. Nothing each time. Cities, roads, buildings, but no human life. Everyone dead. Plague, radiation, or what, we don't know. But *something* killed them. Where did it come from? We don't know. It wasn't there at first, not in our original dips.

"Somehow, *we* introduced it, the lethal factor. *We* brought it, with our meddling. It wasn't there when we started; it was done by us, Hasten." Wood stared at him, his face a white mask. "We brought it and now we've got to find what it is and get rid of it."

"How are you going to do that?"

"We've built a Time Car, capable of carrying one human observer into the future. We're sending a man there to see what it is. Photographs don't tell us enough; we have to know more! When did it first appear? How? What were the first signs? *What is it?* Once we know, maybe we can eliminate it, the factor, trace it down and remove it. Someone must go into the future and find out what it was we began. It's the only way."

Wood stood up, and Hasten rose, too.

"You're that person," Wood said. "You're going, the most competent person available. The Time Car is outside, in an open square, carefully guarded." Wood gave a signal. Two soldiers came toward the desk.

"Sir?"

"Come with us," Wood said. "We're going outside to the square; make sure no one follows after us." He turned to Hasten. "Ready?"

Hasten hesitated. "Wait a minute. I'll have to go over your work, study what's been done. Examine the Time Car itself. I can't—"

The two soldiers moved closer, looking to Wood.

Wood put his hand on Hasten's shoulder. "I'm sorry," he said, "we have no time to waste; come along with me."

ALL AROUND him blackness moved, swirling toward him and then receding. He sat down on the stool before the bank of controls, wiping the perspiration from his face. He was on his way, for better or worse. Briefly, Wood had outlined the operation of the Time Car. A few moments of instruction, the controls set for him, and then the metal door slammed behind him.

Hasten looked around him. It was cold in the sphere; the air was thin and chilly. He watched the moving dials for a while, but presently the cold began to make him uncomfortable. He went over to the equipment-locker and slid the door back. A jacket, a heavy jacket, and a flash gun. He held the gun for a minute, studying it. And tools, all kinds of tools and equipment. He was just putting the gun away when the dull chugging under him suddenly ceased. For one terrible second he was floating, drifting aimlessly, then the feeling was gone.

Sunlight flowed through the window, spreading out over the floor. He snapped the artificial lights off and went to the window to see. Wood had set the controls for a hundred years hence; bracing himself, he looked out.

A meadow, flowers and grass, rolling off into the distance. Blue sky and wandering clouds. Some animals grazed a long way off, standing together in the shade of a tree. He went to the door and unlocked it, stepping out. Warm sunlight struck him, and he felt better at once. Now he could see the animals were cows.

He stood for a long time at the door, his hands on his hips. Could the plague have been bacterial? Air-carried? If it *were* a plague. He reached up, feeling the protective helmet on his shoulders. Better to keep it on.

He went back and got the gun from the locker. Then he returned to the lip of the sphere, checked the door-lock to be certain it would remain closed during his absence. Only then, Hasten stepped down onto the grass of the meadow. He closed the door and looked around him. Presently he began to walk quickly away from the sphere, toward the top of a long hill that stretched out half a mile away. As he strode along, he examined the click-band on his wrist

which would guide him back to the metal sphere, the Time
Car, if he could not find the way himself.

He came to the cows, passing by their tree. The cows
got up and moved away from him. He noticed something
that gave him a sudden chill; their udders were small and
wrinkled. Not herd cows.

When he reached the top of the hill he stopped, lifting
his glasses from his waist. The earth fell away, mile after
mile of it, dry green fields without pattern or design,
rolling like waves as far as the eye could see. Nothing else?
He turned, sweeping the horizon.

He stiffened, adjusting the sight. Far off to the left, at
the very limit of vision, the vague perpendiculars of a city
rose up. He lowered the glasses and hitched up his heavy
boots. Then he walked down the other side of the hill,
taking big steps; he had a long way to go.

HASTEN HAD not walked more than half an hour when he
saw butterflies. They rose up suddenly a few yards in front
of him, dancing and fluttering in the sunlight. He stopped
to rest, watching them. They were all colors, red and blue,
with splashes of yellow and green. They were the largest
butterflies he had ever seen. Perhaps they had come from
some zoo, escaped and bred wild after man left the scene.
The butterflies rose higher and higher in the air. They
took no notice of him but struck out toward the distant
spires of the city; in a moment they were gone.

Hasten started up again. It was hard to imagine the
death of man in such circumstances, butterflies and grass
and cows in the shade. What a quiet and lovely world was
left, without the human race!

Suddenly one last butterfly fluttered up, almost in his
face, rising quickly from the grass. He put his arm up
automatically, batting at it. The butterfly dashed against
his hand. He began to laugh—

Pain made him sick; he fell half to his knees, gasping
and retching. He rolled over on his face, hunching himself
up, burying his face in the ground. His arm ached, and
pain knotted him up; his head swam and he closed his
eyes.

When Hasten turned over at last, the butterfly was
gone; it had not lingered.

He lay for a time in the grass, then he sat up slowly, getting shakily to his feet. He stripped off his shirt and examined his hand and wrist. The flesh was black, hard and already swelling. He glanced down at it and then at the distant city. The butterflies had gone there . . .

He made his way back to the Time Car.

HASTEN REACHED the sphere a little after the sun had begun to drop into evening darkness. The door slid back to his touch and he stepped inside. He dressed his hand and arm with salve from the medicine kit and then sat down on the stool, deep in thought, staring at his arm. A small sting, accidental, in fact. The butterfly had not even noticed. Suppose the whole pack—

He waited until the sun had completely set and it was pitch black outside the sphere. At night all the bees and butterflies disappeared; or at least, those he knew did. Well, he would have to take a chance. His arm still ached dully, throbbing without respite. The salve had done no good; he felt dizzy, and there was a fever taste in his mouth.

Before he went out he opened the locker and brought all the things out. He examined the flash gun but put it aside. A moment later he found what he wanted. A blowtorch, and a flashlight. He put all the other things back and stood up. Now he was ready—if that were the word for it. As ready as he would ever be.

He stepped out into the darkness, flashing the light ahead of him. He walked quickly. It was a dark and lonely night; only a few stars shone above him, and his was the only earthly light. He passed up the hill and down the other side. A grove of trees loomed up, and then he was on a level plain, feeling his way toward the city by the beam of the flashlight.

WHEN HE reached the city he was very tired. He had gone a long way, and his breath was beginning to come hard. Huge ghostly outlines rose up ahead of him, disappearing above, vanishing into darkness. It was not a large city, apparently, but its design was strange to Hasten, more vertical and slim then he was used to.

He went through the gate. Grass was growing from the

stone pavement of the streets. He stopped, looking down. Grass and weeds everywhere; and in the corners, by the buildings were bones, little heaps of bones and dust. He walked on, flashing his light against the sides of the slender buildings. His footsteps echoed hollowly. There was no light except his own.

The buildings began to thin out. Soon he found himself entering a great tangled square, overgrown with bushes and vines. At the far end a building larger than the others rose. He walked toward it, across the empty, desolate square, flashing his light from side to side. He walked up a half-buried step and onto a concrete plaza. All at once he stopped. To his right, another building reared up, catching his attention. His heart thudded. Above the doorway his light made out a word cut expertly into the arch:

Bibliotheca

This was what he wanted, the library. He went up the steps toward the dark entrance. Wood boards gave under his feet. He reached the entrance and found himself facing a heavy wood door with metal handles. When he took hold of the handles the door fell toward him, crashing past him, down the steps and into the darkness. The odor of decay and dust choked him.

He went inside. Spider webs brushed against his helmet as he passed along silent halls. He chose a room at random and entered it. Here were more heaps of dust and grey bits of bones. Low tables and shelves ran along the walls. He went to the shelves and took down a handful of books. They powdered and broke in his hands, showering bits of paper and thread onto him. Had only a century passed since his own time?

HASTEN SAT down at one of the tables and opened one of the books that was in better condition. The words were no language he knew, a Romance language that he knew must be artificial. He turned page after page. At last he took a handful of books at random and moved back toward the door. Suddenly his heart jumped. He went over to the wall, his hands trembling. Newspapers.

He took the brittle, cracking sheets carefully down, holding them to the light. The same language, of course. Bold, black headlines. He managed to roll some of the papers together and add them to his load of books. Then he went through the door, out into the corridor, back the way he had come.

When he stepped out onto the steps cold fresh air struck him, tingling his nose. He looked around at the dim outlines rising up on all sides of the square. Then he walked down and across the square, feeling his way carefully along. He came to the gate of the city, and a moment later he was outside, on the flat plain again, heading back toward the Time Car.

For an endless time he walked, his head bent down, plodding along. Finally fatigue made him stop, swaying back and forth, breathing deeply. He set down his load and looked around him. Far off, at the edge of the horizon, a long streak of gray had appeared, silently coming into existence while he was walking. Dawn. The sun coming up.

A cold wind moved through the air, eddying against him. In the forming gray light the trees and hills were beginning to take shape, a hard, unbending outline. He turned toward the city. Bleak and thin, the shafts of the deserted buildings stuck up. For a moment he watched, fascinated by the first color of day as it struck the shafts and towers. Then the color faded, and a drifting mist moved between him and the city. All at once he bent down and grabbed up his load. He began to walk, hurrying as best he could, chill fear moving through him.

From the city a black speck had leaped up into the sky and was hovering over it.

AFTER A TIME, a long time, Hasten looked back. The speck was still there—but it had grown. And it was no longer black; in the clear light of day the speck was beginning to flash, shining with many colors.

He increased his pace; he went down the side of a hill and up another. For a second he paused to snap on his click-band. It spoke loudly; he was not far from the sphere. He waved his arm and the clicks rose and fell. To the right. Wiping the perspiration from his hands he went on.

A few minutes later he looked down from the top of a ridge and saw a gleaming metal sphere resting silently on the grass, dripping with cold dew from the night. The Time Car; sliding and running, he leaped down the hill toward it.

He was just pushing the door open with his shoulder when the first cloud of butterflies appeared at the top of the hill, moving quietly toward him.

He locked the door and set his armload down, flexing his muscles. His hand ached, burning now with an intense pain. He had no time for that—He hurried to the window and peered out. The butterflies were swarming toward the sphere, darting and dancing above him, flashing with color. They began to settle down onto the metal, even onto the window. Abruptly, his gaze was cut off by gleaming bodies, soft and pulpy, their beating wings mashed together. He listened. He could hear them, a muffled, echoing sound that came from all sides of him. The interior of the sphere dimmed into darkness as the butterflies sealed off the window. He lit the artificial lights.

Time passed. He examined the newspapers, uncertain of what to do. Go back? Or ahead? Better jump ahead fifty years or so. The butterflies were dangerous, but perhaps not the real thing, the lethal factor that he was looking for. He looked at his hand. The skin was black and hard, a dead area that was increasing. A faint shadow of worry went through him; it was getting worse, not better.

The scratching sound on all sides of him began to annoy him, filling him with an uneasy restlessness. He put down the books and paced back and forth. How could insects, even immense insects such as these destroy the human race? Surely human beings could combat them. Dusts, poisons, sprays.

A bit of metal, a little particle drifted down onto his sleeve. He brushed it off. A second particle fell, and then some tiny fragments. He leaped, his head jerking up.

A circle was forming above his head. Another circle appeared to the right of it, and then a third. All around him circles were forming in the walls and roof of the sphere. He ran to the control board and closed the safety switch. The board hummed into life. He began to set the indicator panel, working rapidly, frantically. Now pieces of metal were dropping down, a rain of metal fragments onto the floor. Corrosive, some kind of substance exuded from them. Acid? Natural secretion of some sort. A large piece of metal fell; he turned.

Into the sphere the butterflies came, fluttering and dancing toward him. The piece that had fallen was a circle of metal, cut cleanly through. He did not have time even to notice it; he snatched up the blowtorch and snapped it on. The flame sucked and gurgled. As the butterflies came toward him he pressed the handle and held the spout up. The air burst alive with burning particles that rained down all over him, and a furious odor reeked through the sphere.

He closed the last switches. The indicator lights flickered, the floor chugged under him. He threw the main lever. More butterflies were pushing in, crowding each other eagerly, struggling to get through. A second circle of metal crashed to the floor suddenly, emitting a new horde. Hasten cringed, backing away, the blowtorch up, spouting flame. The butterflies came on, more and more of them.

Then sudden silence settled over everything, a quiet so abrupt that he blinked. The endless, insistent scratching had ceased. He was alone, except for a cloud of ashes and particles over the floor and walls, the remains of the butterflies that had got into the sphere. Hasten sat down on the stool, trembling. He was safe, on his way back to his own time; and there was no doubt, no possible doubt that he had found the lethal factor. It was there, in the heap of ashes on the floor, in the circles neatly cut in the hull of the car. Corrosive secretion? He smiled grimly.

His last vision of them, of the swelling horde had told him what he wanted to know. Clutched carefully against the first butterflies through the circles were tools, tiny cutting tools. They had cut their way in, bored through; they had come carrying their own equipment.

He sat down, waiting for the Time Car to complete its journey.

DEPARTMENT guards caught hold of him, helping him from the Car. He stepped down unsteadily, leaning against them. "Thanks," he murmured.

Wood hurried up. "Hasten, you're all right?"

He nodded. "Yes. Except my hand."

"Let's get inside at once." They went through the door, into the great chamber. "Sit down." Wood waved his hand impatiently, and a soldier hurried a chair over. "Get him some hot coffee."

Coffee was brought. Hasten sat sipping. At last he pushed the cup away and leaned back.

"Can you tell us now?" Wood asked.

"Yes."

"Fine." Wood sat down across from him. A tape recorder whirred into life and a camera began to photograph Hasten's face as he talked. "Go on. What did you find?"

WHEN HE had finished the room was silent. None of the guards or technicians spoke.

Wood stood up, trembling. "God. So it's a form of toxic life that got them. I thought it was something like that. But butterflies? And intelligent. Planning attacks. Probably rapid breeding, quick adaptation."

"Maybe the books and newspapers will help us."

"But where did they come from? Mutation of some existing form? Or from some other planet. Maybe space travel brought them in. We've got to find out."

"They attacked only human beings," Hasten said. "They left the cows. Just people."

"Maybe we can stop them." Wood snapped on the vidphone. "I'll have the Council convene an emergency session. We'll give them your description and recommendations. We'll start a program, organize units all over the planet. Now that we know what it is, we have a chance. Thanks to you, Hasten, maybe we can stop them in time!"

The operator appeared and Wood gave the Council's code letter. Hasten watched dully. At last he got to his feet and wandered around the room. His arm throbbed unmercifully. Presently he went back outside, through the doorway into the open square. Some soldiers were examining the Time Car curiously. Hasten watched them without feeling, his mind blank.

"What is this, sir?" one asked.

"That?" Hasten roused himself, going slowly over. "That's a Time Car."

"No, I mean this." The soldier pointed to something on

the hull. "This, sir; it wasn't on there when the Car went out."

Hasten's heart stopped beating. He pushed past them, staring up. At first he saw nothing on the metal gull, only the corroded metal surface. Then chill fright rushed through him.

Something small and brown and furry was there, on the surface. He reached out, touching it. A sack, a stiff little brown sack. It was dry, dry and empty. There was nothing in it; it was open at one end. He stared up. All across the hull of the Car were little brown sacks, some still full, but most of them already empty.

Cocoons.

A Game of Unchance

WHILE ROLLING A fifty-gallon drum of water from the canal to his potato garden, Bob Turk heard the roar, glanced up into the haze of the midafternoon Martian sky and saw the great blue interplan ship.

In excitement he waved. And then he read the words painted on the side of the ship and his joy became alloyed with care. Because this great pitted hull, now lowering itself to a rear-end landing, was a carny ship, come to this region of the fourth planet to transact business.

The painting spelled out:

FALLING STAR ENTERTAINMENT ENTERPRISES
PRESENTS:
FREAKS, MAGIC, TERRIFYING STUNTS, AND WOMEN!

The final word had been painted largest of all.

I better go tell the settlement council, Turk realized. He left his water drum and trotted toward the shop-area, panting as his lungs struggled to take in the thin, weak air of this unnatural, colonized world. Last time a carnival had come to their area they had been robbed of most of their crops—accepted by the pitchmen in barter—and had wound up with nothing more than an armload of useless plaster figurines. It would not happen again. And yet—

He felt the craving within him, the need to be entertained. And they all felt this way; the settlement yearned for the bizarre. Of course the pitchmen knew this, preyed off this. Turk thought, If only we could keep our heads. Barter excess food and cloth-fibers, not what we need ... not become like a lot of kids. But life in the colony

231

world was monotonous. Carting water, fighting bugs, repairing fences, ceaselessly tinkering with the semi-autonomous robot farm machinery which sustained them...it wasn't enough; it had no—culture. No solemnity.

"Hey," Turk called as he reached Vince Guest's land; Vince sat aboard his one-cylinder plow, wrench in hand. "Hear the noise? Company! More side-shows, like last year—remember?"

"I remember," Vince said, not looking up. "They got all my squash. The hell with traveling shows." His face became dark.

"This is a different outfit," Turk explained, halting. "I never saw them before; they've got a *blue* ship and it looks like it's been everywhere. You know what we're going to do? Remember our plan?"

"Some plan," Vince said, closing the jaw of the wrench.

"Talent is talent," Turk babbled, trying to convince—not merely Vince—but himself as well; he talked against his own alarm. "All right, so Fred's sort of half-witted; his talent's genuine, I mean, we've tried it out a million times, and why we didn't use it against that carny last year I'll never know. But now we're organized. Prepared."

Raising his head Vince said, "You know what that dumb kid will do? He'll join the carny; he'll leave with it and he'll use his talent on their side—we can't trust him."

"I trust him," Turk said, and hurried on toward the buildings of the settlement, the dusty, eroded gray structures directly ahead. Already he could see their council chairman, Hoagland Rae, busy at his store; Hoagland rented tired pieces of equipment to settlement members and they all depended on him. Without Hoagland's contraptions no sheep would get sheared, no lambs would be distailed. It was no wonder that Hoagland had become their political—as well as economic—leader.

STEPPING OUT onto the hard-packed sand, Hoagland shaded his eyes, wiped his wet forehead with a folded handkerchief and greeted Bob Turk. "Different outfit this time?" His voice was low.

"Right," Turk said, his heart pounding. "And we can

take them, Hoag! If we play it right; I mean, once Fred—"

"They'll be suspicious," Hoagland said thoughtfully. "No doubt other settlements have tried to use Psi to win. They may have one of those—what do you call them?—those anti-Psi folks with them. Fred's a p-k and if they have an anti-p-k—" He gestured, showing his resignation.

"I'll go tell Fred's parents to get him from school," Bob Turk panted. "It'd be natural for kids to show up right away; let's close the school for this afternoon so Fred's lost in the crowd, you know what I mean? He doesn't *look* funny, not to me, anyhow." He sniggered.

"True," Hoagland agreed, with dignity. "The Costner boy appears quite normal. Yes, we'll try; that's what we voted to do anyhow, we're committed. Go sound the surplus-gathering bell so these carny boys can see we've got good produce to offer—I want to see all those apples and walnuts and cabbages and squash and pumpkins piled up—" He pointed to the spot. "And an accurate inventory sheet, with three carbons, in my hands, within one hour." Hoagland got out a cigar, lit up with his lighter. "Get going."

Bob Turk went.

As THEY walked through their south pasture, among the black-face sheep who chewed the hard, dry grass, Tony Costner said to his son, "You think you can manage it, Fred? If not, say so. You don't have to."

Straining, Fred Costner thought he could dimly see the carnival, far off, arranged before the up-ended interplan ship. Booths, shimmering big banners and metal streamers that danced in the wind... and the recorded music, or was it an authentic calliope? "Sure," he muttered. "I can handle them; I've been practicing every day since Mr. Rae told me." To prove it he caused a rock lying ahead of them to skim up, pass in an arc, start toward them at high speed and then drop abruptly back to the brown, dry grass. A sheep regarded it dully and Fred laughed.

A small crowd from the settlement, including children, had already manifested itself among the booths now being set up; he saw the cotton candy machine hard at work, smelled the frying popcorn, saw with delight a vast cluster of helium-filled balloons carried by a gaudily-painted dwarf wearing a hobo costume.

His father said quietly, "What you must look for, Fred, is the game which offers the really valuable prizes."

"I know," he said, and began to scan the booths. We don't have a need for hula-hula dolls, he said to himself. Or boxes of salt water taffy.

Somewhere in the carnival lay the real spoils. It might be in the money-pitching board or the spinning wheel or the bingo table; anyhow it was there. He scented it, sniffed it. And hurried.

In a weak, strained voice his father said, "Um, maybe I'll leave you, Freddy." Tony had seen one of the girl platforms and had turned toward it, unable to take his eyes from the scene. One of the girls was already—but then the rumble of a truck made Fred Costner turn, and he forgot about the high-breasted, unclad girl on the platform. The truck was bringing the produce of the settlement, to be bartered in exchange for tickets.

The boy started toward the truck, wondering how much Hoagland Rae had decided to put up this time after the awful licking they had taken before. It looked like a great deal and Fred felt pride; the settlement obviously had full confidence in his abilities.

He caught then the unmistakable stench of Psi.

It emanated from a booth to his right and he turned at once in that direction. This was what the carny people were protecting, this one game which they did not feel they could afford to lose. It was, he saw, a booth in which one of the freaks acted as the target; the freak was a no-head, the first Fred had ever seen, and he stopped, transfixed.

The no-head had no head at all and his sense organs, his eyes and nose and ears, had migrated to other parts of his body beginning in the period before birth. For instance, his mouth gaped from the center of his chest, and from each shoulder an eye gleamed; the no-head was deformed but not deprived, and Fred felt respect for him. The no-head could see, smell and hear as good as anyone. But what exactly did he do in the game?

In the booth the no-head sat within a basket suspended

above a tub of water. Behind the no-head Fred Costner saw a target and then he saw the heap of baseballs near at hand and he realized how the games worked; if the target were hit by a ball the no-head would plunge into the tub of water. And it was to prevent this that the carny had directed its Psi powers; the stench here was overpowering. He could not, however, tell from whom the stench came, the no-head or the operator of the booth or from a third person as yet unseen.

THE OPERATOR, a thin young woman wearing slacks and a sweater and tennis shoes, held a baseball toward Fred. "Ready to play, captain?" she demanded and smiled at him insinuatingly, as if it was utterly in the realm of the impossible that he might play and win.

"I'm thinking," Fred said. He was scrutinizing the prizes.

The no-head giggled and the mouth located in the chest said, "He's thinking—I doubt that!" It giggled again and Fred flushed.

His father came up beside him. "Is this what you want to play?" he said. Now Hoagland Rae appeared; the two men flanked the boy, all three of them studying the prizes. What were they? Dolls, Fred thought. At least that was their appearance; the vaguely male, small shapes lay in rows on the shelves to the left of the booth's operator. He could not for the life of him fathom the carny's reasons for protecting these; surely they were worthless. He moved closer, straining to see . . .

Leading him off to one side Hoagland Rae said worriedly, "But even if we win, Fred, what do we get? Nothing we can use, just those plastic figurines. We can't barter those with other settlements, even." He looked disappointed; the corners of his mouth turned down dismally.

"I don't think they're what they seem," Fred said. "But I don't actually know what they are. Anyhow let me try, Mr. Rae; I know this is the one." And the carny people certainly believed so.

"I'll leave it up to you," Hoagland Rae said, with pessimism; he exchanged glances with Fred's father, then slapped the boy encouragingly on the back. "Let's go," he

announced. "Do your best, kid." The group of them—
joined now by Bob Turk—made their way back to the
booth in which the no-head sat with shoulder eyes
gleaming.

"Made up your mind, people?" the thin stony-faced
girl who operated the booth asked, tossing a baseball and
recatching it.

"Here." Hoagland handed Fred an envelope; it was the
proceeds from the settlement's produce, in the form of
carny tickets—this was what they had obtained in
exchange. This was all there was, now.

"I'll try," Fred said to the thin girl, and handed her a
ticket.

The thin girl smiled, showing sharp, small teeth.

"Put me in the drink!" the no-head babbled. "Dunk me
and win a valuable prize!" It giggled again, in delight.

THAT NIGHT, in the workshop behind his store, Hoagland
Rae sat with a jeweler's loup in his right eye, examining
one of the figurines which Tony Costner's boy had won at
the Falling Star Entertainment Enterprises carnival
earlier in the day.

Fifteen of the figurines lay in a row against the far wall
of Hoagland's workshop.

With a tiny pair of pliers Hoagland pried open the back
of the doll-like structure and saw, within, intricate wiring.
"The boy was right," he said to Bob Turk, who stood
behind him smoking a synthetic tobacco cigarette in jerky
agitation. "It's not a doll; it's fully rigged. Might be UN
property they stole; might even be a microrob. You know,
one of those special automatic mechanisms the government uses for a million tasks from spying to reconstruct
surgery for war vets." Now, gingerly, he opened the front
of the figurine.

More wiring, and the miniature parts which even under
the loup were exceedingly difficult to make out. He gave
up; after all, his ability was limited to repairing power
harvesting equipment and the like. This was just too
much. Again he wondered exactly how the settlement
could make use of these microrobs. Sell them back to the
UN? And meanwhile, the carnival had packed up and
gone. No way to find out from them what these were.

"Maybe it walks and talks," Turk suggested.

Hoagland searched for a switch on the figurine, found none. Verbal order? he wondered. "Walk," he ordered it. The figurine remained inert. "I think we've got something here," he said to Turk. "But—" He gestured. "It'll take time; we've got to be patient." Maybe if they took one of the figurines to M City, where the truly professional engineers, electronics experts and repairmen of all kinds could be found . . . but he wanted to do this himself; he distrusted the inhabitants of the one great urban area on the colony planet.

"Those carny people sure were upset when we won again and again," Bob Turk chuckled. "Fred, he said that they were exerting their own Psi all the time and it completely surprised them that—"

"Be quiet," Hoagland said. He had found the figurine's power supply; now he needed only to trace the circuit until he came to a break. By closing the break he could start the mechanism into activity; it was—or rather it seemed—as simple as that.

SHORTLY, he found the interruption in the circuit. A microscopic switch, disguised as the belt buckle, of the figurine . . . exulting, Hoagland closed the switch with his needle-nose pliers, set the figurine down on his work-bench and waited.

The figurine stirred. It reached into a pouch-like construct hanging at its side, a sort of purse; from the pouch it brought a tiny tube, which it pointed at Hoagland.

"Wait," Hoagland said feebly. Behind him Turk bleated and scuttled for cover. Something boomed in his face, a light that thrust him back; he shut his eyes and cried out in fright. *We're being attacked!* he shouted, but his voice did not sound; he heard nothing. He was crying uselessly in a darkness which had no end. Groping, he reached out imploringly . . .

The settlement's registered nurse was bending over him, holding a bottle of ammonia at his nostrils. Grunting, he managed to lift his head, open his eyes. He lay in his workshop; around him stood a ring of settlement adults, Bob Turk foremost, all with expressions of gray alarm.

"Those dolls or whatever," Hoagland managed to

whisper. "Attacked us; be careful." He twisted, trying to see the line of dolls which he had so carefully placed against the far wall. "I set one off prematurely," he mumbled. "By completing the circuit; I tripped it so now we know." And then he blinked.

The dolls were gone.

"I went for Miss Beason," Bob Turk explained, "and when I got back they had disappeared. Sorry." He looked apologetic, as if it were his personal fault. "But you were hurt; I was worried you were maybe dead."

"Okay," Hoagland said, pulling himself up; his head ached and he felt nauseated. "You did right. Better get that Costner kid in here, get his opinion." He added, "Well, we've been taken. For the second year in a row. Only this time is worse." *This time,* he thought, *we won. We were better off last year when we merely lost.*

He had an intimation of true foreboding.

FOUR DAYS LATER, as Tony Costner hoed weeds in his squash garden, a stirring of the ground made him pause; he reached silently for the pitchfork, thinking, *It's an m-gopher, down under, eating the roots. I'll get it.* He lifted the pitchfork, and, as the ground stirred once more, brought the tines of the fork savagely down to penetrate the loose, sandy soil.

Something beneath the surface squeaked in pain and fright. Tony Costner grabbed a shovel, dug the dirt away. A tunnel lay exposed and in it, dying in a heap of quivering, pulsating fur, lay—as he had from long experience anticipated—a Martian gopher, its eyes glazed in agony, elongated fangs exposed.

He killed it, mercifully. And then bent down to examine it. Because something had caught his eye: a flash of metal.

The m-gopher wore a harness.

It was artificial, of course; the harness fitted snugly around the animal's thick neck. Almost invisible, hair-like wires passed from the harness and disappeared into the scalp of the gopher near the front of the skull.

"Lord," Tony Costner said, picking the gopher and its harness up and standing in futile anxiety, wondering what to do. Right away he connected this with the carnival dolls; they had gone off and done this, made this—the settlement, as Hoagland had said, was under attack.

He wondered what the gopher would have done had he not killed it.

The gopher had been up to something. Tunneling toward—his house!

Later, he sat beside Hoagland Rae in the workshop; Rae, with care, had opened the harness, inspected its interior.

"A transmitter," Hoagland said, and breathed out noisily, as if his childhood asthma had returned. "Short range, maybe half a mile. The gopher was directed by it, maybe gave back a signal that told where it was and what it was doing. The electrodes to the brain probably connect with pleasure and pain areas ... that way the gopher could be controlled." He glanced at Tony Costner. "How'd you like to have a harness like that on you?"

"I wouldn't," Tony said, shivering. He wished, all at once, that he was back on Terra, overcrowded as it was; he longed for the press of the crowd, the smells and sounds of great throngs of men and women, moving along the hard sidewalks, among the lights. It occurred to him then, in a flash, that he had never really enjoyed it here on Mars. Far too lonely, he realized. I made a mistake. My wife; she made me come here.

It was a trifle late, however, to think that now.

"I guess," Hoagland said stonily, "that we'd better notify the UN military police." He went with dragging steps to the wallphone, cranked it, then dialed the emergency number. To Tony he said, half in apology, half in anger, "I can't take responsibility for handling this, Costner; it's too difficult."

"It's my fault too," Tony said. "When I saw that girl, she had taken off the upper part of her garment and—"

"UN regional security office," the phone declared, loudly enough for Tony Costner to hear it.

"We're in trouble," Hoagland said. And explained, then, about the Falling Star Entertainment Enterprises ship and what had happened. As he talked he wiped his streaming forehead with his handkerchief; he looked old and tired, and very much in need of a rest.

AN HOUR later the military police landed in the middle of the settlement's sole street. A uniformed UN officer, middle-aged, with a briefcase, stepped out, glanced around in the yellow late-afternoon light, made out the sight of the crowd with Hoagland Rae placed officially in front. "You are General Mozart?" Hoagland said tentatively, holding his hand out.

"That's correct," the heavy-set UN officer said, as they shook briefly. "May I see the construct, please?" He seemed a trifle disdainful of the somewhat grimy settlement people; Hoagland felt that acutely, and his sense of failure and depression burgeoned.

"Sure, general." Hoagland led the way to his store and the workshop in the rear.

After he had examined the dead m-gopher with its electrodes and harness, General Mozart said, "You may have won artifacts they did *not* want to give up, Mr. Rae. Their final—in other words actual—destination was probably not this settlement." Again his distaste showed, ill-disguised; who would want to bother with this area? "But, and this is a guess, eventually Earth and the more populated regions. However, by your employment of a parapsychological bias on the ball-throwing game—" He broke off, glanced at his wristwatch. "We'll treat the fields in this vicinity with arsine gas, I think; you and your people will have to evacuate this whole region, as a matter of fact tonight; we'll provide a transport. May I use your phone? I'll order the transport—you assemble all your people." He smiled reflexively at Hoagland and then went to the telephone to place his call back to his office in M City.

"Livestock, too?" Rae said. "We can't sacrifice them." He wondered just how he was supposed to get their sheep, dogs and cattle into the UN transport in the middle of the night. What a mess, he thought dully.

"Of course livestock," General Mozart said unsympathetically, as if Rae were some sort of idiot.

The third steer driven aboard the UN transport carried a harness at its neck; the UN military policeman at the entrance hatch spotted it, shot the steer at once, summoned Hoagland to dispose of the carcass.

Squatting by the dead steer, Hoagland Rae examined the harness and its wiring. As with the m-gopher, the harness, connected by delicate leads, the brain of the animal to the sentient organism—whatever it was—which had installed the apparatus, located, he assumed, no further than a mile from the settlement. What was this animal supposed to do? he wondered as he disconnected the harness. Gore one of us? Or—eavesdrop. More likely that; the transmitter within the harness hummed audibly; it was perpetually on, picking up all sounds in the vicinity. So they know we've brought in the military, Hoagland realized. And that we've detected two of these constructs, now.

He had a deep intuition that this meant the abolition of the settlement. This area would soon be a battleground between the UN military and the—whatever they were. Falling Star Entertainment Enterprises. He wondered where they were from. Outside the Sol System, evidently.

KNEELING momentarily beside him a blackjack—a black-clad UN secret police officer—said, "Cheer up. This tipped their hand; we could never prove those carnivals were hostile, before. Because of you they never made it to Terra. You'll be reinforced; don't give up." He grinned at Hoagland, then hurried off, disappearing into the darkness, where a UN tank sat parked.

Yes, Hoagland thought. We did the authorities a favor. And they'll reward us by moving massively into this area.

He had a feeling that the settlement would never be quite the same again, no matter what the authorities did. Because, if nothing else, the settlement had failed to solve its own problems; it had been forced to call for outside help. For the big boys.

Tony Costner gave him a hand with the dead steer; together they dragged it to one side, gasping for breath as they grappled with the still-warm body. "I feel responsible," Tony said, when they had set it down.

"Don't." Hoagland shook his head. "And tell your boy not to feel bad."

"I haven't seen Fred since this first came out," Tony said miserably. "He took off, terribly disturbed. I guess the UN MPs will find him; they're on the outskirts rounding everybody up." He sounded numb, as if he could not quite take in what was happening. "An MP told me that by morning we could come back. The arsine gas would have taken care of everything. You think they've run into this before? They're not saying but they seem so efficient. They seem so sure of what they're doing."

"Lord knows," Hoagland said. He lit a genuine Earth-made Optimo cigar and smoked in glum silence, watching a flock of black-face sheep being driven into the transport. Who would have thought the legendary, classic invasion of Earth would take this form? he asked himself. Starting here at our meager settlement, in terms of small wired figurines, a little over a dozen in all, which we labored to win from Falling Star Entertainment Enterprises; as General Mozart said, the invaders didn't even want to give them up. Ironic.

Bob Turk, coming up beside him, said quietly, "You realize we're going to be sacrificed. That's obvious. Arsine will kill all the gophers and rats but it won't kill the microrobs because they don't breathe. The UN will have to keep blackjack squads operating in this region for weeks, maybe months. This gas attack is just the beginning." He turned accusingly to Tony Costner. "If your kid—"

"All right," Hoagland said in a sharp voice. "That's enough. If I hadn't taken that one apart, closed the circuit—you can blame me, Turk; in fact I'll be glad to resign. You can run the settlement without me."

Through a battery-driven loudspeaker a vast UN voice boomed, "All persons within sound of my voice prepare to board! This area will be flooded with poisonous gas at 14:00. I repeat—" It repeated, as the loudspeakers turned in first one direction and then another; the noise echoed in the night darkness.

STUMBLING, Fred Costner made his way over the unfamiliar, rough terrain, wheezing in sorrow and weariness; he paid no attention to his location, made no effort to see where he was going. All he wanted to do was get away. He had destroyed the settlement and everyone from Hoagland Rae on down knew it. Because of him—

Far away, behind him, an amplified voice boomed, "All persons within sound of my voice prepare to board! This area will be flooded with poisonous gas at 14:00. I repeat, all persons within sound of my voice—" It dinned on and on. Fred continued to stumble along, trying to shut out the racket of the voice, hurrying away from it.

The night smelled of spiders and dry weeds; he sensed the desolation of the landscape around him. Already he was beyond the final perimeter of cultivation; he had left the settlement's fields and now he stumbled over unplowed ground where no fences or even surveyor's stakes existed. But they would probably flood this area, too, however; the UN ships would coast back and forth, spraying the arsine gas, and then after that special forces troops would come in, wearing gas-masks, carrying flame throwers, with metal-sensitive detectors on their backs, to roust out the fifteen microrobs which had taken refuge underground in the burrows of rats and vermin. *Where they belong,* Fred Costner said to himself. *And to think I wanted them for the settlement; I thought, because the carnival wanted to keep them, that they must be valuable.*

He wondered, dimly, if there was any way he could undo what he had done. Find the fifteen microrobs, plus the activated one which had almost killed Hoagland Rae? And—he had to laugh; it was absurd. Even if he found their hideout—assuming that all of them had taken refuge together in one spot—how could he destroy them? And they were armed. Hoagland Rae had barely escaped, and that had been from one acting alone.

A light glowed ahead.

In the darkness he could not make out the shapes which moved at the edge of the light; he halted, waited, trying to orient himself. Persons came and went and he heard their voices, muted, both men's and women's. And the sound of machinery in motion. *The UN would not be sending out women,* he realized. *This was not the authorities.*

A portion of the sky, the stars and faint nocturnal swath of haze, had been blotted out, and he realized all at once that he was seeing the outline of a large stationary object.

It could be a ship, parked on its tail, awaiting take-off; the shape seemed roughly that.

HE SEATED himself, shivering in the cold of the Martian night, scowling in an attempt to trace the passage of the indistinct forms busy with their activity. Had the carnival returned? Was this once more the Falling Star Entertainment Enterprises vehicle? Eerily, the thought came to him: the booths and banners and tents and platforms, the magic shows and girl platforms and freaks and games of chance were being erected here in the middle of the night, in this barren area lost in the emptiness between settlements. A hollow enactment of the festivity of the carny life, for no one to see or experience. Except—by chance—himself. And to him it was revolting; he had seen all he wanted of the carnival, its people and—things.

Something ran across his foot.

With his psycho-kinetic faculty he snared it, drew it back; reaching, he grabbed with both hands until all at once he had snatched out of the darkness a thrashing, hard shape. He held it, and saw with fright one of the microrobs; it struggled to escape and yet, reflexively, he held onto it. The microrob had been scurrying toward the parked ship, and he thought, the ship's picking them up. So they won't be found by the UN. They're getting away, then the carnival can go on with its plans.

A calm voice, a woman's, said from close by, "Put it down, please. It wants to go."

Jumping with shock he released the microrob and it scuttled off, rustling in the weeds, gone at once. Standing before Fred the thin girl, still wearing slacks and a sweater, faced him placidly, a flashlight in her hand; by its circle of illumination he made out her sharply-traced features, her colorless jaw and intense, clear eyes. "Hi," Fred said stammeringly; he stood up, defensively, facing the girl. She was slightly taller than he and he felt afraid of her. But he did not catch the stench of Psi about her and he realized that it had definitely not been she there in the booth who had struggled against his own faculty during the game. So he had an advantage over her, and perhaps one she did not know about.

"You better get away from here," he said. "Did you hear the loudspeaker? They're going to gas this area."

"I heard." The girl surveyed him. "You're the big winner, aren't you, sonny? The master game-player; you dunked out anti-ceph sixteen times in a row." She laughed merrily. "Simon was furious; he caught cold from that and blames you. So I hope you don't run into him."

"Don't call me sonny," he said. His fear began to leave him.

"Douglas, our p-k, says you're strong. You wrestled him down every time; congratulations. Well, how pleased are you with your take?" Silently, she once more laughed; her small sharp teeth shone in the meager light. "You feel you got your produce's worth?"

"Your p-k isn't much good," Fred said. "I didn't have any trouble and I'm really not experienced. You could do a lot better."

"With you, possibly? Are you asking to join us? Is this a proposition from you to me, little boy?"

"No!" he said, startled and repelled.

"There was a rat," the girl said, "in the wall of your Mr. Rae's workshop; it had a transmitter on it and so we knew about your call to the UN as soon as you made it. So we've had plenty of time to regain our—" She paused a moment. "Our merchandise. If we cared to. Nobody meant to hurt you; it isn't our fault that busybody Rae stuck the tip of his screwdriver into the control-circuit of that one microrob. Is it?"

"He started the cycle prematurely. It would have done that eventually anyhow." He refused to believe otherwise; he knew the settlement was in the right. "And it's not going to do you any good to collect all those microrobs because the UN knows and—"

"'Collect'?" The girl rocked with amusement. "We're not collecting the sixteen microrobs you poor little people won. We're going ahead—you forced us to. The ship is unloading the rest of them." She pointed with the flashlight and he saw in that brief instant the horde of microrobs disgorged, spreading out, seeking shelter like so many photophobic insects.

He shut his eyes and moaned.

"Are you still sure," the girl said purringly, "that you don't want to come with us? It'll insure your future, sonny. And otherwise—" She gestured. "Who knows? Who really can guess what'll become of your tiny settlement and you poor tiny people?"

"No," he said. "I'm still not coming."

When he opened his eyes again the girl had gone off.

She stood with the no-head, Simon, examining a clipboard which the no-head held.

Turning, Fred Costner ran back the way he had come, toward the UN military police.

THE LEAN, tall, black-uniformed UN secret police general said, "I have replaced General Mozart who is unfortunately ill-equipped to deal with domestic subversion; he is a military man exclusively." He did not extend his hand to Hoagland Rae. Instead he began to pace about the workshop, frowning. "I wish I had been called in last night. For example I could have told you one thing immediately... which General Mozart did not understand." He halted, glanced searchingly at Hoagland. "You realize, of course, that you did not beat the carnival people. They wanted to lose those sixteen microrobs."

Hoagland Rae nodded silently; there was nothing to say. It now did appear obvious, as the blackjack general had pointed out.

"Prior appearances of the carnival," General Wolff said, "in former years, was to set you up, to set each settlement up in turn. They knew you'd have to plan to win this time. So this time they brought their microrobs. And had their weak Psi ready to engage in an ersatz 'battle' for supremacy."

"All I want to know," Hoagland said, "is whether we're going to get protection." The hills and plains surrounding the settlement, as Fred had told them, were now swarming with the microrobs; it was unsafe to leave the downtown buildings.

"We'll do what we can." General Wolff resumed pacing. "But obviously we're not primarily concerned with you, or with any other particular settlement or locale that's been infested. It's the overall situation that we have to deal with. That ship has been forty places in the last twenty-four hours; how they've moved so swiftly—" He broke off. "They had every step prepared. And you thought you conned them." He glowered at Hoagland Rae. "Every settlement along the line thought that as they won their boxload of microrobs."

"I guess," Hoagland said presently, "that's what we get for cheating." He did not meet the blackjack general's gaze.

"That's what you get for pitting your wits against an adversary from another system," General Wolff said bitingly. "Better look at it that way. And the next time a vehicle *not* from Terra shows up—don't try to master-mind a strategy to defeat them: *call us*."

Hoagland Rae nodded. "Okay. I understand." He felt only dull pain, not indignation; he deserved—they all deserved—this chewing out. If they were lucky their reprimand would end at this. It was hardly the settlement's greatest problem. "What do they want?" he asked General Wolff. "Are they after this area for colonization? Or is this an economic—"

"Don't try," General Wolff said.

"P-pardon?"

"It's not something you can understand, now or at any other time. We know what they're after—and *they* know what they're after. Is it important that you know, too? Your job is to try to resume your farming as before. Or if you can't do that, pull back and return to Earth."

"I see," Hoagland said, feeling trivial.

"Your kids can read about it in the history books," General Wolff said. "That ought to be good enough for you."

"It's just fine," Hoagland Rae said, miserably. He seated himself halfheartedly at his workbench, picked up a screwdriver and began to tinker with a malfunctioning autonomic tractor guidance-turret.

"Look," General Wolff said, and pointed.

IN A corner of the workshop, almost invisible against the dusty wall, a microrob crouched watching them.

"Jeez!" Hoagland wailed, groping around on his workbench for the old .32 revolver which he had gotten out and loaded.

Long before his fingers found the revolver the microrob had vanished. General Wolff had not even moved; he seemed, in fact, somewhat amused: he stood with his arms folded, watching Hoagland fumbling with the antiquated side arm.

"We're working on a central device," General Wolff said, "which would cripple all of them simultaneously. By interrupting the flow of current from their portable power-packs. Obviously to destroy them one by one is absurd; we never even considered it. However—" He paused thoughtfully, his forehead wrinkling. "There's reason to believe they—the outspacers—have anticipated us and have diversified the power-sources in such a way that—" He shrugged philosophically. "Well, perhaps something else will come to mind. In time."

"I hope so," Hoagland said. And tried to resume his repair of the defective tractor turret.

"We've pretty much given up the hope of holding Mars," General Wolff said, half to himself.

Hoagland slowly set down his screwdriver, stared at the secret policeman.

"What we're going to concentrate on is Terra," General Wolff said, and scratched his nose reflectively.

"Then," Hoagland said after a pause, "there's really no hope for us here; that's what you're saying."

The blackjack general did not answer. He did not need to.

As HE bent over the faintly greenish, scummy surface of the canal where botflies and shiny black beetles buzzed, Bob Turk saw, from the corner of his vision, a small shape scuttle. Swiftly he spun, reached for his laser cane; he brought it up, fired it and destroyed—oh happy day!—a heap of rusted, discarded fuel drums, nothing more. The microrob had already departed.

Shakily he returned the laser cane to his belt and again bent over the bug-infested water. As usual the 'robs had been active here during the night; his wife had seen them, heard their rat-like scratchings. What the hell had they done? Bob Turk wondered dismally, and sniffed long and hard at the water.

It seemed to him that the customary odor of the stagnant water was somehow subtly changed.

"Damn," he said, and stood up, feeling futile. The 'robs had put some contaminator in the water; that was obvious. Now it would have to be given a thorough chemical analysis and that would take days. Meanwhile, what would keep his potato crop alive? Good question.

Raging in baffled helplessness, he pawed the laser cane, wishing for a target—and knowing he could never, not in a million years, have one. As always the 'robs did their

work at night; steadily, surely, they pushed the settlement
back.

Already ten families had packed up and taken passage
for Terra. To resume—if they could—the old lives which
they had abandoned.

And, soon, it would be his turn.

If only there was something they could do. Some way
they could fight back. He thought, I'd do anything, give
anything, for a chance to get those 'robs. I swear it. I'd go
into debt or bondage or servitude or anything, just for a
chance of freeing the area of them.

He was shuffling morosely away from the canal, hands
thrust deep in the pockets of his jacket, when he heard the
booming roar of the intersystem ship overhead.

Calcified, he stood peering up, his heart collapsing
inside him. Them back? he asked himself. The Falling
Star Entertainment Enterprises ship . . . are they going to
hit us all over again, finish us off finally? Shielding his
eyes he peered frantically, not able even to run, his body
not knowing its way even to instinctive, animal panic.

The ship, like a gigantic orange, lowered. Shaped like
an orange, colored like an orange . . . it was not the blue
tubular ship of the Falling Star people; he could see that.
But also it was not from Terra; it was not UN. He had
never seen a ship exactly like it before and he knew that he
was definitely seeing another vehicle from beyond the Sol
System, much more blatantly so than the blue ship of the
Falling Star creatures. Not even a cursory attempt had
been made to make it appear Terran.

And yet, on its sides, it had huge letters, which spelled
out words in English.

HIS LIPS moving he read the words as the ship settled to a
landing north-east of the spot at which he stood.

SIX SYSTEM EDUCATIONAL PLAYTIME ASSOCIATES IN A
RIOT OF FUN AND FROLIC FOR ALL!

It was—God in heaven—another itinerant carnival
company.

He wanted to look away, to turn and hurry off. And yet
he could not; the old familiar drive within him, the

craving, the fixated curiosity, was too strong. So he continued to watch; he could see several hatches open and autonomic mechanisms beginning to nose, like flattened doughnuts, out onto the sand.

They were pitching camp.

Coming up beside him his neighbor Vince Guest said hoarsely, "Now what?"

"You can see." Turk gestured frantically. "Use your eyes." Already the auto-mechs were erecting a central tent; colored streamers hurled themselves upward into the air and then rained down on the still two-dimensional booths. And the first humans—or humanoids—were emerging. Vince and Bob saw men wearing bright clothing and then women in tights. Or rather something considerably less than tights.

"Wow," Vince managed to say, swallowing. "You see those ladies? You ever seen women with such—"

"I see them," Turk said. "But I'm never going back to one of these non-Terran carnivals from beyond the system and neither is Hoagland; I know that as well as I know my own name."

How rapidly they were going to work. No time wasted; already faint, tinny music, of a carousel nature, filtered to Bob Turk. And the smells. Cotton candy, roasting peanuts, and with those the subtle smell of adventure and exciting sights, of the illicit. One woman with long braided red hair had hopped lithely up onto a platform; she wore a meager bra and wisp of silk at her waist and as he watched fixedly she began to practice her dance. Faster and faster she spun until at last, carried away by the rhythm, she discarded entirely what little she wore. And the funny thing about it all was that it seemed to him real art; it was not the usual carny shimmying at the midsection. There was something beautiful and alive about her movements; he found himself spellbound.

"I—better go get Hoagland," Vince managed to say, finally. Already a few settlers, including a number of children, were moving as if hypnotized toward the lines of booths and the gaudy streamers that fluttered and shone in the otherwise drab Martian air.

"I'll go over and get a closer look," Bob Turk said, "while you're locating him." He started toward the carnival on a gradually accelerating run, scuffling sand as he hurried.

To HOAGLAND, Tony Costner said, "At least let's *see* what they have to offer. You know they're not the same people; it wasn't them who dumped those horrible damn microrobs off here—you can see that."

"Maybe it's something worse," Hoagland said, but he turned to the boy, Fred. "What do you say?" he demanded.

"I want to look," Fred Costner said. He had made up his mind.

"Okay," Hoagland said, nodding. "That's good enough for me. It won't hurt us to look. As long as we remember what that UN secret police general told us. Let's not kid ourselves into imagining we can outsmart them." He put down his wrench, rose from his workbench, and walked to the closet to get his fur-lined outdoor coat.

When they reached the carnival they found that the games of chance had been placed—conveniently—ahead of even the girly shows and the freaks. Fred Costner rushed forward, leaving the group of adults behind; he sniffed the air, took in the scents, heard the music, saw past the games of chance the first freak platform: it was his favorite abomination, one he remembered from previous carnivals, only this one was superior. It was a no-body. In the midday Martian sunlight it reposed quietly: a bodiless head complete with hair, ears, intelligent eyes; heaven only knew what kept it alive . . . in any case he knew intuitively that it was genuine.

"Come and see Orpheus, the head without a visible body!" the pitchman called through his megaphone, and a group, mostly children, had gathered in awe to gape. "How does it stay alive? How does it propel itself? Show them, Orpheus." The pitchman tossed a handful of food pellets—Fred Costner could not see precisely what—at the head; it opened its mouth to enormous, frightening proportions, managed to snare most of what landed near it. The pitchman laughed and continued with his spiel. The no-body was now rolling industriously after the bits of food which it had missed. Gee, Fred thought.

"Well?" Hoagland said, coming up beside him. "Do you see any games we might profit from?" His tone was drenched with bitterness. "Care to throw a baseball at anything?" He started away, then, not waiting, a tired little fat man who had been defeated too much, who had already lost too many times. "Let's go," he said to the other adults of the settlement. "Let's get out of here before we get into another—"

"Wait," Fred said. He had caught it, the familiar, pleasing stench. It came from a booth on his right and he turned at once in that direction.

A PLUMP, gray-colored middle-aged woman stood in a ringtoss booth, her hands full of the light wicker rings.

Behind Fred his father said to Hoagland Rae, "You get the rings over the merchandise; you win whatever you manage to toss the ring onto so that it stays." With Fred he walked slowly in that direction. "It would be a natural," he murmured, "for a psycho-kinetic. I would think."

"I suggest," Hoagland said, speaking to Fred, "that you look more closely this time at the prizes. At the merchandise." However, he came along, too.

At first Fred could not make out what the neat stacks were, each of them exactly alike, intricate and metallic; he came up to the edge of the booth and the middle-aged woman began her chant-like litany, offering him a handful of rings. For a dollar, or whatever of equal value the settlement had to offer.

"What are they?" Hoagland said, peering. "I—think they're some kind of machines."

Fred said, "I know what they are." And we've got to play, he realized. We must round up every item in the settlement that we can possibly trade these people, every cabbage and rooster and sheep and wool blanket.

Because, he realized, this is our chance. Whether General Wolff knows about it or likes it.

"My God," Hoagland said quietly. "Those are traps."

"That's right, mister," the middle-aged woman chanted. "Homeostatic traps; they do all the work, think for themselves, you just let them go and they travel and travel and they never give up until they catch—" She winked. *"You know what.* Yes, you know what they catch, mister, those little pesky things you can't ever possibly catch by yourselves, that are poisoning your water and killing your steers and ruining your settlement—win a trap, a valuable, useful trap, and you'll see, you'll see!" She tossed a wicker ring and it nearly settled over one of the complex, sleek-metal traps; it might very well have, if she had thrown it just a little more carefully. At least that was the impression given. They all felt this.

Hoagland said to Tony Costner and Bob Turk, "We'll need a couple hundred of them at least."

"And for that," Tony said, "we'll have to hock everything we own. But it's worth it; at least we won't be completely wiped out." His eyes gleamed. "Let's get started." To Fred he said, "Can you play this game? Can you win?"

"I—think so," Fred said. Although somewhere nearby, someone in the carnival was ready with a contrary power of psycho-kinesis. But not enough, he decided. *Not quite enough.*

It was almost as if they had worked it that way on purpose.

Sales Pitch

COMMUTE SHIPS roared on all sides, as Ed Morris made his way wearily home to Earth at the end of a long hard day at the office. The Ganymede-Terra lanes were choked with exhausted, grim-faced businessmen; Jupiter was in opposition to Earth and the trip was a good two hours. Every few million miles the great flow slowed to a grinding, agonized halt; signal-lights flashed as streams from Mars and Saturn fed into the main traffic-arteries.

"Lord," Morris muttered. "How tired can you *get?*" He locked the autopilot and momentarily turned from the control-board to light a much-needed cigarette. His hands shook. His head swam. It was past six; Sally would be fuming; dinner would be spoiled. The same old thing. Nerve-wracking driving, honking horns and irate drivers zooming past his little ship, furious gesturing, shouting, cursing...

And the ads. That was what really did it. He could have stood everything else—but the ads, the whole long way from Ganymede to Earth. And on Earth, the swarms of salesrobots; it was too much. And they were everywhere.

He slowed to avoid a fifty-ship smashup. Repair-ships were scurrying around trying to get the debris out of the lane. His audio-speaker wailed as police rockets hurried up. Expertly, Morris raised his ship, cut between two slow-moving commercial transports, zipped momentarily into the unused left lane, and then sped on, the wreck left behind. Horns honked furiously at him; he ignored them.

"Trans-Solar Products greets you!" an immense voice boomed in his ear. Morris groaned and hunched down in his seat. He was getting near Terra; the barrage was increasing. "Is your tension-index pushed over the

254

safety-margin by the ordinary frustrations of the day? Then you need an Id-Persona Unit. So small it can be worn behind the ear, close to the frontal lobe—"

Thank God, he was past it. The ad dimmed and receded behind, as his fast-moving ship hurtled forward. But another was right ahead.

"Drivers! Thousands of unnecessary deaths each year from inter-planet driving. Hypno-Motor Control from an expert source-point insures your safety. Surrender your body and save your life!" The voice roared louder. "Industrial experts say—"

Both audio ads, the easiest to ignore. But now a visual ad was forming; he winced, closed his eyes, but it did no good.

"Men!" an unctuous voice thundered on all sides of him. "Banish internally-caused obnoxious odors *forever*. Removal by modern painless methods of the gastro-intestinal tract and substitution system will relieve you of the most acute cause of social rejection." The visual image locked; a vast nude girl, blonde hair disarranged, blue eyes half shut, lips parted, head tilted back in sleep-drugged ecstasy. The features ballooned as the lips approached his own. Abruptly the orgiastic expression on the girl's face vanished. Disgust and revulsion swept across, and then the image faded out.

"Does this happen to you?" the voice boomed. "During erotic sex-play do you offend your love-partner by the presence of gastric processes which—"

THE VOICE died, and he was past. His mind his own again, Morris kicked savagely at the throttle and sent the little ship leaping. The pressure, applied directly to the audio-visual regions of his brain, had faded below spark point. He groaned and shook his head to clear it. All around him the vague half-defined echoes of ads glittered and gibbered, like ghosts of distant video-stations. Ads waited on all sides, he steered a careful course, dexterity born of animal desperation, but not all could be avoided. Despair seized him. The outline of a new visual-audio ad was already coming into being.

"You, mister wage-earner!" it shouted into the eyes and ears, noses and throats, of a thousand weary commuters.

"Tired of the same old job? Wonder Circuits Inc. has perfected a marvelous long-range thoughtwave scanner. Know what others are thinking and saying. Get the edge on fellow employees. Learn facts, figures about your employer's personal existence. Banish uncertainty!"

Morris' despair swept up wildly. He threw the throttle on full-blast; the little ship bucked and rolled as it climbed from the traffic-lane into the dead zone beyond. A shrieking roar, as his fender whipped through the protective wall—and then the ad faded behind him.

He slowed down, trembling with misery and fatigue. Earth lay ahead. He'd be home, soon. Maybe he could get a good night's sleep. He shakily dropped the nose of the ship and prepared to hook onto the tractor beam of the Chicago commute field.

"The best metabolism adjuster on the market," the salesrobot shrilled. "Guaranteed to maintain a perfect endocrine-balance, or your money refunded in full."

Morris pushed wearily past the salesrobot, up the sidewalk toward the residential-block that contained his living-unit. The robot followed a few steps, then forgot him and hurried after another grim-faced commuter.

"All the news while it's news," a metallic voice dinned at him. "Have a retinal vidscreen installed in your least-used eye. Keep in touch with the world; don't wait for out-of-date hourly summaries."

"Get out of the way," Morris muttered. The robot stepped aside for him and he crossed the street with a pack of hunched-over men and women.

ROBOT-SALESMEN were everywhere, gesturing, pleading, shrilling. One started after him and he quickened his pace. It scurried along, chanting its pitch and trying to attract his attention, all the way up the hill to his living unit. It didn't give up until he stooped over, snatched up a rock, and hurled it futilely. He scrambled in the house and slammed the doorlock after him. The robot hesitated, then turned and raced after a woman with an armload of packages toiling up the hill. She tried vainly to elude it, without success.

"Darling!" Sally cried. She hurried from the kitchen, drying her hands on her plastic shorts, bright-eyed and excited. "Oh, you poor thing! You look so tired!"

Morris peeled off his hat and coat and kissed his wife briefly on her bare shoulder. "What's for dinner?"

Sally gave his hat and coat to the closet. "We're having Uranian wild pheasant; your favorite dish."

Morris' mouth watered, and a tiny surge of energy crawled back into his exhausted body. "No kidding? What the hell's the occasion?"

His wife's brown eyes moistened with compassion. "Darling, it's your birthday; you're thirty-seven years old today. Had you forgotten?"

"Yeah," Morris grinned a little. "I sure had." He wandered into the kitchen. The table was set; coffee was steaming in the cups and there was butter and white bread, mashed potatoes and green peas. "My golly. A real occasion."

Sally punched the stove controls and the container of smoking pheasant was slid onto the table and neatly sliced open. "Go wash your hands and we're ready to eat. Hurry—before it gets cold."

Morris presented his hands to the wash slot and then sat down gratefully at the table. Sally served the tender, fragrant pheasant, and the two of them began eating.

"Sally," Morris said, when his plate was empty and he was leaning back and sipping slowly at his coffee. "I can't go on like this. Something's got to be done."

"You mean the drive? I wish you could get a position on Mars like Bob Young. Maybe if you talked to the Employment Commission and explained to them how all the strain—"

"It's not just the drive. *They're right out front.* Everywhere. Waiting for me. All day and all night."

"Who are, dear?"

"Robots selling things. As soon as I set down the ship. Robots and visual-audio ads. They dig right into a man's brain. They follow people around until they die."

"I know." Sally patted his hand sympathetically. "When I go shopping they follow me in clusters. All talking at once. It's really a panic—you can't understand half they're saying."

"We've got to break out."

"Break out?" Sally faltered. "What do you mean?"

"'We've got to get away from them. They're destroying us."

MORRIS fumbled in his pocket and carefully got out a tiny fragment of metal-foil. He unrolled it with painstaking care and smoothed it out on the table. "Look at this. It was circulated in the office, among the men; it got to me and I kept it."

"What does it mean?" Sally's brow wrinkled as she made out the words. "Dear. I don't think you got all of it. There must be more than this."

"A new world," Morris said softly. "Where they haven't got to, yet. It's a long way off, out beyond the solar system. Out in the stars."

"Proxima?"

"Twenty planets. Half of them habitable. Only a few thousand people out there. Families, workmen, scientists, some industrial survey teams. Land free for the asking."

"But it's so—" Sally made a face. "Dear, isn't it sort of under-developed? They say it's like living back in the twentieth century. Flush toilets, bathtubs, gasoline driven cars—"

"That's right." Morris rolled up the bit of crumpled metal, his face grim and dead-serious. "It's a hundred years behind times. None of this." He indicated the stove and the furnishings in the livingroom. "We'll have to do without. We'll have to get used to a simpler life. The way our ancestors lived." He tried to smile, but his face wouldn't cooperate. "You think you'd like it? No ads, no salesrobots, traffic moving at sixty miles an hour instead of sixty million. We could raise passage on one of the big trans-system liners. I could sell my commute rocket..."

There was a hesitant, doubtful silence.

"Ed," Sally began. "I think we should think it over more. What about your job? What would you do out there?"

"I'd find something."

"But *what*? Haven't you got that part figured out?" A shrill tinge of annoyance crept into her voice. "It seems to me we should consider that part just a little before we throw away everything and just—take off."

"If we don't go," Morris said slowly, trying to keep his

voice steady, "they'll get us. There isn't much time left. I don't know how much longer I can hold them off."

"Really, Ed! You make it sound so melodramatic. If you feel that bad why don't you take some time off and have a complete inhibition check? I was watching a vidprogram and I saw them going over a man whose psychosomatic system was much worse than yours. A much older man."

She leaped to her feet. "Let's go out tonight and celebrate. Okay?" Her slim fingers fumbled at the zipper of her shorts. "I'll put on my new plastirobe, the one I've never had nerve enough to wear."

Her eyes sparkled with excitement as she hurried into the bedroom. "You know the one I mean? When you're up close it's translucent but as you get farther off it becomes more and more sheer until—"

"I know the one," Morris said wearily. "I've seen them advertised on the way home from work." He got slowly to his feet and wandered into the livingroom. At the door of the bedroom he halted. "Sally—"

"Yes?"

Morris opened his mouth to speak. He was going to ask her again, talk to her about the metal-foil fragment he had carefully wadded up and carried home. He was going to talk to her about the frontier. About Proxima Centauri. Going away and never coming back. But he never had a chance.

The doorchimes sounded.

"Somebody's at the door!" Sally cried excitedly. "Hurry up and see who it is!"

IN THE EVENING darkness the robot was a silent, unmoving figure. A cold wind blew around it and into the house. Morris shivered and moved back from the door. "What do you want?" he demanded. A strange fear licked at him. "What is it?"

The robot was larger than any he had seen. Tall and broad, with heavy metallic grippers and elongated eye-lenses. Its upper trunk was a square tank instead of the usual cone. It rested on four treads, not the customary two. It towered over Morris, almost seven feet high. Massive and solid.

"Good evening," it said calmly. Its voice was whipped around by the night wind; it mixed with the dismal noises of evening, the echoes of traffic and the clang of distant street signals. A few vague shapes hurried through the gloom. The world was black and hostile.

"Evening," Morris responded automatically. He found himself trembling. "What are you selling?"

"I would like to show you a fasrad," the robot said.

Morris' mind was numb; it refused to respond. What was a *fasrad*? There was something dreamlike and nightmarish going on. He struggled to get his mind and body together. "A what?" he croaked.

"A fasrad." The robot made no effort to explain. It regarded him without emotion, as if it was not its responsibility to explain anything. "It will take only a moment."

"I—" Morris began. He moved back, out of the wind. And the robot, without change of expression, glided past him and into the house.

"Thank you," it said. It halted in the middle of the livingroom. "Would you call your wife, please? I would like to show her the fasrad, also."

"Sally," Morris muttered helplessly. "Come here."

Sally swept breathlessly into the livingroom, her breasts quivering with excitement. "What is it? Oh!" She saw the robot and halted uncertainly. "Ed, did you order something? Are we buying something?"

"Good evening," the robot said to her. "I am going to show you the fasrad. Please be seated. On the couch, if you will. Both together."

Sally sat down expectantly, her cheeks flushed, eyes bright with wonder and bewilderment. Numbly, Ed seated himself beside her. "Look," he muttered thickly. "What the hell is a fasrad? *What's going on?* I don't want to buy anything!"

"What is your name?" the robot asked him.

"Morris." He almost choked. "Ed Morris."

The robot turned to Sally. "Mrs. Morris." It bowed slightly. "I'm glad to meet you, Mr. and Mrs. Morris. You are the first persons in your neighborhood to see the fasrad. This is the initial demonstration in this area." Its cold eyes swept the room. "Mr. Morris, you are employed, I assume. Where are you employed?"

"He works on Ganymede," Sally said dutifully, like a little girl in school. "For the Terran Metals Development Co."

The robot digested this information. "A fasrad will be of value to you." It eyed Sally. "What do you do?"

"I'm a tape-transcriber at Histo-Research."

"A fasrad will be of no value in your professional work, but it will be helpful here in the home." It picked up a table in its powerful steel grippers. "For example, sometimes an attractive piece of furniture is damaged by a clumsy guest." The robot smashed the table to bits; fragments of wood and plastic rained down. "A fasrad is needed."

MORRIS leaped helplessly to his feet. He was powerless to halt events; a numbing weight hung over him, as the robot tossed the fragments of table away and selected a heavy floor lamp.

"Oh, dear," Sally gasped. "That's my best lamp."

"When a fasrad is possessed, there is nothing to fear." The robot seized the lamp and twisted it grotesquely. It ripped the shade, smashed the bulbs, then threw away the remnants. "A situation of this kind can occur from some violent explosion, such as an H-bomb."

"For God's sake," Morris muttered. "We--"

"An H-bomb attack may never occur," the robot continued, "but in such an event a fasrad is indispensable." It knelt down and pulled an intricate tube from its waist. Aiming the tube at the floor it atomized a hole five feet in diameter. It stepped back from the yawning pocket. "I have not extended this tunnel, but you can see a fasrad would save your life in case of attack."

The word *attack* seemed to set off a new train of reactions in its metal brain.

"Sometimes a thug or hood will attack a person at night," it continued. Without warning it whirled and drove its fist through the wall. A section of the wall collapsed in a heap of powder and debris. "That takes care of the thug." The robot straightened out and peered around the room. "Often you are too tired in the evening to manipulate the buttons on the stove." It strode into the kitchen and began punching the stove controls; immense quantities of food spilled in all directions.

"Stop!" Sally cried. "Get away from my stove!"

"You may be too weary to run water for your bath." The robot tripped the controls of the tub and water poured down. "Or you may wish to go right to bed." It yanked the bed from its concealment and threw it flat. Sally retreated in fright as the robot advanced toward her. "Sometimes after a hard day at work you are too tired to remove your clothing. In that event—"

"Get out of here!" Morris shouted at it. "Sally, run and get the cops. The thing's gone crazy. *Hurry.*"

"The fasrad is a necessity in all modern homes," the robot continued. "For example, an appliance may break down. The fasrad repairs it instantly." It seized the automatic humidity control and tore the wiring and replaced it on the wall. "Sometimes you would prefer not to go to work. The fasrad is permitted by law to occupy your position for a consecutive period not to exceed ten days. If, after that period—"

"Good God," Morris said, as understanding finally came. "You're the fasrad."

"That's right," the robot agreed. "Fully Automatic Self-Regulating Android (Domestic). There is also the fasrac (Construction), the fasram (Managerial), the fasras (Soldier), and the fasrab (Bureaucrat). I am designed for home use."

"You—" Sally gasped. "You're for sale. You're selling yourself."

"I am demonstrating myself," the fasrad, the robot, answered. Its impassive metal eyes were fixed intently on Morris as it continued, "I am sure, Mr. Morris, you would like to own me. I am reasonably priced and fully guaranteed. A full book of instructions is included. I cannot conceive of taking *no* for an answer."

AT HALF past twelve, Ed Morris still sat at the foot of the bed, one shoe on, the other in his hand. He gazed vacantly ahead. He said nothing.

"For heaven's sake," Sally complained. "Finish untying that knot and get into bed; you have to be up at five-thirty."

Morris fooled aimlessly with the shoelace. After awhile

he dropped the shoe and tugged at the other one. The house was cold and silent. Outside, the dismal night-wind whipped and lashed at the cedars that grew along the side of the building. Sally lay curled up beneath the radiant-lens, a cigarette between her lips, enjoying the warmth and half-dozing.

In the livingroom stood the fasrad. It hadn't left. It was still there, was waiting for Morris to buy it.

"Come on!" Sally said sharply. "What's wrong with you? It fixed all the things it broke; it was just demonstrating itself." She sighed drowsily. "It certainly gave me a scare. I thought something had gone wrong with it. They certainly had an inspiration, sending it around to sell itself to people."

Morris said nothing.

Sally rolled over on her stomach and languidly stubbed out her cigarette. "That's not so much, is it? Ten thousand gold units, and if we get our friends to buy one we get a five per cent commission. All we have to do is show it. It isn't as if we had to *sell* it. It sells itself." She giggled. "They always wanted a product that sold itself, didn't they?"

Morris untied the knot in his shoelace. He slid his shoe back on and tied it tight.

"What are you doing?" Sally demanded angrily. "You come to bed!" She sat up furiously, as Morris left the room and moved slowly down the hall. "Where are you going?"

In the livingroom, Morris switched on the light and sat down facing the fasrad. "Can you hear me?" he said.

"Certainly," the fasrad answered. "I'm never inoperative. Sometimes an emergency occurs at night: a child is sick or an accident takes place. You have no children as yet, but in the event—"

"Shut up," Morris said, "I don't want to hear you."

"You asked me a question. Self-regulating androids are plugged in to a central information exchange. Sometimes a person wishes immediate information; the fasrad is always ready to answer any theoretical or factual inquiry. Anything not metaphysical."

Morris picked up the book of instructions and thumbed it. The fasrad did thousands of things; it never wore out; it was never at a loss; it couldn't make a mistake. He threw the book away. "I'm not going to buy you," he said to it. "Never. Not in a million years."

"Oh, yes you are," the fasrad corrected. "This is an opportunity you can't afford to miss." There was calm, metallic confidence in its voice. "You can't turn me down, Mr. Morris. A fasrad is an indispensable necessity in the modern home."

"Get out of here," Morris said evenly. "Get out of my house and don't come back."

"I'm not your fasrad to order around. Until you've purchased me at the regular list price, I'm responsible only to Self-Regulating Android Inc. Their instructions were to the contrary; I'm to remain with you until you buy me."

"Suppose I never buy you?" Morris demanded, but in his heart ice formed even as he asked. Already he felt the cold terror of the answer that was coming; there could be no other.

"I'll continue to remain with you," the fasrad said; "eventually you'll buy me." It plucked some withered roses from a vase on the mantel and dropped them into its disposal slot. "You will see more and more situations in which a fasrad is indispensable. Eventually you'll wonder how you ever existed without one."

"Is there anything you can't do?"

"Oh, yes; there's a great deal I can't do. But I can do anything *you* can do—and considerably better."

MORRIS LET out his breath slowly. "I'd be insane to buy you."

"You've got to buy me," the impassive voice answered. The fasrad extended a hollow pipe and began cleaning the carpet. "I am useful in all situations. Notice how fluffy and free of dust this rug is." It withdrew the pipe and extended another. Morris coughed and staggered quickly away; clouds of white particles billowed out and filled every part of the room.

"I am spraying for moths," the fasrad explained.

The white cloud turned to an ugly blueblack. The room faded into ominous darkness; the fasrad was a dim shape moving methodically about in the center. Presently the cloud lifted and the furniture emerged.

"I sprayed for harmful bacteria," the fasrad said.

It painted the walls of the room and constructed new furniture to go with them. It reinforced the ceiling in the bathroom. It increased the number of heat-vents from the furnace. It put in new electrical wiring. It tore out all the fixtures in the kitchen and assembled more modern ones. It examined Morris' financial accounts and computed his income tax for the following year. It sharpened all the pencils; it caught hold of his wrist and quickly diagnosed his high blood-pressure as psychosomatic.

"You'll feel better after you've turned responsibility over to me," it explained. It threw out some old soup Sally had been saving. "Danger of botulism" it told him. "Your wife is sexually attractive, but not capable of a high order of intellectualization."

Morris went to the closet and got his coat.

"Where are you going?" the fasrad asked.

"To the office."

"At this time of night?"

Morris glanced briefly into the bedroom. Sally was sound asleep under the soothing radiant-lens. Her slim body was rosy pink and healthy, her face free of worry. He closed the front door and hurried down the steps into the darkness. Cold night wind slashed at him as he approached the parking lot. His little commute ship was parked with hundreds of others; a quarter sent the attendant robot obediently after it.

In ten minutes he was on his way to Ganymede.

THE FASRAD boarded his ship when he stopped at Mars to refuel.

"Apparently you don't understand," the fasrad said. "My instructions are to demonstrate myself until you're satisfied. As yet, you're not wholly convinced; further demonstration is necessary." It passed an intricate web over the controls of the ship until all the dials and meters were in adjustment. "You should have more frequent servicing."

It retired to the rear to examine the drive jets. Morris numbly signalled the attendant, and the ship was released from the fuel pumps. He gained speed and the small sandy planet fell behind. Ahead, Jupiter loomed.

"Your jets aren't in good repair," the fasrad said, emerging from the rear. "I don't like that knock to the main brake drive. As soon as you land I'll make extensive repair."

"The Company doesn't mind your doing favors for me?" Morris asked, with bitter sarcasm.

"The Company considers me your fasrad. An invoice will be mailed to you at the end of the month." The robot whipped out a pen and a pad of forms. "I'll explain the four easy-payment plans. Ten thousand gold units cash means a three per cent discount. In addition, a number of household items may be traded in—items you won't have further need for. If you wish to divide the purchase in four parts, the first is due at once, and the last in ninety days."

"I always pay cash," Morris muttered. He was carefully resetting the route positions on the control board.

"There's no carrying charge for the ninety day plan. For the six month plan there's a six percent per annum charge which will amount to approximately—" It broke off. "We've changed course."

"That's right."

"We've left the official traffic lane." The fasrad stuck its pen and pad away and hurried to the control board. "What are you doing? There's a two unit fine for this."

Morris ignored it. He hung on grimly to the controls and kept his eyes on the viewscreen. The ship was gaining speed rapidly. Warning buoys sounded angrily as he shot past them and into the bleak darkness of space beyond. In a few seconds they had left all traffic behind. They were alone, shooting rapidly away from Jupiter, out into deep space.

The fasrad computed the trajectory. "We're moving out of the solar system. Toward Centaurus."

"You guessed it."

"Hadn't you better call your wife?"

Morris grunted and notched the drive bar farther up. The ship bucked and pitched, then managed to right itself. The jets began to whine ominously. Indicators showed the main turbines were beginning to heat. He ignored them and threw on the emergency fuel supply.

"I'll call Mrs. Morris," the fasrad offered. "We'll be beyond range in a short while."

"Don't bother."

"She'll worry. The fasrad hurried to the back and examined the jets again. It popped back into the cabin buzzing with alarm. "Mr. Morris, this ship is not equipped for inter-system-travel. It's a Class D four-shaft domestic model for home consumption only. It was never made to stand this velocity."

"To get to Proxima," Morris answered, "we need this velocity."

THE FASRAD connected its power cables to the control board. "I can take some of the strain off the wiring system. But unless you rev her back to normal I can't be responsible for the deterioration of the jets."

"The hell with the jets."

The fasrad was silent. It was listening intently to the growing whine under them. The whole ship shuddered violently. Bits of paint drifted down. The floor was hot from the grinding shafts. Morris' foot stayed on the throttle. The ship gained more velocity as Sol fell behind. They were out of the charted area. Sol receded rapidly.

"It's too late to vid your wife," the fasrad said. "There are three emergency-rockets in the stern; if you want, I'll fire them off in the hope of attracting a passing military transport."

"Why?"

"They can take us in tow and return us to the Sol system. There's a six hundred gold unit fine, but under the circumstances it seems to me the best policy."

Morris turned his back to the fasrad and jammed down the throttle with all his weight. The whine had grown to a violent roar. Instruments smashed and cracked. Fuses blew up and down the board. The lights dimmed, faded, then reluctantly came back.

"Mr. Morris," the fasrad said, "you must prepare for death. The statistical probabilities of turbine explosion are seventy-thirty. I'll do what I can, but the danger-point has already passed."

Morris returned to the view-screen. For a time he gazed hungrily up at the growing dot that was the twin star Centaurus. "They look all right, don't they? Prox is the important one. Twenty planets." He examined the wildly fluttering instruments. "How are the jets holding up? I can't tell from these; most of them are burned out."

The fasrad hesitated. It started to speak, then changed its mind. "I'll go back and examine them," it said. It moved to the rear of the ship and disappeared down the short ramp into the thundering, vibrating engine chamber.

Morris leaned over and put out his cigarette. He waited a moment longer, then reached out and yanked the drives full up, the last possible notch on the board.

The explosion tore the ship in half. Sections of hull hurtled around him. He was lifted weightless and slammed into the control board. Metal and plastic rained down on him. Flashing incandescent points winked, faded, and finally died into silence, and there was nothing but cold ash.

THE DULL *swish-swish* of emergency air-pumps brought consciousness back. He was pinned under the wreckage of the control board; one arm was broken and bent under him. He tried to move his legs but there was no sensation below his waist.

The splintered debris that had been his ship was still hurtling toward Centaurus. Hull-sealing equipment was feebly trying to patch the gaping holes. Automatic temperature and grav feeds were thumping spasmodically from self-contained batteries. In the view-screen the vast flaming bulk of the twin suns grew quietly, inexorably.

He was glad. In the silence of the ruined ship he lay buried beneath the debris, gratefully watching the growing bulk. It was a beautiful sight. He had wanted to see it for a long time. There it was, coming closer each moment. In a day or two the ship would plunge into the fiery mass and be consumed. But he could enjoy this interval; there was nothing to disturb his happiness.

He thought about Sally, sound asleep under the radiant-lens. Would Sally have liked Proxima? Probably not. Probably she would have wanted to go back home as soon as possible. This was something he had to enjoy alone. This was for him only. A vast peace descended over him. He could lie here without stirring, and the flaming magnificence would come nearer and nearer...

A sound. From the heaps of fused wreckage something was rising. A twisted, dented shape dimly visible in the flickering glare of the viewscreen. Morris managed to turn his head.

The fasrad staggered to a standing position. Most of its trunk was gone, smashed and broken away. It tottered, then pitched forward on its face with a grinding crash. Slowly it inched its way toward him, then settled to a dismal halt a few feet off. Gears whirred creakily. Relays popped open and shut. Vague, aimless life animated its devastated hulk.

"Good evening," its shrill, metallic voice grated.

Morris screamed. He tried to move his body but the ruined beams held him tight. He shrieked and shouted and tried to crawl away from it. He spat and wailed and wept.

"I would like to show you a fasrad," the metallic voice continued. "Would you call your wife, please? I would like to show her a fasrad, too."

"Get away!" Morris screamed. "Get away from me!"

"Good evening," the fasrad continued, like a broken tape. "Good evening. Please be seated. I am happy to meet you. What is your name? Thank you. You are the first persons in your neighborhood to see the fasrad. Where are you employed?"

Its dead eyelenses gaped at him empty and vacant.

"Please be seated," it said again. "This will take only a second. Only a second. This demonstration will take only a—"

Precious Artifact

BELOW THE 'COPTER of Milt Biskle lay newly fertile lands. He had done well with his area of Mars, verdant from his reconstruction of the ancient water-network. Spring, two springs each year, had been brought to this autumn world of sand and hopping toads, a land once made of dried soil cracking with the dust of former times, of a dreary and unwatered waste. Victim of the recent Prox-Terra conflict.

Quite soon the first Terran emigrants would appear, stake their claims and take over. He could retire. Perhaps he could return to Terra or bring his own family here, receive priority of land-acquisition—as a reconstruct engineer he deserved it. Area Yellow had progressed far faster than the other engineers' sections. And now his reward came.

Reaching forward, Milt Biskle touched the button of his long-range transmitter. "This is Reconstruct Engineer Yellow," he said. "I'd like a psychiatrist. Any one will do, so long as he's immediately available."

WHEN MILT BISKLE entered the office Dr. DeWinter rose and held out his hand. "I've heard," Dr. DeWinter said, "that you, of all the forty odd reconstruct engineers, have been the most creative. It's no wonder you're tired. Even God had to rest after six days of such work, and you've been at it for years. As I was waiting for you to reach me I received a news memo from Terra that will interest you." He picked the memo up from his desk. "The initial transport of settlers is about to arrive here on Mars . . . and they'll go directly into your area. Congratulations, Mr. Biskle."

270

Rousing himself Milt Biskle said, "What if I returned to Earth?"

"But if you mean to stake a claim for your family, here—"

Milt Biskle said, "I want you to do something for me. I feel too tired, too—" He gestured. "Or depressed, maybe. Anyhow I'd like you to make arrangements for my gear, including my wug-plant, to be put aboard a transport returning to Terra."

"Six years of work," Dr. DeWinter said. "And now you're abandoning your recompense. Recently I visited Earth and it's just as you remember—"

"How do you know how I remember it?"

"Rather," DeWinter corrected himself smoothly, "I should say it's just as it was. Overcrowded, tiny conapts with seven families to a single cramped kitchen. Autobahns so crowded you can't make a move until eleven in the morning."

"For me," Milt Biskle said, "the overcrowding will be a relief after six years of robot autonomic equipment." He had made up his mind. In spite of what he had accomplished here, or perhaps because of it, he intended to go home. Despite the psychiatrist's arguments.

Dr. DeWinter purred, "What if your wife and children, Milt, are among the passengers of this first transport?" Once more he lifted a document from his neatly-arranged desk. He studied the paper, then said, "Biskle, Fay, Mrs. Laura C. June C. Woman and two girl children. Your family?"

"Yes," Milt Biskle admitted woodenly; he stared straight ahead.

"So you see you can't head back to Earth. Put on your hair and prepare to meet them at Field Three. And exchange your teeth. You've got the stainless steel ones in, at the moment."

Chagrined, Biskle nodded. Like all Terrans he had lost his hair and teeth from the fallout during the war. For everyday service in his lonely job of re-reconstructing Yellow Area of Mars he made no use of the expensive wig which he had brought from Terra, and as to the teeth he personally found the steel ones far more comfortable than the natural-color plastic set. It indicated how far he had drifted from social inter-action. He felt vaguely guilty; Dr. DeWinter was right.

But he had felt guilty ever since the defeat of the Proxmen. The war had embittered him; it didn't seem fair that one of the two competing cultures would have to suffer, since the needs of both were legitimate.

Mars itself had been the locus of contention. Both cultures needed it as a colony on which to deposit surplus populations. Thank God Terra had managed to gain tactical mastery during the last year of the war . . . hence it was Terrans such as himself, and not Proxmen, patching up Mars.

"By the way," Dr. DeWinter said. "I happen to know of your intentions regarding your fellow reconstruct engineers."

MILT BISKLE glanced up swiftly.

"As a matter of fact," DeWinter said, "we know they're at this moment gathering in Red Area to hear your account." Opening his desk drawer he got out a yo-yo, stood up and began to operate it expertly doing *walking the dog*. "Your panic-stricken speech to the effect that something is wrong, although you can't seem to say just what it might be."

Watching the yo-yo Biskle said, "That's a toy popular in the Prox system. At least so I read in a homeopape article, once."

"Hmm. I understood it originated in the Philippines." Engrossed, Dr. DeWinter now did *around the world*. He did it well. "I'm taking the liberty of sending a disposition to the reconstruct engineers' gathering, testifying to your mental condition. It will be read aloud,—sorry to say."

"I still intend to address the gathering," Biskle said.

"Well, then there's a compromise that occurs to me. Greet your little family when it arrives here on Mars and then we'll arrange a trip to Terra for you. At our expense. And in exchange you'll agree not to address the gathering of reconstruct engineers or burden them in any way with your nebulous forebodings." DeWinter eyed him keenly. "After all, this is a critical moment. The first emigrants are arriving. We don't want trouble; we don't want to make anyone uneasy."

"Would you do me a favor?" Biskle asked. "Show me that you've got a wig on. And that your teeth are false. Just so I can be sure that you're a Terran."

Dr. DeWinter tilted his wig and plucked out his set of false teeth.

"I'll take the offer," Milt Biskle said. "If you'll agree to make certain that my wife obtains the parcel of land I set aside for her."

Nodding, DeWinter tossed him a small white envelope. "Here's your ticket. Round trip, of course, since you'll be coming back."

I hope so, Biskle thought as he picked up the ticket. But it depends on what I see on Terra. Or rather on what they *let* me see.

He had a feeling they'd let him see very little. In fact as little as Proxmanly possible.

WHEN HIS SHIP reached Terra a smartly uniformed guide waited for him. "Mr. Biskle?" Trim and attractive and exceedingly young she stepped forward alertly. "I'm Mary Ableseth, your Tourplan companion. I'll show you around the planet during your brief stay here." She smiled brightly and very professionally. He was taken aback. "I'll be with you constantly, night and day."

"Night, too?" he managed to say.

"Yes. Mr. Biskle. That's my job. We expect you to be disoriented due to your years of labor on Mars . . . labor we of Terra applaud and honor, as is right." She fell in beside him, steering him toward a parked 'copter. "Where would you like to go first? New York City? Broadway? To the night clubs and theaters and restaurants . . ."

"No, to Central Park. To sit on a bench."

"But there is no more Central Park, Mr. Biskle. It was turned into a parking lot for government employees while you were on Mars."

"I see," Milt Biskle said. "Well, then Portsmouth Square in San Francisco will do." He opened the door of the 'copter.

"That, too, has become a parking lot," Miss Ableseth said, with a sad shake of her long, luminous red hair. "We're so darn overpopulated. Try again. Mr. Biskle; there are a few parks left, one in Kansas, I believe, and *two* in Utah in the south part near St. George."

"This is bad news," Milt said. "May I stop at that amphetamine dispenser and put in my dime? I need a stimulant to cheer me up."

"Certainly," Miss Ableseth said, nodding graciously.

Milt Biskle walked to the spaceport's nearby stimulant dispenser, reached into his pocket, found a dime, and dropped the dime in the slot.

The dime fell completely through the dispenser and bounced onto the pavement.

"Odd," Biskle said, puzzled.

"I think I can explain that," Miss Ableseth said. "That dime of yours is a Martian dime, made for a lighter gravity."

"Hmm," Milt Biskle said, as he retrieved the dime. As Miss Ableseth had predicted he felt disoriented. He stood by as she put in a dime of her own and obtained the small tube of amphetamine stimulants for him. Certainly her explanation seemed adequate. But—

"It is now eight p.m. local time," Miss Ableseth said. "And I haven't had dinner, although of course you have, aboard your ship. Why not take me to dinner? We can talk over a bottle of Pinot Noir and you can tell me these vague forebodings which have brought you to Terra, that something dire is wrong and that all your marvelous reconstruct work is pointless. I'd adore to hear about it." She guided him back to the 'copter and the two of them entered, squeezing into the back seat together. Milt Biskle found her to be warm and yielding, decidedly Terran; he became embarrassed and felt his heart pounding in effort-syndrome. It had been some time since he had been this close to a woman.

"LISTEN," he said, as the automatic circuit of the 'copter caused it to rise from the spaceport parking lot, "I'm married. I've got two children and I came here on business. I'm on Terra to prove that the Proxmen really won and that we few remaining Terrans are slaves of the Prox authorities, laboring for—" He gave up; it was hopeless. Miss Ableseth remained pressed against him.

"You really think," Miss Ableseth said presently, as the 'copter passed above New York City, "that I'm a Prox agent?"

"N-no," Milt Biskle said. "I guess not." It did not seem likely, under the circumstances.

"While you're on Terra," Miss Ableseth said, "why stay in an over-crowded, noisy hotel? Why not stay with me at my conapt in New Jersey? There's plenty of room and you're more than welcome."

"Okay," Biskle agreed, feeling the futility of arguing.

"Good." Miss Ableseth gave an instruction to the 'copter; it turned north. "We'll have dinner there. It'll save money, and at all the decent restaurants there's a two-hour line this time of night, so it's almost impossible to get a table. You've probably forgotten. How wonderful it'll be when half our population can emigrate!"

"Yes," Biskle said tightly. "And they'll like Mars; we've done a good job." He felt a measure of enthusiasm returning to him, a sense of pride in the reconstruct work he and his compatriots had done. "Wait until you see it, Miss Ableseth."

"Call me Mary," Miss Ableseth said, as she arranged her heavy scarlet wig; it had become dislodged during the last few moments in the cramped quarters of the 'copter.

"Okay," Biskle said, and, except for a nagging awareness of disloyalty to Fay, he felt a sense of well-being.

"Things happen fast on Terra," Mary Ableseth said. "Due to the terrible pressure of over-population." She pressed her teeth in place; they, too, had become dislodged.

"So I see," Milt Biskle agreed, and straightened his own wig and teeth, too. *Could I have been mistaken?* he asked himself. After all he could see the lights of New York below; Terra was decidedly not a depopulated ruin and its civilization was intact.

Or was this all an illusion, imposed on his percept-system by Prox psychiatric techniques unfamiliar to him? It was a fact that his dime had fallen completely through the amphetamine dispenser. Didn't that indicate something was subtly, terribly wrong?

Perhaps the dispenser hadn't really been there.

THE NEXT day he and Mary Ableseth visited one of the few remaining parks. In the southern part of Utah, near the mountains, the park although small was bright green and attractive. Milt Biskle lolled on the grass watching a squirrel progressing toward a tree in wicket-like leaps, its tail flowing behind it in a gray stream.

"No squirrels on Mars," Milt Biskle said sleepily.

Wearing a slight sunsuit, Mary Ableseth stretched out on her back, eyes shut. "It's nice here, Milt. I imagine Mars is like this." Beyond the park heavy traffic moved along the freeway; the noise reminded Milt of the surf of the Pacific Ocean. It lulled him. All seemed well, and he tossed a peanut to the squirrel. The squirrel veered, wicket-hopped toward the peanut, its intelligent face twitching in response.

As it sat upright, holding the nut, Milt Biskle tossed a second nut off to the right. The squirrel heard it land among the maple leaves; its ears pricked up, and this reminded Milt of a game he once had played with a cat, an old sleepy tom which had belonged to him and his brother in the days before Terra had been so overpopulated, when pets were still legal. He had waited until Pumpkin—the tomcat—was almost asleep and then he had tossed a small object into the corner of the room. Pumpkin woke up. His eyes had flown open and his ears had pricked, turned, and he had sat for fifteen minutes listening and watching, brooding as to what had made the noise. It was a harmless way of teasing the old cat, and Milt felt sad, thinking how many years Pumpkin had been dead, now, his last legal pet. On Mars, though, pets would be legal again. That cheered him.

In fact on Mars, during his years of reconstruct work, he had possessed a pet. A Martian plant. He had brought it with him to Terra and it now stood on the living room coffee table in Mary Ableseth's conapt, its limbs draped rather unhappily. It had not prospered in the unfamiliar Terran climate.

"Strange," Milt murmured, "that my wug-plant isn't thriving. I'd have thought in such a moist atmosphere . . ."

"It's the gravity," Mary said, eyes still shut, her bosom rising and falling regularly. She was almost asleep. "Too much for it."

Milt regarded the supine form of the woman, remembering Pumpkin under similar circumstances. The hypnogogic moment, between waking and sleeping, when

consciousness and unconsciousness became blended
... reaching, he picked up a pebble.

He tossed the pebble into the leaves near Mary's head.

At once she sat up, eyes open startled, her sunsuit
falling from her.

Both her ears pricked up.

"But we Terrans," Milt said, "have lost control of the
musculature of our ears, Mary. On even a reflex basis."

"What?" she murmured, blinking in confusion as she
retied her sunsuit.

"Our ability to prick up our ears has atrophied," Milt
explained. "Unlike the dog and cat. Although to examine
us morphologically you wouldn't know because the
muscles are still there. So you made an error."

"I don't know what you're talking about," Mary said,
with a trace of sullenness. She turned her attention
entirely to arranging the bra of her sunsuit, ignoring him.

"Let's go back to the conapt," Milt said, rising to his
feet. He no longer felt like lolling in the park, because he
could no longer believe in the park. Unreal squirrel,
unreal grass ... was it actually? Would they ever show him
the substance beneath the illusion? He doubted it.

The squirrel followed them a short way as they walked
to their parked 'copter, then turned its attention to a
family of Terrans which included two small boys; the
children threw nuts to the squirrel and it scampered in
vigorous activity.

"Convincing," Milt said. And it really was.

Mary said, "Too bad you couldn't have seen Dr.
DeWinter more, Milt. He could have helped you." Her
voice was oddly hard.

"I have no doubt of that," Milt Biskle agreed as they
re-entered the parked 'copter.

WHEN THEY arrived back at Mary's conapt he found his
Martian wug-plant dead. It had evidently perished of
dehydration.

"Don't try to explain this," he said to Mary as the two
of them stood gazing down at the parched, dead stalks of
the once active plant. "You know what it shows. Terra is
supposedly more humid than Mars, even reconstructed
Mars at its best. Yet this plant has completely dried out.

There's no moisture left on Terra because I suppose the Prox blasts emptied the seas. Right?"

Mary said nothing.

"What I don't understand," Milt said, "is why it's worth it to you people to keep the illusion going. *I've finished my job.*"

After a pause Mary said, "Maybe there're more planets requiring reconstruct work, Milt."

"Your population is that great?"

"I was thinking of Terra. Here," Mary said. "Reconstruct work on it will take generations; all the talent and ability you reconstruct engineers possess will be required." She added, "I'm just following your hypothetical logic, of course."

"So Terra's our next job. That's why you let me come here. In fact I'm going to *stay* here." He realized that, thoroughly and utterly, in a flash of insight. "I won't be going back to Mars and I won't see Fay again. You're replacing her." It all made sense.

"Well," Mary said, with a faint wry smile, "let's say I'm attempting to." She stroked his arm. Barefoot, still in her sunsuit, she moved slowly closer and closer to him.

Frightened, he backed away from her. Picking up the dead wug-plant he numbly carried it to the apt's disposal chute and dropped the brittle, dry remains in. They vanished at once.

"And now," Mary said busily, "we're going to visit the Museum of Modern Art in New York and then, if we have time, the Smithsonian in Washington, D.C. They've asked me to keep you busy so you don't start brooding."

"But I am brooding," Milt said as he watched her change from her sunsuit to a gray wool knit dress. Nothing can stop that, he said to himself. And you know it now. And as each reconstruct engineer finishes his area it's going to happen again. I'm just the first.

At least I'm not alone, he realized. And felt somewhat better.

"How do I look?" Mary asked as she put on lipstick before the bedroom mirror.

"Fine," he said listlessly, and wondered if Mary would meet each reconstruct engineer in turn, become the mistress of each. Not only is she not what she seems, he thought, but I don't even get to keep her.

It seemed a gratuitous loss, easily avoided.

He was, he realized, beginning to like her. *Mary was alive*; that much was real. Terran or not. At least they had not lost the war to shadows; they had lost to authentic living organisms. He felt somewhat cheered.

"Ready for the Museum of Modern Art?" Mary said briskly, with a smile.

LATER, at the Smithsonian, after he had viewed the Spirit of St. Louis and the Wright brothers' incredibly ancient plane—it appeared to be at least a million years old—he caught sight of an exhibit which he had been anticipating.

Saying nothing to Mary—she was absorbed in studying a case of semi-precious stones in their natural uncut state—he slipped off and, a moment later, stood before a glass-walled section entitled

PROX MILITARY OF 2014

Three Prox soldiers stood frozen, their dark muzzles stained and grimy, side arms ready, in a makeshift shelter composed of the remains of one of their transports. A bloody Prox flag hung drably. This was a defeated enclave of the enemy; these three creatures were about to surrender or be killed.

A group of Terran visitors stood before the exhibit, gawking. Milt Biskle said to the man nearest him, "Convincing, isn't it?"

"Sure is," the man, middle-aged, with glasses and gray hair, agreed. "Were you in the war?" he asked Milt, glancing at him.

"I'm in reconstruct," Milt said. "Yellow Engineer."

"Oh." The man nodded, impressed. "Boy, those Proxmen look scary. You'd almost expect them to step out of that exhibit and fight us to the death." He grinned. "They put up a good fight before they gave in, those Proxmen; you have to give 'em credit for that."

Beside him the man's gray, taut wife said, "Those guns of theirs make me shiver. It's too realistic." Disapproving, she walked on.

"You're right," Milt Biskle said. "They do look

frighteningly real, because of course they are." There was no point in creating an illusion of this sort because the genuine thing lay immediately at hand, readily available. Milt swung himself under the guard rail, reached the transparent glass of the exhibit, raised his foot and smashed the glass; it burst and rained down with a furious racket of shivering fragments.

As Mary came running, Milt snatched a rifle from one of the frozen Proxmen in the exhibit and turned it toward her.

She halted, breathing rapidly, eyeing him but saying nothing.

"I am willing to work for you," Milt said to her, holding the rifle expertly. "After all, if my own race no longer exists I can hardly reconstruct a colony world for them; even I can see that. But I want to know the truth. Show it to me and I'll go on with my job."

Mary said, "No, Milt, if you knew the truth you wouldn't go on. You'd turn that gun on yourself." She sounded calm, even compassionate, but her eyes were bright and enlarged, wary.

"Then I'll kill you," he said. And, after that, himself.

"Wait." She pondered. "Milt—this is so difficult. You know absolutely nothing and yet look how miserable you are. How do you expect to feel when you can see your planet as it is? It's almost too much for me and I'm—" She hesitated.

"Say it."

"I'm just a—" she choked out the word—"a visitor."

"But I am right," he said. "Say it. Admit it."

"You're right, Milt," she sighed.

Two UNIFORMED museum guards appeared, holding pistols. "You okay, Miss Ableseth?"

"For the present," Mary said. She did not take her eyes off Milt and the rifle which he held. "Just wait," she instructed the guards.

"Yes ma'am." The guards waited. No one moved.

Milt said, "Did any Terran women survive?"

After a pause, Mary said, "No, Milt. But we Proxmen are within the same genus, as you well know. We can interbreed. Doesn't that make you feel better?"

"Sure," he said. "A lot better." And he did feel like turning the rifle on himself now, without waiting. It was all he could do to resist the impulse. So he had been right; that thing had not been Fay, there at Field Three on Mars. "Listen," he said to Mary Ableseth, "I want to go back to Mars again. I came here to learn something. I learned it, now I want to go back. Maybe I'll talk to Dr. DeWinter again, maybe he can help me. Any objection to that?"

"No." She seemed to understand how he felt. "After all, you did all your work there. You have a right to return. But eventually you have to begin here on Terra. We can wait a year or so, perhaps even two. But eventually Mars will be filled up and we'll need the room. And it's going to be so much harder here . . . as you'll discover." She tried to smile but failed; he saw the effort. "I'm sorry, Milt."

"So am I," Milt Biskle said. "Hell, I was sorry when that wug-plant died. I knew the truth then. It wasn't just a guess."

"You'll be interested to know that your fellow reconstruct engineer Red, Cleveland Andre, addressed the meeting in your place. And passed your intimations on to them all, along with his own. They voted to send an official delegate here to Terra to investigate; he's on his way now."

"I'm interested," Milt said. "But it doesn't really matter. It hardly changes things." He put down the rifle. "Can I go back to Mars now?" He felt tired. "Tell Dr. DeWinter I'm coming." Tell him, he thought to have every psychiatric technique in this repertory ready for me, because it will take a lot. "What about Earth's animals?" he asked. "Did any forms at all survive? How about the dog and the cat?"

Mary glanced at the museum guards; a flicker of communication passed silently between them and then Mary said, "Maybe it's all right after all."

"WHAT'S ALL RIGHT?" Milt Biskle said.

"For you to see. Just for a moment. You seem to be standing up to it better than we had expected. In our opinion you *are* entitled to that." She added, "Yes, Milt, the dog and cat survived; they live here among the ruins. Come along and look."

He followed after her, thinking to himself, Wasn't she right the first time? Do I really want to look? Can I stand up to what exists in actuality—what they've felt the need of keeping from me up until now?

At the exit ramp of the museum Mary halted and said, "Go on outside, Milt. I'll stay here. I'll be waiting for you when you come back in."

Haltingly, he descended the ramp.

And saw.

It was, of course, as she had said, ruins. The city had been decapitated, leveled three feet above ground-level; the buildings had become hollow squares, without contents, like some infinite arrangement of useless, ancient courtyards. He could not believe that what he saw was *new*; it seemed to him as if these abandoned remnants had always been there, exactly as they were now. And—how long would they remain this way?

To the right an elaborate but small-scale mechanical system had plopped itself down to a debris-filled street. As he watched, it extended a host of pseudopodia which burrowed inquisitively into the nearby foundations. The foundations, steel and cement, were abruptly pulverized; the bare ground, exposed, lay naked and dark brown, seared over from the atomic heat generated by the repair autonomic rig—a construct, Milt Biskle thought, not much different from those I employ on Mars. At least to some meager extent the rig had the task of clearing away the old. He knew from his own reconstruct work on Mars that it would be followed, probably within minutes, by an equally elaborate mechanism which would lay the groundwork for the new structures to come.

And, standing off to one side in the otherwise deserted street, watching this limited clearing-work in progress, two gray, thin figures could be made out. Two hawk-nosed Proxmen with their pale, natural hair arranged in high coils, their earlobes elongated with heavy weights.

The victors, he thought to himself. Experiencing the satisfaction of this spectacle, witnessing the last artifacts of the defeated race being obliterated. Some day a purely Prox city will rise up here: Prox architecture, streets of the odd, wide Prox pattern, the uniform boy-like buildings with their many subsurface levels. And citizens such as these will be treading the ramps, accepting the high-speed runnels in their daily routines. And what, he thought, about the Terran dogs and cats which now inhabit these ruins, as Mary said? Will even they disappear? Probably not entirely. There will be room for them, perhaps in museums and zoos, as oddities to be gaped at. Survivals of an ecology which no longer obtained. Or even mattered.

And yet—Mary was right. The Proxmen were within the same genus. Even if they did not interbreed with the remaining Terrans the species as he had known it would go on. And they would interbreed, he thought. His own relationship with Mary was a harbinger. As individuals they were not so far apart. The results might even be good.

The results, he thought as he turned away and started back into the museum, may be a race not quite Prox and not quite Terran; something that is genuinely new may come from the melding. At least we can hope so.

Terra would be rebuilt. He had seen slight but real work in progress with his own eyes. Perhaps the Proxmen lacked the skill that he and his fellow reconstruct engineers possessed . . . but now that Mars was virtually done they could begin here. It was not absolutely hopeless. Not *quite*.

Walking up to Mary he said hoarsely, "Do me a favor. Get me a cat I can take back to Mars with me. I've always liked cats. Especially the orange ones with stripes."

One of the museum guards, after a glance at his companion, said, "We can arrange that, Mr. Biskle. We can get a—cub, is that the word?"

"Kitten, I think," Mary corrected.

ON THE trip back to Mars, Milt Biskle sat with the box containing the orange kitten on his lap, working out his plans. In fifteen minutes the ship would land on Mars and Dr. DeWinter—or the thing that posed as Dr. DeWinter anyhow—would be waiting to meet him. And it would be too late. From where he sat he could see the emergency escape hatch with its red warning light. His plans had become focused around the hatch. It was not ideal but it would serve.

In the box the orange kitten reached up a paw and batted at Milt's hand. He felt the sharp, tiny claws rake across his hand and he absently disengaged his flesh, retreating from the probing reach of the animal. You wouldn't have liked Mars anyhow, he thought, and rose to his feet.

Carrying the box he strode swiftly toward the emergency hatch. Before the stewardess could reach him he had thrown open the hatch. He stepped forward and the hatch locked behind him. For an instant he was within the cramped unit, and then he began to twist open the heavy outer door.

"Mr. Biskle!" the stewardess' voice came, muffled by the door behind him. He heard her fumbling to reach him, opening the door and groping to catch hold of him.

As he twisted open the outer door the kitten within the box under his arm snarled.

You, too? Milt Biskle thought, and paused.

Death, the emptiness and utter lack of warmth of 'tween space, seeped around him, filtering past the partly opened outer door. He smelled it and something within him, as in the kitten, retreated by instinct. He paused, holding the box, not trying to push the outer door any farther open, and in that moment the stewardess grabbed him.

"Mr. Biskle," she said with a half-sob, "are you out of your mind? Good God what are you doing?" She managed to tug the outer door shut, screw the emergency section back into shut position.

"You know exactly what I'm doing," Milt Biskle said as he allowed her to propel him back into the ship and to his seat. And don't think you stopped me, he said to himself. Because it wasn't you. I could have gone ahead and done it. But I decided not to.

He wondered why.

LATER, at Field Three on Mars, Dr. DeWinter met him as he had expected.

The two of them walked to the parked 'copter and DeWinter in a worried tone of voice said, "I've just been informed that during the trip—"

"That's right. I attempted suicide. But I changed my

mind. Maybe you know why. You're the psychologist, the authority as to what goes on inside us." He entered the 'copter, being careful not to bang the box containing the Terran kitten.

"You're going to go ahead and stake your land parcel with Fay?" Dr. DeWinter asked presently as the 'copter flew above green, wet fields of high protein wheat. "Even though—you know?"

"Yes." He nodded. After all, there was nothing else for him, as far as he could make out.

"You Terrans." DeWinter shook his head. "Admirable." Now he noticed the box on Milt Biskle's lap. "What's that you have there? A creature from Terra?" He eyed it suspiciously; obviously to him it was the manifestation of an alien form of life. "A rather peculiar-looking organism."

"It's going to keep me company," Milt Biskle said. "While I go on with my work, either building up my private parcel or—" Or helping you Proxmen with Terra, he thought.

"Is that what was called a 'rattlesnake'? I detect the sound of its rattles." Dr. DeWinter edged away.

"It's purring." Milt Biskle stroked the kitten as the autonomic circuit of the 'copter guided it across the dully red Martian sky. Contact with the one familiar life-form, he realized, will keep me sane. It will make it possible for me to go on. He felt grateful. My race may have been defeated and destroyed, but not all Terran creatures have perished. When we reconstruct Terra maybe we can induce the authorities to allow us to set up game preserves. We'll make that part of our task, he told himself, and again he patted the kitten. At least we can hope for that much.

Next to him, Dr. DeWinter was also deep in thought. He appreciated the intricate workmanship, by engineers stationed on the third planet, which had gone into the simulacrum resting in the box on Milt Biskle's lap. The technical achievement was impressive, even to him, and he saw clearly—as Milt Biskle of course did not. This artifact, accepted by the Terran as an authentic organism from his familiar past, would provide a pivot by which the man would hang onto his psychic balance.

But what about the other reconstruct engineers? What would carry each of them through and past the moment of discovery as each completed his work and had to—whether he liked it or not—awake?

IT WOULD vary from Terran to Terran. A dog for one, a more elaborate simulacrum, possibly that of a nubile human female, for another. In any case each would be provided with an "exception" to the true state. One essential surviving entity, selected out of what had in fact totally vanished. Research into the past of each engineer would provide the clue, as it had in Biskle's instance; the cat-simulacrum had been finished weeks before his abrupt, panic-stricken trip home to Terra. For instance, in Andre's case a parrot-simulacrum was already under construction. It would be done by the time he made *his* trip home.

"I call him Thunder," Milt Biskle explained.

"Good name," Dr. DeWinter—as he titled himself these days—said. And thought, A shame we could not have shown him the real situation on Terra. Actually it's quite interesting that he accepted what he saw, because on some level he must realize that nothing survives a war of the kind we conducted. Obviously he desperately wanted to believe that a remnant, even though no more than rubble, endures. But it's typical of the Terran mind to fasten onto phantoms. That might help explain their defeat in the conflict; they were simply not realists.

"This cat," Milt Biskle said, "is going to be a mighty hunter of Martian sneak-mice."

"Right," Dr. DeWinter agreed, and thought, *As long as its batteries don't run down*. He, too, patted the kitten.

A switch closed and the kitten purred louder.

Small Town

VERNE HASKEL crept miserably up the front steps of his house, his overcoat dragging behind him. He was tired. Tired and discouraged. And his feet ached.

"My God," Madge exclaimed, as he closed the door and peeled off his coat and hat. "You home already?"

Haskel dumped his briefcase and began untying his shoes. His body sagged. His face was drawn and gray.

"Say something!"

"Dinner ready?"

"No, dinner isn't ready. What's wrong this time? Another fight with Larson?"

Haskel stumped into the kitchen and filled a glass with warm water and soda. "Let's move," he said.

"Move?"

"Away from Woodland. To San Francisco. Anywhere." Haskel drank his soda, his middle-aged flabby body supported by the gleaming sink. "I feel lousy. Maybe I ought to see Doc Barnes again. I wish this was Friday and tomorrow was Saturday."

"What do you want for dinner?"

"Nothing. I don't know." Haskel shook his head wearily. "Anything." He sank down at the kitchen table. "All I want is rest. Open a can of stew. Pork and beans. Anything."

"I suggest we go out to Don's Steakhouse. On Monday they have good sirloin."

"No. I've seen enough human faces today."

"I suppose you're too tired to drive me over to Helen Grant's."

"The car's in the garage. Busted again."

"If you took better care of it—"

"What the hell do you want me to do? Carry it around in a cellophane bag?"

"Don't shout at me, Verne Haskel!" Madge flushed with anger. "Maybe you want to fix your own dinner."

HASKEL got wearily to his feet. He shuffled toward the cellar door. "I'll see you."

"Where are you going?"

"Downstairs in the basement."

"Oh, Lord!" Madge cried wildly. "Those trains! Those toys! How can a grown man, a middle-aged man—"

Haskel said nothing. He was already half way down the stairs, feeling around for the basement light.

The basement was cool and moist. Haskel took his engineer's cap from the hook and fitted it on his head. Excitement and a faint surge of renewed energy filled his tired body. He approached the great plywood table with eager steps.

Tracks ran everywhere. Along the floor, under the coal bin, among the steam pipes of the furnace. The tracks converged at the table, rising up on carefully graded ramps. The table itself was littered with transformers and signals and switches and heaps of equipment and wiring. And—

And the town.

The detailed, painfully accurate model of Woodland. Every tree and house, every store and building and street and fireplug. A minute town, each facet in perfect order. Constructed with elaborate care throughout the years. As long as he could remember. Since he was a kid, building and glueing and working after school.

Haskel turned on the main transformer. All along the track signal lights glowed. He fed power to the heavy Lionel engine parked with its load of freight cars. The engine sped smoothly into life, gliding along the track. A flashing dark projectile of metal that made his breath catch in his throat. He opened an electric switch and the engine headed down the ramp, through a tunnel and off the table. It raced under the work bench.

His trains. And his town. Haskel bent over the miniature houses and streets, his heart glowing with pride. He had built it—himself. Every inch. Every perfect inch. The whole town. He touched the corner of Fred's Grocery Store. Not a detail lacking. Even the windows. The displays of food. The signs. The counters.

The Uptown Hotel. He ran his hand over its flat roof. The sofas and chairs in the lobby. He could see them through the window.

Green's Drugstore. Bunion pad displays. Magazines. Frazier's Auto Parts. Mexico City Dining. Sharpstein's Apparel. Bob's Liquor Store. Ace Billiard Parlor.

The whole town. He ran his hands over it. He had built it: the town was his.

THE TRAIN came rushing back, out from under the workbench. Its wheels passed over an automatic switch and a drawbridge lowered itself obediently. The train swept over and beyond, dragging its cars behind it.

Haskel turned up the power. The train gained speed. Its whistle sounded. It turned a sharp curve and grated across a cross-track. More speed. Haskel's hands jerked convulsively at the transformer. The train leaped and shot ahead. It swayed and bucked as it shot around a curve. The transformer was turned up to maximum. The train was a clattering blur of speed, rushing along the track, across bridges and switches, behind the big pipes of the floor furnace.

It disappeared into the coal bin. A moment later it swept out the other side, rocking wildly.

Haskel slowed the train down. He was breathing hard, his chest rising painfully. He sat down on the stool by the workbench and lit a cigarette with shaking fingers.

The train, the model town, gave him a strange feeling. It was hard to explain. He had always loved trains, model engines and signals and buildings. Since he was a little kid, maybe six or seven. His father had given him his first train. An engine and a few pieces of track. An old wind-up train. When he was nine he got his first real electric train. And two switches.

He added to it, year after year. Track, engines, switches, cars, signals. More powerful transformers. And the beginnings of the town.

He had built the town up carefully. Piece by piece. First, when he was in junior high, a model of the Southern

Pacific Depot. Then the taxi stand next door. The cafe where the drivers ate. Broad Street.

And so on. More and more. Houses, buildings, stores. A whole town, growing under his hands, as the years went by. Every afternoon he came home from school and worked. Glued and cut and painted and sawed.

Now it was virtually complete. Almost done. He was forty-three years old and the town was almost done.

Haskel moved around the big plywood table, his hands extended reverently. He touched a miniature store here and there. The flower shop. The theater. The Telephone Company. Larson's Pump and Valve Works.

That, too. Where he worked. His place of business. A perfect miniature of the plant, down to the last detail.

Haskel scowled. Jim Larson. For twenty years he had worked there, slaved day after day. For what? To see others advanced over him. Younger men. Favorites of the boss. Yes-men with bright ties and pressed pants and wide, stupid grins.

Misery and hatred welled up in Haskel. All his life Woodland had got the better of him. He had never been happy. The town had always been against him. Miss Murphy in high school. The frats in college. Clerks in the snooty department stores. His neighbors. Cops and mailmen and bus drivers and delivery boys. Even his wife. Even Madge.

HE HAD never meshed with the town. The rich, expensive little suburb of San Francisco, down the peninsula beyond the fog belt. Woodland was too damn upper-middle class. Too many big houses and lawns and chrome cars and deck chairs. Too stuffy and sleek. As long as he could remember. In school. His job—

Larson. The Pump and Valve Works. Twenty years of hard work.

Haskel's fingers closed over the tiny building, the model of Larson's Pump and Valve Works. Savagely, he ripped it loose and threw it to the floor. He crushed it underfoot, grinding the bits of glass and metal and cardboard into a shapeless mass.

God, he was shaking all over. He stared down at the remains, his heart pounding wildly. Strange emotions, crazy emotions, twisted through him. Thoughts he never had had before. For a long time he gazed down at the crumpled wad by his shoe. What had once been the model of Larson's Pump and Valve Works.

Abruptly he pulled away. In a trance he returned to his workbench and sat stiffly down on the stool. He pulled his tools and materials together, clicking the power drill on.

It took only a few moments. Working rapidly, with quick, expert fingers, Haskel assembled a new model. He painted, glued, fitted pieces together. He lettered a microscopic sign and sprayed a green lawn into place.

Then he carried the new model carefully over to the table and glued it in the correct spot. The place where Larson's Pump and Valve Works had been. The new building gleamed in the overhead light, still moist and shiny.

WOODLAND MORTUARY

Haskel rubbed his hands in an ecstasy of satisfaction. The Valve Works was gone. He had destroyed it. Obliterated it. Removed it from the town. Below him was Woodland—without the Valve Works. A mortuary instead.

His eyes gleamed. His lips twitched. His surging emotions swelled. He had got rid of it. In a brief flurry of action. In a second. The whole thing was simple— amazingly easy.

Odd he hadn't thought of it before.

SIPPING a tall glass of ice-cold beer thoughtfully, Madge Haskel said, "There's something wrong with Verne. I noticed it especially last night. When he came home from work."

Doctor Paul Tyler grunted absently. "A highly neurotic type. Sense of inferiority. Withdrawal and introversion."

"But he's getting worse. Him and his trains. Those damn model trains. My God, Paul! Do you know he has a whole town down there in the basement?"

Tyler was curious. "Really? I never knew that."

"All the time I've known him he's had them down

there. Started when he was a kid. Imagine a grown man playing with trains! It's—it's disgusting. Every night the same thing."

"Interesting." Tyler rubbed his jaw. "He keeps at them continually? An unvarying pattern?"

"Every night. Last night he didn't even eat dinner. He just came home and went directly down."

Paul Tyler's polished features twisted into a frown. Across from him Madge sat languidly sipping her beer. It was two in the afternoon. The day was warm and bright. The living room was attractive in a lazy, quiet way. Abruptly Tyler got to his feet. "Let's take a look at them. The models. I didn't know it had gone so far."

"Do you really want to?" Madge slid back the sleeve of her green silk lounge pajamas and consulted her wristwatch. "He won't be home until five." She jumped to her feet, setting down her glass. "All right. We have time."

"Fine. Let's go down." Tyler caught hold of Madge's arm and they hurried down into the basement, a strange excitement flooding through them. Madge clicked on the basement light and they approached the big plywood table, giggling and nervous, like mischievous children.

"See?" Madge said, squeezing Tyler's arm. "Look at it. Took years. All his life."

Tyler nodded slowly. "Must have." There was awe in his voice. "I've never seen anything like it. The detail. . . . He has skill."

"Yes, Verne is good with his hands." Madge indicated the workbench. "He buys tools all the time."

TYLER walked slowly around the big table, bending over and peering. "Amazing. Every building. The whole town is here. Look! There's my place."

He indicated his luxurious apartment building, a few blocks from the Haskel residence.

"I guess it's all there," Madge said. "Imagine a grown man coming down here and playing with model trains!"

"Power." Tyler pushed an engine along a track. "That's why it appeals to boys. Trains are big things. Huge and noisy. Power-sex symbols. The boy sees the train rushing along the track. It's so huge and ruthless it scares him. Then he gets a toy train. A model, like these. He controls it. Makes it start, stop. Go slow. Fast. He runs it. It responds to him."

Madge shivered. "Let's go upstairs where it's warm. It's so cold down here."

"But as the boy grows up, he gets bigger and stronger. He can shed the model-symbol. Master the real object, the real train. Get genuine control over things. Valid mastery." Tyler shook his head. "Not this substitute thing. Unusual, a grown person going to such lengths." He frowned. "I never noticed a mortuary on State Street."

"A mortuary?"

"And this. Steuben Pet Shop. Next door to the radio repair shop. There's no pet shop there." Tyler cudgeled his brain. "What *is* there? Next to the radio repair place."

"Paris Furs." Madge clasped her arms. "Brrrrr. Come on, Paul. Let's go upstairs before I freeze."

Tyler laughed. "Okay, sissy." He headed toward the stairs, frowning again. "I wonder why. Steuben Pets. Never heard of it. Everything is so detailed. He must know the town by heart. To put a shop there that isn't—" He clicked off the basement light. "And the mortuary. What's supposed to be there? Isn't the—"

"Forget it," Madge called back, hurrying past him, into the warm living room. "You're practically as bad as he is. Men are such children."

Tyler didn't respond. He was deep in thought. His suave confidence was gone; he looked nervous and shaken.

Madge pulled the venetian blinds down. The living room sank into amber gloom. She flopped down on the couch and pulled Tyler down beside her. "Stop looking like that," she ordered. "I've never seen you this way." Her slim arms circled his neck and her lips brushed close to his ear. "I wouldn't have let you in if I thought you were going to worry about *him*."

Tyler grunted, preoccupied. "Why *did* you let me in?"

The pressure of Madge's arms increased. Her silk pajamas rustled as she moved against him. "Silly," she said.

BIG RED-HEADED Jim Larson gaped in disbelief. "What do you mean? What's the matter with you?"

"I'm quitting." Haskel shoveled the contents of his desk into his briefcase. "Mail the check to my house."

"But—"

"Get out of the way." Haskel pushed past Larson, out into the hall. Larson was stunned with amazement. There was a fixed expression on Haskel's face. A glazed look. A rigid look Larson had never seen before.

"Are you—all right?" Larson asked.

"Sure." Haskel opened the front door of the plant and disappeared outside. The door slammed after him. "Sure I'm all right," he muttered to himself. He made his way through the crowds of late-afternoon shoppers, his lips twitching. "You damn right I'm all right."

"Watch it, buddy," a laborer muttered ominously, as Haskel shoved past him.

"Sorry." Haskel hurried on, gripping his briefcase. At the top of the hill he paused a moment to get his breath. Behind him was Larson's Pump and Valve Works. Haskel laughed shrilly. Twenty years—cut short in a second. It was over. No more Larson. No more dull, grinding job, day after day. Without promotion or future. Routine and boredom, months on end. It was over and done for. A new life was beginning.

He hurried on. The sun was setting. Cars streaked by him, businessmen going home from work. Tomorrow they would be going back—but not him. Not ever again.

He reached his own street. Ed Tildon's house rose up, a great stately structure of concrete and glass. Tildon's dog came rushing out to bark. Haskel hastened past. Tildon's dog. He laughed wildly.

"Better keep away!" he shouted at the dog.

He reached his own house and leaped up the front steps two at a time. He tore the door open. The living room was dark and silent. There was a sudden stir of motion. Shapes untangling themselves, getting quickly up from the couch.

"Verne!" Madge gasped. "What are you doing home so early?"

VERNE HASKEL threw his briefcase down and dropped his hat and coat over a chair. His lined face was twisted with emotion, pulled out of shape by violent inner forces.

"What in the world!" Madge fluttered, hurrying toward him nervously, smoothing down her lounge

pajamas. "Has something happened? I didn't expect you
so—" She broke off, blushing. "I mean, I—"

Paul Tyler strolled leisurely toward Haskel. "Hi there,
Verne," he murmured, embarrassed. "Dropped by to say
hello and return a book to your wife."

Haskel nodded curtly. "Afternoon." He turned and
headed toward the basement door, ignoring the two of
them. "I'll be downstairs."

"But Verne!" Madge protested. "What's happened?"

Verne halted briefly at the door. "I quit my job."

"You *what*?"

"I quit my job. I finished Larson off. There won't be
anymore of him." The basement door slammed.

"Good Lord!" Madge shrieked, clutching at Tyler
hysterically. "He's gone out of his mind!"

Down in the basement, Verne Haskel snapped on the
light impatiently. He put on his engineer's cap and pulled
his stool up beside the great plywood table.

What next?

Morris Home Furnishings. The big plush store. Where
the clerks all looked down their noses at him.

He rubbed his hands gleefully. No more of them. No
more snooty clerks, lifting their eyebrows when he came
in. Only hair and bow ties and folded handkerchiefs.

He removed the model of Morris Home Furnishings
and disassembled it. He worked feverishly, with frantic
haste. Now that he had really begun he wasted no time. A
moment later he was glueing two small buildings in its
place. Ritz Shoeshine. Pete's Bowling Alley.

Haskel giggled excitedly. Fitting extinction for the
luxurious, exclusive furniture store. A shoeshine parlor
and a bowling alley. Just what it deserved.

The California State Bank. He had always hated the
Bank. They had once refused him a loan. He pulled the
Bank loose.

Ed Tildon's mansion. His damn dog. The dog had bit
him on the ankle one afternoon. He ripped the model off.
His head spun. He could do anything.

Harrison Appliance. They had sold him a bum radio.
Off came Harrison Appliance.

JOE'S CIGAR and Smoke Shop. Joe had given him a lead
quarter in May, 1949. Off came Joe's.

The Ink Works. He loathed the smell of ink. Maybe a bread factory, instead. He loved baking bread. Off came the Ink Works.

Elm Street was too dark at night. A couple of times he had stumbled. A few more streetlights were in order.

Not enough bars along High Street. Too many dress shops and expensive hat and fur shops and ladies' apparel. He ripped a whole handful loose and carried them to the workbench.

AT THE top of the stairs the door opened slowly. Madge peered down, pale and frightened. "Verne?"

He scowled up impatiently. "What do you want?"

Madge came downstairs hesitantly. Behind her Doctor Tyler followed, suave and handsome in his gray suit. "Verne—is everything all right?"

"Of course."

"Did—did you really quit your job?"

Haskel nodded. He began to disassemble the Ink Works, ignoring his wife and Doctor Tyler.

"But *why*?"

Haskel grunted impatiently. "No time."

Doctor Tyler had begun to look worried. "Do I understand you're too busy for your job?"

"That's right."

"Too busy doing *what*?" Tyler's voice rose; he was trembling nervously. "Working down here on this town of yours? Changing things?"

"Go away," Haskel muttered. His deft hands were assembling a lovely little Langendorf Bread Factory. He shaped it with loving care, sprayed it with white paint, brushed a gravel walk and shrubs in front of it. He put it aside and began on a park. A big green park. Woodland had always needed a park. It would go in place of State Street Hotel.

Tyler pulled Madge away from the table, off in a corner of the basement. "Good God." He lit a cigarette shakily. The cigarette flipped out of his hands and rolled away. He ignored it and fumbled for another. "You see? You see what he's doing?"

Madge shook her head mutely. "What is it? I don't—"

"How long has he been working on this? All his life?"

Madge nodded, white-faced. "Yes, all his life."

Tyler's features twisted. "My God, Madge. It's enough to drive you out of your mind. I can hardly believe it. We've got to do something."

"What's happening?" Madge moaned. "What—"

"He's losing himself into it." Tyler's face was a mask of incredulous disbelief. "Faster and faster."

"He's always come down here," Madge faltered. "It's nothing new. He's always wanted to get away."

"Yes. Get away." Tyler shuddered, clenched his fists and pulled himself together. He advanced across the basement and stopped by Verne Haskel.

"What do you want?" Haskel muttered, noticing him.

Tyler licked his lips. "You're adding some things, aren't you? New buildings."

Haskel nodded.

TYLER TOUCHED the little bread factory with shaking fingers. "What's this? Bread? Where does it go?" He moved around the table. "I don't remember any bread factory in Woodland." He whirled. "You aren't by any chance *improving* on the town? Fixing it up here and there?"

"Get the hell out of here," Haskel said, with ominous calm. "Both of you."

"Verne!" Madge squeaked.

"I've got a lot to do. You can bring sandwiches down about eleven. I hope to finish sometime tonight."

"Finish?" Tyler asked.

"Finish," Haskel answered, returning to his work.

"Come on, Madge." Tyler grabbed her and pulled her to the stairs. "Let's get out of here." He strode ahead of her, up to the stairs and into the hall. "Come on!" As soon as she was up he closed the door tightly after them.

Madge dabbed at her eyes hysterically. "He's gone crazy, Paul! What'll we do?"

Tyler was deep in thought. "Be quiet. I have to think this out." He paced back and forth, a hard scowl on his features. "I'll come soon. It won't be long, not at this rate. Sometime tonight."

"*What*? What do you mean?"

"His withdrawal. Into his substitute world. The

improved model he controls. Where he can get away."

"Isn't there something we can do?"

"Do?" Tyler smiled faintly. "Do we want to do something?"

Madge gasped. "But we can't just—"

"Maybe this will solve our problem. This may be what we've been looking for." Tyler eyed Mrs. Haskel thoughtfully. "This may be just the thing."

IT WAS after midnight, almost two o'clock in the morning, when he began to get things into final shape. He was tired—but alert. Things were happening fast. The job was almost done.

Virtually perfect.

He halted work a moment, surveying what he had accomplished. The town had been radically changed. About ten o'clock he had begun basic structural alterations in the lay-out of the streets. He had removed most of the public buildings, the civic center and the sprawling business district around it.

He had erected a new city hall, police station, and an immense park with fountains and indirect lighting. He had cleared the slum area, the old run-down stores and houses and streets. The streets were wider and well-lit. The houses were now small and clean. The stores modern and attractive—without being ostentatious.

All advertising signs had been removed. Most of the filling stations were gone. The immense factory area was gone, too. Rolling countryside took its place. Trees and hills and green grass.

The wealthy district had been altered. There were now only a few of the mansions left—belonging to persons he looked favorably on. The rest had been cut down, turned into uniform two-bedroom dwellings, one story, with a single garage each.

The city hall was no longer an elaborate, rococo structure. Now it was low and simple, modeled after the Parthenon, a favorite of his.

There were ten or twelve persons who had done him special harm. He had altered their houses considerably. Given them war-time housing unit apartments, six to a building, at the far edge of town. Where the wind came off the bay, carrying the smell of decaying mud-flats.

Jim Larson's house was completely gone. He had erased Larson utterly. He no longer existed, not in this new Woodland—which was now almost complete.

Almost. Haskel studied his work intently. All the changes had to be made *now*. Not later. This was the time of creation. Later, when it had been finished, it could not be altered. He had to catch all the necessary changes now—or forget them.

THE NEW Woodland looked pretty good. Clean and neat—and simple. The rich district had been toned down. The poor district had been improved. Glaring ads, signs, displays, had all been changed or removed. The business community was smaller. Parks and countryside took the place of factories. The civic center was lovely.

He added a couple of playgrounds for smaller kids. A small theater instead of the enormous Uptown with its flashing neon sign. After some consideration he removed most of the bars he had previously constructed. The new Woodland was going to be moral. Extremely moral. Few bars, no billiards, no red light district. And there was an especially fine jail for undesirables.

The most difficult part had been the microscopic lettering on the main office door of the city hall. He had left it until last, and then painted the words with agonizing care:

Mayor
Vernon R. Haskel

A few last changes. He gave the Edwards a '39 Plymouth instead of a new Cadillac. He added more trees in the downtown district. One more fire department. One less dress shop. He had never liked taxis. On impulse, he removed the taxi stand and put in a flower shop.

Haskel rubbed his hands. Anything more? Or was it complete...Perfect...He studied each part intently. What had he overlooked?

The high school. He removed it and put in two smaller high schools, one at each end of town. Another hospital. That took almost half an hour. He was getting tired. His hands were less swift. He mopped his forehead shakily. Anything else? He sat down on his stool wearily, to rest and think.

ALL DONE. It was complete. Joy welled up in him. A bursting cry of happiness. His work was over.

"Finished!" Verne Haskel shouted.

He got unsteadily to his feet. He closed his eyes, held his arms out, and advanced toward the plywood table. Reaching, grasping, fingers extended, Haskel headed toward it, a look of radiant exaltation on his seamed, middle-aged face.

Upstairs, Tyler and Madge heard the shout. A distant booming that rolled through the house in waves. Madge winced in terror. "What was that?"

Tyler listened intently. He heard Haskel moving below them, in the basement. Abruptly, he stubbed out his cigarette. "I think it's happened. Sooner than I expected."

"It? You mean he's—"

Tyler got quickly to his feet. "He's gone, Madge. Into his other world. We're finally free."

Madge caught his arm. "Maybe we're making a mistake. It's so terrible. Shouldn't we—try to do something? Bring him out of it—try to pull him back."

"Bring him back?" Tyler laughed nervously. "I don't think we could, now. Even if we wanted to. It's too late." He hurried toward the basement door. "Come on."

"It's horrible." Madge shuddered and followed reluctantly. "I wish we had never got started."

Tyler halted briefly at the door. "Horrible? He's happier, where he is, now. And you're happier. The way it was, nobody was happy. This is the best thing."

He opened the basement door. Madge followed him. They moved cautiously down the stairs, into the dark, silent basement, damp with the faint night mists.

The basement was empty.

Tyler relaxed. He was overcome with dazed relief. "He's gone. Everything's okay. It worked out exactly right."

"BUT I don't understand," Madge repeated hopelessly, as

Tyler's Buick purred along the dark, deserted streets. "*Where* did he go?"

"You know where he went," Tyler answered. "Into his substitute world, of course." He screeched around a corner on two wheels. "The rest should be fairly simple. A few routine forms. There really isn't much left, now."

The night was frigid and bleak. No lights showed, except an occasional lonely streetlamp. Far off, a train whistle sounded mournfully, a dismal echo. Rows of silent houses flickered by on both sides of them.

"Where are we going?" Madge asked. She sat huddled against the door, face pale with shock and terror, shivering under her coat.

"To the police station."

"Why?"

"To report him, naturally. So they'll know he's gone. We'll have to wait; it'll be several years before he'll be declared legally dead." Tyler reached over and hugged her briefly. "We'll make out in the meantime, I'm sure."

"What if—they find him?"

Tyler shook his head angrily. He was still tense, on edge. "Don't you understand? They'll never find him—he doesn't exist. At least, not in our world. He's in his own world. You saw it. The model. The improved substitute."

"He's *there?*"

"All his life he's worked on it. Built it up. Made it real. He brought that world into being—and now he's in it. That's what he wanted. That's why he built it. He didn't merely dream about an escape world. He actually constructed it—every bit and piece. Now he's warped himself right out of our world, into it. Out of our lives."

Madge finally began to understand. "Then he really *did* lose himself in his substitute world. You meant that, what you said about him—getting away."

"It took me awhile to realize it. The mind constructs reality. Frames it. Creates it. We all have a common reality, a common dream. But Haskel turned his back on our common reality and created his own. And he had a unique capacity—far beyond the ordinary. He devoted his whole life, his whole skill to building it. He's there now."

• • •

Tyler hesitated and frowned. He gripped the wheel tightly and increased speed. The Buick hissed along the dark street, through the silent, unmoving bleakness that was the town.

"There's only one thing," he continued presently. "One thing I don't understand."

"What is it?"

"The model. It was also gone. I assumed he'd—shrink, I suppose. Merge with it. But the model's gone, too." Tyler shrugged. "It doesn't matter." He peered into the darkness. "We're almost there. This is Elm."

It was then Madge screamed. *"Look!"*

To the right of the car was a small, neat building. And a sign. The sign was easily visible in the darkness.

WOODLAND MORTUARY

Madge was sobbing in horror. The car roared forward, automatically guided by Tyler's numb hands. Another sign flashed by briefly, as they coasted up before the city hall.

STEUBEN PET SHOP

The city hall was lit by recessed, hidden illumination. A low, simple building, a square of glowing white. Like a marble Greek temple.

Tyler pulled the car to a halt. Then suddenly shrieked and started up again. But not soon enough.

The two shiny-black police cars came silently up around the Buick, one on each side. The four stern cops already had their hands on the door. Stepping out and coming toward him, grim and efficient.

The Pre-Persons

PAST THE grove of cypress trees Walter—he had been playing king of the mountain—saw the white truck, and he knew it for what it was. He thought, That's the abortion truck. Come to take some kid in for a postpartum down at the abortion place.

And he thought, Maybe my folks called it. For me.

He ran and hid among the blackberries, feeling the scratching of the thorns but thinking, It's better than having the air sucked out of your lungs. That's how they do it; they perform all the P.P.s on all the kids there at the same time. They have a big room for it. For the kids nobody wants.

Burrowing deeper into the blackberries, he listened to hear if the truck stopped; he heard its motor.

"I am invisible," he said to himself, a line he had learned at the fifth-grade play of *Midsummer Night's Dream*, a line Oberon, whom he had played, had said. And after that no one could see him. Maybe that was true now. Maybe the magic saying worked in real life; so he said it again to himself, "I am invisible." But he knew he was not. He could still see his arms and legs and shoes, and he knew they—everyone, the abortion truck man especially, and his mom and dad—they could see him too. If they looked.

If it was him they were after this time.

He wished he was a king; he wished he had magic dust all over him and a shining crown that glistened, and ruled fairyland and had the Puck to confide to. To ask for advice from, even. Advice even if he himself was a king and bickered with Titania, his wife.

I guess, he thought, saying something doesn't make it true.

303

Sun burned down on him and he squinted, but mostly he listened to the abortion truck motor; it kept making its sound, and his heart gathered hope as the sound went on and on. Some other kid, turned over to the abortion clinic, not him; someone up the road.

He made his difficult exit from the berry brambles shaking and in many places scratched and moved step by step in the direction of his house. And as he trudged he began to cry, mostly from the pain of the scratches but also from fear and relief.

"Oh, good lord," his mother exclaimed, on seeing him. "What in the name of God have you been doing?"

He said, stammeringly, "I—saw—the abortion—truck."

"And you thought it was for you?"

Mutely, he nodded.

"Listen, Walter," Cynthia Best said, kneeling down and taking hold of his trembling hands, "I promise, your dad and I both promise, you'll never be sent to the County Facility. Anyhow you're too old. They only take children up to twelve."

"But Jeff Vogel—"

"His parents got him in just before the new law went into effect. They couldn't take him now, legally. They couldn't take you now. Look—you have a soul; the law says a twelve-year-old boy has a soul. So he can't go to the County Facility. See? You're safe. Whenever you see the abortion truck, it's for someone else, not you. Never for you. Is that clear? It's come for another younger child who doesn't have a soul yet, a pre-person."

Staring down, not meeting his mother's gaze, he said, "I don't feel like I got a soul; I feel like I always did."

"It's a legal matter," his mother said briskly. "Strictly according to age. And you're past the age. The Church of Watchers got Congress to pass the law—actually they, those church people, wanted a lower age; they claimed the soul entered the body at three years old, but a compromise bill was put through. The important thing for you is that you are legally safe, however you feel inside; do you see?"

"Okay," he said, nodding.

"You knew that."

He burst out with anger and grief, "What do you think it's like, maybe waiting every day for someone to come and put you in a wire cage in a truck and—"

"Your fear is irrational," his mother said.

"I saw them take Jeff Vogel that day. He was crying, and the man just opened the back of the truck and put him in and shut the back of the truck."

"That was two years ago. You're weak." His mother glared at him. "Your grandfather would whip you if he saw you now and heard you talk this way. Not your father. He'd just grin and say something stupid. Two years later, and intellectually you know you're past the legal maximum age! How—" She struggled for the word. "You are being *depraved*."

"And he never came back."

"Perhaps someone who wanted a child went inside the County Facility and found him and adopted him. Maybe he's got a better set of parents who really care for him. They keep them thirty days before they destroy them." She corrected herself. "Put them to sleep, I mean."

He was not reassured. Because he knew "put him to sleep" or "put them to sleep" was a Mafia term. He drew away from his mother, no longer wanting her comfort. She had blown it, as far as he was concerned; she had shown something about herself or, anyhow, the source of what she believed and thought and perhaps did. What all of them did. I know I'm no different, he thought, than two years ago when I was just a little kid; if I have a soul now like the law says, then I had a soul then, or else we have no souls—the only real thing is just a horrible metallic-painted truck with wire over its windows carrying off kids their parents no longer want, parents using an extension of the old abortion law that let them kill an unwanted child before it came out: because it had no "soul" or "identity," it could be sucked out by a vacuum system in less than two minutes. A doctor could do a hundred a day, and it was legal because the unborn child wasn't "human." He was a pre-person. Just like this truck now; they merely set the date forward as to when the soul entered.

Congress had inaugurated a simple test to determine

the approximate age at which the soul entered the body: the ability to formulate higher math like algebra. Up to then, it was only body, animal instincts and body, animal reflexes and responses to stimuli. Like Pavlov's dogs when they saw a little water seep in under the door of the Leningrad laboratory; they "knew" but were not human.

I guess I'm human, Walter thought, and looked up into the gray, severe face of his mother, with her hard eyes and rational grimness. I guess I'm like you, he thought. Hey, it's neat to be a human, he thought; then you don't have to be afraid of the truck coming.

"You feel better," his mother observed. "I've lowered your threshold of anxiety."

"I'm not so freaked," Walter said. It was over; the truck had gone and not taken him.

But it would be back in a few days. It cruised perpetually.

Anyhow he had a few days. And then the sight of it—if only I didn't know they suck the air out of the lungs of the kids they have there, he thought. Destroy them that way. Why? Cheaper, his dad had said. Saves the taxpayers money.

He thought then about taxpayers and what they would look like. Something that scowled at all children, he thought. That did not answer if the child asked them a question. A thin face, lined with watch-worry grooves, eyes always moving. Or maybe fat; one or the other. It was the thin one that scared him; it didn't enjoy life nor want life to be. It flashed the message, "Die, go away, sicken, don't exist." And the abortion truck was the proof—or the instrument—of it.

"Mom," he said, "how do you shut a County Facility? You know, the abortion clinic where they take the babies and little kids."

"You go and petition the county legislature," his mother said.

"You know what I'd do?" he said. "I'd wait until there were no kids in there, only county employees, and I'd firebomb it."

"Don't talk like that!" his mother said severely, and he saw on her face the stiff lines of the thin taxpayer. And it frightened him; his own mother frightened him. The cold and opaque eyes mirror nothing, no soul inside, and he thought, *It's you who don't have a soul*, you and your skinny messages not-to-be. Not us.

And then he ran outside to play again.

A BUNCH more kids had seen the truck; he and they stood around together, talking now and then, but mostly kicking at rocks and dirt, and occasionally stepping on a bad bug.

"Who'd the truck come for?" Walter said.

"Fleischhacker. Earl Fleischhacker."

"Did they get him?"

"Sure, didn't you hear the yelling?"

"Was his folks home at the time?"

"Naw, they split earlier on some shuck about 'taking the car in to be greased.'"

"*They* called the truck?" Walter said.

"Sure, it's the law; it's gotta be the parents. But they were too chickenshit to be there when the truck drove up. Shit, he really yelled; I guess you're too far away to hear, but he really yelled."

Walter said, "You know what we ought to do? Firebomb the truck and snuff the driver."

All the other kids looked at him contemptuously. "They put you in the mental hospital for life if you act out like that."

"Sometimes for life," Pete Bride corrected. "Other times they 'build up a new personality that is socially viable.'"

"Then what should we do?" Walter said.

"You're twelve; you're safe."

"But suppose they change the law." Anyhow it did not assuage his anxiety to know that he was technically safe; the truck still came for others and still frightened him. He thought of the younger kids down at the Facility now, looking through the Cyclone fence hour by hour, day after day, waiting and marking the passage of time and hoping someone would come in and adopt them.

"You ever been down there?" he said to Pete Bride. "At the County Facility? All those really little kids, like babies some of them, just maybe a year old. And they don't even know what's in store."

"The babies get adopted," Zack Yablonski said. "It's the old ones that don't stand a chance. They're the ones that get you; like, they talk to people who come in and put on a good show, like they're desirable. But people know they wouldn't be there if they weren't—you know, undesirable."

"Let the air out of the tires," Walter said, his mind working.

"Of the truck? Hey, and you know if you drop a mothball in the gas tank, about a week later the motor wears out. We could do that."

Ben Blaire said, "But then they'd be after us."

"They're after us now," Walter said.

"I think we ought to firebomb the truck," Harry Gottlieb said, "but suppose there're kids in it. It'll burn them up. The truck picks up maybe—shit, I don't know. Five kids a day from different parts of the county."

"You know they even take dogs too?" Walter said. "And cats; you see the truck for that only about once a month. The pound truck it's called. Otherwise it's the same; they put them in a big chamber and suck the air out of their lungs and they die. They'd do that even to animals! Little animals!"

"I'll believe that when I see it," Harry Gottlieb said, derision on his face, and disbelief. "A truck that carries off dogs."

HE KNEW it was true, though. Walter had seen the pound truck two different times. Cats, dogs, and mainly us, he thought glumly. I mean, if they'd start with us, it's natural they'd wind up taking people's pets, too; we're not that different. But what kind of a person would do that, even if it is the law? "Some laws are made to be kept, and some to be broken," he remembered from a book he had read. We ought to firebomb the pound truck first, he thought; that's the worst, that truck.

Why is it, he wondered, that the more helpless a creature, the easier it was for some people to snuff it? Like a baby in the womb; the original abortions, "pre-partums," or "pre-persons" they were called now. How could they defend themselves? Who would speak for them? All those lives, a hundred by each doctor a day ... and all helpless and silent and then just dead. The fuckers, he thought. That's why they do it; they know they can do it; they get off on their macho power. And so a little thing that wanted to see the light of day is vacuumed out in less than two minutes. And the doctor goes on to the next chick.

There ought to be an organization, he thought, similar to the Mafia. Snuff the snuffers, or something. A contract man walks up to one of those doctors, pulls out a tube, and sucks the doctor into it, where he shrinks down like an unborn baby. A unborn baby doctor, with a stethoscope the size of a pinhead ... he laughed, thinking of that.

Children don't know. But children know everything, knew too much. The abortion truck, as it drove along, played a Good Humor Man's jingle:

> Jack and Jill
> Went up the hill
> To fetch a pail of water.

A tape loop in the sound system of the truck, built especially by Ampex for GM, blared that out when it wasn't actively nearing a seize. Then the driver shut off the sound system and glided along until he found the proper house. However, once he had the unwanted child in the back of the truck, and was either starting back to the County Facility or beginning another pre-person pick-up, he turned back on

> Jack and Jill
> Went up the hill
> To fetch a pail of water.

Thinking to himself, Oscar Ferris, the driver of truck Three, finished, "Jack fell down and broke his crown and Jill came tumbling after." What the hell's a crown? Ferris wondered. Probably a private part. He grinned. Probably Jack had been playing with it, or Jill, both of them together. Water, my ass, he thought. I know what they went off into the bushes for. Only, Jack fell down, and his thing broke right off. "Tough luck, Jill," he said aloud as he expertly drove the four-year-old truck along the winding curves of California Highway One.

Kids are like that, Ferris thought. Dirty and playing with dirty things, like themselves.

This was still wild and open country, and many stray children scratched about in the canyons and fields; he kept his eye open, and sure enough—off to his right scampered a small one, about six, trying to get out of sight. Ferris at once pressed the button that activated the siren of the truck. The boy froze, stood in fright, waited as the truck, still playing "Jack and Jill," coasted up beside him and came to a halt.

"Show me your D papers," Ferris said, without getting out of the truck; he leaned one arm out the window, showing his brown uniform and patch; his symbols of authority.

The boy had a scrawny look, like many strays, but, on the other hand, he wore glasses. Tow-headed, in jeans and T-shirt, he stared up in fright at Ferris, making no move to get out his identification.

"You got a D card or not?" Ferris said.

"W-w-w-what's a 'D card'?"

In his official voice, Ferris explained to the boy his rights under the law. "Your parent, either one, or legal guardian, fills out form 36-W, which is a formal statement of desirability. That they or him or her regard you as desirable. You don't have one? Legally, that makes you a stray, even if you have parents who want to keep you; they are subject to a fine of $500."

"Oh," the boy said. "Well, I lost it."

"Then a copy would be on file. They microdot all those documents and records. I'll take you in—"

"To the County Facility?" Pipe-cleaner legs wobbled in fear.

"They have thirty days to claim you by filling out the 36-W form. If they haven't done it by then—"

"My mom and dad never agree. Right not I'm staying with my dad."

"He didn't give you a D card to identify yourself with." Mounted transversally across the cab of the truck was a shotgun. There was always the possibility that trouble might break out when he picked up a stray. Reflexively, Ferris glanced up at it. It was there, all right, a pump shotgun. He had used it only five times in his

law-enforcement career. It could blow a man into
molecules. "I have to take you in," he said, opening the
truck door and bringing out his keys. "There's another kid
back there; you can keep each other company."

"No," the boy said. "I won't go." Blinking, he
confronted Ferris, stubborn and rigid as stone.

"Oh, you probably heard a lot of stories about the
County Facility. It's only the warpies, the creepies, that
get put to sleep; any nice normal-looking kid'll be
adopted—we'll cut your hair and fix you up so you look
professionally groomed. We want to find you a home.
That's the whole idea. It's just a few, those who are—you
know—ailing mentally or physically that no one wants.
Some well-to-do individual will snap you up in a minute;
you'll see. Then you won't be running around out here
alone with no parents to guide you. You'll have new
parents, and listen—they'll be paying heavy bread for
you; hell, they'll *register* you. Do you see? It's more a
temporary lodging place where we're taking you right
now, to make you available to prospective new parents."

"But if nobody adopts me in a month—"

"Hell, you could fall off a cliff here at Big Sur and kill
yourself. Don't worry. The desk at the Facility will
contact your blood parents, and most likely they'll come
forth with the Desirability Form (15A) sometime today
even. And meanwhile you'll get a nice ride and meet a lot
of new kids. And how often—"

"No," the boy said.

"This is to inform you," Ferris said, in a different tone,
"that I am a County Official." He opened his truck door,
jumped down, showed his gleaming metal badge to the
boy. "I am Peace Officer Ferris and I now order you to
enter by the rear of the truck."

A tall man approached them, walking with wariness;
he, like the boy, wore jeans and a T-shirt, but no glasses.

"You the boy's father?" Ferris said.

The man, hoarsely, said, "Are you taking him to the
pound?"

"We consider it a child protection shelter," Ferris said.
"The use of the term 'pound' is a radical hippie slur, and
distorts—deliberately—the overall picture of what we
do."

Gesturing toward the truck, the man said, "You've got

kids locked in there in those cages, have you?"

"I'd like to see your ID," Ferris said. "And I'd like to know if you've ever been arrested before."

"Arrested and found innocent? Or arrested and found guilty?"

"Answer my question, sir," Ferris said, showing his black flatpack that he used with adults to identify him as a County Peace Officer. "Who are you? Come on, let's see your ID."

The man said, "Ed Gantro is my name and I have a record. When I was eighteen, I stole four crates of Coca-Cola from a parked truck."

"You were apprehended at the scene?"

"No," the man said. "When I took the empties back to cash in on the refunds. That's when they seized me. I served six months."

"Have you a Desirability Card for your boy here?" Ferris asked.

"We couldn't afford the $90 it cost."

"Well, now it'll cost you five hundred. You should have gotten it in the first place. My suggestion is that you consult an attorney." Ferris moved toward the boy, declaring officially, "I'd like you to join the other juveniles in the rear section of the vehicle." To the man he said, "Tell him to do as instructed."

The man hesitated and then said. "Tim, get in the goddamn truck. And we'll get a lawyer; we'll get the D card for you. It's futile to make trouble—technically you're a stray."

"'A stray,'" the boy said, regarding his father.

Ferris said, "Exactly right. You have thirty days, you know, to raise the—"

"Do you also take cats?" the boy said. "Are there any cats in there? I really like cats; they're all right."

"I handle only P.P. cases," Ferris said. "Such as yourself." With a key he unlocked the back of the truck. "Try not to relieve yourself while you're in the truck; it's hard as hell to get the odor and stains out."

The boy did not seem to understand the word; he gazed from Ferris to his father in perplexity.

"Just don't go to the bathroom while you're in the truck," his father explained. "They want to keep it sanitary, because that cuts down their maintenance costs." His voice was savage and grim.

"With stray dogs or cats," Ferris said, "they just shoot them on sight, or put out poison bait."

"Oh, yeah, I know that Warfarin," the boy's father said. "The animal eats it over a period of a week, and then he bleeds to death internally."

"With no pain," Ferris pointed out.

"Isn't that better than sucking the air from their lungs?" Ed Gantro said. "Suffocating them on a mass basis?"

"Well, with animals the county authorities—"

"I mean the children. Like Tim." His father stood beside him, and they both looked into the rear of the truck. Two dark shapes could be dimly discerned, crouching as far back as possible, in the starkest form of despair.

"Fleischhacker!" the boy Tim said. "Didn't you have a D card?"

"Because of energy and fuel shortages," Ferris was saying, "population must be radically cut. Or in ten years there'll be no food for anyone. This is one phase of—"

"I had a D card," Earl Fleischhacker said, "but my folks took it away from me. They didn't want me any more; so they took it back, and then they called for the abortion truck." His voice croaked; obviously he had been secretly crying.

"And what's the difference between a five-month-old fetus and what we have here?" Ferris was saying. "In both cases what you have is an unwanted child. They simply liberalized the laws."

Tim's father, staring at him, said, "Do you agree with these laws?"

"Well, it's really all up to Washington and what they decide will solve our needs in these days of crisis," Ferris said. "I only enforce their edicts. If this law changed— hell. I'd be trucking empty milk cartons for recycling or something and be just as happy."

"*Just* as happy? You enjoy your work?"

Ferris said, mechanically, "It gives me the opportunity to move around a lot and to meet people."

Tim's father Ed Gantro said, "You are insane. This postpartum abortion scheme and the abortion laws before it where the unborn child had no legal rights—it was removed like a tumor. Look what it's come to. If an unborn child can be killed without due process, why not a born one? What I see in common in both cases is their helplessness; the organism that is killed had no chance, no ability, to protect itself. You know what? I want you to take me in, too. In back of the truck with the three children."

"But the President and Congress have declared that when you're past twelve you have a soul," Ferris said. "I can't take you. It wouldn't be right."

"I have no soul," Tim's father said. "I got to be twelve and nothing happened. Take me along, too. Unless you can find my soul."

"Jeez," Ferris said.

"Unless you can show me my soul," Tim's father said, "unless you can specifically locate it, then I insist you take me in as no different from these kids."

Ferris said, "I'll have to use the radio to get in touch with the County Facility, see what they say."

"You do that," Tim's father said, and laboriously clambered up into the rear of the truck, helping Tim along with him. With the other two boys they waited while Peace Officer Ferris, with all his official identification as to who he was, talked on his radio.

"I HAVE here a Caucasian male, approximately thirty, who insists that he be transported to the County Facility with his infant son," Ferris was saying into his mike. "He claims to have no soul, which he maintains puts him in the class of subtwelve-year-olds. I don't have with me or know any test to detect the presence of a soul, at least any I can give out here in the boondocks that'll later on satisfy a court. I mean, he probably can do algebra and higher math; he seems to possess an intelligent mind. But—"

"Affirmative as to bringing him in," his superior's voice on the two-way radio came back to him. "We'll deal with him here."

"We're going to deal with you downtown," Ferris said to Tim's father, who, with the three smaller figures, was crouched down in the dark recesses of the rear of the truck. Ferris slammed the door, locked it—an extra precaution, since the boys were already netted by electronic bands—and then started up the truck.

> Jack and Jill went up the hill
> To fetch a pail of water.
> Jack fell down
> And broke his crown

Somebody's sure going to get their crown broke, Ferris thought as he drove along the winding road, and it isn't going to be me.

"I CAN'T do algebra," he heard Tim's father saying to the three boys. "So I can't have a soul."

The Fleishhacker boy said, snively, "I can, but I'm only nine. So what good does it do me?"

"That's what I'm going to use as my plea at the Facility," Tim's father continued. "Even long division was hard for me. I don't have a soul. I belong with you three little guys."

Ferris, in a loud voice, called back, "I don't want you soiling the truck, you understand? It costs us—"

"Don't tell me," Tim's father said, "because I wouldn't understand. It would be too complex, the proration and accrual and fiscal terms like that."

I've got a weirdo back there, Ferris thought, and was glad he had the pump shotgun mounted within easy reach. "You know the world is running out of everything," Ferris called back to them, "energy and apple juice and fuel and bread; we've got to keep the population down, and the embolisms from the Pill make it impossible—"

"None of us knows those big words," Tim's father broke in.

Angrily, and feeling baffled, Ferris said, "Zero population growth; that's the answer to the energy and food crisis. It's like—shit, it's like when they introduced the rabbit in Australia, and it had no natural enemies, and so it multiplied until, like people—"

"I do understand multiplication," Tim's father said. "And adding and subtraction. But that's all."

Four crazy rabbits flopping across the road, Ferris

thought. People pollute the natural environment, he thought. What must this part of the country have been like before man? Well, he thought, with the postpartum abortions taking place in every county in the U.S. of A. we may see that day; we may stand and look once again upon a virgin land.

We, he thought. I guess there won't be any we. I mean, he thought, giant sentient computers will sweep out the landscape with their slotted video receptors and find it pleasing.

The thought cheered him up.

"LET'S HAVE an abortion!" Cynthia declared excitedly as she entered the house with an armload of synthogroceries. "Wouldn't that be neat? Doesn't that turn you on?"

Her husband Ian Best said drily, "But first you have to get pregnant. So make an appointment with Dr. Guido—that should cost me only fifty or sixty dollars—and have your I.U.D. removed."

"I think it's slipping down anyhow. Maybe, if—" Her pert dark shag-haired head tossed in glee. "It probably hasn't worked properly since last year. So I could be pregnant now."

Ian said caustically. "You could put an ad in the *Free Press:* 'Man wanted to fish out I.U.D. with coathanger.'"

"But you see," Cynthia said, following him as he made his way to the master closet to hang up his status-tie and class-coat, "it's the in thing now, to have an abortion. Look, what do we have? A kid. We have Walter. Every time someone comes over to visit and sees him, I know they're wondering, 'Where did you screw up?' It's embarrassing." She added, "And the kind of abortions they give now, for women in early stages—it only costs one hundred dollars...the price of ten gallons of gas! And you can talk about it with practically everybody who drops by for hours."

Ian turned to face her and said in a level voice. "Do you get to keep the embryo? Bring it home in a bottle or sprayed with special luminous paint so it glows in the dark like a night light?"

"In any color you want!"

"The *embryo?*"

"No, the bottle. And the color of the fluid. It's in a preservative solution, so really it's a lifetime acquisition. It even has a written guarantee, I think."

Ian folded his arms to keep himself calm: alpha state condition. "Do you know that there are people who would want to have a child? Even an ordinary dumb one? That go to the County Facility week after week looking for a little newborn baby? These ideas—there's been this world panic about overpopulation. Nine trillion humans stacked like kindling in every block of every city. Okay, if that were going on—" He gestured. "But what we have now is not *enough* children. Or don't you watch TV or read the *Times*?"

"It's a drag," Cynthia said. "For instance, today Walter came into the house freaked out because the abortion truck cruised by. It's a drag taking care of him. *You* have it easy; you're at work. But *me*—"

"You know what I'd like to do to that Gestapo abortion wagon? Have two ex-drinking buddies of mine armed with BARs, one on each side of the road. And when the wagon passes by—"

"It's a ventilated air-conditioned truck, not a wagon."

He glared at her and then went to the bar in the kitchen to fix himself a drink. Scotch will do, he decided. Scotch and milk, a good before-"dinner" drink.

As he mixed his drink, his son Walter came in. He had, on his face, an unnatural pallor.

"The 'bort truck went by today, didn't it?" Ian said.

"I thought maybe—"

"No way. Even if your mother and I saw a lawyer and had a legal document drawn up, an un-D Form, you're too old. So relax."

"I know intellectually," Walter said, "but—"

"'Do not seek to know for whom the bell tolls; it tolls for thee,'" Ian quoted (inaccurately). "Listen, Walt, let me lay something on you." He took a big, long drink of Scotch and milk. "The name of all this is, *kill me*. Kill them when they're the size of a fingernail, or a baseball, or later on, if you haven't done it already, suck the air out of the lungs of a ten-year-old boy and let him die. It's a certain kind of woman advocating this all. They used to call them 'castrating females.' Maybe that was once the right term, except that these women, these hard cold women, didn't just want to—well, they want to do in the *whole* boy or man, make all of them dead, not just the part that makes him a man. Do you see?"

"No," Walter said, but in a dim sense, very frightening, he did.

After another hit of his drink, Ian said, "And we've got one living right here, Walter. Here in our very house."

"What do we have living here?"

"What the Swiss psychiatrists call a *kindermörder*," Ian said, deliberately choosing a term he knew his boy wouldn't understand. "You know what," he said, "you and I could get onto an Amtrak coach and head north and just keep on going until we reached Vancouver, British Columbia, and we could take a ferry to Vancouver Island and never be seen by anybody down here again."

"But what about mom?"

"I would send her a cashier's check," Ian said. "Each month. And she would be quite happy with that."

"It's cold up there, isn't it?" Walter said. "I mean, they have hardly any fuel and they wear—"

"About like San Francisco. Why? Are you afraid of wearing a lot of sweaters and sitting close to the fireplace? What did you see today that frightened you a hell of a lot more?"

"Oh, yeah." He nodded somberly.

"We could live on a little island off Vancouver Island and raise our own food. You can plant stuff up there and it grows. And the truck won't come there; you'll never see it again. They have different laws. The women up there are different. There was this one girl I knew when I was up there for a while, a long time ago; she had long black hair and smoked Players cigarettes all the time and never ate anything or ever stopped talking. Down here we're seeing a civilization in which the desire by women to destroy their own—" Ian broke off; his wife had walked into the kitchen.

"If you drink any more of that stuff," she said to him, "you'll barf it up."

"Okay," Ian said irritably. "Okay!"

"And don't yell," Cynthia said. "I thought for dinner tonight it'd be nice if you took us out. Dal Rey's said on TV they have steak for early comers."

Wrinkling his nose, Walter said, "They have raw oysters."

"Blue points," Cynthia said. "In the half shell, on ice. I love them. All right, Ian? Is it decided?"

To his son Walter, Ian said, "A raw blue point oyster looks like nothing more on earth than what the surgeon—" He became silent, then, Cynthia glared at him, and his son was puzzled. "Okay," he said, "but I get to order steak."

"Me too," Walter said.

Finishing his drink, Ian said more quietly, "When was the last time you fixed dinner here in the house? For the three of us?"

"I fixed you that pigs' ears and rice dish on Friday," Cynthia said. "Most of which went to waste because it was something new and on the nonmandatory list. Remember, *dear*?"

Ignoring her, Ian said to his son, "Of course, that type of women will sometimes, even often, be found up there, too. She has existed throughout all time and all cultures. But since Canada has no law permitting postpartum—" He broke off. "It's the carton of milk talking," he explained to Cynthia. "They adulterate it these days with sulfur. Pay no attention or sue somebody; the choice is yours."

Cynthia, eying him, said, "Are you running a fantasy number in your head again about splitting?"

"Both of us," Walter broke in. "Dad's taking me with him."

"Where?" Cynthia said, casually.

Ian said, "Wherever the Amtrak track leads us."

"We're going to Vancouver Island in Canada," Walter said.

"Oh, really?" Cynthia said.

After a pause Ian said, "Really."

"And what the shit am I supposed to do when you're gone? Peddle my ass down at the local bar? How'll I meet the payments on the various—"

"I will continually mail you checks," Ian said. "Bonded by giant banks."

"Sure. You bet. Yep. Right."

"You could come along," Ian said, "and catch fish by

leaping into English Bay and grinding them to death with your sharp teeth. You could rid British Columbia of its fish population overnight. All those ground-up fish, wondering vaguely what happened ... swimming along one minute and then this—ogre, this fish-destroying monster with a single luminous eye in the center of its forehead, falls on them and grinds them into grit. There would soon be a legend. News like that spreads. At least among the last surviving fish."

"Yeah, but Dad," Walter said, "suppose there are no surviving fish."

"Then it will have been all in vain," Ian said, "except for your mother's own personal pleasure at having bitten to death an entire species in British Columbia, where fishing is the largest industry anyhow, and so many other species depend on it for survival."

"But then everyone in British Columbia will be out of work," Walter said.

"No," Ian said, "they will be cramming the dead fish into cans to sell to Americans. You see, Walter, in the olden days, before your mother multitoothedly bit to death all the fish in British Columbia, the simple rustics stood with stick in hand, and when a fish swam past, they whacked the fish over the head. This will *create* jobs, not eliminate them. Millions of cans of suitably marked—"

"You know," Cynthia said quickly, "he believes what you tell him."

Ian said, "What I tell him is true." Although not, he realized, in a literal sense. To his wife he said, "I'll take you out to dinner. Get our ration stamps, put on that blue knit blouse that shows off your boobs; that way you'll get a lot of attention and maybe they won't remember to collect the stamps."

"What's a 'boob'?" Walter asked.

"Something fast becoming obsolete," Ian said, "like the Pontiac GTO. Except as an ornament to be admired and squeezed. Its function is dying away." As is our race, he thought, once we gave full rein to those who would destroy the unborn—in other words, the most helpless creatures alive.

"A boob," Cynthia said severely to her son, "is a mammary gland that ladies possess which provides milk to their young."

"Generally there are two of them," Ian said. "Your operational boob and then your backup boob, in case there is power failure in the operational one. I suggest the elimination of a step in all this pre-person abortion mania," he said. "We will send all the boobs in the world to the County Facilities. The milk, if any, will be sucked out of them, by mechanical means of course; they will become useless and empty, and then the young will die naturally, deprived of many and all sources of nourishment."

"There's formula," Cynthia said, witheringly. "Similac and those. I'm going to change so we can go out." She turned and strode toward their bedroom.

"You know," Ian said after her, "if there was any way you could get me classified as a pre-person, you'd send me there. To the Facility with the greatest facility." And, he thought, I'll bet I wouldn't be the only husband in California who went. There'd be plenty others. In the same bag as me, then as now.

"Sounds like a plan," Cynthia's voice came to him dimly; she had heard.

"It's not just a hatred for the helpless," Ian Best said. "More is involved. Hatred of what? Of everything that grows?" You blight them, he thought, before they grow big enough to have muscle and the tactics and skill for fight—big like I am in relation to you, with my fully developed musculature and weight. So much easier when the other person—I should say pre-person—is floating and dreaming in the amniotic fluid and knows nothing about how to nor the need to hit back.

Where did the motherly virtues go to? he asked himself. When mothers *especially* protected what was small and weak and defenseless?

Our competitive society, he decided. The survival of the strong. Not the fit, he thought; just those who hold the *power*. And are not going to surrender it to the next generation: it is the powerful and evil old against the helpless and gentle new.

"Dad," Walter said, "are we really going to Vancouver Island in Canada and raise real food and not have anything to be afraid of any more?"

Half to himself, Ian said, "Soon as I have the money."

"I know what that means. It's a 'we'll see' number you

say. We aren't going, are we?" He watched his father's face
intently. "She won't let us, like taking me out of school
and like that; she always brings up that . . . right?"

"It lies ahead for us someday," Ian said doggedly.
"Maybe not this month but someday, sometime. I
promise."

"And there's no abortion trucks there."

"No. None. Canadian law is different."

"Make it soon, Dad. Please."

His father fixed himself a second Scotch and milk and
did not answer; his face was somber and unhappy, almost
as if he was about to cry.

IN THE rear of the abortion truck three children and one
adult huddled, jostled by the turning of the truck. They
fell against the restraining wire that separated them, and
Tim Gantro's father felt keen despair at being cut off
mechanically from his own boy. A nightmare during day,
he thought. Caged like animals; his noble gesture had
brought only more suffering to him.

"Why'd you say you don't know algebra?" Tim asked,
once. "I know you know even calculus and trig-
something; you went to Stanford University."

"I want to show," he said, "that either they ought to kill
all of us or none of us. But not divide along these
bureaucratic arbitrary lines. 'When does the soul enter the
body?' What kind of rational question is that in this day
and age? It's Medieval." In fact, he thought, it's a
pretext—a pretext to prey on the helpless. And he was not
helpless. The abortion truck had picked up a fully grown
man, with all his knowledge, all his cunning. How are they
going to handle me? he asked himself. Obviously I have
what all men have; if they have souls, then so do I. If not,
then I don't, but on what real basis can they "put me to
sleep"? I am not weak and small, not an ignorant child
cowering defenselessly. I can argue the sophistries with
the best of the county lawyers; with the D.A. himself, if
necessary.

If they snuff me, he thought, they will have to snuff
everyone, including themselves. And that is not what this
is all about. This is a con game by which the established,
those who already hold all the key economic and political

posts, keep the youngsters out of it—murder them if necessary. There is, he thought, in the land, a hatred by the old of the land, a hatred by the old of the young, a hatred and a fear. So what will they do with me? I am in their age group, and I am caged up in the back of this abortion truck. I pose, he thought, a different kind of threat; I am one of them but on the other side, with the stray dogs and cats and babies and infants. Let them figure it out; let a new St. Thomas Aquinas arise who can unravel this.

"All I know," he said aloud, "is dividing and multiplying and subtracting. I'm even hazy on my fractions."

"But you use to know that!" Tim said.

"Funny how you forget it after you leave school," Ed Gantro said. "You kids are probably better at it than I am."

"Dad, they're going to *snuff* you," his son Tim said, wildly. "Nobody'll adopt you. Not at your age. You're too *old*."

"Let's see," Ed Gantro said. "The binomial theorem. How does that go? I can't get it all together: something about a and b." And as it leaked out of his head, as had his immortal soul . . . he chuckled to himself. I cannot pass the soul test, he thought. At least not talking like that. I am a dog in the gutter, an animal in a ditch.

The whole mistake of the pro-abortion people from the start, he said to himself, was the *arbitrary* line they drew. An embryo is not entitled to American Constitutional rights and can be killed, legally, by a doctor. But a fetus was a "person," with rights, at least for a while; and then the pro-abortion crowd decided that even a seven-month fetus was not "human" and could be killed, legally, by a licensed doctor. And, one day, a newborn baby—it is a vegetable; it can't focus its eyes, it understands nothing, nor talks . . . the pro-abortion lobby argued in court, and won, with their contention that a newborn baby was only a fetus expelled by accident or organic processes from the womb. But, even then, where was the line to be drawn finally? When the baby smiled its first smile? When it spoke its first word or reached for its initial time for some toy it enjoyed? The legal line was relentlessly pushed back and back. And now the most savage and arbitrary definition of all: when it could perform "higher math."

That made the ancient Greeks, of Plato's time, nonhumans, since arithmetic was unknown to them, only geometry; and algebra was an Arab invention, much later in history. *Arbitrary*. It was not a theological arbitrariness either; it was a mere legal one. The Church had long since—from the start, in fact—maintained that even the zygote, and the embryo that followed, was as sacred a life form as any that walked the earth. They had seen what would come of arbitrary definitions of "Now the soul enters the body," or in modern terms, "Now it is a person entitled to the full protection of the law like everyone else." What was so sad was the sight now of the small child playing bravely in his yard day by day, trying to hope, trying to pretend a security he did not have.

Well, he thought, we'll see what they do with me; I am thirty-five years old, with a Master's Degree from Stanford. Will they put me in a cage for thirty days, with a plastic food dish and a water source and a place—in plain sight to relieve myself—and if no one adopts me, will they consign me to automatic death along with the others?

I am risking a lot, he thought. But they picked up my son today, and the risk began then, when they had him, not when I stepped forward and became a victim myself.

He looked about at the three frightened boys and tried to think of something to tell them—not just his own son but all three.

"'Look,'" he said, quoting. "'I tell you a sacred secret. We shall not all sleep in death. We shall—'" But then he could not remember the rest. Bummer, he thought dismally. "'We shall wake up,'" he said, doing the best he could. "'In a flash. In the twinkling of an eye.'"

"Cut the noise," the driver of the truck, from beyond his wire mesh, growled. "I can't concentrate on this fucking road." He added, "You know, I can squirt gas back there where you are, and you'll all pass out; it's for obstreperous pre-persons we pick up. So you want to knock it off, or have me punch the gas button?"

"We won't say anything," Tim said quickly, with a look of mute terrified appeal at his father. Urging him silently to conform.

His father said nothing. The glance of urgent pleading was too much for him, and he capitulated. Anyhow, he reasoned, what happened in the truck was not crucial. It was when they reached the County Facility—where there would be, at the first sign of trouble newspaper and TV reporters.

So they rode in silence, each with his own fears, his own schemes. Ed Gantro brooded to himself, perfecting in his head what he would do—what he *had* to do. And not just for Tim but all the P.P. abortion candidates; he thought through the ramifications as the truck lurched and rattled on.

As soon as the truck parked in the restricted lot of the County Facility and its rear doors had been swung open, Sam B. Carpenter, who ran the whole goddamn operation, walked over, stared, said, "You've got a grown man in there, Ferris. In fact, you comprehend what you've got? A protester, that's what you've latched onto."

"But he insisted he doesn't know any math higher than adding," Ferris said.

To Ed Gantro, Carpenter said, "Hand me your wallet. I want your actual name. Social Security number, police region stability ident—come on, I want to know who you really are."

"He's just a rural type," Ferris said, as he watched Gantro pass over his lumpy wallet.

"And I want confirm prints offa his feet," Carpenter said. "The full set. Right away—priority A." He liked to talk that way.

An hour later he had the reports back from the jungle of inter-locking security-data computers from the fake-pastoral restricted area in Virginia. "This individual graduated from Stanford College with a degree in math. And then got a master's in psychology, which he has, no doubt about it, been subjecting us to. We've got to get him out of here."

"I did have a soul," Gantro said, "but I lost it."

"How?" Carpenter demanded, seeing nothing about that on Gantro's official records.

"An embolism. The portion of my cerebral cortex, where my soul was, got destroyed when I accidentally inhaled the vapors of insect spray. That's why I've been living out in the country eating roots and grubs, with my boy here, Tim."

"We'll run an EEG on you," Carpenter said.

"What's that?" Gantro said. "One of those brain tests?"

To Ferris, Carpenter said, "The law says the soul enters at twelve years. And you bring in this individual male adult well over thirty. We could be charged with murder. We've got to get rid of him. You drive him back to exactly where you found him and dump him off. If he won't voluntarily exit from the truck, gas the shit out of him and then throw him out. That's a national-security order. Your job depends on it, also your status with the penal code of this state."

"I belong here." Ed Gantro said. "I'm a dummy."

"And his kid," Carpenter said. "He's probably a mathematical mental mutant like you see on TV. They set you up; they've probably already alerted the media. Take them all back and gas them and dump them wherever you found them or, barring that, anyhow out of sight."

"You're getting hysterical," Ferris said, with anger. "Run the EEG and the brain scan on Gantro, and probably we'll have to release him, but these three juveniles—"

"All geniuses," Carpenter said. "All part of the setup, only you're too stupid to know. Kick them out of the truck and off our premises, and deny—you get this?— deny you ever picked any of the four of them up. Stick to that story."

"Out of the vehicle," Ferris ordered, pressing the button that lifted the wire mesh gates.

The three boys scrambled out. But Ed Gantro remained.

"He's not going to exit voluntarily," Carpenter said. "Okay, Gantro, we'll physically expel you." He nodded to Ferris, and the two of them entered the back of the truck. A moment later they had deposited Ed Gantro on the pavement of the parking lot.

"Now you're just a plain citizen," Carpenter said, with relief. "You can claim all you want, but you have no proof."

"Dad," Tim said, "how are we going to get home?" All

three boys clustered around Ed Gantro.

"You could call somebody from up there," the Fleischhacker boy said. "I bet if Walter Best's dad has enough gas he'd come and get us. He takes a lot of long drives; he has a special coupon."

"Him and his wife, Mrs. Best, quarrel a lot," Tim said. "So he likes to go driving at night alone; I mean, without her."

Ed Gantro said, "I'm staying here. I want to be locked up in a cage."

"But we can *go*," Tim protested. Urgently, he plucked at his dad's sleeve. "That's the whole point, isn't it? They let us go when they saw you. We did it!"

Ed Gantro said to Carpenter, "I insist on being locked up with the other pre-persons you have in there." He pointed at the gaily imposing, esthetic solid-green-painted Facility Building.

To Mr. Sam B. Carpenter, Tim said, "Call Mr. Best, out where we were, on the peninsula. It's a 669 prefix number. Tell him to come and get us, and he will. I promise. Please."

The Fleischhacker boy added, "There's only one Mr. Best listed in the phonebook with a 669 number. Please, mister."

Carpenter went indoors, to one of the Facility's many official phones, looked up the number. Ian Best. He punched the number.

"You have reached a semiworking, semiloafing number," a man's voice, obviously that of someone half-drunk, responded. In the background Carpenter could hear the cutting tones of a furious woman, excoriating Ian Best.

"Mr. Best," Carpenter said, "several persons whom you know are stranded down at Fourth and A Streets in Verde Gabriel, an Ed Gantro and his son Tim, a boy identified as Ronald, or Donald Fleischhacker, and another unidentified minor boy. The Gantro boy suggested you would not object to driving down here to pick them up and take them home."

"Fourth and A Streets," Ian Best said. A pause. "Is that the pound?"

"The County Facility," Carpenter said.

"You son of a bitch," Best said. "Sure I'll come get them; expect me in twenty minutes. You have *Ed* Gantro there as a pre-person? Do you know he graduated from Stanford University?"

"We are aware of this," Carpenter said stonily. "But they are not being detained; they are merely—here. Not—I repeat not—in custody."

Ian Best, the drunken slur gone from his voice, said, "There'll be reporters from all the media there before I get there." Click. He had hung up.

Walking back outside, Carpenter said to the boy Tim, "Well, it seems you mickey-moused me into notifying a rabid anti-abortionist activist of your presence here. How neat, how really neat."

A few moments passed, and then a bright-red Mazda sped up to the entrance of the Facility. A tall man with a light beard got out, unwound camera and audio gear, walked leisurely over to Carpenter. "I understand you may have a Stanford MA in math here at the Facility," he said in a neutral, casual voice. "Could I interview him for a possible story?"

Carpenter said, "We have booked no such person. You can inspect our records." But the reporter was already gazing at the three boys clustered around Ed Gantro.

In a loud voice the reporter called, "Mr. Gantro?"

"Yes, sir," Ed Gantro replied.

Christ, Carpenter thought. We did lock him in one of our official vehicles and transport him here; it'll hit all the papers. Already a blue van with the markings of a TV station had rolled onto the lot. And, behind it, two more cars.

ABORTION FACILITY SNUFFS STANFORD GRAD

That was how it read in Carpenter's mind. Or.

COUNTY ABORTION FACILITY FOILED IN ILLEGAL ATTEMPT TO...

And so forth. A spot on the 6:00 evening TV news. Gantro, and when he showed up, Ian Best who was probably an attorney, surrounded by tape recorders and mikes and video cameras.

We have mortally fucked up, he thought. Mortally fucked up. They at Sacramento will cut our appropriation; we'll be reduced to hunting down stray dogs and cats again, like before. Bummer.

When Ian Best arrived in his coal-burning Mercedes-Benz, he was still a little stoned. To Ed Gantro he said, "You mind if we take a scenic roundabout route back?"

"By way of what?" Ed Gantro said. He wearily wanted to leave now. The little flow of media people had interviewed him and gone. He had made his point, and now he felt drained, and he wanted to go home.

Ian Best said, "By way of Vancouver Island, British Columbia."

With a smile, Ed Gantro said, "These kids should go right to bed. My kid and the other two. Hell, they haven't even had any dinner."

"We'll stop at a McDonald's stand," Ian Best said. "And then we can take off for Canada, where the fish are, and lots of mountains that still have snow on them, even this time of year."

"Sure," Gantro said, grinning. "We can go there."

"You want to?" Ian Best scrutinized him. "You really want to?"

"I'll settle a few things, and then, sure, you and I can take off together."

"Son of a bitch," Best breathed. "You mean it."

"Yes," he said. "I do. Of course, I have to get my wife's agreement. You can't go to Canada unless your wife signs a document in writing where she won't follow you. You become what's called a 'landed Immigrant.'"

"Then I've got to get Cynthia's written permission."

"She'll give it to you. Just agree to send support money."

"You think she will? She'll let me go?"

"Of course," Gantro said.

"You actually think our wives will let us go," Ian Best said as he and Gantro herded the children into the Mercedes-Benz. "I'll bet you're right; Cynthia'd love to get rid of me. You know what she calls me, right in front of Walter? 'An aggressive coward,' and stuff like that. She has no respect for me."

"Our wives," Gantro said, "will let us go." But he knew better.

He looked back at the Facility manager, Mr. Sam B. Carpenter, and at the truck driver, Ferris, who, Carpenter had told the press and TV, was as of this date fired and was a new and inexperienced employee anyhow.

"No," he said. "They won't let us go. None of them will."

Clumsily, Ian Best fiddled with the complex mechanism that controlled the funky coal-burning engine. "Sure they'll let us go; look, they're just standing there. What can they do, after what you said on TV and what that one reporter wrote up for a feature story?"

"I don't mean them," Gantro said tonelessly.

"We could just run."

"We are caught," Gantro said. "Caught and can't get out. You ask Cynthia, though. It's worth a try."

"We'll never see Vancouver Island and the great ocean-going ferries steaming in out of the fog, will we?" Ian Best said.

"Sure we will, eventually." But he knew it was a lie, an absolute lie, just like you know sometimes when you say something that for no rational reason you know is absolutely true.

They drove from the lot, out onto the public street.

"It feels good," Ian Best said, "to be free . . . right?" The three boys nodded, but Ed Gantro said nothing. Free, he thought. Free to go home. To be caught in a larger net, shoved into a greater truck than the metal mechanical one the County Facility uses.

"This is a great day," Ian Best said.

"Yes," Ed Gantro agreed. "A great day in which a noble and effective blow has been struck for all helpless things, anything of which you could say, 'It is alive.'"

Regarding him intently in the narrow tricky light, Ian Best said, "I don't want to go home; I want to take off for Canada now."

"We *have* to go home," Ed Gantro reminded him. "Temporarily, I mean. To wind things up. Legal matters, pick up what we need."

Ian Best, as he drove, said, "We'll never get there, to British Columbia and Vancouver Island and Stanley Park and English Bay and where they grow food and keep horses and where they have the ocean-going ferries."

"No, we won't," Ed Gantro said.

"Not now, not even later?"

"Not ever," Ed Gantro said.

"That's what I was afraid of," Best said and his voice broke and his driving got funny. "That's what I thought from the beginning."

They drove in silence, then, with nothing to say to each other. There was nothing left to say.

Story Notes

By Philip K. Dick

"The Golden Man."

Here I am saying that mutants are dangerous to us
ordinaries, a view which John W. Campbell, Jr. deplored. We
were supposed to view them as our leaders. But I always felt
uneasy as to how they would view us. I mean, maybe they
wouldn't *want* to lead us. Maybe from their superevolved lofty
level we wouldn't seem worth leading. Anyhow, even if they
agreed to lead us, I felt uneasy as to where we would wind up
going. It might have something to do with buildings marked
SHOWERS but which really weren't.

"Return Match."

The theme of dangerous toys runs like a tattered thread
throughout my writing. The dangerous disguised as the
innocent... and what could be more innocent than a toy? This
story makes me think of a set of huge speakers I looked at last
week; they cost six thousand dollars and were larger than
refrigerators. Our joke about them was that if you didn't go to
the audio store to see them, they'd come to see *you*.

"The King of the Elves."

This story, of course, is fantasy, not SF. Originally it had a
downbeat ending on it, but Horace Gold, the editor who bought
it, carefully explained to me that prophecy always came true; if it
didn't ipso facto it wasn't prophecy. I guess, then, there can be
no such thing as a false prophet; "false prophet" is an oxymoron.

"The Mold of Yancy."

Obviously, Yancy is based on President Eisenhower. During
his reign we all were worrying about the man-in-the-gray-
flannel-suit problem; we feared that the entire country was
turning into one person and a whole lot of clones. (Although in
those days the word "clone" was unknown to us.) I liked this

story enough to use it as the basis for my novel THE PENULTIMATE TRUTH; in particular the part where everything the government tells you is a lie. I still like that part; I mean, I still believe it's so. Watergate, of course, bore the basic idea of this story out.

"Not By Its Cover."

Here I presented what used to be a wish on my part: that the Bible was true. Obviously, I was at a sort of halfway point between doubt and faith. Years later I'm still in that position; I'd *like* the Bible to be true, but—well, maybe if it isn't we can make it so. But, alas, it's going to take plenty of work to do it.

"The Little Black Box."

I made use of this story when I wrote my novel DO ANDROIDS DREAM OF ELECTRIC SHEEP? Actually, the idea is better put forth in the story. Here, a religion is regarded as a menace to all political systems; therefore it, too, is a kind of political system, perhaps even an ultimate one. The concept of *caritas* (or *agape*) shows up in my writing as the key to the authentic human. The android, which is the unauthentic human, the mere reflex machine, is unable to experience empathy. In this story it is never clear whether Mercer is an invader from some other world. But he must be; in a sense all religious leaders are... but not from another planet as such.

"The Unreconstructed M."

If my main theme throughout my writing is, "Can we consider the universe real, and if so, in what way?" my secondary theme would be, "Are we all humans?" Here a machine does not imitate a human being, but instead fakes evidence *of* a human being, a given human being. Fakery is a topic which absolutely fascinates me; I am convinced that anything can be faked, or anyhow evidence pointing to any given thing. Spurious clues can lead us to believe anything *they* want us to believe. There is really no theoretical upper limit to this. Once you have mentally opened the door to reception of the notion of *fake*, you are ready to think yourself into another kind of reality entirely. It's a trip from which you never return. And, I think, a healthy trip... unless you take it too seriously.

"The War with the Fnools."

Well, once again we are invaded. And, humiliatingly, by a life form which is absurd. My colleague Tim Powers once said that

Martians could invade us simply by putting on funny hats, and we'd never notice. It's a sort of low-budget invasion. I guess we're at the point where we can be amused by the idea of Earth being invaded. (And this is when they really zap you.)

"The Last of the Masters."

Now I show trust of a robot as leader, a robot who is the suffering servant, which is to say a form of Christ. Leader as servant of man; leader who should be dispensed with—perhaps. An ambiguity hangs over the morality of this story. Should we have a leader or should we think for ourselves? Obviously the latter, in principle. But—sometimes there lies a gulf between what is theoretically right and that which is practical. It's interesting that I would trust a robot and not an android. Perhaps it's because a robot does not try to deceive you as to what it is.

"Meddler."

Within the beautiful lurks the ugly; you can see in this rather crude story the germ of my whole theme that nothing is what it seems. This story should be read as a trial run on my part; I was just beginning to grasp that obvious form and latent form are not the same thing. As Heraclitus said in fragment 54: "Latent structure is master of obvious structure," and out of this comes the later more sophisticated Platonic dualism between the phenomenal world and the real but invisible realm of forms lying behind it. I may be reading too much into this simpleminded early story, but at least I was beginning to see in a dim way what I later saw so clearly; in fragment 123, Heraclitus said, "The nature of things is in the habit of concealing itself," and therein lies it all.

"A Game of Unchance."

I feel the same way about this little story as I do about Harlan Ellison: I love the little bastard. It's a well-constructed story, with what for me (in rereading it) is a totally unexpected ending. A carnival is feral; another carnival shows up and is pitted against the first one; and the antithetical interaction is preplanned in such a way that the first carnival wins. It's as if the two opposing forces that underlie all change in the universe are rigged; in favor of thanatos, the dark force, yin or strife, which is to say, the force of destruction.

●　　●　　●

"Sales Pitch."

When this story first appeared, the fans detested it. I read it over, perplexed by their hostility, and could see why: it is a superdowner story, and relentlessly so. Could I rewrite it, I would have it end differently. I would have the man and the robot, i.e. the fasrad, form a partnership at the end and become friends. The logic of paranoia of this story should be deconstructed into its opposite; Y, the human-against-robot theme, should have been resolved into null-Y, human-and-robot-against-the-universe. I really deplore the ending. So when you read the story, try to imagine it as it ought to have been written. The fasrad says, "Sir, I am here to help you. The hell with my sales pitch. Let's be together forever." Yes, but then I would have been criticized for a false upbeat ending, I guess. Still, this ending is not good. The fans were right.

"Precious Artifact."

I insisted that this story be included in this collection. It utilized a peculiar logic which I generally employ, which Professor Patricia Warrick pointed out to me. First you have Y. Y. Then you do a cybernetics flipflop and you have null-Y. Okay, now you reverse it again and have null-null-Y. Okay, the question is: Does null-null-Y equal Y^3? Or is it a deepening of null-Y? In this story, what appears to be the case is Y but we find out the opposite is true (null-Y). But then *that* turns out not to be true, so are we back to Y? Professor Warrick says that my logic winds up with Y equals null-Y. I don't agree, but I'm not sure what I do wind up with. Whatever it is, in terms of logic, it is contained in this particular story. Either I've invented a whole new logic or, ahem, I'm not playing with a full deck.

"Small Town."

Here the frustrations of a defeated small person—small in terms of power, in particular power over others—gradually become transformed into something sinister: the force of death. In rereading this story (which is of course a fantasy, not science fiction) I am impressed by the subtle change which takes place in the protagonist from Trod-Upon to Treader. Verne Haskel initially appears as the prototype of the impotent human being, but this conceals a drive at his core self which is anything but weak. It is as if I am saying, The put-upon person may be very dangerous. Be careful as to how you misuse him; he may be a mask for thanatos: the antagonist of life; he may not secretly wish to rule; he may wish to *destroy*.

• • •

"The Pre-Persons."

In this, the most recent of the stories in this collection, I incurred the absolute hate of Joanna Russ who wrote me the nastiest letter I've ever received; at one point she said she usually offered to beat up people (she didn't use the word "people") who expressed opinions such as this. I admit that this story amounts to special pleading, and I am sorry to offend those who disagree with me about abortion on demand. I also got some unsigned hate mail, some of it not from individuals but from organizations promoting abortion on demand. Well, I have always managed to offend people by what I write. Drugs, communism, and now an anti-abortion stand; I really know how to get myself into hot water. Sorry, people. But for the pre-persons' sake I am not sorry. I stand where I stand: "Hier steh' Ich; Ich kann nicht anders," as Martin Luther is supposed to have said.

Afterword

By Philip K. Dick

In my introduction to this volume I said that SF is a field of rebellion: against accepted ideas, institutions, against all that is. In my writing I even question the universe; I wonder out loud if it is real, and I wonder out loud if all of us are real. So I have left nothing untouched. Throughout this volume of short stories the theme of fakes, of deception, the theme of guile and cunning, are evident, but I would also like to have a theme of human trust noted, even though it may be submerged at times under the ominous. In "The Pre-Persons" it is love for the children that I feel, not anger toward those who would destroy them. My anger is generated out of love; it is love baffled. I hope you can see this in even this story. If not, then I've failed. I would ask you to read "The Little Black Box" last of all the stories, because it is closer to being my credo than any of the other stories here. As with "Precious Artifact" I asked that it be included. It is a story about trust. Caritas in the final analysis is emotional trust. I trust, then, that you will not misread me and see dislike and anger only; please reach out to me at the core below that, the core of love.

Science Fiction and Fantasy from Methuen Paperbacks

While every effort is made to keep prices low, it is sometimes necessary to increase prices at short notice. Methuen Paperbacks reserves the right to show new retail prices on covers which may differ from those previously advertised in the text or elsewhere.

The prices shown below were correct at the time of going to press.

☐ 413 55450 3	**Half-Past Human**	T J Bass	£1.95
☐ 413 58160 8	**Rod of Light**	Barrington J Bayley	£2.50
☐ 417 04130 6	**Colony**	Ben Bova	£2.50
☐ 413 57910 7	**Orion**	Ben Bova	£2.95
☐ 417 07280 5	**Voyagers**	Ben Bova	£1.95
☐ 417 06760 7	**Hawk of May**	Gillian Bradshaw	£1.95
☐ 413 56290 5	**Chronicles of Morgaine**	C J Cherryh	£2.95
☐ 413 51310 6	**Downbelow Station**	C J Cherryh	£1.95
☐ 413 51350 5	**Little Big**	John Crowley	£3.95
☐ 417 06200 1	**The Golden Man**	Philip K Dick	£1.75
☐ 417 02590 4	**The Man Who Japed**	Philip K Dick	£1.75
☐ 413 58860 2	**Wasp**	Eric Frank Russell	£2.50
☐ 413 59770 9	**The Alchemical Marriage of Alistair Crompton**	Robert Sheckley	£2.25
☐ 413 59990 6	**All Flesh is Grass**	Clifford D Simak	£2.50
☐ 413 58800 9	**A Heritage of Stars**	Clifford D Simak	£2.50
☐ 413 55590 9	**The Werewolf Principle**	Clifford D Simak	£1.95
☐ 413 58640 5	**Where the Evil Dwells**	Clifford D Simak	£2.50
☐ 413 52000 5	**The Buccaneers of Lan-Kern**	Peter Tremayne	£1.95
☐ 413 54600 4	**Raven of Destiny**	Peter Tremayne	£1.95
☐ 413 56840 7	**This Immortal**	Roger Zelazny	£1.95
☐ 413 56850 4	**The Dream Master**	Roger Zelazny	£1.95

All these books are available at your bookshop or newsagent, or can be ordered direct from the publisher. Just tick the titles you want and fill in the form below.

Methuen Paperbacks, Cash Sales Department,
PO Box 11, Falmouth,
Cornwall TR10 109EN.

Please send cheque or postal order, no currency, for purchase price quoted and allow the following for postage and packing:

UK	55p for the first book, 22p for the second book and 14p for each additional book ordered to a maximum charge of £1.75.
BFPO and Eire	55p for the first book, 22p for the second book and 14p for each next seven books, thereafter 8p per book.
Overseas Customers	£1.00 for the first book plus 25p per copy for each additional book.

NAME (Block Letters) ....

ADDRESS..

....